MW01037471

DELVEON

THE HELLSTROMM LEGACY
BOOK 1

THE KNIGHT AND THE HALF-DRAGON

Becky
Thanks for being a
great friend all these years

Kelly Ross

All Rights Reserved.

No part of this book may be used or reproduced by any means, graphic, electronic, or mechanical, including photocopying, recording, taping, or by any information storage retrieval system without the written permission of the publisher except in the case of brief quotations embodied in critical articles and reviews.

Kelly Ross
Visit me on Facebook: World of Delveon
Email: Worldofdelveon@gmail.com
ISBN# E-Book: 979-8-9876127-0-5
ISBN# Print: 979-8-9876127-1-2
Copyright © 2022
First published 2023

CHAPTER 1
(THE CITY OF MAGIC AND STEAM)

The morning sun crests over the mountains, casting the first rays of the new day onto the gold and silver spires of Rose Harbor, which has been the capital city of the Rose Empire for over two hundred years. Rainbow hues form for a few moments as those rays pass through the magical dome which protects the city. This can be quite the spectacle for those citizens up this early. Years of invention, technology, and magic have shaped the empire into a formidable economic powerhouse. The city's ten Houses control everything including shipping, manufacturing, and finances. The head of each House sits on a special city council dedicated to deciding the direction of city affairs, but everyone knows the Emperor holds all the power.

The morning rays hit the red brick streets, signaling everyone to ready themselves for the new day. Vehicles kick on, windows open, horses and oxen are hitched, and the city's workers head to their places of employment. The city's many vendors open for business with virtually everything you can imagine being found there… all forms of powerful magical items, rare animals, materials of every kind, and various contraptions. The aroma of fresh food cooking for breakfast permeates the streets of the massive city.

A tall, foreboding Human stands on his balcony looking over the city. He is deep tanned from standing there many mornings with the cool mountain breeze passing through his hair. *Hard to imagine I built all this from being a humble farmer so long ago.* He laughs to himself, thinking about it. He perks up hearing his wife approaching. *Had I not met her, none of the legends about me would be true.*

His first wife, Skylar, places her soft hands on his hips. "You're up early. Couldn't sleep, my love?"

"Something is amiss in my empire." He turns to his Empress. "Something is going on under my nose."

"And what would that be?"

"I'm not sure, but it's not a problem for me to solve. We are getting too old to deal with such matters ourselves." He turns back, leaning on the railing, and listening to the city come to life.

She smiles and joins him. "There is more to it than that." She turns to him, her blond hair flowing in the wind. "I know you."

Turning to her, he smiles. Her blue eyes are sparkling, as beautiful as ever. "I believe the time is right to add to the family, and this would be an excellent test to see who it is."

She grins. "You have a plan to find the one we are missing."

"And more. I think Daniel will appreciate it as well."

"Been a long time since you ran with him. Think he's doing well?" She looks out over the city as lamps turn off with the morning sun.

"I believe so. He hasn't complained much. I'm sure this news will excite him, however."

She tilts her head at him. "So, when do we begin?"

"Today feels right. The stars are in place and if things are to go as they should, I need to get things started now."

"Can it wait till after breakfast? I'm famished."

"We can do both." He turns around and walks back inside. "Summon my scribe and the record keeper!"

In the Third House (the House of Hellstromm) the aromas of freshly baked bread, eggs cooking, and fresh-cut fruit fill the massive home. Jack Hellstromm, a short dark-skinned Human with long black braided hair, sits at the head of a large ironwood table in the dining hall. He wears a simple suit of green and gold and on his left ring finger is a plain gold band with his House's insignia. The table itself is inlaid with gold and adamantium with decorative patterns laminated into it. It now has many scratches and scars from years of Jack's tinkering with his inventions, much to the dismay of his wife, Jasmine. He sits stoically at this majestic table reading the morning newspaper dated Saturday March twelfth, eighteen sixty-five. Cline, Jack's butler and longtime friend, a tall light-skinned Human male wearing a simple white shirt and pants, accentuated by a vibrant blue vest, brings him fresh-squeezed orange juice and a report from his holdings.

"Thank you, Cline." Jack looks up from his paper. "How are you this morning?"

Cline puts down the tall glass of orange juice and hands Jack the report. "I'm doing well sir, as always." Cline's eyebrow shoots up, spotting some minute amount of grease and oil on the table. "I see you've been tinkering again. What new idea do you have this time?"

Jack notes Cline's inquiry and change of tone and then looks down at the table. Disappointment crosses his face as he realizes he wasn't successful in cleaning up after himself. "Well, it's an improvement over a previous model of a loading system. I've been trying to fine-tune it a bit more to get a better response time and make it safer to use." Jack peers around the room searching, and in a hushed tone, he puts his paper down. "Just remember to keep that to yourself. You know how upset she gets when I work on weapon systems instead of common goods, but I don't want the guard getting hurt by faulty designs."

Cline nods in understanding and gestured toward the rest of the house. "Sir, breakfast will be ready shortly. Shall I summon the family?"

Jack pauses a moment, keeping Cline's attention and motioning to the table. "Uh sure, but before you go, let's get this grease cleaned up quickly." Cline nods and walks back into the other room to get cleaning rags and solvent. Upon his return, Jack folded up his paper and drinks in the fresh juice. "Thanks, Cline." He takes the cleaning supplies. "Go ahead and wake the kids and let them know breakfast is ready. I should be done with this in a minute."

"Of course, sir." Cline bows and proceeds out of the room.

Upstairs in the manor, Jasmine, a Half-White Dragon woman, is already awake and picking out her attire. Her light brown hair is tied back and her white Dragon scales glimmer in the sunlight. If not for the scales, she could almost pass for a normal Human. She is a petite woman barely standing over five feet tall, and stronger than some of the bigger men in Jack's guard. She's also a powerful sorceress, and Jack's adventuring partner many years ago, saving his life. Now, not only is she the wife of a successful engineer, but she's also a professor at the Third House's academy within Rose Harbor teaching Evocation Magic.

Looking through her wardrobe she pulls out a crimson red dress with dark adamantium accents laced into it. She smiles as she thinks of how the red dress contrasts nicely with her pearl white scales and ivory white skin. She places the dress on the bed and moves to her dressing table to start her morning rituals. Sitting down and picking up her brush, she looks into the mirror to see the icy blue of her eyes staring back at her. She reaches up and brushes the knots and kinks from her locks when a knock at the chamber door is preceded by Cline's upbeat voice.

"Ma'am, breakfast is being served. Is there anything you would like to drink?"

Jasmine thinks about it for but a moment and turns to face the door. "Yes, I would like some fresh tea." She turns back to the mirror. "I'll be down in a moment!"

Cline writes it down on a small parchment he's carrying and proceeds further up the hallway. Crossing over to the other wing of the house, he makes his way to the room of Jack's son, Andrew. He knocks on the chamber door and waits patiently, but receives no answer. He knows Andrew could be praying and peeks inside to see him doing just that. Andrew worships the god Daniel, a god known for healing, fire, and good fortune. He has been studying to become part of the priesthood for some time and today he is hoping to finally be accepted.

Cline speaks up, keeping respect in his voice, knowing he's interrupting. "Master Andrew, breakfast is ready when you are finished." Andrew, a lighter-skinned version of his father, gives the faintest of nods but doesn't speak a word, something Cline has gotten used to after all these years. He knows Andrew is very religious and only drinks water, so there was no need to ask him for his order. *Twenty-two years it's been. He's all grown up.* He thinks, as he closes the door quietly before proceeding.

Cline comes to the last door and holds out his hand to knock on it, but it opens. Crystal, a petite young girl, standing barely five feet tall, stares up at him with the same icy blue eyes as her mother, with her skin being just as white. Her hair, black as coal, like her father's, is braided to the small of her back and makes a striking contrast with her skin tone. She is adorned in a sky-blue dress with gold and silver threads embroidered into it, making him think of snow falling on it.

6

She looks up at him, sounding innocent. "Can I help you, Cline?"

"Yes, Mistress Crystal, I was wondering what you wanted to drink with your breakfast. It is now ready, so I'm here to take your order."

An impish grin crosses her face. "I'll take some orange juice, please. I'm sure Shadow has it freshly squeezed."

Cline wrinkles his nose at Crystal calling the Master Chef by her nickname. "Yes, Penelope has prepared fresh orange juice this morning. Your father is currently down there enjoying a tall glass."

Crystal's eyes widen. "Well, in that case. I better get down there before daddy drinks it all."

Cline recalls her birth nineteen years ago. She's always been a handful... impish and playful. However, her greatest attribute was being naturally gifted with magic, like her mother. Meanwhile, Andrew finishes his morning prayers several minutes later and straightens out his plain brown clothing. Looking into the mirror in his room, he makes sure he looks presentable. Just as Andrew steps out of his room, Crystal steps around and dashes past him, almost knocking him over, heading down the hallway.

Elsewhere in the city, the hustle and bustle fills the streets, as traders go about their business. Steam and horse-drawn carts, loaded with fresh goods from other cities, show up to unload their wares. Vehicles of all kinds and colors make their way along the streets, for those who can afford them. Each of the ten districts is distinct from one another, as each has its own basic culture and is run differently, but all must follow the Emperor's codes and laws.

Down on the docks, a steamship of red and gold comes into port. Seagulls squawk while swooping down, picking at dropped scraps on the dock as the waves crash onto the shore. Sounds of ships honking for right of way pulling in and out of the slips can be heard from as far out as the channel markers. On one ship, the Seventh House's crest is painted on the side of the hull, with the Rose Empire's flag flying high from its center mast.

On the docks, inspecting cargo as it comes in, stands a short-haired, clean-shaven young man, with skin the color of bronze from countless days standing in the sun. He stands an intimidatingly six and a half feet tall, towering over the other dock workers. Of his near-perfect and brightly polished armor, he wears only the red and gold breastplate adorned with decorations of his achievements from the Royal Academy. The robust and athletic young man of only twenty-one looks as if he's been working this dock for years. Ornamentations on his armor tell everyone he's a member of the Seventh House, and that he's the authority on the dock. His leather pants and white cotton shirt, sleeves torn showing off his muscles from his training and hard work, are already dirty from checking the odd selection of cargo as it comes in. He scrutinizes some Kobolds that unload a ship onto the dock.

These Kobolds, a species of short reptilian humanoids, work feverishly to get unloaded. They make splendid sailors due to how well balanced they are and their ability to squeeze into tight places, but everyone knows they have a knack for sneaking in contraband and must be closely watched. A tan and blonde furred Minotaur, wearing only black leather pants with a large rapier strapped and antique blunderbuss to his belt, and upon his head, he wears a distinctive black captain's hat with a long tan feather, and he crosses over the gangplank onto the dock. The immense creature, standing well over nine feet tall, towers over the Kobold crew.

The Minotaur bellows in greeting, waving for attention. "William Blakely, is that you hiding behind all those fruits?"

William looks up from inspecting a crate of fresh pineapples. "Farvrak Steelpelt! You pirate!" He closes the distance to greet him.

They shake hands, both men's arms flexing, but William finally breaks away, unable to match the large humanoid. Farvrak laughs, slapping William on the back. "Got some new armor, I see." He hands over his shipping manifest with everything he's unloading here. "And you're getting stronger."

William nods with a smile and looks over the manifest with a glance. "Guns get more advanced, so does the armor. Dad makes sure I get the latest protection." William turns back to his tasks. "So, what do you have for us this week, Farv?" He flips through pages, running numbers in his head. "Your crew trying to sneak in some stuff I should know about?"

The Minotaur shakes his head. "Not this time. I can't afford to get my shipping license pulled." He taps his muzzle for emphasis. "I've been keeping my nose on them." He shrugs, scanning over the horde. "They work hard if you can keep them in line, but they are like children. Same size, and same knack for getting into mischief, but they work well collectively. Just keeping them focused is the hard part." Farv motions to the paperwork. "Everything's there. Fresh shipment from the Silvian Empire of fruits and vegetables." He turns and looks back at the ship and then glances off in the distance with his nose up, sniffing the air.

He looks back down at William and his smile gets larger. "Those magical cold units invented by the wizards of the Tenth House worked out well. These should be fresh for a whole week."

William nods in agreement. "Was an excellent investment for sure." He looks over at the dock crew, then flips the pages back down. "Let's get these crates loaded onto a transport as soon as they are inspected." Dwarves and a handful of Half-Orcs load as inspectors clear them, but William can see the Dwarves are eyeballing the Kobold crew and looking over the crates as they go.

Farv sighs and sticks his nose back up, sniffing the air. "Since this is going to take a while, I'm going off to get something to eat at the Gastrognome." He looks down at William. "Those guys make some really good coffee there, and Provider knows I'm ready for something not seafood-related."

William acknowledges him with a wave and gets back to work inspecting the crates and comparing them to the papers in his hands. The sea breeze comes across the dock, blowing the salty spray up, covering those on the dock with brine. Kobolds argue with the Dwarves as they try to load their steam-powered transports. Things can get heated between them because they never see things the same way. A tumultuous history between the groups fuels animosity as they accuse each other of things neither has done, but under the Emperor's laws, they never let it get out of hand. However, the Dwarves are raising a point on the dock that the Kobolds could try to pull another fast one.

9

William intercedes, addressing the female Dwarf crew leader. "Look, Ms. Amberjaw. I understand your suspicions, but so far, we haven't turned up anything, and we are being very thorough with these guys." He looks down at the manifest and back at her. "Unless you have something solid, you can't harass the crew. Just load the crates and get them on their way to the rightful owners."

She glowers and speaks with a heavily accented quip, putting her finger on his armor. "I know they're up to something. They're always up to something." She relents and puts her hand down, then glances back at her crew. "You heard the officer. Let's get loaded up." She turns, looking back at William, and he can tell immediately that she still doesn't trust him. "But double-check everything."

William just shakes his head. *This is not what I had in mind when I went to the academy.*

As the morning sun creeps along to close to ten-thirty a.m. a steam car pulls up with the distinctive markings of the Rose Empire's First House. A long, white-bearded Gnome steps out of the vehicle, wearing some high-end clothing and walking like he's been a noble his whole life. He marches up to William and tugs on his pants. This startles the big man as he looks down to see the tiny Gnome.

"Can I help you with something?"

The white-bearded Gnome asks in a squeaky voice. "Are you Sir William Blakely, Son of Gerald Blakely, head of the Seventh House?" He flashes the signet ring with the crest of the First House to the young knight.

William reacts with a start. "Yes, I am. What is this about?" The Gnome courier hands him an official-looking document, wax sealed with the seal of the Emperor.

"You are hereby summoned to the Emperor's court today at one p.m. Do not be late!" Looking at and smelling how dirty William is, he then speaks with disdain. "And clean yourself up. You smell like fish and brine." With that, the Gnome turns on his heel and goes back to the car, and leaves.

William stares at the document in his hands. *Wonder what this is about?*

CHAPTER 2
(Fate of Strangers)

Sitting at the temple of Daniel, a fair-skinned Half-Elven woman kneels at a white marble altar and speaks her morning prayers, her holy symbol clutched in her hands. As a priestess of Daniel, she is married to her God and has taken a vow of chastity, giving her full devotion only to her beliefs. Wearing the common brown robes of the order, she murmurs her prayers with others as she has done for so many years. The morning sun hits the top of the church, triggering its bells to play their song.

The head priestess, a tall fair skinned Elven lady named Lyndis, steps up to her after they have finished. She speaks up with a cheerful voice, grabbing the younger lady's attention. "Tia!" Tia stands and turns to the head priestess, awaiting her orders. She is handed a piece of parchment. "Here's your list of chores for the day." Lyndis clears her throat. "Services tonight are going to be a little larger than usual. Not only are the spring solstice farmers going to be coming in to pray for good weather, but we have a new member joining the church." Tia notes she's happy as always, as they all are when serving their god.

Tia turns to go to her first task and Lyndis walks with her, continuing. "He's a member of the Third House, so he's going to need some time to adjust. It's difficult for someone to give up royalty and become a servant. He's making an enormous sacrifice." Lyndis places a hand on Tia's shoulder. "Could you make sure that he transitions easily? Your knack for talking to people and putting them at ease will be most useful here."

Sounds of the bustling city outside echo in the main hall of the church. Tia cleans the table of melted wax from the candles burning all night. Unlike the rest of the city, the church of Daniel still uses natural firelight instead of the new technological magical light invented by the Third House. The church is always kept well-lit, with windows positioned to allow the most natural light in with mirrors used to reflect it into the building for other times of the day, and candles burning at night.

As time passes and the morning transitions into midday. Tia notices a well-dressed, white-bearded Gnome enter the church. He marches up to Lyndis and flashes something at her. She bows her head as he hands her a document. He tips his hat to her politely, turns, and walks away.

Crystal barges into the dining hall full of energy and walks up to her father, giving him a huge morning hug, as she's done since she could walk. Nineteen years and he hasn't changed. She does occasionally if it's momma's doing with her magic or the "legend" he never speaks of. "Morning daddy." She glides around the table without care. "You've been tinkering again, haven't you?" She takes her place at the table setting.

Jack looks up from his production reports. "How?"

"You can clean up the grease, but the smell lingers." She gleefully takes a pastry from the table's center. "And there're new scratches."

Jack looks down in disbelief, then eyeballs her. "There is no way you can tell that."

Meanwhile, Penelope steps in wearing her customary white hat and rose-colored jacket. She is a female Halfling standing only three feet tall and is the House's head chef. Carrying breakfast for Jack, she lays it on the table in front of him. "She's right, you can still smell the grease from that thing." She taps her nose. "And with your wife's nose, if we can smell it, she definitely *will*." Penelope walks around the table to where Crystal is sitting. "Doesn't help with that stink from the solvents trying to clean up either."

Jack looks at Crystal, opening his mouth, but she puts her hand up and nods, knowing what he will ask before he does. She chants a short set of magical words and with a wave of her glowing yellow hand, the smell disappears.

"What would you like for breakfast, Mistress?"

Crystal holds up the pastry with a bite still in her mouth. "This is fine."

Penelope points to Crystal's midsection. "You're not going to keep that figure eating pastries. How about some Dwarven-style sausages and a fresh-sliced apple?" Crystal acquiesces but says nothing with another mouthful of the sweet delight.

Shortly after, Andrew walks in and takes his place at the table, followed by Jasmine wearing her new red dress. She walks past Jack's old power armor and tings it with a finger flick. It has sat in the corner unused for decades but looks just as new as the day he fashioned it. She had preserved it with her magic when they both were much younger. Jack looks back at her, causing her to smile. She then leans down and kisses him and points to the report. "So, how is the family business doing?" With that, her hand drags along his shoulder, making her way to her place at the table, snagging the morning paper as she goes.

Cline walks in carrying their morning drinks and sets them down. Penelope, Cline, and other staff members bring in food and take away the dirty plates as the family discusses the day ahead.

Jack puts the report down. "Looking good. Marcus is ordering more power suits." The excitement in his voice causes Jasmine to wrinkle her nose at the mention of the war machines. "And Seventh House put in an order for another one thousand stasis units for shipping." This news gets her smile to return.

She exhales heavily. "I wish you would have never invented those things." She takes a drink of her tea.

"I know, I know." He's heard her complaints often now. "But if it wasn't for the prototype I made, Cline over here," thumbing back at him, "would have beaten us."

A knock at the door brings the conversation to a momentary halt. Cline bows before exiting the room to go get the door. Cline has served the family and has been their Estate Steward for as long as Crystal can remember, and like her Father, he hasn't aged a day to her. Opening the door, a long, white-bearded Gnome with a short top hat and a very well-tailored black suit greets him. They exchange words that the others can't hear from the dining hall and then the Gnome hands Cline a document and departs. Cline looks down at the document with puzzlement crossing his face.

Walking back in, Jack speaks up. "What was that all about?" Cline hands the document to Crystal.

"It appears His Majesty, Emperor Marcus, is summoning Mistress Crystal." Clines' perplexed tone at the news echoes their thoughts.

Everyone there, even Penelope and her kitchen staff, stops and turns to look at Crystal. She looks nervous as she stares at the official document, sealed with the wax seal of the First House.

Jack breaks Crystal out of her thoughts. "Well, what does it say, dear?"

"Uh, well…" she breaks the seal and reads it. "It says: 'Ms. Crystal Hellstromm, His Majesty, is summoning you for an interview for a new project, as yet undisclosed, and possibly more'." She swallows nervously and continues reading. "Your potential is to be tested and will be personally interviewed by me, Emperor Marcus Rose. If you are receiving this message, it is because you have been recommended by your teachers at the academies. Be at the Palace by one p.m."

Andrew drinks some water. "Well, that's quite the honor, Sis."

Crystal looks at her parents, and Jasmine speaks up. "I suggest you prepare and get underway."

Crystal travels nobly to the palace in the family vehicle. One of the first few steam cars in the empire and is heavily armored with adamantium plates. Her father takes the family's safety seriously and built it himself years ago. Arriving at the palace a full thirty minutes before anyone else, the Hellstromm's Human chauffeur stops at the gate awaiting permission to enter. A royal guard steps to Crystal's window, where she hands him the summons from His Majesty. The guard examines it, then with a signal, the gate opens, allowing them to pass. The vehicle makes its way up the long drive to the palace entrance where yet another guard awaits.

Once the vehicle is stopped, Crystal awaits as her chauffeur comes around to open her door. Taking her time, she dramatically exits the vehicle. Once standing outside the vehicle door, she slowly straightens out her backless sky-blue dress. The dress is adorned with gold embroidery in a 'magical' themed pattern. She went all out to look stunning. Her hair is done with a single large braid, wrapped with gold and silver lace, ending at the small of her back. One doesn't get summoned to the Palace and show up not looking their best. That's the fastest way to be thrown out on their backside, plus a way to become the laughingstock of the entire town. She would not let her family and the academy down by looking like a commoner.

After exiting the vehicle, the palace guard escorts her inside to further ensure her safety. She must be very important for His Majesty to summon her. As Crystal and the guard walk up the palace steps, the chauffeur informs her; that he will stay close by watching and waiting for her to exit. She nods and dismissively waves to him in acknowledgment.

Walking in, she is overwhelmed by what she sees. She stops to take it all in. The foyer looks to be as large as her entire home. The pillars of the hall are made of black marble with gold bands. Light from the stained glass fills the foyer beautifully, bringing one's attention to the centerpiece of the foyer, an intricate inlaid map of the entire Rose Empire. The map itself must be a few hundred feet across and she can't even fathom what it cost. The city itself was represented as a rose, made up of thousands of sparkling red rubies with its many roads laid out as white marble. Its massive land is represented by deep green emeralds, its majestic mountains with layers of adamantium, and the oceans surrounding it made of deep blue sapphires. Crystal is mesmerized taking it all in. The guard, who has seen this reaction from every visitor, lightly coughs, breaking her from her introspection to keep her moving along. *Maybe one day daddy will be this rich.* Crossing the giant map of the Rose Empire fills her with pride that her family helped build this powerful nation.

Walking into the throne room, it looks empty and perplexes her. She knows she is early, but the fact that there is no one here doesn't feel right to her somehow. *Anyone summoned by the Emperor should arrive early to show respect to him.* The room is impossibly huge and structurally; it shouldn't be possible to be this large. She scans the room and detects magic all over the place. Detect magic, a basic spell, and she's been using it since she could walk. This spell is traditionally used to find things out of place, magical, or hidden by magical means. However, Crystal often uses this spell for her impish side. It can provide her with knowledge of what presents she is about to receive. Even though it makes it difficult to feign surprise, it doesn't dissuade her from using it to her advantage.

The guard doesn't leave the room but allows her to walk around lost in thought, looking at all the paintings, tapestries, and artifacts from faraway lands she will most likely never get to see. A deep voice from behind her startles her out of her speculation. She spins to see Emperor Marcus Rose and Skylar standing there. She has excellent hearing, but they walked in without making a sound. Her proper training kicks in and she immediately kneels to the emperor and bows her head, not looking up till she is addressed.

His voice booms throughout the room. "Hello Crystal."

Still looking straight at the floor, bowing her head as she replies. "Greetings Your Highness." She stammers, getting the words out in surprise. "I received your letter and am here at your behest."

Tia strolls up to the outside gate, dressed in her traditional brown priestess robes, looking no different from any other member of Daniel's church. She is greeted by a member of the Royal Guard, and she hands him her summons. Arriving virtually simultaneously comes William riding upon his heavily barded warhorse and regal looking in his dress uniform. His rank insignia of being a sergeant in the Royal Guard, prevalent on his left breast, is polished and gleams in the sunlight. Tia enters as William produces his documentation, also allowing his entrance to the palace grounds.

A few moments later, he kicks his steed to catch up to her and introduces himself. She smiles up at him in a friendly manner and returns the gesture, but doesn't break her stride. He looks down at her, sounding polite. "Do you have any idea why you were summoned to see the emperor?"

She pulls the letter from her robe. "His Majesty has asked my head priestess to send a member of her congregation to represent the faith, and to make sure it was one of her best, but youthful." She looks at the letter and adds, "From what priestess Lyndis stated to me, after being handed the letter and reading it, she had an overwhelming feeling it was meant for me, so here I am."

William nods, pulling out a similar letter. "I was summoned because my commanding officer believes am naturally gifted for command. I thought I was just paying attention more than others." He turns and looks up at the palace. "I wonder who else was summoned?" Tia shakes her head, indicating she doesn't know.

Looking back down at her, and smiling, he offers his hand. "Would you like a ride to the door? You could get on the back with me and make your trip a little easier."

She shakes her head. "It wouldn't be appropriate in my faith. Riding with a man would look to be intimate, and that's not permitted."

William nods in understanding and dismounts. The sound of his heavy armor sliding against the barding of his horse rings until his feet hit heavily on the ground with a clear clank of metal. Motioning her to precede him to the palace door. "Then I shall walk with you so we can continue our conversation, but let's not keep His Majesty waiting." The palace guard meets them, and the stable boy takes William's horse to be kept safe while he's inside. William meanwhile mentally notes the heavily armored steam car not too far away with the Third House's marking on it, knowing that someone of extreme importance must also be here to warrant that protection.

CHAPTER 3
(Adventure Within an Adventure)

Tia and William walk into the throne room where several others have gathered in the Emperor's presence. William quickly counts at least twenty individuals, including himself and Tia. It looks like representatives from every House are here along with several members of the religious sects. He notes them in his head… standing on a stool to see, a Halfling wearing a noble outfit from the Tenth House. An Elf from the Fourth House whom, going by the crest and signet, he believes is the grandson of its head. A stocky male Dwarf with his beard tucked into his greaves, wearing full plate colored with that of the Ninth House's guard. An ivory-white female in a blue dress with a long black braid dressed like royalty. A female silver Dragonborn adorned with the Symbol of Johnathan, the God of Paladins, with all gold-colored armor, and several others he can't place. *What possibly can be happening that so many people from all walks of life are gathered here?* Emperor Marcus is speaking to the ivory white female in the blue dress at the moment at the far end of the room. *I can't hear what they are saying, and there is no echo for a room this size. A room such as this with so many should be louder. Must be an enchantment preventing sound from carrying and interrupting the proceedings.* After a few moments, the ivory-skinned female curtsies with a smile on her face, possibly receiving some good news. She exits into a side chamber that the emperor points to, giving his attention to the next representative. William watches the young girl and notes her perfect walk and stride is that of someone of high class and nobility, then realizes he is looking at her too intently as her leaving breaks his concentration.

Each person in the room speaks with the emperor and his wife, but each is summarily dismissed one after another. William is finally called up and successfully stamps out his nervousness. As a member of the Royal Guard, he is trained to serve the Emperor no matter what, showing nervousness in the face of his Majesty would be frowned upon. However, being this close to the man who built the Rose Empire is awe-inspiring. He walks up to the throne and takes a knee, bowing his head before His Highness.

Emperor Marcus speaks to him clearly with deep bass in his voice. "Stand sergeant." He waves his hand in an upward direction. William does, and Emperor Marcus continues. "Tell me, sergeant, do you know *why* I have summoned you here?" He pauses a moment and starts a new question before William can formulate an answer. "Let me put it in another way. What is your assessment of why I may have summoned you, of all the other Royal Guardsmen, at my command?" The emperor holds an arm outward, showing he's expecting him to give him an exceptional answer.

William pauses and clenches his lips, thinking of what to say. He knows he is being tested by the emperor. He then speaks with confidence he doesn't feel. "I believe you're looking for exceptional young people within the highest ranks of each field for a special mission, sire."

The emperor does not respond immediately, and the moment stretches into what seems forever before the Emperor speaks again. "Please continue, sergeant."

William standing ridged as his training kicks in. He wets his lips while doing his best in trying to keep the fear from his voice from being so close to Emperor Marcus. "Several things, sir. Upon inspecting the people gathered here, I believe I was recommended to you because my commanding officer believes I could be naturally gifted in an area of which you have a need for with this mission." He then motions to Tia stating, which causes her to look down and away, covering her torso with her arms. "She was chosen because her head priestess had a feeling it should be her." He pauses, gathering his words carefully. "And as you spoke to others, they were dismissed, well, except for the first woman you interviewed." He stops continuing to gather his thoughts and the look from His Majesty tells him he's expected to continue. "I believe you're judging your needs based on how people are answering your questions, which means it must be a specialized mission that needs specific kinds of people for it to be successful."

Emperor Marcus looks at the Empress. "The boy is extremely close. I believe I found another qualified candidate." She nods and then he turns back to William. "Please go to the room on my right." He motions in the direction the Ivory woman had left in. "I'll be in there a moment." William bows and moves along as ordered.

Marcus interviews a few others and finally comes to Tia as she is the last in his sight. She did her best to make it that way by hiding behind others so he wouldn't pick her over the others. She walks up to the emperor and bows her head respectfully and kneels. Marcus looks at her, and her eyes stay looking at the floor. "Why do you believe you are here?"

She keeps looking down and responds. "Because my God has chosen for me to be here." Her voice shakes as she continues. "Out of everyone Lyndis could have chosen in that church, she said Daniel chose me." She continues, but the softness of her voice strains the emperor's ear. "So maybe Daniel thinks I'm what you're looking for?"

Marcus casually looks at his wife, who gives a subtle nod. "So do you disagree with Daniel for choosing you to represent him here in front of me in my court?"

"No, no, sire." She looks up for a moment, then looks back down, seeing he is looking directly at her. "It is just I do not believe I am worthy. I do not dare speak on Daniel's behalf, nor assume what he may want." Emperor Marcus stands up and puts his hand on her shoulder, causing her to flinch.

"And that's why I'm choosing you. Because you have potential." She looks up, finding some courage to face him finally. "I have much respect for Daniel and he would not send me someone I could not count on." He motions and turns her in the direction he sent the others. "You just have to realize it yourself, so please join the others." With a gentle push on her back, she folds her hands in front of her and goes to where she is told.

Tia turns to him before she walks in. "Thank you, sire."

As Marcus is interviewing the others, William and Crystal talk about what could happen and why they were chosen. William walks around and examines the room as she speaks. He views the tapestries and paintings and notices the table is made from a wood he can't identify, all making him that much more curious. *This is one hell of an office.* He speaks up and faces her. "So, do you know why he chose you?"

"As I spoke with his highness, he asked me several questions about magic." She looks at her well-manicured hand. "I graduated top of my class in the magic academy of the Fifth House." William looks back at her, noting her tone is that of someone high born and well mannered, and very arrogant. "I even have my own, *personally researched*, spells that differ from the '*common*' spells used by wizards. They are *infused* into my blood." Sitting down and crossing her legs, she leans back in the chair with an air of smugness and touches her hand to her chest. "He obviously sees my potential and chose me."

William looks away, trying hard not to shake his head. *She's going to be fun to work with.* After taking in the room more, he looks back at her. "Going by the crest on your signet, you're a member of the Third House. Why did you go to the Fifth House's Academy?"

She sighs heavily and rolls her eyes away from him. "Because my mother is a professor in the academy in the Third House district. They didn't want my success to be attributed to her influence." Her hands come down on the arms of the chair hard and she looks up at him with her piercing icy blue eyes. "So, they sent me across town to school."

He paces the room looking at artifacts. *It's her skills and status Marcus is after, not her attitude. Hopefully, she is as good as she thinks she is, but she is a pompous ass and needs a good dose of reality.*

She interrupts his train of thought. "So, how about you? Do you wonder why he chose you over the Dragonborn or the Dwarf?" She crosses her arms and looks back at the desk. "They looked pretty tough."

William thinks about it for a moment. "To be honest, like you, I also graduated at the top of my class at the Royal Guard Academy." He shrugs. "And I have a knack for noticing things that my commanding officer claims are an advantage with military tactics and investigation."

She motions to the chair next to her. "Could you please sit down? You walking around the office like that is making me nervous and I think the Emperor wouldn't take too kindly to others snooping around, even if it is 'casual'."

William thinks for a moment and believes she has a point. He's been looking around the room to gather information, but she looks like royalty and obviously knows more about proper etiquette than he does.

Crystal and William continue to talk about different things and speculate about why they were chosen when Tia walks in. She sheepishly finds a chair as the other two look at her.

Crystal turns her attention to Tia. "Soooo, you were chosen as well?" Tia nods from her chair but doesn't speak up. Crystal stares on as if expecting an answer any time, but William interjects first.

"Tia is a member of Daniel's religious sect. We met at the front gate. Her letter said something to the effect that her God chose her for this." William motions at her with his hand to add weight to his words. "I take it that's why she is here."

Crystal is about to speak up but is interrupted by the deep voice of Emperor Marcus. "That is correct, young William." The emperor steps into the large office. All three jump to their feet and bow respectfully. "Please have a seat. In here you can talk casually with no fear of reprisal from me." He makes his way and sits down behind his massive red and gold desk. "I think of this place as a hidey-hole where I can get honest opinions." He leans forward, resting his elbows on the desktop. "I've summoned the best young people, the academies, and the sects offered." He looks at the three. Crystal and William both keep eye contact, but Tia looks to her feet. "You three made it out of twenty candidates because my wife and I both see potential in you and so much more."

Marcus casually talks to the three, judging their interactions for what seems like hours to them. Food and drinks, to everyone's liking, are brought in as they talk from subject to subject. He silently judges their character and potential based on answers and interactions with each other and with himself. After all the work he had just gone through, he had to be sure of whom he selected.

He asks questions of faith to Tia, judging her knowledge of Daniel. As a healer, she must be reliable in an emergency and as counsel. Being a priestess isn't just a one-dimensional job. Crystal is tested about magic and nobility, seeing if she has what it takes to awaken the power inside before telling her how. He knows of Crystal's parentage and the powerful potential she has for both magic and leadership. William is asked about scenarios in different situations to see if he can think beyond conventional tactics. Marcus notes William could do well in a position of military authority but still needs experience.

The light from the window works its way off the desk and onto the wall, and the noise of the city changes to the lull of those going home and settling in for the evening. Marcus finally comes down to the real reason they are all there.

"Well, it's getting late. I'm sure your families are wondering what news you bring from the great emperor himself." His laugh bellows and echoes in the room as he leans back. "So here is what I want from you three. Up north, on the border of my empire, is a small town of about five thousand, named Black Rock. It's about two hundred miles along the coastal road." He pulls out a map and lays it out on his desk for the three to see, and points to this road. "This road leading north along the mountains is mostly safe, but as you get closer to the border, it gets a bit…" He looks at the trio, "… wilder." Tia and William look up at Marcus as he says that, but Crystal stays focused on the map. *Interesting.* "Black Rock is responsible for the mining and shipping of obsidian and coal, hence the name." He shrugs with a slight chuckle. "Not very original, but what can you do?" Marcus continues, turning his hand upright. "Here lately the shipments of obsidian have been reduced but the coal and other things they send us have been steady."

Marcus pauses and Crystal almost instinctively picks up from there. "And they haven't sent a notice to why the shipments are in decline, and you need someone to go there and investigate." It was a statement, not a question, and Marcus can see some of her dad has rubbed off on her.

William looks at her and his eyebrows raise and he purses his lips with a slight nod.

Marcus continues. "Yes, that is correct, but that's not all. I haven't been getting the same amount of taxes from the town." He pulls out some other paperwork. "Now granted, less obsidian sold does mean fewer taxes, but the lower rate and lower tax aren't equal. With the strange difference in the math, I fear something odd is happening up there." He looks at the trio. "I want you three to gather up the things you need for the trip there and back to investigate the problem in the town. If it's just a shipping error, then get all the information on why. Is it a labor shortage? Is the source drying up? Was there a natural disaster they don't want to tell us about?" He taps Black Rock on the map. "Figure out what's happening and report back to me." Marcus rolls the map back up and puts it away. "I'll give you two days to get your affairs in order and gather supplies you believe you will need. This shouldn't take but a few weeks to figure out. Most of it will be travel time."

Tia was the first to leave the room, followed by William. Crystal standing up is stopped by Marcus, placing a hand on her left shoulder.

"Ms. Hellstromm, if you could wait a moment?"

She bows her head, keeping her voice soft. "Anything for you, sire."

Marcus shakes his head. "You're not as strong as you think you are, girl. Overconfidence can get you killed." He reaches into his desk and pulls out a small token of a Dragon. "Your mother is a Half-Dragon, but you show only the faintest of your Dragon heritage. The raw magical power is there yet to be awakened, only then you will be as strong, if not more so than her." His words ring in her mind as he hands the token over. "You have the intelligence and the charisma to be a powerful sorceress and the bloodline to back it up." He points to the Dragon in her hands. "Take this to the Sanctuary of the Dragon Order. They will help you awaken your true potential." She almost believes he is being fatherly with the tone of his voice. "But only when you have the wisdom to wield such power should you take that path."

She looks up at him but keeps her mouth shut. *When is power a bad thing? I'm going to be the best the world has ever seen.*

"It won't be easy, but the payoff, in the end, is unbelievable." He removes his hand as she looks down at the tiny artifact.

She can feel the power radiating from it and into her mind. *I can't explain it, but it feels like it's calling me. I must know more.*

Skylar watches as Crystal leaves and when she's clear of the room, gets up off her throne and saunters into her husband's den. A grin crosses his face as she closes the door behind her. Her gaze falls upon him and closes her proximity. "Are they all that we hoped they are?"

Marcus' grin grows. "They are. The girl has the most potential and I believe the boy is going to be the catalyst for it."

She steps behind him, placing her hands on his shoulders. "And the priestess girl?"

"Daniel picked the one that's going to free him of his burden. She and Crystal will help him tremendously." He leans back in his chair as she comforts him. "I just hope Crystal's ambition doesn't get the better of her. She has a lot of room to grow."

"Is she the one?"

He closes his eyes, feeling her powerful hands. "I'm relatively certain. This test will tell me more."

Tia and William make their way out and say their goodbyes, but William stays at the front gate, waiting for Crystal. Tia, seeing the sun is setting, remembers there is an important ceremony she is missing and hurriedly makes her way back across town. *She's dodging traffic and showing a nimbleness you wouldn't think a priestess would have.*

A few moments pass by and Crystal walks out of the palace carrying something in her hands. He can't make it out at this distance, but she seems very excited about it judging by how large her smile is. As she comes down the steps, the large car of the Third House pulls up. *Driver must have been watching intently for hours for her to come out. That's dedication.*

As she approaches the car, the chauffeur gets out, but William reaches over and opens the door for the young lady first. Crystal stops a moment and looks up at William, stunned. *He is rather handsome and strong. Odd how I didn't notice sooner.* She mentally shakes the sensation away. *Not important right now. Artifact to analyze.* She puts on a genuine smile. "Thank you, Sergeant Blakely." He then offers his hand to steady herself. "Very kind of you." She smiles, taking his hand to lower her down into the car. The driver nods to him and gets back into the vehicle himself. William closes the door carefully, and she cranks down the window. "I will see you in two days," William notes the kindness in her voice quickly faded back to the pompousness he's familiar with and looks up at him with those ice-blue eyes of hers. She waves at him as the car pulls away, then fades into the distance. *It's a rather odd design that the Hellstromm's car has such small tires compared to the other steam cars. Wonder what the thought was on making is so low to the ground.*

CHAPTER 4
(Gathering of farewells)

Tia makes her way across town to the Temple of Daniel, desperately trying to beat the sun as it set. She is part of the congregation for the night, but the meeting with Marcus took way longer than expected. Getting back to the church with little time to spare, Lyndis has gotten most preparations already set as Tia rushes into the Priestess' chamber.

She pants hard. "High Priestess, I'm back." Her face is flushed from having run clear across town in such a short time.

"Ah yes, welcome back, Tia!" Lyndis walks over to Tia and hugs her, embracing her tightly. "So, tell me, what happened? How did it go with Marcus?" She beams a smile and holds Tia at arm's length with her hands still on Tia's shoulders.

Tia stammers with her words but details the whole meeting. She also tells the priestess about Crystal and William and why they were chosen. "It's still a whirlwind in my head. I'm excited but also scared. I've known nothing outside of the city." Tia looks down and away from the Priestess.

Lyndis notices her shyness and uncertainty. "It's obvious that Daniel wants you to go forth and help Marcus by helping these other two young people as well." Lyndis continues as she lets go and walks back to her desk. "They will need your wisdom on this trip, and you should look to Daniel for that wisdom to advise them."

Tia nods and looks back up, making eye contact with Lyndis. She opens her arms outwards at her sides. "But I don't know how to counsel others, and I'm scared. What am I supposed to bring? Do I need extra sets of robes?"

"Well, you have two days to prepare. For now, we have a new member to welcome." Lyndis remarks wrinkling her nose. "You might want to put on a new robe and have that one washed. That one is a little gamey from the cornucopia of smells you ran through on the way here."

William walks back home rather than ride his horse. He felt it appropriate to walk through the heart of his city so he may reflect inwards on the mission he was about to partake in and the consequences of failure to complete it successfully. With his horse's reins in his right hand, his trusty steed walks calmly on his right side. They cause quite a spectacle while passing by the common folk walking in his dress uniform and armored steed

Why is Marcus sending three young adults with virtually no experience? Especially when he has an airship that could make the trip in hours or a steam vehicle? He waves friendlily as some citizens as he crosses different intersections. *But he said it would take weeks. Are we walking the entire way on our own?* William shakes his head in dismissal. *Emperor Marcus wouldn't do that. He would most likely provide horses at least, but I can't see that rich girl Crystal riding on a horse. At least not for something more than fun.* William dodges children playing ball in the street as it goes flying past his head. His thoughts turn to her. *She was such a pristine ivory white; you would think she must bathe several times a day to keep every speck of dirt off herself. Her hair, although black as night, makes a complete contrast to her skin but has a shimmer on its own.* He continues his thoughts crossing a busy street, with the traffic dying down for the night. *I don't even know how she would get on a horse because she's so short. I've seen Dwarves taller than her.* He chuckles to himself, picturing her trying to jump up. He shakes his head again, this time to clear his mind. *I'm thinking of her too much and the mission is important. Just get a Dwarven pony and be done with it, maybe?*

William makes more mental notes. *Tia is another mystery. A Half-Elven woman worshiper of Daniel. Daniel is a god of healing, fortune, and fire, if I remember correctly. Is the mission going to be so dangerous that a healer is needed? That's something to consider when packing for the trip along with armor and weapons.*

His mind switches back to the mission at hand once more as he continues his journey home. *Marcus mentioned the farther away from the city, the wilder things become. Tia is going to be integral to keeping us alive and dealing with the animals and what of the possibility of bandits?* He arrives at his home after walking for hours. The city's magical lamps have kicked on as the sun hit the ocean to the west, keeping the streets illuminated as if the sun didn't move from high in the sky. *Time to get my stuff together and inform Father of what's going on.* He walks in the front door, preparing to speak with him.

Crystal arrives back at the Hellstromm manor, having not stopped anywhere else at Crystal's behest. She hops out excitedly before the chauffeur could even get out himself and runs up the stairs, barging into the house. She closes the large oaken door behind her and composes herself. She can't hide her smile, but can at least act a little dignified.

Along the way to her father's workshop behind the house, Cline spots her along with Penelope. He figures Crystal wanted to tell her father first what happened, but his curiosity was getting to him. He places a hand on his chin. "She looks rather happy. What do you think, Penelope?" He looks down at her as they both look out the back door of the kitchen.

The Halfling cook smiles to herself. "Well then, I believe I need to make something very special for dinner because something tells me this is going to be an extra special occasion." She looks up at Cline. "But I believe Master Jack and Mistress Jasmine are going to be upset. Both of their children are leaving at the same time and going their own ways."

Cline nods in agreement, watching as Crystal practically skips across the yard to the old shop. Billowing smoke from the chimney tells him Master Jack is busy forging some new hardware. He turns away and looks down at his tiny companion. "Let me know what you need, and I'll go get it right away."

Penelope grabs some parchment and a pen and writes up a list of exotic ingredients and hands it to Cline. "I need to start as soon as possible. Master Andrews's ceremony starts in a few hours." The urgency in her tone lets Cline know how serious she is.

Cline smiles, knowing he's getting a rare chance to cut loose a little. "Guess I'll have to use some of my talents then. I'll be back soon." Penelope is confident in his abilities as he looks at the list, then utters an incantation and, in an instant, he disappears, teleporting to his first destination.

Within the Hellstromm's backyard stands a building almost as large as the house itself. The once red building is covered in soot from years of Jack's inventing and use of the forge inside. The sounds of pounding metal and grinding can be heard as Jack works on his next invention. Crystal walks carefree into the building, knowing full well that it's probably the filthiest place on the planet, but it's her dad's and so she loves it. Jack notices her entering almost immediately. The natural light from the opening door illuminates the area much brighter than his lamps, which gives her away. Looking up, he puts his tools down on the anvil and tosses the metal to the side into some sand. "Hey monster, so how did it go? What is it the Emperor wanted of you?" She notes his curiosity and concern all at once. She walks up and gives him a big hug, knowing full well it will cover her and her expensive dress in grease, soot, and only the Provider knows what else. He is surprised but closes his arms around her, knowing the maids will be very upset.

"Emperor Marcus selected me to do a mission for him." Before Jack could say anything, she breaks the embrace and then holds up the Dragon trinket he gave her. "And he gave me this! It's magical, but I couldn't discern any other information from it." Jack can tell she's curious and excited about this little bauble as she continues. "He told me to take it to the Dragon order."

Jack looks at it, not having a clue what it means. "What has your mom said?"

Crystal shakes her head and gives a subtle shrug. "I haven't told mom yet." She is fascinated by the trinket. "I wanted to tell you first."

Jack looks at his grease-covered daughter and smiles. "Go get cleaned up, then. Penelope should have dinner ready soon, so you can tell us all about it then."

Crystal beams a smile and rushes off to change. Dinner is served just over an hour later and no one can get a word in as Crystal just keeps talking excitedly about everything that happened. Finally, she takes a bite of food and Jasmine speaks up. "Tomorrow we can go check out what that trinket does. I *personally* have seen nothing like it." She continues after taking a drink of wine. "But I've heard of objects like this. It's used in rituals as a focus." She looks up to notice Crystal looking at the trinket as if expecting it to do something.

Andrew speaks up after finishing his meal. "I believe it's about time for me to get going."

Jack hurriedly chews his mouthful and swallows, looking up at the clock. "Ah yes, it's about that time, isn't it?"

Penelope walks in as if cued and motions to the kitchen staff. "I'll go ahead and handle this, you should get going."

The family stands up and prepares to leave. "Thanks, Penelope." She nods, and she summons the kitchen staff to gather the plates from dinner. "Cline, get the car around, and let's all get going." Cline nods and steps out while the family puts on their evening wears. Within moments, the chauffeur brings the car around and they embark, ladies first, and proceed to the Temple of Daniel.

Arriving just as the evening services are about to start, Andrew is greeted by Lyndis at the car. She looks him over in his robes and fixes his holy symbol hanging from his neck. "You're just in time. We will start in a few minutes if you want to go to the back and get ready." Lyndis directs Andrew with a wave of her hand. He turns, hugs each member of his family, and follows Lyndis to the back.

Jack waves his hand to the main doors. "Shall we go?"

Andrews's family walks into the church, and Tia spots Crystal almost immediately. She ducks back behind the door, barely peering around the corner. Lyndis catches this and with a quizzical look on her face addresses the woman. "What's wrong Tia? You look spooked."

Tia points towards the congregation, peeking from her cover with just a single finger. "That pale white girl out there is Crystal. That's the girl I told you about that Marcus chose to be part of the team." Lyndis notes the fear in her voice, but looking at Crystal can't see what makes her so scared.

Andrew, getting the final preparations done, looks to the congregation, and Tia. "Yes, that's my sister." He looks at the frightened Half-Elf. "So, you were there at the meeting too?"

Tia is flabbergasted but notes his curiosity in his question. "She's *your* sister? You don't look anything alike except for the eyes. She's pale white and you're a dark tan, she's short, you're tall, she's mean and you're…"

31

Andrew snickers, cutting her off, and smiles widely as if stifling a laugh. "I get that a lot. Mother is a Half-White Dragon, but my father is that short black man." He points to Jack sitting next to Crystal. He shrugs. "So technically I'm a one-quarter White Dragon, but in me, my father's side is more dominant, well, except for the height. Got lucky there." He straightens out his collar in the mirror, making sure everything is perfect. "But my sister takes after my mother more. They both have that ivory skin, but Mother has white scales while Crystal doesn't. She's got mom's talent for magic and the Dragon heritage in her is shown through her appearance. It's why she's such a natural at spell casting. She almost does it reflexively." Andrew finishes, turning to Tia. He holds his arms out so she can get a good look at him. "How do I look?"

She looks up at him, breaking her intent stare at the ivory girl, and smiles. "Very handsome." She chuckles. "There are girls whose hearts are breaking because you're going to be married to your faith instead of them."

Lyndis interrupts their conversation. "Time to get this going. We have many prayers to ask of Daniel for this year for our farmers." She then gestures to Tia and Andrew to get into their positions.

The next day, as the sun's morning rays just crested over the mountains, William is out in the training yard practicing when approached by his father, Gerald. He watches the young man go through the motions of hand-to-hand combat. "Good morning, son."

William, breathing hard and taking more swings on the practice dummy, doesn't turn to face him. "Morning, father."

"Couldn't sleep, son?"

William turns for a moment to look at the old man and returns to his task. "What makes you ask that?"

Gerald gestures to encompass the whole yard. "Well, the day hasn't technically started, but yet you're out here in full armor practicing." He puts his cup down and lowers his arm outwards to the side. "Have you even had breakfast yet?"

William stops and puts the sword down to his side. Sweating heavily even in the cool air, he looks over at his dad. "No, I haven't."

He breathes heavily and wipes sweat from his brow. "And no, I couldn't."

The older man puts his arm around his son and pulls him towards the house. "Come, let's eat and talk. You're worried about something, and I can tell." They walk inside and the kitchen maid serves them their breakfast. William explains to his father all the questions in his head and the older man listens intently and nods.

"One thing I've always had as a constant is that the Emperor always knows more than he's letting on." He stabs a piece of fruit with his fork, then points it at William. "But not dishonestly. It's like he wants us to figure out the rest on our own." Gerald then takes the bite, letting his son fill in the silence.

William nods in acknowledgment and swallows. "That's why I've been thinking so hard. Things don't add up, but as you said, maybe we need to figure things out on our own." William takes a drink of fresh milk and continues to analyze things internally.

"Well, we have all day." Putting his fork down, the elder man sits up and grabs some bacon. "Did Marcus give you an exact time for when you are supposed to be there tomorrow?"

William thinks about it, and realization dawns on him. He looks at his father making eye contact. "No, he didn't mention it. He only said to bring what you needed for the trip. He didn't say a time."

Gerald nods, finishing his bite. "Then what does that tell you?"

William finishes his glass and stands up. "That it's up to us to get this trip going. I guess I need to find Ms. Moonglow and Ms. Hellstromm and get them organized."

The elderly man smiles forcing more wrinkles. "Very good. Now get on with your day then."

William formulates an idea and, before getting up from the table, pens two brief letters and seals them. One for both Crystal and Tia, to meet him at the Sugar Rose restaurant tonight at six to discuss the mission over dinner. The Dwarven courier for his House takes the messages and hurries off to deliver them.

At the Church of Daniel, Tia, Andrew, and the others do their morning prayers prepping for the day. The Dwarven courier walks in and gets one of the cleric's attention. The cleric speaks with him a moment, then points towards Tia and Andrew.

The short man nods and walks up to Tia, getting both of their attention. "I have a message for Ms. Moonglow." He shows the crest of the Seventh House to her and hands her the letter. "I hope I have the correct person."

Tia nods, accepts the letter and whispers to him. "Thank you." Before she can open it, the Dwarven man tips his hat, turns, and heads out of the church.

Andrew's eyebrow shoots up. "What was that all about?"

Tia shrugs and opens the seal, then reads it, then summarizes as she goes along. "Sergeant Blakely wants to meet at a restaurant tonight." She pauses, continuing to read. "He wants to plan out the mission and get us all on the same page so we can be ready."

Andrew tilts his head, thinking about it. "Not a bad idea. You going to go?"

Tia nods, confirming she would. "Yes, if we're going to be working together, might as well get organized, right?" Then she turns back to Andrew. "Let's get our chores done first, so I'm not leaving you with extra work."

At the Hellstromm manor, the same Dwarven man walks up to the gate and speaks with the guards. After a few moments, the courier explains he must hand this to Ms. Hellstromm. The guards speak amongst themselves, then one guard motions to the other to go summon her. After a good thirty minutes, Crystal comes out in a shimmering green dress embroidered with silver decorative patterns. She walks with grace, but her eyes and slight frown give them all pause.

She crosses her arms over her chest and leans slightly to her right. "What is it that I'm dragged out here for so early in the morning for?" The guards flinch as she moves her hands.

The Dwarven courier straightens up and shows his signet ring with the Seventh House crest. "I have a message for a *Ms. Crystal Hellstromm* from Master William Blakely."

Her frown disappears, replaced by a smile. Stepping forward, she uncrosses her arms and looks the Dwarf over. "Oh, why didn't you say so?" Holding out her hand and making a *give me* motion with her fingers. He hands the letter over to her, tips his hat in acknowledgment, and leaves. Crystal handles the letter, staring down at it for a long moment as she looks at his seal.

One guard interrupts her thoughts. "Mistress, maybe you should proceed inside?" She nods without a word, nor looks up and walks back into the manner lost in thought. Entering the house, she shuts the large oaken door behind her with the echo bouncing off the far walls. Standing in the foyer, she doesn't notice her mother at the top of the stairs as she continues to just stare at the letter.

"What's that, honey?" Jasmine's voice breaks Crystal from her thoughts, bringing her back from wherever her mind had wandered.

Crystal shakes her head, clearing her mind more, and sounds confused. "Sorry, what mom?"

Jasmine points to the letter in her hand from the top of the stairs. "You're holding a letter in your hand." She glides down as if she was barely touching the steps, making her way to her daughter's side.

Crystal looks back and forth between her and the letter. She speaks as though it's not of real importance, flipping it around in her hands. "It's from William of the Seventh House."

Jasmine stops in front of her daughter and smiles, causing Crystal to flush a little pink. "Ah yes, the tall strapping knight you were telling us about at dinner yesterday. He was selected to go with you on this journey, if I recall correctly?"

Crystal notes the rise in her voice, as if she's expecting her to elaborate a little more. "Yes, mother." Jasmine stands there a moment, prompting Crystal to continue. "I haven't opened it yet." Jasmine reaches out as if to take the letter, but Crystal pulls back and out of her mother's reach. "What?"

Jasmine pulls her hand back slightly, looking into her daughter's eyes. "You going to open it? It's probably important if he wrote to you."

Crystal tilts her head up and throws her hands down before looking back down at the letter giving in and opening the letter. "Fiiine!"

After they've both read it, Jasmine smiles, placing a hand on Crystal's shoulder. "Guess you won't be home for dinner." She turns with a fluid motion, then casually strolls into the dining hall. She waves with a single hand. "I'll let your father know."

CHAPTER 5
(Start of a new beginning)

Jasmine and her daughter Crystal arrive at the Dragon Order's Sanctuary around midafternoon. Crystal insisted on getting this done before her dinner meeting with William and Tia and her mom relented, also curious about the trinket. The mother and daughter pair walk up to the main doors made of dark wood and knock. Crystal is surprised to see the female silver Dragonborn paladin from the day before and answers the door.

She looks them both over and recognizes them immediately. Bowing her head in respect, she addresses them. "Mrs. and Ms. Hellstromm. To what do we owe the honor?"

Jasmine speaks up first, motioning past the doors. "May we enter? My daughter has something to present to the Pontiff."

The paladin waves them to follow her inside, keeping her head lowered. "Yes, this way ma'am." Heading to the center of the sanctuary, she motions them to a set of pews and to wait there. She disappears into the back and moments later, is joined by a male Dragonborn with copper scales draped in purple robes.

Smiling with a toothy grin, he addresses them, taking their hands and shaking them. "Jasmine, Crystal, how are you both? What brings you back to our humble sanctuary?"

Crystal reaches out and hands him the Dragon token. Looking up at him, she explains her case. "Emperor Marcus handed this to me and instructed me to come here."

The Pontiff looks at it, turning it over in his hands. "Ah yes, it's a ritual item. It's used to awaken the Dragon blood within you. Make it more potent, so you're more in tune with the surrounding magic." He looks it over with a smile and then addresses Crystal. "Are you wanting to partake in this ritual?"

Crystal looks to her mother, then back to the Pontiff. "Yes, I do."

"Excellent." He looks at the young lady. "First, you must gather some items for the ritual." He touches her forehead gently. "Only when you gather them, all will you be strong enough to awaken the blood within your veins."

Crystal's smile fades and she crosses her arms. "What's that supposed to mean?"

"It means you are not yet strong enough, but your willingness to partake of the journey is the first step of many." He holds the trinket back out. "Hold on to this child." She takes it into her hands and he wraps his hands around hers with it trapped inside. "Don't lose it." He holds one hand up and points his finger up as if it was the most important step. "Bring it back to us when you have gathered everything. Only then will you be ready." Crystal looks thoughtful, but he interrupts her pondering. He writes up a list of materials she will need. "You must gather the items personally, not buy them in a store." Crystal makes a soured face. "Then we will see if you are wise enough to handle this gift." Crystal nods as if understanding. "I look forward to performing this with you, when you're wise enough."

At the Sugar Rose, William is wearing a bright blue and silver suit with the Seventh House crest on the right breast, as he sits waiting for the other two in his party. It's one of the most expensive restaurants in town. He figured it would be the only way to get Ms. Hellstromm to even take him seriously. The First House's district is one of the best in the city. He fidgets with some notes he had made for the meeting ahead of time, so he would get everything addressed before they leave in the morning. Music is playing in the background as people enjoy their meals and, as predicted, Tia arrives first in her traditional brown robes issued to her by her religion. Her long blond hair shines well in the artificial magical light of the establishment. She shows the letter to the maître d', and he escorts the young lady to William's table, where he stands up there and pulls the chair out for her.

She looks so uncomfortable. He adopts a friendly face for her. "I expect our other guest will be here any moment."

Tia nods, acknowledging what he had said, but doesn't reply. A waitress brings her some water and asks her what she would like to drink. Tia just points to the water. "This is fine, thanks."

William holds his hand up, stopping the waitress from going, and turns to Tia. "You can have whatever you want. It's on me. Indulge yourself."

Tia shakes her head. "It's not my way. Water is fine. Thanks anyway."

William understands she is shy and puts his hand down. The waitress shrugs and asks if he needs anything. "Not yet. I have one more I'm waiting on before we get started. Thank you." The waitress nods and goes to another table.

William talks a little, and Tia listens, but seldom speaks as they wait. But they didn't have to wait long. The familiar black adamantine and gold car of the Third House pulls up outside the Sugar Rose just moments later. A different chauffeur this time, however. The previous one was a regular Human male, but this one is a large Half-Orc-looking fella. *He looks out of place and uncomfortable in the black and white suit.* The Half-Orc walks around the car to the rear passenger door and opens it, reaches out and Crystal extends her hand, taking his. At that moment, it seems as if the whole place stops in time as she steps out. Even the musicians stop playing.

She's stunningly beautiful, almost entrancing. She's wearing a stunning ice blue dress that matches her eyes, with what looks to be diamonds sewn in a decorative pattern into seams around the collar and sleeves. They sparkle in the artificial firelight with a life of their own. Her hair is formed into three braids then braided into themselves again with gold wire strands holding it all together. Her cheeks and lipstick are also an icy blue, making her look almost like a frozen princess. She runs her hands along her hourglass frame, straightens her dress, then walks with a grace he's only seen the Empress manage. She walks up to the maître d's podium and presents the letter William had written to her. The Half-Orc chauffer stands stoically by the car longer than he should, watching her and everyone else's every move.

William surveys the area. *No, he's not a chauffeur, he's a bodyguard. Guess Mr. Hellstromm is very protective of his daughter to hire someone that big.* Once she's inside safely, he gets back into the car and drives around, and positions himself so he can see her every move. William notes that he's not the only one entranced by the Third House's daughter. Most conversations stopped when she got out. As she walks over, William stands up and pulls her chair out. She sits, and he effortlessly pushes her up to the table, and a whiff of a sweet-smelling fragrance is about her, further enhancing her beauty. She looks up at him, and he catches the faintest hint of a smile. *She really went all out for a dinner meeting. She must be showing off her status and wealth.* He and Tia look way underdressed compared to her.

She motions to a random waitress just walking by. "I'll take a Flaming Shadow to start as a drink."

The waitress bows and hurries off, and leaves William floored. *That's a twenty-gold drink, one of the more expensive drinks in town. I'm regretting the dinner already.* He keeps his smile. *I wanted to make a good first impression.*

William opens first, placing his hands on the table in front of him, and looking at his two guests. "So tomorrow we are going to be leaving, but the Emperor didn't say what *time* we were to show up. So we need to decide when we are going to get started on our journey." He smiles broadly, opening his hands outwards, hoping to get the girls to engage him. The waitress returns with Crystal's drink and sets it down, and she dismisses the help with a flick of the wrist.

Tia sits quietly, but Crystal speaks up. "Well, if it's up to us, I say we start mid-morning. This way, we have time to pack and spend some time with our families before we take off." She holds the drink to her mouth, then looks over its rim at William, her eyes gazing into his. "What about eleven a.m.? This way we could stop for lunch on the way out of town before leaving it behind?" She imbibes the drink, taking in its sweet taste with a slight spice to it.

Before William can answer, their original waitress arrives, taking out a small notepad. "Are you ready to order?"

Crystal doesn't hesitate for a moment. "Yes, I would like the chef's special salad with rich Elven dressing, a pan-fried catfish, a side of potatoes with a slice of Silvian orange, and a Dragon turtle strudel for dessert." Then hands the menu to the waitress with a flick of the wrist, almost hitting her. William and Tia sit stunned, and he can physically feel his wallet screaming for mercy.

The waitress turns and addresses Tia. "And for you, ma'am?"

She gently holds the menu up. "I'll just have a house salad and a steamed marsh puffin." The waitress turns to William after taking the menu from Tia.

"Well, I'll have the chef's special salad as well with Dwarven vinaigrette, a medium-rare twelve-ounce Porterhouse steak, and an Elven strawberry yogurt for dessert." He hands the menu to the waitress and catches a casual nod of approval from Crystal.

After the waitress leaves, Crystal starts up again. "I noticed you're wearing a bright blue jacket with a white undershirt and silver buttons." She picks up her glass again, looking at its diminished contents swirling it a little. "Almost like we planned our outfits somehow." Her icy blue eyes connect with his and he sits up.

He tries sounding dismissive in his response, as if it's coincidental, and waves a hand outward. "Yes, well, I figured it would be a pleasant change from the red and purple I normally wear while being part of the guard." He lets out an uneasy chuckle.

She looks down and drinks the last of her Flaming Shadow. "Or you guessed I liked the color blue and thought I would approve?" She turns those icy blue eyes back in his direction. "Are you trying to impress me?"

He feels as if she is looking into his very soul when the waitress arrives with their food, freeing him from the uncomfortable stare of her gaze. "Being we are going to be traveling together, we should get to know each other a little better." William hurriedly takes a drink of his wine.

"What would you like to know..." She looks across at him. "Sergeant?" She holds her glass up for the waitress to take, then starts on her catfish. William notices immediately that she is referring to his rank and not by name. *Either she's keeping this formal or she's doing just like me and judging me by my own reactions.*

"Well, what are your strengths?" He adjusts himself and motions with an open palm at her. "You seem very confident in yourself, but self-confidence can only carry you so far. I take it you're skilled in the ways of magic?"

Crystal rolls her eyes at the question. "I'm *very* skilled in magic." Putting her hand to her chest "And I believe I'm a natural leader." She then leans down, taking a bite of her salad.

Tia chimes in, still sounding nervous, especially seeing how Crystal and William are verbally dueling right in front of her. "I don't know why I'm here." She turns back and forth to them both as they both stopped looking at each other and focused on her. "Daniel says I'm needed as part of this group, but that's all."

William's smile returns, looking at her and gestures openly in her direction. "Then that makes you the most important member." He takes a bite of his steak, chews, and finishes. "Without you, who's going to keep us healed up if we are attacked?"

Tia thinks about it and looks down at her food. She picks up her fork. "I guess you're right."

Crystal casts her gaze upon him once again. "What are your strengths, sergeant?"

He looks up with his eye as he chews his food, then back at her. "I'm pretty good at thinking on my feet, analyzing a situation, and figuring out solutions." He thinks about it a little more the points his fork at her. "Plus, I'm very well practiced in swordplay."

She wipes her mouth with a napkin as the waitress returns with another drink. Once again, she flicks her away and scrunches up her face for a moment. "And to finish your question from earlier, I can cast spells I study directly from the connection in my blood. Once I commit a spell to it, it's there to be used whenever I want." She takes a drink and savors the flavor, closing her eyes but a moment. "Or till I replace it with another I like or if I research something better." She demonstrates by reciting a short incantation, icing over the drink in her hand.

The evening continues as they talk. Tia opens more from being shy, at least around them. *Crystal has a very dominant personality. She doesn't just think she's a leader; she projects it like a spotlight. William is also strong that way, but nothing like Crystal. He's going to be a great military leader someday, I can tell, but Crystal is either going to shine bright or burn out. I see why Daniel sent her along. To curb her personality and grant her wisdom with all that brashness she presents and to give him the confidence he needs to take action instead of being reactive.*

As the evening concludes and the only light in the city is the artificial flames from the streetlamps, the three finally agree to a time of ten a.m. to meet at the Emperor's palace. Tia elects to walk home as usual and departs, waving as she heads along her way. The richness of Crystal's car is too much for her to even fathom and wants nothing to do with it. Not that she's taken a vow of poverty or anything, but she explains that such extravagant wealth looks to be a waste to her. William walks Crystal to her car and the huge Half-Orc is standing there like a stone monolith as if daring the young man to pull anything to give him an excuse to rip him apart. William smiles up at him, not backing down. *He's big, but I highly doubt he's trained as well as I am.*

Crystal turns slowly back to the large man, keeping her hands folded in front of her respectfully. "Thank you, Sergeant Blakely, for the wonderful evening." Crystal smiles up at him and it's almost alluring as if daring him to make a move on her. "I look forward to working together on our endeavor tomorrow."

William smiles back, leaning forward, but then opens the door for the young woman. "Remember to bring only what you need to survive and a little extra. It's going to take a week to travel there by horse." He offers his hand for her to steady herself with and she takes it, doing her best to stay composed. Her hand is so soft compared to his that's all callused up from hard labor. "So, hope you dress appropriately for the trip."

She sits down in the luxurious vehicle and looks up at him with those icy blue eyes. "Of course…" She flutters her eyes a little. 'Sergeant.' He swallows nervously, and at that very moment he realized she is going to do exactly what she wants to do, and he doesn't have any control over it. He lets her hand go, and she places it back on her lap. Then suddenly the Half-Orc closes the door, barely missing William.

He growls, putting his large hand on Williams's chest, pushing him away. "Step back, sir."

William catches the drift immediately. *He's under some very strict orders for Crystal's safety. Wonder what's going to happen tomorrow?* He watches as the bodyguard gets into the car and drives away. Crystal waves from the window and she passes into the distance, leaving him alone, and lighter in the wallet. He smiles as his horse is brought to him. *She's going to be a handful. I hope I can keep her reined in during this trip.*

CHAPTER 6
(The Gathering)

As ten a.m. approaches, Tia, in her usual cleric's robes, has arrived, burdened with an overfilled traveler's pack and bedroll. She watches but hears a heavily clad horse approaching long before she can see him. William's armor is polished to a mirror finish and its trim is decorated with the colors of his House's traditional red and gold and even the horse's barding is polished to a pristine finish. *You can't miss him coming. Is he really going that over the top for a trip?*

As William approaches the palace gate, he can easily see several squads of troops along with a female Dwarven Lieutenant. He knows this Dwarf by her name of Gelga Orefall. The stout Dwarf wears full plate unlike the rest of the soldiers with just a breastplate. Also, unlike the rest of the troops, the lieutenant wears a galea with the mane running front to back with the red and purple colors alternating three times. William, doing the quick math, sees it's roughly fifty men and women of all kinds standing at attention. They are all in battle dress, rifles at the ready and swords at their side, ready to deploy to a battlefield along with several standard military wagons loaded with supplies. William notes that if the emperor was coming out, he would want to be well protected, and quickly spots Tia, looking out of place among the contingent.

He dismounts with the sound of metal sliding against metal. "Has Ms. Hellstromm arrived yet?" Tia just shakes her head no, but she can see her coming from this distance. She points down the roadway from the other direction. William turns following her arm to see a large Vardo pulled by four horses. Painted a bright red with gold filigree with black accents, highlighting it with bright white and gold wheels, and easily forty or fifty feet long. William's forehead wrinkles as a sigh escapes him. Throwing his hand out toward the oncoming wagon. "I expressly told her to only bring what she needed."

Tia smiles, and holding back a giggle, turns back to speak. "You and she have very different ideas about what constitutes as *necessary,* it appears, sergeant."

William paces a little and stares back at the oncoming wagon, then lets his arms drop to his sides. "I should have expected nothing less, to be honest." He pauses a moment as the wagon gets closer. "But I had hoped that she would just show up with a horse and casual supplies."

Tia shakes her head negatively, having known better, but perks up at another sight. "The driver of that wagon sure is an odd choice. Is that a Halfling?" William also noticed that, wondering where the Half-Orc went.

Both Tia and William jump and turn as one as a deep voice from behind them both booms past them. "I expected nothing less from her myself." William and Tia turn to see the emperor standing right behind them as if he was always there. Tia bows her head and William hits the pavement with a knee as if he weighed a ton.

They both speak in unison. "Your Highness."

Marcus smiles, waving them up. "You may rise sergeant and you both please, look up." As William stands, the fancy Vardo carrying Crystal pulls up in front of the palace. The Halfling female driver, dressed simply in a white cotton shirt, with a brown leather vest and leggings, stands up to dismount. Marcus puts his right hand up, looking at her, and she immediately bows her head and sits back down, knowing exactly who that is. Marcus walks around to the back, then opens the door to the luxurious carriage, triggering the steps to fold down to the ground.

Crystal reflexively extends her hand out to be helped down, not realizing it's Emperor Marcus standing there. She's done it so often before without ever checking who was on the other end. She clambers out in her rose-colored red dress that fits her form snugly. Her hair freely flows to the small of her back with rose-colored lipstick and blush on her cheeks. She keeps her focus on the stairs as she walks down, making sure she doesn't fall or get tangled in her dress, only to look up to see it's the emperor is the one holding her hand. William notices the entire spectrum of emotions cross her face as a surprise, fear, shock, embarrassment, and confusion just seem to hit her all at once and had to stifle a laugh not to embarrass himself. Crystal is glad for the choice of the coloring of her makeup, or everyone would notice how red she just turned.

Crystal curtsies as best she can, with Marcus still holding her hand. Her words are a jumbled mess, which just makes Marcus smile larger. "Breathe child. It's alright." Stepping back, Marcus walks back to where he was before. Crystal straightens herself out, regaining some composure, and walks over to join William and Tia. Marcus is addressing a lieutenant by the guards, but too quietly for them to hear.

William addresses Crystal under his breath. "I thought for sure I told you to bring only what you needed."

She retorts under her breath back at him, "And I did. I have food, shelter, a driver, maps, a table, and everything else a civilized person of my stature needs for trips." Tia lets out a quick snort at the two, trying to argue in hushed tones, but cuts it off immediately. *Wouldn't be right to laugh in this situation, but the contrast between these two is comical.*

"I'm surprised it's not steam-powered."

"Daddy didn't have time to convert it. Two days is too short, even for his genius." She flips her hand contemptuously. "So, he did what any reasonable person would do. He bought what I needed."

"Speaking of the driver." William motions to Penelope. "Who is the Halfling?"

Crystal responds quietly. "Her name is Shadow. She's not just my driver, but my personal chef as well."

Why does that name sound familiar? William shakes his head slightly, trying his best to control his own emotions, but fails. He turns his head and looks down to face her. His eyes turn hard, and he extends his right arm outwards. He no longer whispers, having lost all pretense. "Personal chef? I said to bring what you needed—"

She cuts him off mid-sentence with a cutting motion with her right hand, bringing her voice up to match his and putting a finger to his armored chest. "And I need my personal chef. I have particular tastes." Her gesture gets grander, pointing towards the street. "You don't expect me to just eat roadkill that you scrape up with a shovel, do you?"

William visibly bristles and Tia whispers her two cents. "Now is not the time to argue." They both stop to look at her. "She is who she is. You should expect that of her, and Ms. Hellstromm, William, is

46

a military man. His idea of needs doesn't include a refrigerator." Crystal was about to retort when Marcus turns and calls to William. William, snapping to attention, immediately answering him. Marcus motions to come to him and William marches over with military precision.

Crystal watches William intently. *He's so ridged. If he doesn't learn to relax, he's going to snap.*

William stands at attention in front of the assembled guards next to the lieutenant. Marcus looks down at them both. Reaching out, Marcus removes the insignia marker on Williams's right pauldron. "William," the Emperor starts. "I hereby promote you to the rank of Captain." Placing the new insignia where the old one was, he continues. "These troops here are yours to command for this trip." This time Crystal must stifle a laugh as William does his best to keep himself in check. Tia just glances back and forth between the two.

William sounds surprised, unable to keep it from his voice. "Thank you, Your Highness." He wets his lips that suddenly went dry. "But shouldn't the lieutenant be promoted before me?"

Marcus raises an eyebrow and scrutinizes the new captain by leaning into him. "Are you questioning my decision to put you in charge of these troops?" William swallows hard, noting the deeper tone in the emperor's voice and it sends chills up his spine and Tia and Crystal straighten up more. Even Penelope reflexively hides, virtually vanishing as if she never existed.

William responds with his voice cracking a little. "No, Sire. I was just." He stops and tries to start again but is cut off by the emperor.

"You believe the lieutenant should be next in line to be promoted?" Marcus finishes his sentence. William stands there like a statue. "I chose you over the lieutenant because I believe you're a better fit for this assignment to command the troops." Marcus leans in closer, mere inches from William's face. "Leave it at that, Captain." He steps back a few steps, having made his point.

William bows respectfully. *Captain at my age. I didn't expect to get a promotion like this for another ten years. What did I do to jump two ranks?* His mind races back to his father's words. *The emperor has a plan, and it's only for me to figure it out.*

Marcus smiles again and places his hand on the young man's shoulder. "Keep those under your charge safe. That's your standing order from me."

William responds reflexively. "Yes, Your Highness."

Marcus turns to face Crystal and gestures for her to stand next to William. "Come here, child." She walks over with the grace of years of practice and stops to stand next to William. "Crystal, I'm placing you in charge of the mission. You're acting as a representative of my House and my Empire." He hands her official documents. "William is to answer to you, but he has the sole discretion of military deployments. These guards are your personal retinue." Marcus sees her beaming with pride and William's face changes ever so slightly, but just enough that Marcus noticed. "They are to guard you with their very lives as my representative, but it's on you to find out everything I wanted to know in Black Rock, understand?" Crystal nods but doesn't speak up. "Tia." Marcus motions her to join the others. Tia comes to stand next to Crystal. Being almost comical, as she's almost a full foot taller than Crystal and then William, another half foot taller than her. "Tia, keep everyone safe and give them council as they need it." Tia looks down and folds her hands in front of her. "As a servant of Daniel, I'm counting on you to be the heart of this group."

Marcus takes a few steps towards his palace and then turns back to the trio. "It's time to get started. I will see you all in a few weeks." He scans all three and his next words weigh heavy on them all. "Do not fail me." Marcus waves and leaves, accompanied by his personal guards back into his home.

Crystal takes a few steps forward and turns about. "Well, Captain, shall we get on the road?" William nods in agreement and turns to the troops. He issues orders to move out. Crystal asks Tia if she would like to ride with her in the wagon.

Tia looks up at the wagon and back to Crystal, then shakes her head. "I'll ride up front with the driver. I don't feel like I should ride in the back."

Crystal shrugs. "Whatever you want." She turns back to William. "Captain, help me back into my wagon." William marches alongside her to the large carriage and stands next to the door on the back. Crystal extends her right-hand allowing William to take it, as she climbs in. She leans back out as he bends down to get the steps.

"Thank you, Captain. Do you think we have time to stop for lunch before we leave?"

William folds the stairs up and then looks back at her. "No ma'am. Every moment we aren't on the road is a moment we aren't getting back." He takes hold of the door, preparing to close it.

Crystal frowns while looking down at him for once. "But I think we should. You heard the Emperor, I'm in charge."

William sighs and shakes his head and with almost no emotion, he answers her. "That would be rather expensive, don't you think?"

Crystal looks at the assembled troops, seeing how many there are. "On second thought, I don't believe I brought enough money for everyone. Let us just go."

William visibly relaxes and goes to shut the door but is stopped by Crystal, placing her hand on it. "See Captain, I can be reasonable," then lets the door shut. Crystal finds a seat in her carriage and picks up some maps with markers that list the names of items on them. *I have my own mission to accomplish while doing this one.*

William orders one squad and supply wagon to the front of the Vardo, and one squad along each side of the supply wagons behind it. He figures Crystal would want her home away from home to be in the forward part of the convoy. Each wagon is carrying enough food and supplies for the detachment as they move along for the trip and will be supplemented with whatever game and resources they find along the way. Traffic and citizens move aside as they proceed out the front gate and into the open prairie to the north.

CHAPTER 7
(The wilderness beckons)

The group exits the city, and they approach the shimmering rainbow veil of the magical dome. William has been past this point often in his life, out on training exercises, and it brings back memories. The temperature difference from the eternal summer of the city to the cool spring air doesn't faze him. Tia and Penelope, riding on the front of Crystal's wagon, however, notice the stark change from constant mid to high seventies to the low to mid-fifties in an instant, reflexively crossing their arms. Crystal watches as they pass through from a window, observing everything, seemingly unaffected by the change. The extensive fields of grass and spaced trees are so different from the city. Farmers out with teams of mules and even some of the more advanced steam plows are planting this year's crops. She smiles to herself, knowing her dad helped invent some of those devices. She opens her window on the right side to peek out and notices a sharp drop in temperature, but unlike the others, she enjoys the cold. *It must be no more than fifty-five degrees out here. It feels amazing. I should have left the dome sooner.*

William, not too far away, slows his horse, leaving the lieutenant upfront. Pulling alongside her open window, William addresses her. "So, is this your first time coming outside, *princess*?"

Crystal, with her elbows perched on the windowsill, looks over at him. "Yes, it is, Captain. Surprised?" Her long black hair flows down the side of the enormous house on wheels as the breeze catches it.

William turns to her with a half-grin. "Not really." He turns back to the road a moment, then back to her, and chuckles a little. "I had a feeling you've been cooped up in your *tower* your whole life." The sounds of the metal barding on the horse hitting his armor are constant. It's not an irritating sound, she notes, almost comforting knowing he's there watching over her and is at her disposal.

"So, how long till we get to our destination, you think?"

"Well, if we keep pace, and take breaks to let the horses and men rest." William thinks, looking onward up the road, then returns his attention to her. "About five days, maybe six, depending on the terrain and weather."

Crystal, still smiling out her gilded window. "Thank you, Captain." She brushes her hair behind her ear and her tone shifts just a little to be almost flirty. "Are you going to ride there the entire trip and watch over me?"

William, knowing it's a loaded question, turns away to look forward back to the road, but she notices his eye shift to look at her but a moment. "That's on you. If you order me to, I shall."

Crystal presses the issue. "But if I don't order you, you wouldn't want to on your own?"

William doesn't take the bait. "*Princess*, I have a convoy to run. I'm going to have to constantly move about and check on things." Looking from her to the front and back again. "I couldn't even if I wanted to."

Crystal notices that's twice he's called her, "princess", but can't tell if he means it as an insult, or as a compliment. Crystal sits back down with the open window to her back, enjoying the cool breeze. Reaching over into a cabinet nearby, she pulls out a book titled *Spells and Rituals: A Guide to Finding Rare Spell Components* along with the map of the area. She has more work to do to find all the components she needs to complete this ritual.

William rides back to the front of the column when Tia speaks up. "You know, she was dropping a hint back there." William nods, but doesn't look at Tia.

"I know, but I have more important things to do right now."

Tia looks onward up the winding and hilly road. "I suppose you're right. Once we hit those woods up ahead, we will be watching over our shoulders for bandits." William just nods and kicks his steed up to the front to speak with the Lieutenant. Several hours go by and the plains are slowly turning into light woods. The sounds of animals in the distance and the wind rustling the leaves of the trees replace the sounds of the city and agriculture. Penelope nudges Tia with an elbow and points. "Company."

Tia strains her eyes. "You can see that from here?"

Penelope nods, confirming Tia's inquiry. "Not much escapes me. You should tell the Captain." Tia, looking down on the Halfling, then shouts to William. The shouting also catches Crystal's attention, causing her to lean her head out the window to hear what's happening.

William says something to the lieutenant, then pulls back on the reins to slow his horse again. Coming up on the right side of the Vardo, but never took his eyes off the road ahead. "What's wrong, Tia?"

She points out ahead, in the far distance. "We spotted some travelers on the road ahead of us. Figured you would like to know."

William squints. "I don't see anyone."

"Oh, they are there, Captain." Penelope grabs his attention, speaking up. "I can see them just fine from here. Maybe two miles ahead?" Her voice rose at the end as if not sure of the distance.

Crystal overhears the conversation. "We should stop and talk to them. Maybe they have news from Black Rock."

I can't see a reason to stop, but if I don't, she will argue with me. Turning his head to the side, to make it easier for Crystal to hear better. "As you command."

Returning to the front, he informs the lieutenant of the plan. William takes point as the Dwarven knight makes her way back along the column, notifying each sergeant of the planned stop. Within twenty minutes, they are finally close enough that the oncoming traffic is easily seen by everyone. The sun is well on their left and casting long shadows. It's easily seven in the evening, going by Penelope's instinct and training. The travelers approach with their wagon of supplies and move over to allow them to pass on each other's left.

William rides up ahead a short distance and hails the other caravan's wagon master. A tall, scrawny man, also on a horse, with no armor to speak of. The opposite of William and his steed that's heavily clad in red steel plating. The lieutenant holds his hand up, signaling to the rest to stop where they are. Crystal feels her Vardo come to a halt and leans out the window again, doing her best to see what's happening without falling out. She sees the other caravan and squints, trying to see more. *I can't see or hear anything. I'm in charge. I should be negotiating.* She sits back down and looks over her map. She almost has all six locations mapped out to find the stuff she needs, but it would help her needs to talk to the locals. Opening the door on her wagon, the stairs unfold with an audible *"thunk"* of wood hitting the gravel pathway. This perks up Tia and Penelope as they both felt and heard the stairs coming down. The dark-skinned Human sergeant in front of the wagon behind the Vardo speaks up, trying to stop her. "Ma'am, it's not safe yet. You can't just depart like that."

Crystal climbs down the steps with feminine grace, hanging onto the railing since no one helped her down, then walks right up to his horse and looks up at him with those icy blue eyes. "Don't presume you can tell me what to do, sergeant."

He swallows hard, feeling as if his blood turned to ice. He snaps his face back to face the front of the caravan. "Yes, ma'am!" Not missing a beat, she turns towards the other caravan only a few hundred feet away. As she walks along the side, Tia and Penelope immediately notice her walking by. That rose-red dress sticks out against the green of the surrounding area, hiding from no one. Tia immediately tries to disembark but notices that Penelope is not just already down, but hot on Crystal's tail.

How did she get down that fast? Did she jump from way up here? She makes her way down the side, using the ladder, as the commotion has caught the attention of the Lieutenant who turns to see what's going on. She watches Crystal makes her way past her horse with the little Halfling behind her, trying her best to get a word in to slow her down, and Tia fumbling with getting down off the giant wagon.

"Mistress, please wait till Captain Blakely gives the all-clear before approaching, is all I'm saying."

She waves Penelope off. "Oh please, Shadow. I can handle myself and with the Captain standing there, there is no way anyone would try anything." She breathes a little harder than usual, not used to faster-paced walking. "Besides, I just want to ask them a few questions. It's not like I'm trying to mug them."

The lieutenant begins to speak up but then thinks better of it. Looking back, Tia finally gets down, but she's so far behind the other two she doubts the priestess can do anything to stop them. The argument between Crystal and Penelope catches William's attention and that of the other wagon master. Noticing she's approaching fast with the Halfling hot on her heels, William thinks fast. "Ah, I was about to come and get you." He introduces her to the other wagon master with a gesture. "This is Master Cain from Mossy Fields, the next town up from here." Turning to Cain and introducing Crystal with a matching gesture, trying to keep things flowing. "Master Cain, this is Ms. Crystal Hellstromm, heiress to the Third House of Rose Harbor and Emperor Marcus Rose's representative on our trip."

Cain nods in acknowledgment, tipping his wide-brimmed hat. "How do you do, Madam?"

Crystal smiles and does a small curtsey, speaking cheerfully. "I do well. How's the road ahead?"

William slightly raises an eyebrow. *Small talk? I figured she would blast right into whatever it is she's after.*

"Well, there are no bandits that we ran across, and even if there were, you have quite the army there. I doubt anyone would even try anything if they were smart."

She holds her smile. "And how far ahead is your humble town? Could we make it there by nightfall?"

Cain looks to the west and sees how far the sun has set. "Not a chance." Turning back to her. "Maybe by afternoon tomorrow you could. It's at least another day away or so. Usually takes us a day and a half to get to the Capital one way."

Crystal nods her head, turning to look at the sunset for a moment, then back again to him. "Thanks for the information." Before he can get in another word, she continues onward to another question. "You wouldn't so happen to know where we could find a basilisk around here, would you?"

William, Cain, and Penelope all stop in wonderment, and even Tia, as she walks up to the group, wonders what she's talking about. Tia speaks up first, asking what everyone else is thinking. "What's a basilisk?"

Cain interrupts before Crystal can answer. "No, I don't know where to find one. Even if I did, I wouldn't want to find it."

William looks down at Crystal, puzzled. "Why do you need to find a basilisk?"

She looks at William. "That's personal, Captain. I'll tell you later." Then, turning back to Cain. "Do you have anything to trade?

You said you were heading to the Capital to sell some things. Could I look?"

Cain blinks and grips the horn of the saddle a little harder. "For what, exactly? We are heading into town to sell stuff, sure, but—"

Crystal walks towards the other caravan, cutting him off. "Well, let's see what you have, and maybe we can make a deal. I wouldn't mind getting some fresh fruits for the troops. That dried jerky just doesn't look good for them."

William objects. "There is nothing wrong with standard rations for the troops."

She turns her attention back to William. "I understand that, Captain, but they are my troops, too. If I want them to eat better when we can, we will."

Cain moves his horse to block Crystal, stopping her. "Listen, madam." He licks his lips and takes in a deep breath. "I have specific orders to take this stuff to Rose Harbor. I can't authorize any trades."

Crystal boils inside and it's showing outward as she turns slightly pink. "How rude to use your beast to block me like that." She runs her hands along her sides and the pinkness disappears. "I just want to see what you have as cargo. If I buy it here, it means you don't have to haul it to the city."

Cain moves his horse backward. "Sorry, but I can't allow that. If you're interested in trade, you need to go to Mossy Fields and talk to them there." Cain moves his horse backward, giving space between them. "I don't have the authority to do that from here."

William can see Crystal is doing her best to hold back her temper. "Mistress."

"What!" she exclaims, breathing a little heavier.

He thumbs towards the setting sun. "We should get moving along." This turns her attention back to the setting sun. "We have about two or three hours of light. We can cover some ground before setting camp if we get going now."

She runs her hands along her sides again, pulling the wrinkles from her dress. "You're right, Captain." She turns back, walking towards her wagon.

"Ms. Hellstromm, would you like a ride back to your Vardo?"

Crystal turns and looks up at him, then at everyone else, noting the situation. "I would like that, yes. Saves me a walk on this rocky road and that's very nice of you, Captain." She walks up to the heavily clad horse. "How exactly do I get up here?"

William reaches out his arm and leans down. "Grab my elbow and hang on." She reaches up and does as he gives her more instruction. "When I pull, just swing your left leg over." She nods, and he yanks her gently onto the back of the horse as if she weighed nothing. She then instinctively wraps her arms around him as he kicks the steed into motion. Tia and Penelope begin their long walk back. They both notice that Crystal went from furious to calm to happy in just a few moments.

Penelope keeps her tone soft to not be overheard. "I think she likes him."

Tia responds, keeping her tone down. "How can you tell?"

"Years of being around her. She only calms down for two other men I've known. Her father and her brother." They walk back to the wagon themselves, watching William take her all the way. "Even Cline can't calm her down and he scares me, but Master Jack and Master Andrew's very presence can turn her temper down with some kind words."

Tia looks onward as they make their way back to the wagon. Penelope climbs up first, then Tia as William and Crystal talk at the back of the wagon in hushed tones. "If I can inquire about something, Ms. Penelope?"

"Sure. What would you like to know?" She hears the door and stairs in the back get set in place.

"Why does Crystal call you Shadow instead of Penelope?"

Penelope's demeanor doesn't change, and William advances and they take off again. With confidence that catches Tia off-guard, Penelope confesses her sins. "I was a thief." She turns for the briefest of moments and gives Tia an evil grin. "A damn good one at that. Had two passions in my life, cooking and stealing." She turns back to the road again and continues. "I was being referred to as *The Shadow* because I was a master at hiding in plain sight and couldn't be spotted unless I wanted to be."

Tia nods, trying to understand. "If you were so good, what happened?"

Penelope gives a short chortle. "Jack happened."

They pass the other caravan wavering as they do and showing common roadside courtesies.

Tia shakes her head, not understanding what Penelope means. "I don't get it, who's Jack?"

Penelope thumbs towards the wagon. "Her father is Jack, and he caught me. I was going to rob his house blind, you know, big score." She makes grandiose gestures, giving weight to her story. "I disabled the mechanical and magical triggers for the house and got in." She continues after taking a drink from her canteen. "Dead of night, and I thought everyone was asleep, well, till I got the scare of a lifetime."

Tia hasn't taken her eyes off the Halfling since her story started. "So, what happened?"

"As I said, Jack happened." She laughs. "He was still up, testing some new prototype armor that could not only see me in the dark, but the guy was invisible and soundless!" She continues to smile. "I'm making my way into the family room to pick up something of value and out of nowhere, he just picks me off the ground." Penelope waves her arms and legs frantically for emphasis. "I had no way to run, nowhere to go, and couldn't even see the bastard's hand that was holding me." She drinks more water. "Next thing I know the suit opens up in front of me and this short black man steps out of a seven-foot-tall steam-powered armor that's still clear as glass, at least on the outside, but with it open, I could see it for what it was." She puts the canteen down

Tia still staring down at her. "So, what did you do?"

Penelope continues watching the road. "There was nothing I could do. That suit's vice-like grip held me there till the guard showed up and took me away. The next day, Jack shows up at the station and asks for me. They dragged me out of the cell and propped me up in front of him. He asked if I could do anything else in the world but steal; what would it be? So I thought about it, then I told him I liked to cook."

"And then what?" Tia prompts, eager to hear the rest.

"He said that he requires a new head chef. *If* I could cook him and his family a meal that none of them could forget, he would take me in and give me a job and home. I had nothing to lose." She takes her eyes off the road for a moment to look at Tia. "I was going to be set in indentured servitude anyway for all the other houses I robbed so might as well take him up on the offer and try."

"You cooked them a meal they loved?"

"Oh, hell no." Penelope laughs loudly, getting William and Gelga to look back for a moment. "It was a passion, but I didn't have a clue what I was doing over basics. I could hear Mrs. Hellstromm cough and gag and Andrew pray to Daniel for help with the aftertaste."

Tia laughs as Penelope continues. "I thought for sure I was going to be shipped right back to the station." She continues to laugh. "Jack came into the kitchen and put his plate down, looked at me, and asked in all seriousness. 'Do you know how to cook at all'?" Penelope tries to calm herself. "I told him I could cook, but nothing fancy. I enjoyed cooking, but having to steal to make my way didn't leave much time to learn."

Penelope leans back in reflection. "My life changed at that moment. Jack tossed the plate in the sink and turned to Cline, who I thought for sure was going to kill me with a glance." She turns her head to Tia. "That man scared me more than any guard, and to an extent, still does." She sits upright and looks back at the path ahead. "And Jack told him to get me cooking lessons from the top chef of the First House."

Tia gasps. "He paid to have you learn from the best?"

Penelope nods. "And I learned. I wanted to be the best cook Jack has ever known." Penelope glances at Tia and goes back to the road again. "No one ever gave me a break like this. I was nothing more than a common thief stealing to survive, but this black Human just offered to turn my life around out of compassion." Penelope's grin goes from friendly to more sinister for a moment before going back again. "And he kept my secondary talents up to speed, too. I never lost my edge for being a thief, but I used my talents to help protect the family now instead of taking from it, testing new security systems he invents as part of his competition with the Fifth House."

Tia turns away, looking at the shadows cast from the trees, noticing they are getting exceptionally long as the sun is barely above the ocean now. Twilight is setting in and the brightest of stars are coming into view. Even the moon is bright enough for them to see coming over the mountains to the east. "So why are you here on this trip instead of serving Mr. Hellstromm?"

She thumbs backward towards the Vardo. "Because Ms. Hellstromm needs her favorite chef to prepare her meals." Penelope turns, winking at Tia, and the sinister grins return. Tia's skin gets goosebumps from the look alone. "And if anyone makes a move to harm her, or other things, I'm ordered to kill them without consequence." The coldness of how Penelope said that causes a slight tinge of fear in the priestess. Tia can tell that Penelope wasn't exaggerating and feels sorry for anyone who makes Crystal mad or tries to harm her. She notices William motion to Gelga pointing to a camping spot ahead. Trees line the roads, but it's not too heavily wooded yet. They pull the wagons in and set up defensively with Crystal's Vardo in the center.

CHAPTER 8
(Feed me)

Setting camp for the night, William barks orders at the troops to get tents set up and fires started. It's going to get cold at night out here. As the sun drops below the ocean's surface, replacing the daylight with darkness, the temperature goes with it. Dropping into the low forties or possibly lower, they will be lucky if the ground doesn't frost over tonight. Penelope and Tia disembark from their perch atop the wagon. The curtains on the wagon are drawn so no one can see inside, meaning Crystal wants her privacy. Penelope hitches the horses to a tree stump nearby so they can't take off, and then proceeds to the back of the Vardo. Knocking on the door, Crystal's muffled voice comes from inside. "Who is it?"

Penelope speaks loudly to be heard through the wood. "It's Penelope, Mistress."

"Come in then." Penelope opens the door and climbs the stairs to get inside, closing the ironwood door behind her. Within minutes, smoke from the stovepipe billows out and the scent of something good hits the area.

William, still helping set camp, mutters to himself. "She's eating well tonight."

"Well, maybe you can eat well too if you but knock. Maybe she will share with you?" Tia's voice ascends, sounding almost musical.

William turns to see she's sitting several dozen feet away looking as if praying and then remembers she's Half-Elven. *She could have easily heard that.* "No, no, it wouldn't be right, nor is it protocol." Turning back to his work. "Besides, I have my trail rations." He holds one up. "It's why we brought them." He then points it towards the red wagon, whose scent is growing more alluring by the moment. "And I know she won't eat them, but I'm a soldier."

Tia turns her head slightly to look at him, then shakes her head, going back to her thoughts. *As if that's supposed to be an excuse?*

The commander's tent is assembled, illuminated with lamps, and the cot is set up, along with the folding chairs and table. William walks in and sits down, enjoying a cup of coffee percolated over one of the camp's many fires. He sips the caffeinated nectar of the gods, looking over the maps spread out on the table, and the lieutenant brings in a report of the current stock of supplies. Gelga turns her attention to the wagon, then back to William. "Whatever that Halfling is cooking up sure smells good, don't you think, sir?"

William nods in agreement, looking at the report. "Don't lose focus, Lieutenant. We have a long way to go yet." Looking up from his papers. "Is the camp finished and secured?"

The lieutenant straightens up, and she speaks with confidence. "Yes, Sir. Each squad is going to take rotations to watch for bandits or other dangers." William nods, for he expected no less from her and this outfit, each trained to perfection by the academies. The hours go by, and he steps out of his tent into the chill of the air. Soldiers, in their bedrolls, lay close to the campfires for warmth, including Tia, who is curled up there, twitching occasionally. *Wonder what she could possibly be dreaming about?* The nearly full moon faintly lights up the area beyond the fires, but also tells him it is close to midnight. The squads rotate shifts on guard duty and keep the fires stoked.

Continuing his journey around the camp, he notices the door on Crystal's "home on wheels" is open. It's dim inside but not dark. His heart skips hoping she's all right and looks inside for her. He can see Penelope is asleep in her little bed in the overhang, but curiously, he doesn't see Crystal. He feels his heartbeat in his ears as he looks inside more intently, but is startled by a soft voice behind him. "Looking for anything in particular... Captain?" Crystal's voice is soft, almost seductive sounding. He spins in place blushing slightly, seeing her wreathed in the moonlight with her hands behind her back looking completely innocent. Her head is cocked slightly and an impish grin on her face gets him to swallow.

How can someone that bright white and wearing a bright blue dress be so unnoticeable? Then it dawns on him that's not the same dress she wore when they left. "You should stay in your Vardo, Ms. Hellstromm. It would be safer in there."

She takes a hand from behind her back and steps into him, placing a single finger on his breastplate, making her dangerously close. "But you're supposed to be keeping me safe, remember?" She stares up at him, locking eyes with him for a long moment.

William, flustered and frustrated by her just doing whatever she wants, snaps him back to reality. He can feel his hands sweating and rubs them on his sides. "Why do you insist on making my job harder?"

Crystal takes in the cool night air with a smile and deep inhales through her nose. "I'm not making your job harder." Her impish grin grows, getting him to swallow again. "I'm making it more… fascinating?"

He smiles in return, seeing what she is up to. "I don't need it to be more 'fascinating' thank you very much." She takes her hand from his breastplate, turns, and walks off toward the woods, away from the warmth of the fires. He follows instinctively, knowing it's his charge to keep her safe. As they stare up into the darkness, and the stars twinkle above them, the moon hasn't reached its pinnacle, but it will soon. His breath is noticeable in the cool night air, and he shivers slightly as the temperature dives below forty. He tilts his head slightly down in her direction. "You should get back inside. It's getting cold out here and that dress is not going to keep you warm."

Crystal just stares up at the stars, taking it all in. "I'm not cold." She pauses for but a moment. "Captain." She doesn't turn to look at him, but he can tell her tone was flat.

He's not sure how, but he's wearing full leathers under his armor and it's cold to him, but she just stands in a sheer dress made of silk and doesn't seem phased. "Nonetheless." He places a hand on her back gently. "I need to continue my rounds." He looks down at her, giving her his attention and she takes notice, looking into his eyes once again. "As fun as it would be to sit and look at the stars all night with you, I need to get to sleep myself for the journey tomorrow."

Her smile returns, tapping his chest plate as she goes. "I'll hold you to that." She drags a finger across his polished armor as she turns back to her Vardo. He moves his hand to the center of her back and escorts her back to the wagon. He doesn't know why he did it. It felt right to do, and knows contact like that is unprofessional. He's further baffled that she didn't react, as if she didn't mind. He removes it when they get to the wagon, and he extends it again to stabilize her. She reaches out and takes his hand, gripping it softly, and climbs up the stairs.

"Good night, Captain." She turns, closes the door, and locks it.

William stays up a little longer to make sure the midnight rotation goes well, and then he wakes the lieutenant to take over so he can finally catch some sleep himself.

Waking up to the smell of cooking eggs and freshly toasted bread made his stomach rumble. Donning his armor, he picks up the cup of coffee from last night and tosses it out. Asking no one he addresses the troops. "We have freshly brewed coffee around here somewhere?"

"Yes, sir." A Human officer hands him a fresh cup.

Taking the cup, he slaps the man on the shoulder. "Thanks, soldier, I needed this." William walks around the camp. "Make sure these fires are completely out. Don't want to start a wildfire and accidentally destroy everything." The smell from Crystal's wagon is so tempting and then he notices Tia is missing. "Anyone see where the cleric lady went?"

Troopers look around, and one of them speaks up, pointing at the woods. "She's over here." William walks over and sees a small portable altar and some sacramental cloth laid out. He nods in understanding. *At least I know where she is.*

Taking almost an hour, they finally finish packing up camp. Penelope opens the door to the Vardo and climbs down, and Crystal steps out behind her. Stretching in the morning light, she has changed yet again into a nice dark green dress with matching makeup. *Must be her attempt at camouflage, I guess?* Birds, squirrels, and other animals make noises as the woods come to life in the morning. He looks up and notices the clouds in the sky are looking heavy. "Looks like it could rain soon."

The wagon's now ready, and they head back onto the road. The first few hours are uneventful. The temperature comes up as the sun crests high noon, causing complaints to come from Crystal's wheeled apartment. The windows are already open on both sides to get the best cross breeze possible. Tia and Penelope glance back at the wagon occasionally as she cusses about something inside the Vardo. Crystal wipes the sweat from her brow. *I need a bath. I'm filthy and need to be clean. This is unacceptable.* She sighs. *I guess I could just keep using my magic, but I really want a bath.* Her body *craves* the feel of cool, clean water on her ivory skin. *Not to mention spells do nothing to moisturize nor get my hair silky-smooth as I love.* She leans out the window, her hair flowing in the wind behind them. "Shadow!"

"Yes, Ms. Hellstromm?" Penelope leans over to the side to hear her better.

"If you spot a water source, *ANY* water source like a pond or something, let me know!"

Penelope nods reflexively. "Yes, Mistress."

Tia, chewing on some jerky she brought with her, just sits there watching the road, "What's going on Penelope?"

She just shrugs from her seat. "Haven't a clue. Last I checked, the water tank and the canteens were full."

The forest gets heavier, and soon they are covered in shadows from the trees. Still brightly lit as it's midday, and the shade is welcome from all those present. Rolling hills rock the wagons and the cussing coming from the Vardo intensifies. William and Gelga casually look back at the noise, then at each other, but neither dare approach it. Penelope and Tia can clearly hear Crystal's complaints as things fall over inside the cabin, making a mess and causing windows to flop open and closed.

They pass into the heaviest part of the woods and the sounds of the creatures living there come from all directions. Chirps and squawks, growls and barks, and the rustling of bushes as the game takes off from the sounds of the oncoming troops and wagons. They continue traveling and the noises die down. William takes notice, as does Penelope, as they both look around at their surroundings. Reflexively, Penelope stands up and takes a better look, breaking Tia out of her thoughts.

"What is it?"

Penelope shakes her head, not knowing what has her spooked. Her tone is reserved, almost hushed. "Something isn't right."

William pulls his sword from the scabbard as a vine lashes out from above and right side of the woods, grabbing him. The horse bucks in protest, but more vines lash out, grabbing Gelga and her pony. The guards react in an instant, as the sound of steel on leather punctuates the air as swords are readied into position. Penelope yanks the reins, bringing the wagon to an abrupt halt, causing more things to fall over and more cursing from the back. More vines entangle men, horses, and wheels of the carriage coming from all directions now, including from the canopy.

William barks orders. "Defensive positions! And someone cut this damn thing off of me!"

Penelope pulls daggers from nowhere and leaps off the wagon, onto the horses, and slashes the diabolical branches. Tia drops the food she was snacking on, taking in the scene. Thinking fast, she jumps down and runs up to the captain and the lieutenant. She speaks a brief prayer and fans her fingers outward, glowing red. Bolts of flames shoot out from her fingertips, striking everything in front of her. The vines burn away and instantly let go, dropping man and steed.

William, standing up, brushes off a few flames that started on his armor. Gelga pats her head, putting out the flames started on her galea. William turns to Tia. "Thanks for saving our tails, even if you did set them on fire."

Farther back, soldiers drop their rifles and pull swords, swinging at the plants, and cutting vines back. Metal clangs against wood as they try to cover each other from the whip-like appendages coming from all directions. Penelope yells for help as the carriage is being dragged off the pathway.

The right window flings open, and Crystal's ire is broadcast for all to hear. "I HAVE HAD ENOUGH!" This is followed by a muffled chant only heard by Penelope and the closest guards. A small cone of ice and snow flies out the right side, striking the bushes in a wide area. An audible screech is heard from all directions. Vines lash with a new intensity as several troopers disappear into the underbrush, dragged to an unknown fate.

Vines whip out and smash on top of the carts, destroying and dragging away crates and casks. Troops are hauled into the air, swinging at their legs, trying to cut themselves free. Gelga takes swings with her hand axe as the vines get more intense. "I think you only ticked it off, Ms. Hellstromm." William swings his sword, trying to keep the vines at bay. Penelope frees one horse, but the vines come for her too. Using her small size, she dodges and cuts them, freeing the other horses. Vines strain, holding the carriage wheels in place as the horses pull with everything they have. A sergeant comes forward behind the carriage, striking the plants holding one of the back wheels, severing it.

William cuts his own mount free, as it bucks wildly against the strange plant's grasp. Tia, muttering another prayer, reaches out and touches him with her hands glowing blue. The minor burns he suffered from her earlier attack vanish as if they had never happened. He turns in her direction. "Thanks." He mounts up and quickly surveys the situation. The vines from the right are more animated than the ones on the left. He's dealing with multiple assailants of whatever this is.

"Ms. Moonglow!" Tia looks up at him. "That fire trick you just pulled. Can you pull it again and focus it on the right? I think Crystal's attack wounded this thing, and it's trying to protect that part of itself from another assault!"

Tia nods and turns to Gelga. "Lieutenant, do you need healing?"

The Dwarven woman continues to chop at branches. "Do as you're ordered. It will take more than a cursed tree to bring me down!" Tia nods and moves back towards the center of the attack.

Crystal is frustrated deeply with her situation. Sticky and sweaty from the heat, her home trashed from poor roads and now a damn fern is making things worse. She is livid with everything right now. She throws open the back door and steps down onto the road. "Get the hell off my wagon, you infernal plant!" Chanting a new incantation, her right hand glows red as a ball of ice forms out of the ethereal in front of it, and rockets into the woods, exploding into a small shower of shards.

The screeching increases and vines whip frantically in every direction. One from behind Crystal lashes out and wraps itself around her leg, tripping her face-first into the mud from the busted casks, and drags her towards the woods. She screams in pain and claws at the ground as it drags her away. The sergeant standing there goes to grab for her, but he gets snared from the opposite direction and is pulled into the air away from her.

William kicks his steed hard, seeing Crystal in trouble. He rides right into the whipping branches and jumps from his mount, landing face down in the dirt behind her. Grabbing the offending plant, he digs in his heels and pulls his dagger from his belt. He chops at the thing, swinging harder and harder with his considerable strength till it lets go. Crystal is dropped unceremoniously, into the blood and mud forming from the battle. Troops swinging at anything, trying their best to keep more horses and each other alive.

Penelope continues to spur the horses. Vines and branches snap as they can't hold on any longer, setting the wagon into motion. The lieutenant, seeing an opportunity, rushes over to Tia to protect her as she begins her prayers. Tia's eyes open and she fans her fingers once again as flames of divine fire leap from her red glowing fingers, burning the woods and setting plants alight. Exhausted from casting so much so fast, Tia is caught by the lieutenant, who lowers her down gently.

The noise coming from the forest is almost deafening as the plants around them shake violently in no real direction. One trooper takes a chance and reaches into one wagon and pulls out a small container. He tosses it into the burning flames, and it breaks, causing a shower of flames to erupt. *Good idea.* William continues swinging at vines. *Tossing lamp oil on it should really do some damage.*

Crystal, covered in mud, bleeding from her leg, and dress torn, gets up but slips and falls again, causing her to sob. She just sits in the mud, not knowing what to do, pounding her fists on the soaked ground. William crawls up to her, looking over her wounds. The thorns on the branches did a number on her leg all the way up, but it doesn't look deep. Waving his hand, he shouts, "Medic!" bringing the attention of everyone who isn't in immediate danger.

Penelope, having pulled the wagon clear, dives off and runs back into the fray. Slashing at anything green and moving as she makes her way back to Crystal. Tia rises to her feet. "Lass you're in no shape to be moving right now." Gelga puts herself into a defensive stance. "But I think we got this thing beat; it's retreating."

Tia gets up anyway. "I'm a cleric of Daniel. If someone is hurt, I must help." She wills herself onward to discover what she can do.

Vines from overhead grab Tia and haul her into the air. Gelga jumps up and grabs the Half-Elf, adding her weight and arresting Tia's assent. Tia screams for help and Crystal looks up. She looks at him and grits her teeth. "Pick me up." William stands holding Crystal upright. She starts a new incantation, pulling power from her blood and pointing in Tia's direction. Another ball of ice forms in front of her red glowing hand and rockets into the vine holding Tia, freezing and shattering it. Tia and Gelga fall to the ground and Crystal, being exhausted from pushing herself and the pain, passes out in Williams's arms. Between the fire and the freezing cold, the axes and swords, the whipping vines cease to move and they believe it's dead. Crystal isn't out for long, slowly coming to as William lowers her back to the ground so he can bandage her wounds.

Tia runs up and sees what happened. "How bad?"

"Looks like some deep scratches from the thorns. Taoni hasn't had a chance to test for poison, but for now, she's just in a lot of pain."

"I have a little strength left in me. I could cast a healing spell on her."

William shakes his head. "We have others wounded much worse than this. Help Taoni first. As our only field medic, she's going to have her hands full here." He turns back to work on Crystal. "I'm going to bandage her up and get this under control."

Tia nods in understanding. She doesn't enjoy leaving Crystal like this, but William is right. Serious wounds need to be treated first. She walks back over to the makeshift medical area where Taoni is setting a fracture.

"Where can I help best?"

Taoni looks up at Tia, then directs her to a serious case. "This trooper has a fractured rib. It was trying to crush him to death."

"Is he the most wounded person here? I have very little spiritual power left, so I want it to count."

"Everyone else is either dead, suffering from sprains and scrapes, or made it out alright." She turns back to the Human she was treating with a broken femur. "Well, and his leg is broken, but aside from a lot of pain, he should be ok." She looks at the current patient. "But all I really know is he has some fractured ribs and his breathing is labored. He might have bone splinters poking him in the lungs, or maybe internal damage. We almost didn't get him free from those vines in time."

Tia nods, closing her eyes as she begins her prayer to Daniel and her hands glow with a faint blue light. She touches the man on his chest and a blue glow envelops him and just from the look on his face, some of the pain went away.

"Thanks, lady." His eyes roll back and he falls unconscious. Taoni reacts instantly, checking for a pulse.

She feels relieved. "He's alive."

Tia, weakened from her spell casting, clutches the cart. "I need to rest." She sits down on the edge with sweat pouring off her face.

The medic nods and does another check over the wounded trooper. "You're healing is good. The broken ribs are at least better. Only time will tell now." She takes a testing kit. "I need to know if this thing is poisonous. If it is, we could all be in serious trouble."

William goes to stand up but Crystal grabs his arm. He turns his attention to her and can see a tear in her eye, and her lip quivers a little. "Where are you going?"

William kneels back down. "I have to check on everyone else, get an idea of what we were fighting and see what our losses are."

She let's him go, sounding defeated. "So, I'm just going to sit here in the mud till you get back then?"

"No, you're not. I'll take care of you first." He stands up and lifts Crystal off the ground, putting his arms under her shoulders and knees. She reflexively places her hands around his neck and buries her face in his massive chest as he carries her to her now filthy Vardo. Her frown disappears and even a tiny smile appears, having almost forgotten about the situation. Penelope shakes her head and re-hides her daggers as if they don't exist and follows the tall knight and Crystal, keeping only a few steps behind. Carrying her up into her mobile home, he places her carefully onto the divan. She lays in her torn dress and mud and mouths *thank you.* He nods and turns to the exit, only to bump into Penelope.

"I'll take it from here, Captain." Walking around him to the stove, she lights it up and grabs a pot. "I know a recipe that will help with the pain. She will be right as rain in no time."

William glances back at Crystal, with her eyes closed as if sleeping, looks back to the Halfling, and departs. He walks to Tia, Gelga, and Taoni by the medical wagon. "Casualties?"

Taoni removes her helmet and cradles it on her side. Sweat-soaked strawberry blond hair cascades down to her shoulders.

"Currently, sir, we have four officially dead, one missing presumed dead, one seriously wounded, and a dozen minor injuries."

William sighs, but it's a part of the job. All kinds of weird stuff out there and can't be prepared for everything. He turns to Gelga. "What supplies have we lost, lieutenant?"

"I haven't finished the count yet, but I know at least four flasks of lamp oil were used to kill the monster plant. We lost a horse in the battle as well. Other than that, everything looks intact, but going by the mud and the scattered food, we lost some other supplies. I'll have a full report for you tonight when we break for camp."

CHAPTER 9
(Vices)

William smiles in thought at the smell of freshly brewed tea coming from the carriage. After a few minutes, Crystal emerges and stumbles down the steps, almost falling. William moves to intercept her before she hurts herself again.

"You really should stay in your wagon, Ms. Hellstromm."

Crystal grabs him by the waist to steady herself. "Has anyone searched the area where the creature was?"

William's eyebrows raise slightly, looking confused. "We recovered our dead to be buried properly. Why?"

Crystal shakes her head. "No, that's not what I mean. Take me to its center. I want to look for something."

William sighs and his brow furls a little. "I don't think so, Ms. Hellstromm. I must keep you and everyone else safe and if it's not dead, taking you to the heart of it would place you in danger."

Crystal looks at him with those icy blue eyes filled with anger and defeat. "Fine, but in its bed, could you check for unusual items?"

William looks to where they found the body of his soldier, then to her. "What do you mean by 'unusual items,' ma'am?"

She does her best to hold herself upright, wincing a little as she puts weight on her leg. "Like, I don't know." She shrugs. "A basilisk shell, or some Minotaur fur?" William's face is stoic and he just stands there. She sighs and waves her hand dismissively. "Never mind." Turning, she walks back to her Vardo. William walks with her and helps board her once again.

Closing the door and setting the steps up, Penelope gets his attention while standing under one wheel. "We really should get a move on. I know you're in charge, but if that thing is still alive, we're still in its kill box."

William nods in agreement. Penelope leaves and he approaches Gelga. "I'll hitch my horse to the wagon that doesn't have one, so we don't have to leave anything behind." He points forward. "Gelga, take point. I'm counting on you."

She nods and circles her hand in the air, motioning to form up. Mounting her pony, she moves upfront and they venture out again.

What seems to be an eternity to Crystal, but only a few hours, the hills level off and the forest thins again. The tea Penelope made makes her feel a hundred times better. She opens and looks out the left window for a time. The trees relent to open grasslands once again, and she can feel the cross breeze. It's only about four or five in the afternoon, but it feels much later. Another thirty minutes pass as she just enjoys the breeze when she spots a small pond close to the road ahead. Internally, she becomes giddy. *It's a pond! I can finally get my bath and get all this mud off me.* Looking around the mess, she grabs some soaps, oils, and other items, then packs them in a small bag.

As they get as close as they can to the water when Crystal shouts, "STOP!" from the window. Everyone in the convoy stops in an instant, wondering what she is shouting about now. The back door opens and the stairs come down with that familiar 'thunk'. Crystal comes down the steps way too fast, prompting William to jump from his horse just behind her cart. By then, she's already running into the tall grasses, hair billowing behind her. William gives chase, clanking as he goes. Penelope and Tia stand up, looking onward at the strange spectacle.

Gelga pulls her pony around and comments from next to the large wagon. "What in Sturm's name is happening now?" Penelope smirks and Tia shakes her head silently, not having the faintest of clues.

Coming up on the flowing water, Crystal wastes no time standing on the bank. She utters an incantation before William can grab her, and in an instant, her torn dress and bandages just hit the ground. William, who was just barely trailing behind her grinds to a dead halt, almost tripping over himself. He quickly turns around, only glimpsing her bare, petite ivory body.

Penelope lets out a hearty laugh and is caught by Tia before she falls from her perch. The Dwarven lieutenant looks up, confused at the Halfling, not seeing anything but grass. "What's so funny?"

Penelope, trying her best to catch her breath, can't speak. Tia looks down. "I can't see as far as you can, but from what I can tell."

73

She pauses a moment to catch her breath and to confirm what she's about to say. "The Captain was chasing Ms. Hellstromm till she got to the bank and then he just stopped and turned around. He's doing one heck of a statue impression."

Penelope finally gets enough air. "He finally got more than he bargained for with her."

Tia, not understanding, gives a subtle shake of her head, looking down. "What do you mean?"

Penelope calms. "You're a priestess of Daniel. I doubt you would understand unless I got basic with it."

The medic, Taoni, walks up to the others. "Why did we stop? Are we setting camp here? It's not even nightfall yet."

Back at the pond sitting neck-deep in the water, a grin of pure pleasure crosses Crystal's face. William can't understand it. *It's springtime, and that water has to be ice cold.* He dares not look in her direction, but he's supposed to keep her safe. *What the hell am I supposed to do? My training didn't cover situations like this.*

Thinking fast, he waves one of his arms frantically at the convoy. Each of those looking on takes turns glancing at each other, trying to figure out what he could be signaling. He stops moving as Crystal clears her throat from somewhere behind him.

"Captain?" He stands there like a statue, not acknowledging anything. She waits but a moment, then calls to him again. He realizes he's in a no-win situation.

Willian doesn't turn around. "Yes, Ms. Hellstromm?"

Her voice softens. "Could you hand me the rose-scented soap I dropped on the shore?"

William changes colors, as he does not know what to do. "You want me to come out there and hand you soap, ma'am?" His eyes dart around, looking for something, anything, to get out.

"Yes I do, Captain." The sound of the water sloshing gives him no comfort. "Unless you rather I come up there and get it instead?"

He's such a bright shade of red that Penelope can tell the color shift from there. She looks down at the lieutenant and medic. "I think your captain is in danger." She covers her mouth, trying not to laugh more. "One of you should intervene before he does something unexpected, or she kills him out of embarrassment." The two soldiers look at each other, not knowing what Penelope means, but Tia speaks up.

"I'll go. If Penelope is correct, Crystal could be trying to tease him to death."

Taoni looks at Gelga. "I have wounded to treat." She turns and walks away, leaving Gelga holding the short straw.

Gelga sighs. "Fine, I'll go with ya before anything turns bad."

Tia and Gelga make their way to the water as Crystal comes out of it, bare for all to see, as if she doesn't care. She walks up behind the captain but Tia shouts, "stop!" before she can go any further. William has his eyes shuttered shut and is as red as his armor.

"Sir, I'll take it from here. You look like you need a break from guard duty."

William feels relieved and marches away. Crystal shrugs and gathers her soaps and walks back into the water as if nothing happened. William opens his eyes after hearing her enter the water again. "Thanks, lieutenant."

Tia turns to Crystal soaping up and humming to herself. "Why did you tease him like that?"

Crystal, not missing a beat, looks back at the shore at them. "I didn't ask him to chase me down here. I just wanted a bath after all that mud and fighting." She shrugs her shoulders and turns her back to the shore once again.

"But you had to have known that he would chase you down for your own safety." Crystal looks over her left shoulder, looking at Tia with a smirk on her face, and shrugs gently again then looks away once more.

She takes more than a full hour to bathe and play in the water. William, looking at the setting sun, decides that they might as well-set camp here since they will not make much more time. Ordering the wagons off the road and into the tall grass, they make camp by knocking down an area.

Gelga comes back up first. "Ms. Hellstromm wants her, and I quote 'black evening dress' to be brought down to her."

William looked at the Dwarven lady, letting a hand drift outward. "And what should I do about it?"

Gelga continues. "She also said if no one brings it to her, she will just have to walk up here and get it herself, and she is refusing to put on the old dress because it's filthy and…" She holds her hands up in air quotes. "'Doesn't want it to touch her fresh silken skin'."

Panic crosses William's face with a hard swallow, looking back at the Vardo. Penelope speaks up, breaking his thoughts. "I know where it is. I'll get it and save you the hassle, captain." Relief visibly crosses his face, getting a chuckle from her.

Crystal, standing on the shore, towels off. Tia muses, motioning with her hand at the ivory woman. "So let me get this straight. You remembered everything but a change of clothes?" Tia notices the scratches on Crystal's leg have led to some light scarring and scabbing over. *Hopefully, those will go away on their own.* She takes the bandages out, ready to redress her leg. She had prayed for a remove disease spell to remove any infections that could have come from the water.

Crystal dries her hair and stands there exposed in the cool night air. "I'm used to having a private bathroom and not having to worry about bringing stuff like that with me. So, it slipped my mind."

Tia kneels, dressing Crystal's leg. "But does it bother you standing there like that with others around? It's not very ladylike."

Crystal pauses a moment, letting her gaze drift. "Yes, and no. You're a woman, so it's not a big deal. I'm comfortable around you."

"And what about Captain Blakely?"

Crystal's face flushes a little and her body turns a light shade of pink. "He's cute, but he's so stuck up."

Tia stands up, shaking her head. *He's stuck up? Pot, this is my friend kettle.* Looking over her dressing. "That's not an answer."

Crystal tosses the towel down and picks up some perfume she brought with her. Spraying it in the air, she walks through the cloud of the sweet-smelling fragrance. "I don't know. I tease him to see what he will do. He's so prim and proper, like me, I suppose, but I don't think he's fun at all."

Penelope comes through the tall grass with her pack. "Here is your dress, mistress."

She gathers up her bathing items. "Thank you, Shadow. Go ahead and take these. I'll be up there in a moment." Penelope packs the soaps and fragrances, picks up the dirty dress, and takes them back to the camp. Tia stands there silently, as if expecting more. "What?"

"It's getting cold to me. We should go warm up by the fire."

Crystal shrugs indifferently and turns around and points to her back. "Button me up before we go."

They walk back up to camp. The commander's and medical tents are set up and Tia feels bad she can't help more magically. Crystal walks around the main fire, but the sun hasn't set yet. Twilight is coming and the sky changes shades from red to purple. Temperature is dropping with the setting sun and Penelope prepares a meal for Crystal as William sits is in his tent alone, looking at the reports Gelga brought him.

He reads it aloud, pacing back and forth. "Four casks of water destroyed, six bags of feed destroyed, six pints of oil used, down one horse, four men lost."

A squeaky voice interrupts him. "Knock, knock." Turning to the sound, Penelope stands there holding a covered plate. "I made an extra plate just for you." She places it down on his table. "After what you were through today back at the river, I thought you deserved it."

William laughs nervously. "Yeah, I wasn't expecting that at all." Steam rises from around the edges of the lid. "Thank you for thinking of me." Sitting down at his table, he prepares for the meal but turns to her first because she hasn't left. "Is there something else, Penelope?"

She puts her hands behind her back. "No sir. Just let me know when you're finished, and I'll come to pick up the plate. Enjoy." She turns and exits.

William pulls the lid off and sees fresh steamed vegetables and a side of beef. It smells amazing and he can't wait to try it. Picking up his fork, he digs in. The tenderness of the seasoned steak just melts in his mouth, and the steamed vegetables are wonderfully balanced. A few moments later, Crystal enters his tent, closing the flap behind her. William stands up reflexively.

"It's alright, Captain. Go ahead and eat. I just want to talk about tomorrow's plans. You can eat while I talk." She finds a chair at the table and then sits down.

The troops set up their watches to account for the missing members. Extra wood is stacked neatly, and tall torches are set up farther out to give them a better field of view overnight. Crystal exits the commander's tent after an hour as Penelope watches from her hiding spot nearby. With Crystal leaving, she enters, seeing the commander is looking over some reports. "Knock, knock again."

"Ah yes, I didn't forget." Grabbing the plate and utensils, he hands them over. "Wonderfully cooked. I can see why she wanted you along."

"Glad you enjoyed it, Captain." She exits, heading back to the Vardo.

CHAPTER 10
(Mossy Fields)

The night goes without incident and the next morning; the sun comes up over the mountains, signaling that time to wake up the troops. The convoy packs up and extinguishes the fires. Getting back onto the road, they make good time for once and they get to Mossy Fields by eleven.

William studies the area. *Not a very large town. A dilapidated general store that has siding falling off and peeled up roofing. The houses in the area look in disrepair with peeling paint and old wood.* William would have believed the place was abandoned if it wasn't for the occasional glance he catches from the people still here. Penelope and Tia riding on top have a much better view. Gelga sits on her pony upfront, taking in as much as she can. William whistles loudly. That signals her to pull the convoy over in town.

Crystal, with her wide-open windows, looks out over the town. "Definitely a farming town." *Not much to see here, but we need supplies. Time to see if I can strike a deal like my dad.*

The convoy comes to a halt close to the general store. William dismounts, taking the area in. Looking up, the cloud cover is getting heavier. *That looks ominous. We need to get what we can, and soon.* The door to the Vardo opens and William walks over. Crystal stands in another one of her fancy lime green dresses. She offers her hand and William takes it, helping her down. Penelope jumps down before Tia can even stand up.

Penelope calls up to her. "Watch the horses." Tia standing there looks around and sees there are guards everywhere.

"Let the guards watch them. If I don't stretch my legs, I'll get a cramp."

Penelope smirks. S*he's finally getting a personality. Only took three days of constantly talking to her to break her out of her shell.* Tia makes her way to a Half-Orc corporal and gets his attention.

"Can I help you, cleric?"

Tia takes a half step back to open a little space between them. "Could you feed and water the horses on the Vardo when you and the troops are doing the others?"

The Half-Orc glances at the Vardo and back to Tia. "Yeah, sure. I'll just add it to the list of everything else I must do."

Tia, missing the fact that he was being sarcastic, just smiles. "Thank you so much." She turns back and runs to join Crystal and Penelope.

Crystal, William, and Penelope, during all this, come up with a plan of action.

Crystal motions to the papers in his hands. "So, what do we need in the way of supplies, Captain?" She gets up on her tippy toes, trying to look at them. "I know we lost some supplies in that odd plant attack, so I want to try my hand at negotiating for replacements."

William, looking around himself, places his empty hand on his left hip and holds up the report. "*You* want to negotiate?"

She stands upright confidently, brushing her hair behind her ears. "My father didn't rise to become the third richest person in Rose Harbor for nothing." She acts so proudly. "I was raised watching him make deals in the hundreds of thousands of gold pieces." She crosses her arms as if daring to be challenged. "Surely a dinky town like this would be easy for me."

William sees that further argument would be a complete waste of time and energy. "Ok, ok, fine." Taking his hand off his hip and putting it up as if to surrender. He extends the paperwork to her. "This is everything we lost. Get what you can. Our budget is limited, so I really hope you're half as good as you are boasting about."

She reaches out with her left hand, not taking her right arm from its current place, takes the paperwork and glances down at it. "How much of a budget do we have?" She studies the list.

William opens his pocketbook, pulling out some paper banknotes. "About two hundred and fifty gold worth here."

With lightning-fast snake-like precision, she snatches the notes right out of his hand before he could even react, catching him completely by surprise. She thumbs through it. "Two hundred and fifty-three, to be exact."

Penelope's eyes widen and mutters under her breath. "Damn."

William's forehead wrinkles. "Don't spend it all at once. That's for buying more food for the trip back if we stay out too long."

Crystal smiles with a big grin. "Don't worry, Captain, I'm good with money, and counting money."

Penelope butts in. "And spending money." Crystal shoots a dirty look at the poor Halfling, causing her to let out a laugh.

"Oh!" William reaches out and takes a few banknotes. "Going to need this if I'm going to buy some replacement horses." He then walks away.

Crystal watches in disbelief and then turns to Penelope. "I want you to scout the town a bit. Any information I can use that can help with strengthening our position would be most helpful."

Penelope nods, already noticing that someone has been trying their best to be covert and spy on them far away. "I'll turn up everything I can, Mistress." She walks between two houses and vanishes.

Tia finally catches up to Crystal just to see William go on his way and Penelope just vanishes as if she didn't exist. "What did I miss?" Crystal turns to her with an impish smile that makes her uneasy.

She holds up the money. "We are going shopping." She puts the notes in her purse, grabs Tia's hand, and drags her off to the general store.

William makes his way up the road a little, looking around for anything that could be a stable. Thunder echoes over his head as the storm gets closer, prompting him to pick up his pace. He walks a few blocks and sees a rotund and graying elderly white Human male sweeping his porch. *Great, a local.*

Calling out to him from the street, William waves a hand at him. "Excuse me, sir." A moment passes and either the portly man didn't hear him, or he's being ignored. William walks up the pathway to the porch and tries again. "Pardon me, sir."

The old man turns to face William, his face covered in wrinkles and a few scars from a hard life. "Can I help you with something, *knight?*"

He can't help but notice the disdain in the old man's voice as he says the word knight. "Sorry to bother you, but do you have a stable in this town? I'm needing to buy a few horses so we can continue our way."

The old man stops sweeping and looks at William. "You're a member of the 'Royal Guard', aren't you? Why not just go back to the city and get more?" The contempt is almost palpable.

"I would if it was an option." William chuckles and looks back towards the city for a moment. "But we are rather far away." William pauses and looks around as the old man just stands there, staring. "Look, I can tell you're not happy I'm here. So, if you can help me, the faster I can leave, ok?"

He grumbles and points to his left. "Fine. Go two blocks north, turn left. It's on the northern edge of town can't miss it."

"Thank you." William waves and turns away. "Have a pleasant day." The elderly man sweeps again and just grunts a reply.

Penelope, doing what she does best, works her way around to the person spying on them. The thunder of the coming storm helps mask her movements, and the sunlight is dimming. She watches her prey for several minutes and when Crystal and Tia walk into the general store, the wannabe spy crouch walks out of the bush away from them, trying his best to be undetected. He makes his way to a nearby house, looks around, and then enters. Penelope smiles to herself, *Been a long time since I got to do something like this.*

Following the target, she walks around the house to an open window. Taking a place so she can overhear. Sounds from inside tell her she's in a suitable spot and she waits. She believes the man from the bushes is talking to others in the house. "Those are Royal guards in the town square."

Another man's voice, deeper than the first, answers him. What are they doing here?

"They seem to be escorting some noble girl, but I've never seen her before."

A third person, a female's voice, joins the conversation. "A noblewoman?"

The first voice answers her. "I believe so. Must be royalty going by how she was dressed, and how well guarded she is." The sound of thunder in the distance gives them all pause as it's accompanied by a flash of lightning.

The deeper voice cuts in. "What does she look like? I've been to the city. Maybe I can figure out who she is."

"Uh let's see. She's white. But not like regular Humans or Elf-like white. I mean *WHITE*. Like she's made of marble or ivory. You could lose her in a snowstorm kind of white." There is a pause with some false starts. "Uh, very long black hair. Like the opposite of white. Like obsidian black. Goes all the way down her back. Small to medium chested."

Penelope hears something like a punch, followed by the female's voice. "Of course you would notice that."

"As I was saying, she walked with a grace of nobility, and she's short and skinny. Like everyone else, there is taller than her except the Dwarves. Can't weigh much more than one hundred pounds. She's wearing a lime green dress that has a shimmer to it. Must be expensive."

The female voice continues to interrogate. "Anything else? Any jewelry like a crown to note nobility? She just could just be rich with a well-paid guard."

The deep voice man cuts in. "I would have remembered a woman like that. I don't think she's of the First House, so she's not technically royalty, but all that hardware around her, she has to be from one of the stronger houses."

The first voice continues. "What if they know?"

The deeper voice cuts off the lady's voice as she objects. "They don't. If they did, they would be running the town right now, not feeding horses."

Penelope perks up, intent on discovering more. *What is going on? These people don't sound like typical bandits.*

The woman speaks up. "So, what should we do? If they don't know, we could leave 'em alone, but if they are here to check things out, we could lose everything."

The deep voice answers here with the sound of a hand slapping a table. "Then we have but one choice. We need to talk to this noblewoman and find out what she knows."

The first male's voice sounds scared. "What are you going to do? Walk up to her and just ask?"

The deep voice answers and Penelope can hear leather sliding across a wooden surface. "Not really." The sound of thunder echoes across the plains. "But I have an idea."

Penelope's eyes are as wide as dinner plates. *Oh, I don't like the sound of that, but I don't know what they are armed with. I must let her or William know what's about to happen.* She departs, staying as quiet as she can.

Crystal is towing Tia behind her, dragging her up onto the store's porch. The sound of thunder in the distance tells her she has little time. The old boards of the porch creek even under her light frame. Stepping inside, there isn't much, but she thinks she can find what they need. Ringing the bell on the counter, a minute or two passes. Tia wanders the store looking at all the wares when a middle-aged dark Human steps out from the back.

He looks at the two women. "Can I help you, girls?"

Crystal smiles broadly and places her hands on the counter. She tries her best to sound friendly as she unfolds the list and reads it. "Why yes, you can. I need a few things to continue my journey. I need some casks of water, at least four, but I think I could use a few extra just in case." Looking at him and back at the report. "Six bags of horse feed and six pints of lamp oil."

"Is that all?"

Crystal thinks a moment, looking out the window at the troops. "Do you have any fresh fruits and vegetables?"

He makes a noise of disgust. "Girl, the crops haven't been planted yet. Where would we get fresh produce?"

Crystal's smile fades for a moment but forces it back, trying to keep her composure. "You don't order fresh food from Rose Harbor?"

Walking around the counter, he gathers the items she wanted. "No, we don't. We aren't important to them. Till harvest time comes, we aren't worth visiting."

Crystal's smile fades and almost turns into a frown. She cocks her head a little to the right. "But you're on the main road to Rose Harbor from the north. Surely you get travelers who stop in?"

He drops a bag of feed on the countertop next to her, getting Tia to look up. "Not travelers with money. Refugees maybe." He grabs another bag of feed and drops it on the counter. "Speaking of money, this will be twenty-five gold for everything you asked for." He grabs another fifty-pound bag of feed and drops it on the other two. Crystal nods and pulls out the notes and counts out the twenty-five they need. The shopkeeper stops her, putting a hand on hers. "We don't take banknotes here, only gold." He then let's her go.

She holds the notes up. "But these are as good as gold."

"In the city they are. If you haven't noticed." He waves his arm to the outside. "We are almost two days from the city." He points to himself and lowers himself a little. "I'm not riding two days one way to get twenty-five gold coins."

Crystal batted her eyes and smiled, trying to look innocent. Tia notes her voice even changes a little to sound a little more child-like. "But I really need this stuff, and banknotes are all I have. I can't carry that much gold on my tiny person."

He picks up the feed and puts it back on the shelf. "No gold, no supplies. Your notes are no good here."

Crystal drops the good girl routine. Her voice becomes harder, stepping into the man. This stops him from putting more stuff away. "You're a citizen of the Rose Empire." She holds the notes up, waving them in front of him. "These are as good as gold anywhere within the Empire. You can't refuse these."

He steps around her, grabbing another bag. "A citizen I am, but as I said, I can't use those here." Tossing it back down on the floor by the shelf. He then pats his hands together and points outside. "Real gold or get out, girly."

Tia looks to the old man and to Crystal and can see her other hand twitching. Crystal is also turning red and knows these things in combination are bad. Tia takes Crystal's hand grabbing her attention before she boils over. "We should get going, Ms. Hellstromm."

Crystal calms and jerks her hand from Tia's, turning back to the shopkeeper. "What if we traded something else? I have other valuables. Maybe we can work something out? We could trade goods?"

The shopkeeper shakes his head. "I doubt you have anything I want." He then waves his hands in a shooing manner.

Crystal's face turns pink and Tia knows she's about to go off again. She places a hand on Crystal's shoulder to grab her attention once again. "Please, Ms. Hellstromm, maybe one of the troops has some hard currency. Couldn't hurt to ask."

Crystal calms down and sighs. "That's not a bad idea. Let's go." Crystal turns her nose up and, with Tia in tow, she exits the store.

William makes his way in the direction he was given and sure enough, finds the stable. The sound of thunder and a flash of lightning in the distance tells him he has little time to get back. Walking in, he can see several horses and some oxen. "Hello!" William shouts, as he just wanders about, lightly petting one horse.

A small boy carrying a bucket of water enters the barn. Looking at the knight, he drops it, spilling the water inside and runs back the way he came, crying out. "PA!"

He mutters to himself. "Not exactly the welcome I was expecting, but can't say I'm surprised after dealing with the old man."

Several minutes pass and he's about to walk away when a large man like himself walks in covered in mud and dirt. "Greetings there, sir knight. He rubs the mud off his hands, then extends it to William. They shake hands and William has a genuine smile since the first time getting here. "My son said we had a stranger in our stable. Is there something you need?"

This is better than I thought it would go. "I sure hope so. I need three good steeds or one good steed and two good oxen."

The tall burly Human turns to a brown and white horse next to him and rubs its head. "I have an extra horse and two oxen to spare." He pats the mare and looks back at William. "Fifty gold for the horse, thirty per oxen."

William nods, taking out the notes; the stable master stops him holding up his hand. "I don't take vouchers here. Too far from the city or bank for us to use them."

William stops and tilts a little to the side. "But we crossed one of your caravans on the way here that was heading to the city. You can just send the notes on their next trip and get your gold that way."

The stable master shakes his head, but his tone doesn't change. "I don't want to have to do that. Hard currency only, soldier. Sorry."

William puts the bills away. "Well, thanks for your time." William leaves, not wanting to push the matter. *What is going on with this town? Most of the people are unfriendly if not hostile, and the one man I run into who's respectful won't take my money. There is something strange happening here.*

Crystal, startled by Penelope popping up out of nowhere, steps back into Tia. "Mistress! I believe you're in danger. Please get back to your Vardo immediately!" Penelope grabs Crystal's hand and tugs.

Tia speaks up before Crystal can. "What's happening?"

"I followed a kid who I caught spying on us. He ended up in a house with at least two other individuals." The three ladies cross the open ground to the wagons. "They seem very interested in you and were very concerned about your presence." She looks back at Crystal. "And I fear for your safety."

"Why would anyone not be interested in me? I'm beautiful and rich."

Penelope shakes her head and Tia explains it differently. "I think what Penelope means is not in a good way, Ms. Hellstromm."

Crystal, thinking a moment, understands. "Why would they want to harm me? I don't know these people."

Penelope pulls harder, getting Crystal to move faster. "I don't know, Mistress. But I'd rather have you in a well-guarded area instead of out here in the open."

Crystal relents when the rain starts. It's a light sprinkle, but it doesn't take long for it to turn into a straight downpour. The trio runs towards the wagon, barely able to see. Lightning crackles overhead as Tia and Penelope shiver from the biting cold water. The troops scramble to settle the horses from the thunder that breaks above them. Penelope's heart races. *This would be an opportune moment to strike with all the confusion.*

CHAPTER 11
(Mud, Blood, and Rage)

Penelope, still pulling, trying to get Crystal to move faster, is suddenly jerked backward off her feet, falling into the mud. Looking up, she sees Crystal lying face down in the water. Tia reacting instantly bends down to pick up the fallen maiden. Penelope jumps back to her feet in an instant, but Crystal is motionless.

Tia cries. "Please don't be dead." She leans down and with Penelope's help, gets Crystal off the ground and tries to get to the caravan.

Gelga calls out over the noise. "We're under attack!" Troopers are already reacting to the unseen assailants taking cover behind wagons. They ready weapons to return fire but can't see where the shots are coming from.

William picks up the pace as the water comes pouring down. He can barely make out the caravan in the distance. He can see the brown robes of Tia and the lime green dress of Crystal as they go sprinting to the Vardo. Seconds later, Crystal collapses to the ground, sparking his adrenaline into overdrive. He runs at full speed and he hears Gelga shout out that they are under attack.

Tia and Penelope do their best to get Crystal to the Vardo and the Half-Orc corporal comes rushing up. "I'll take her. You two get going." He goes to take her, but a crossbow bolt strikes, penetrating his breastplate, then collapses himself. Another crossbow bolt hits the side of the Vardo near Tia passing through her robes, and leaving a hole. Trying to get around the fallen soldier, they hear sounds of a galloping horse and a large man on horseback comes into view through the fog. Slowing and leaning over, he latches onto Crystal, getting a handful of her dress, lifting her into the air. Tia reacts, grasping at her body, but she can't hold on in the rain. William closes the distance as the rider still has his head turned, looking back at Tia when he grabs Crystal right out of his hands, tearing the dress and freeing her.

The kidnapper pulls hard on the reins to turn around for another chance, but a shout from William and the report from a rifle from a second direction makes him think better of it and turns away. A bullet hits the rider in the back but doesn't drop him and he rides off into the rain and vanishes with only the sound of hooves hitting wet gravel and mud fading into the distance.

William hands Crystal back to Tia and Penelope and crouches down in front, acting as a shield. "Report Lieutenant!"

"If I had to guess, Captain." Gelga catches a crossbow bolt to the shield. "There are only two attackers. Shots coming in too slow to be more than that, but it's a crossfire."

William yanks a crossbow bolt from the dead Half-Orc and examines it. "Armor Piercing. Expensive." Looking at the impacts from the bolts, William calculates where the shots could come from. "I think it's coming from one of those two houses." He points in the directions she can follow. "Lieutenant, take a squad and start flanking. These guys are going to run as soon as we move on them, so we must act fast." He ducks as a bolt hit the wagon next to him. "And be careful. They are using armor-piercing bolts. Our armor won't stop these like they would normal bullets." Gelga shouts orders and troops react instantly, returning fire with shots from their rifles into those homes. *I don't like innocents getting hurt, but I can't let my people die out here.*

Pulling his sword, he turns to the trio, concern in his voice is evident to both. "Is she alive?"

Tia is holding her head up out of the mud and presses a finger to her neck. "Yes, sir, but her pulse and breathing are slow."

William looks out at the house he suspects a shooter is at. "Stay here and keep her alive. I'm going after the bastards that attacked us."

She points to his sword. "You're going to take them on with a sword, with them shooting at you?"

"Less likelihood of hitting someone who doesn't deserve it." Pointing to several troopers watching him. "Cover fire on those two houses." Then pointing to three others. "You three, with me. GO!" Penelope and Tia watch as he charges into the oncoming fire.

Tia looks over Crystal's body looking for a wound and on her right side she pulls out a small dart. "Hey, what's this?" She hands it to Penelope.

Penelope looks at it, puts it to her nose, and takes a whiff. "It's poison of some kind." Looking up to the Vardo. "It's only a few steps. If we can get her in there, you can purge her of the poison, right?"

Tia wipes the water from her face and her arm collapses to the ground. "Yes, I can't focus out here. I feel worthless."

Penelope yanks on Tia's robe, bringing her face within inches of Tia's. Tia's eyes widen as Penelope bares her teeth. "We are in a battle." She points down at Crystal. "And she needs you to pull it together." Sitting back in the mud, she glances over at the corpse of the fallen soldier and then up, watching the action. William and the three soldiers are running for the nearest house, "and the enemy is distracted. Let's go!" The two women heave and drag the poor girl up the stairs and into the wagon out of the rain. Tia starts her prayer as Penelope closes the door and locks it.

Running to the closest house, William leads the charge, as he is struck in the shoulder by a crossbow bolt. He barely feels the impact, though, due to the sound of his heart racing and adrenaline pumping throughout his system. Kicking in the door, a lady cowers in the corner, using her body to shield her two children. Surveying the area, he can hear running coming from inside the house.

He turns to the soldiers behind him. "Circle around back before he gets out." They react, splitting around the house. "I want prisoners!" Looking at the woman and children, he holds his empty hand up. "Stay here and stay down. I'm not after you." He takes chase and comes around the kitchen. The entire area was in shambles as the assailant turned over the table to slow him down. He turns and takes a shot, but it bounces off William's armor. This fuels his rage, driving him onward. Kicking the back door open, the figure runs into the rain, but two of the troopers come around the house and are right behind him. William grins. *He has nowhere to go. He's not getting away from the guard.*

Tackling him to the ground, the armored soldiers pin the guy to the wet grass. He desperately tries to get away, but William and the last trooper get right upon him. Kicking the crossbow away, William reaches down and grabs the would-be assassin by the shirt, yanking him to his feet.

"Sir, you're bleeding!"

"Bleeding can wait. This is what I wanted." Turning to the others. "Tell the lieutenant to kill the other."

The mystery man squeaks. "Please don't. I surrender. Don't kill her." William, with his one good arm, pulls the scrawny man a full foot off the ground and brings him face to face with him. "Should have thought of that before firing on us." The boy whimpers, holding onto William's arm. William almost rubs noses with the kid, then tosses him back to the ground. "Belay that last order. Take him back to the convoy. He's going to answer some questions."

Getting back to the convoy, Gelga has the girl assailant already tied up. The girl has a bullet wound through her thigh, immobilizing her.

Gelga salutes as William marches up. "Crystal, Tia, and Penelope are in the wagon, sir." The boy is dropped next to the girl. The rain still coming down hard muffles the sounds coming from inside the Vardo.

"So which one of you wants to live and tell me what's going on here?" William yanks the bolt from his shoulder and snaps it with his thumb. "I want to know why you shot at us and why that other guy tried to take the girl."

The girl speaks up first. "We aren't talking to you. Kill us. We will tell you nothing, knight."

William turns to the boy, pointing his sword. "You feel the same?" The boy looks at the girl but says nothing. William crouches down and grabs her leg pushing his thumb into the hole, causing her to scream in pain.

Through gritted teeth, she continues her defiance. "I'll tell you nothing!" She continues to scream as he grinds his thumb around.

The boy cries. "Enough already! Please stop."

William let's go, and she visibly relaxes. "Speak up, boy."

"Don't tell them anyth—" Gelga silences her with a slug to the face with the butt of her axe.

He looks at her, then back at William. He sits there silently and William reaches out for her leg again. "We don't like the royal guard here." He swallows and looks to the ground. "You only come here to take from us and never give back."

William stands back up. "You think I'm going to buy that excuse? You're paid for your crops." William looks at the boy, but he doesn't continue. "I know there is more to it than just this, and if you're not going to tell me." He looks at the girl, placing his massive boot on her leg, causing her to cry out. "I have all day." He looks back at the boy. "And that doesn't answer my question about why you were trying to take the girl."

He sits there and William puts more weight on the girl's leg, causing her to scream. He turns to the girl, then up at William. "We thought we could ransom her. She looks rich. We thought we could take a few potshots at you and run and grab her in the confusion."

William looks to Gelga, then back at the boy. "That actually sounds feasible, but the armor-piercing bolts tell me there is something else." He's about to ask another question when he's interrupted. The back door to the Vardo opens violently, and William can hear Tia and Penelope pleading with Crystal.

Inside the Vardo, Tia prays to Daniel to remove the poison from her system. A glow forms around her hands and Crystals eye's creep open.

"What happened?" She sounds weak now, but Tia is glad she's all right.

"Oh, thanks be to Daniel; you're ok, Mistress!" Crystal sits up in her torn dress. Tia sits back on the couch and takes a breather. Penelope holds up the dart. "They poisoned you with this and it knocked you out."

Crystal, going from confusion to anger, snatches the dart from Penelope's hand. Outside, they can hear a girl screaming in pain, and with the rain, she can faintly hear William asking questions. She clambers up, dress was torn beyond repair, mud, blood, bruised up, and insulted. Rage boils up from inside her as she hears William finish his little interrogation. Going for the door, Tia and Penelope object in unison. The door flings open as she exits into the rain. Penelope and

Tia tell her she's not decent and shouldn't be out there, but she only hears the blood pounding in her ears.

Everyone turns around to face the commotion, but the troopers quickly turn away. Crystal comes down and grits her teeth. "STAY!" That is all she shouts, and no one knows who she is referring to, so they all freeze at once. One of her breasts hangs exposed because of the torn cloth and William, with his eyes partially closed, tries his best to cover her up. She swats away his hand in defiance and she stands in front of the prisoners.

With her teeth still gritted, malice drips with every word she speaks. "One of you is going to pay for what you did to me!" She points a finger and utters an incantation. Her hand glows black, and a black bolt of lightning shoots from her finger, striking the bound girl in the chest, causing her to fall over. Her face is barely above the rising water, but her eyes moving around and the fact she's still breathing are the only clues she wasn't killed instantly but is paralyzed. Pointing to the boy. "Tell me who did this or I'm going to make her watch what I do to you." Troopers and even Gelga reflexively step back, not knowing what she will do next.

William, with a blanket he grabbed from a wagon, wraps it around her. Her eyes contact his and he realizes she's beyond reason. The glance was enough to tell him there is no compromise, no compassion, only rage. He looks at the boy as he sits there frozen in fear, unable to speak. She starts a new incantation, her hand glows red, and a ball of ice forms in front of her palm. William has seen this spell before and knows what it's capable of. William grabs her hand, causing the ice ball to fly past the boy's head and impact the ground, erupting in a shower of icy shards. She turns to him and opens her mouth to yell, but the girl speaks up first.

The girl cries from the ground. "The Black Rose."

Crystal and William stop before they start their fight and turn to the girl. "What did you say?" she points her hand at the boy again.

"We are members of The Black Rose."

William holds the blanket up covering Crystal but looks at the girl. "What's the Black Rose?"

She turns her eyes askance, trying to look up at them, her body limp from having the lack of strength to even pick up her own head.

"I've said too much." She relents, looking back at the puddle forming in front of her. "We don't like the control of the Empire. They don't do anything for us, but we work ourselves to death to support it." Water continues to pool up around her head.

William crouches down and picks her upright, getting her face out of the mud. "You're paid for that work. If you think you're not getting enough for your labor, renegotiate. We will pay you what we both think is fair."

Crystal, still furious from the embarrassment. "I don't care." She starts a new incantation. William drops the girl and steps in front of Crystal's hand, causing her to stop.

"Out of the way, William."

"Crystal, you made your point. You don't have to kill them." He puts his hand on top of hers, trying to calm her down.

"They shot me, ripped my dress, and embarrassed me in front of everyone. Someone has to pay for this blood on my body." Her makeup running on her face made her look much scarier in the rain.

"I get that." He holds her hand, getting her to look down, then back up at him. "But it's not for you to murder them for it." She visibly fumes and he continues with a softer voice. "Please let me handle this and go get cleaned up."

She goes from pink back to white as she calms down at William's words. She hangs her head and turns about. Grabbing the soggy blanket, the anger in her voice fades a little. "Fine." She walks back over to the Vardo. Tia helps her inside and the door closes.

William turns back to the duo. "Well, that could have gone better."

"So, are you going to let us go?" The boy looks up. "We told you what you wanted to know."

"Not yet. How many are in this 'Black Rose' thing you're a part of? Is it the whole town? Is that why we are given such a cold welcome?"

The boy shakes his head. "It's just us and the guy who got away, but they don't like you for the same reason we don't. It's just, that we found others who are willing to help us. The townspeople are too scared to do anything about it."

William picks up the sword he dropped when stopping Crystal, and Gelga, taking the cue, readies her axe. "Unfortunately, you murdered two Royal Guards, wounded four others plus me, and assaulted then attempted to kidnap a member of the Third House and representative to the crown." Turning to the two prisoners. "And I have to uphold the law." He sighs. "I don't like this part of the job, but the law is quite clear." Fear races over both of their faces and they close their eyes. William nods and moments later the two prisoners lay motionless in the mud and rain.

Gathering up the dead guards, the soldiers place them in the rearmost wagon. The rain lets up a little, and William gets first aid from Taoni to stop the bleeding. Tia exits the Vardo first and closes the door behind her. William is trying to mount everyone up to move out, being it's not safe here.

Tia, seeing the bandage, points to it. "Are you in need of healing?"

William shakes his head. "Taoni treated it. I'll be fine."

"But I can heal you." She starts a prayer, but William stops her.

"Maybe later, but right now, we need to get on the road. That rider got a huge head start and we don't know where he was headed."

"How long till we leave?"

William walks to his horse not far away. "As soon as we can mount up. Get Penelope in her seat."

Tia turns and knocks on the Vardo's door and Penelope answers. "Penelope, Captain Blakely wants to get underway right now. You need to get to your station."

Penelope, having changed from her soaked clothing from earlier, sighs. "Is he aware of just how cold it is in the rain right now?"

Tia looks at him as he mounts up. "I don't think he cares. It's unsafe here, and he wants to get underway before we are attacked again."

Penelope nods and looks around in the cabin. Grabbing the blanket that William wrapped Crystal in, she disembarks into the pouring rain and makes her way to the seat, using it as a cover. Tia climbs in to check on Crystal. She's laying on the bed having changed into her nightgown.

"How are you feeling, Ms. Hellstromm?"

Crystal just lays there looking up at the ceiling. "I don't feel like talking right now, Tia. I'm sorry."

"Captain Blakely has ordered us to get back underway. He fears for our safety here."

"You mean *MY* safety." Tia stands silent, unable to find a proper response. "It's ok Tia. I'm just a fragile little rich girl."

Tia sits down in a chair and shakes her head. "But you're magically strong. Physically, yes, you're not very intimidating, *but* you have raw magical power, and those Black Rose people were scared to death of you."

Crystal sits up and faces Tia. "They were scared because they should have been dead." Her face flushes again as the fresh memory replays in her head. "Had William not grabbed my hand, that boy's head would be a frozen pile of slush on the ground."

Tia, looking down. "And I'm glad he stopped you. You would have hated yourself for killing in cold blood like that." The wagon moves as William shouts the order to move out. The rain outside lightens up more, but doesn't look like it will let up completely soon.

Crystal bends over, putting her head in her hands as she calms down again. "I don't know, Tia. I really wanted to kill that boy. I was ready too."

Tia looks up with her eyes. "He actually looked older than you, so he wasn't a boy, per se." She collects herself. "In any case, I'm glad he stopped you." She looks around the Vardo. "Guess we're going to be riding together a while. So we can talk about whatever you want."

Crystal straightens back up and looks up at the ceiling. "I'm being punished, aren't I?"

CHAPTER 12
(All-Nighter)

Hours go by and the rain finally stops. Crystal and Tia talk for most of that time and bond a little. The clouds still block the view of the sunset, causing it to get dark sooner. The woods are thickening up again, but it's not too dense yet. As the night drags on, the air turns brisk, causing Tia and Crystal to note the complaints coming from outside. Penelope, having used the blanket as an umbrella, now regrets she can't use it to keep warm. She can hear William ordering a halt but to stay on the road. He dismounts and jogs past the Vardo and up to Gelga. They seem to exchange words and he walks back and stops to speak to the shaking Halfling.

"How tired are you, Penelope?"

She looks down at him and he can tell she is miserable. "I'm cold, I'm wet, I'm hungry, I'm tired, and I'm dying to get next to a fire and warm up. I can't feel my ears or my toes."

William nods and looks at the rest of the convoy. "We have a slight problem." He looks back up at her. "If we pull off the main road, there is a good chance this wagon will get stuck, being how heavy it is, and with the odd attack from these so-called 'Black Rose' people, I don't want to take a chance the rider returns."

Penelope looks down at her feet, unable to feel them. "What are you wanting to do? I'm freezing up here."

"I'm going to rotate the guards and let some of them sleep on the wagons while we keep driving."

"But I have no one to rotate with." Penelope points with her thumb to the back. "I don't think Tia can drive."

He interrupts her tirade. "Penelope, I'll drive. You can get some sleep. I'm sure Crystal won't mind having you back there to cook for her."

"Then who's going to ride your horse, Captain?"

"Well, I'll have one of my guys ride. I'll happily skip the formalities if it means keeping everyone on the road and alive."

Penelope stretches and wiggles her toes, then points to the sling. "If you think you can with that one good arm."

He looks down at it. "Yeah, I guess I should have Tia fix that real fast, shouldn't I?"

Penelope climbs down and the two walk to the back. William knocks and Crystal opens the door wearing a lavender-colored evening dress, causing William to swallow visibly.

"What's going on, Captain? Why are we stopped?"

William brings Crystal and Tia up to speed and Tia heals his arm so he can drive. Penelope climbs on in and Tia follows. Tia turns around to help Crystal up and extends a hand, but she doesn't go for it.

She turns to William. "Actually... I've slept for most of the day after my incident. I want to ride up front with the Captain to help keep him awake."

Penelope peeks from under Tia. "And how exactly are you planning on doing that?"

"By talking about our mission, and the 'Black Rose' people, and whatever else I want to talk about, that's none of your concern." She crosses her arms and looks away. "We have to keep coordinated if this mission is going to move forward, and that means communication along the chain of command."

Penelope shakes her head, and one of her long ears catches Tia's pant leg, causing her to wince. "I think that's a great idea." Tia looks down at Penelope. "Would be good for the people in charge to trade ideas."

William just shakes his head and holds his hands up. "It's your wagon. I can't stop you if you want to sit there." Crystal shrugs and moves up to the front of the wagon. William finishes issuing orders and getting the troops organized. He grabs a few extra blankets, being the temperature is going down. Getting back up to the Vardo, Crystal is already sitting in the passenger seat. William makes his way up the ladder and sits in the driver's seat. He hands a blanket to Crystal and wraps one around himself. She refuses and indicates she has no need.

"Aren't you going to cover up?" William looks her over, then picks up the reins. "It can't be much above forty out here, and that dress sure doesn't look insulated."

"As I've said, Captain, I'm not cold." She places her hands in her lap and casually looks up. "And I'm hoping that I'll get to see some more stars tonight since you didn't let me see that much last night."

William looks up as twilight sets and the clouds are clearing. Crystal looks to William. "I wasn't lying to Shadow when I said we need to talk about the mission and the 'Black Rose' people." William turns to her, looking into her eyes. "Plus, I want to bring you up to speed on something else I'm wanting to do while we are out here."

They get underway and after a few minutes; she speaks up to him. "Also, I would like to thank you for saving my life back there." She looks off into the distance. "Had you not grabbed me, who knows what would have happened?"

William looks at her and back to the road. "I swear on my life that I will always protect you." This gets her attention and looks at him for more. "It's my duty to make sure that you live and you return to the Emperor."

She doesn't look away, fixating on him. "Is that all?"

He looks back at her, seeing how she looks at him. "No, even if it wasn't my duty, my honor would still demand I do whatever I can to protect you." He goes back to the road when he spots the slimmest of smiles appear on her face. "Is this what you're wanting to talk to me about? Me rescuing you?"

She shakes her head. "There are a few other things I want to ask you about."

Half the night goes by. A waxing moon, more than three quarters full above their heads and the surrounding area thinned out to just a few trees. William is getting tired and dozes off a few times. Crystal is trying her best to talk about anything to keep him awake, but she thinks he's done for the night. She whistles to the point man to stop as William falls unconscious, exhausted. He turns around, and she flags him to a stop as she grabs the reins of her own wagon.

"Something the matter, ma'am?"

"Yes trooper, I think it's time for us to switch drivers." She gets William to wake up by smacking him gently on the face. "William, you fell asleep. It's time to switch the guards out." He snaps out of it a little when she says "William," bringing him right out of his grogginess as she has never called him by his first name before.

"Yeah, yeah, I know, let's get new drivers." He climbs down and then helps her reach the ground. They walk to the back, but she stops him at the back of the Vardo.

"William, sleep in my cabin."

Now he's awake as his eyes widen. "I don't think that would be appropriate, ma'am."

Her pale ivory face glows bright pink, and she punches him in his bad shoulder, getting him to let out a yelp. "I'm going to drive the wagon; I'm not going back there with you. What kind of lady do you take me for?"

"Wait for a second. You know how to drive one of these?"

She looks a little uneasy, and she grinds a foot in the dirt. "Technically, no, but I've been watching you all night and I believe I can manage it a few hours while you get some sleep. Doesn't look that hard." She crosses her arms and her tone changes. "I've helped my dad reassemble steam engine components and hydraulic fittings. I think I can handle a few horses tied to a stick."

I'm not sure how to respond to that. She clearly is more complicated than I gave her credit for.

Crystal knocks on the door and a few moments later Penelope pokes her head out, looking like she's a little better off than William. She turns to her. "The Captain is going to take a nap back here." Penelope looks at Crystal as if she's speaking draconic. William clambers into the back and the sound of the armor hitting the floor echoes. "Don't let him rifle through my things. If he does anything unsavory, cut his fingers off."

William speaks up from inside. "I heard that."

Crystal shouts back. "Good, because I mean it. Hate to return you to the Emperor, unable to hold your sword anymore."

Penelope just shakes her head and "Do you want me to drive, Mistress?"

"No, I think I got it handled. Besides, you need to keep the Captain on the straight and narrow."

Looking back and seeing he's already asleep on the floor. "I don't think that will be a problem, Mistress."

Crystal goes back to her perch and picks up the reins. *So, this is what it's like to be common folk. It's so… simple.* The cool night air keeps them on their toes. Crystal catches herself looking up and seeing stars revealed as the overhead clouds break up and dissipate. She even glimpses the waxing moon. *Only a few more days till it's full.* The nighttime sounds of nocturnal animals come from all directions, only to quiet down as they get closer to the clanging of metal and stomping of hooves. Shadows seem to jump and move, keeping the whole column jumping at nothing.

The morning dawn slowly makes its appearance, as the darkness recedes and colors of blue, yellow, and red slowly replace the blackness of the night. What few clouds that remain make it look as if the sky itself is on fire. Crystal lets out a yawn and the poor corporal at the head of the line looks like he's been on autopilot most of the night. She can hear Tia getting up in the wagon. Crystal never noticed that you can hear what's going on inside, but it's very muffled. The wagon shifts under her bottom as the Half-Elven woman tries to step around the large knight sleeping on the floor. Crystal motions to the corporal and he slows up and pulls alongside.

"Yes, Ma'am?"

She yawns. "How long till rotation again? I'm not good at this whole time-keeping thing you guys do out here. I'm getting tired."

"You're in command, my lady." He keeps his eyes on the road ahead. "If you want to do a rotation, you have but to order it."

She stretches and a few popping sounds come from her. "Let me know when another hour goes by and then we will change shifts. Should be enough daylight by then."

The corporal rides up, and she calls out to him. "Unless you see a body of water first, then we stop." The corporal turns with a quizzical look on his face but doesn't question his order.

The hour passes by with only the sounds of life coming from the Vardo. It's obvious everyone is awake in there going but the muffled conversations and the smell of fresh food being cooked. Crystal can feel her stomach rumble as she realized that she's been lost in thought most of the night. *I still can't believe I trust William enough that I told him about the spell components I needed, but if I don't get his help, I may never get them.* Her belly rumbles again. *I just don't want the rest to know. A few are dangerous to obtain.* She sighs, watching the trees pass by, trying to keep herself motivated. *He seemed to understand that I have my own personal life goals, and this was one of them. What I didn't tell him is what the ritual was for. Then*

101

again, I don't know one hundred percent either what 'awakening your Dragon blood' means. Dragons are powerful, magical entities. Having a Dragon blood heritage has been linked to possessing powerful, innate magical abilities.

The corporal motions there is a place they can pull over that doesn't look like they will sink. The Rose Empire installed camping spots along its main roads decades ago before the emergence of airships and steam power. Not everyone has access to such advances in technology. They try to at least keep them somewhat maintained. She stands up and gets a better look around her, and catches sight of a pond nearby. *Oh good, I can get a bath and finally get this mud and who knows what else off me?* She clambers down the ladder. "Corporal, tie up the horses for me!"

The occupants of the wagon only get that much of a warning too as she opens the door. "We are on a roadside rest area, everyone." She then clambers in and the wagon is getting crowded.

William just waking up says something, but Penelope speaks up first. "Breakfast is almost ready, Mistress."

Crystal stops what she is doing and remembers how hungry she is. "So, what do you have cooking, Shadow?"

William is wondering too. "It smells good, but I need to get out there and address the troops. Get reorganized and figure out a new plan."

Tia chimes in. "May Daniel bring you guidance, Captain."

He mutters as he climbs out. "I can use all the help I can get at this point."

Penelope, finally getting a moment to speak. "I made you a two-egg and cheese omelet with salted pork and a side of mashed potatoes, Mistress, and I even got some fresh orange juice ready for you to drink."

Crystal sits down at the table. "You're a lifesaver." She picks up her glass and drinks. "What are you having, Tia?"

Tia shakes her head. "I'm going to go pray and then just eat one of my ration packs."

Crystal interrupts, grabbing her robe. "No, you're going to sit here and have a proper breakfast. Yesterday you didn't tell me about any vow of poverty or anything like that." She lets go and points to the table. "So, there is no reason for you not to sit here with us and not have a decent meal."

Tia, surprised, just nods and has a seat as ordered. Penelope puts a plate of eggs down in front of her and some fresh toast on the table. She herself sits down with an omelet of her own. The table is small, and they are crammed together, but at least it's civilized. The trio talk and listen to William, Gelga, and Taoni exchange notes and make plans of their own for the upcoming day.

Tia has a look of satisfaction on her face as she eats. "I've never had a meal this good before." She points with her fork at the food. "No wonder Ms. Hellstromm wanted you with her."

"Thanks." Penelope motions with her glass to Crystal. "Her dad is amazing for giving me the opportunity."

Tia swallows. "Daniel works in wonderful ways, doesn't he?"

Crystal finishes first, placing her utensils on the now empty plate. "Wonderfully delicious, as always." Patting her dirty belly, she looks for her soaps and other supplies for bathing. Scrounging through cabinets, trying to find where she put everything from the day before when it was all unceremoniously dropped everywhere.

Penelope and Tia take notice, but Tia speaks first. "Where are you going?"

Crystal takes out some soaps and puts them in a bag. Penelope sounds disparaged. "Oh no, she found a pond or something."

Crystal wrinkles her nose at Penelope's criticism. "I have to clean up. I can't just run around dirty, like those troopers out there. I have an image to maintain."

"But that water is probably dirtier than you are."

"That's what magic is for." Crystal disappears out the door, leaving them at the table.

Penelope snickers. "Think William will chase her again?"

William, in his meeting with the troops, is getting the overnight reports. As he is eating his ration bar and jerky, Crystal comes flying out the back of her Vardo. She's still in her lavender dress from last night, but she's carrying a small bag with her and walks off into the tall grass. William quickly asks everyone if there is water around here. The corporal from overnight, speaks up and points in the direction she was leaving in.

"Gelga, go with her and make sure she doesn't get attacked. She's off to go bathe again and I dare not go over there."

"Yes, Sir." She picks up her food and follows the ivory maiden.

William studies the map and does rough calculations on how far it still is to Black Rock. "Well, with us going overnight like that, we should get there tomorrow night." He looks over at the wounded and thinks a break is in order. "We are going to keep up the pace, but we're taking a quick break for now. So, relax, get some food, and change clothes if you need to." Looking back towards the pond and then back at the assembled troops. "And if you need a bath, wait till she returns." He thumbs in that direction. "I don't want any of you to be killed." This gets a chorus of laughs.

Tia and Penelope finally leave the wagon, shutting the door behind them. Tia walks over to the wounded troops and casts a few healing spells, getting them back up to full strength and leaving the walking wounded at two. She gets William's attention and points to a secluded area at the edge. "I'll be over there praying for the day."

William acknowledges with a nod and lets out another yawn. That floor wasn't the most comfortable place he ever slept, but at least it was warm. He speaks to no one. "Help me get my armor on." He gathers pieces and other soldiers help him strap it on.

The camp gets louder as each member does their tasks. Feeding of horses, cooking of meals and maintenance of the wagons. Crystal stands neck deep in the water, enjoying herself to no end, just lost in the moment, as the cool water caresses her skin. She looks back to the shore and sees Gelga standing in full armor. "Could you bring me out my lavender soap?"

Gelga looks down at the bag and back out to Crystal and shakes her head. "I'm in full armor. I'll sink to the bottom." She motions to the water itself. "Plus, I don't care much for cold water."

Crystal lets out a sigh of disgust. "Must I do everything myself?" She walks out of the pond and Gelga immediately turns around. Crystal rolls her eyes. "You're a girl too. What are you all shy about?"

Gelga's voice is crisp, but a tinge of fear can be heard in it. "You're the C.O. of this expedition. I wouldn't dare." Crystal rolls her eyes again and walks back up onto the grass and gets her things.

"Besides, why didn't you take it with you when you initially walked in?"

"Because, silly, I want to enjoy it first." She smiles as she goes back into the water. "I don't know what it is, but I just love the water. I can't get enough."

That water must be barely above freezing right now. How can anyone enjoy it? Gelga shutters just thinking about it.

Penelope comes out of the tall grass and looks at Gelga and to Crystal. "Gelga, you can go. I'll take it from here." Gelga looks visibly relieved as she departs. Penelope strips down to her bathing suit and grabs her own soaps. She touches the water and jumps back. "Holy crap, Mistress!"

Crystal, turning around in a panic, expecting to see a monster or something. "What? What?!" She only sees Penelope standing at the edge of the water. "You see something?"

She shakes her head. "How are you standing in that? I put my foot in there and it's biting cold."

Crystal looks down at the water and back to the Halfling, then shrugs. "Feels fine to me."

Penelope starts a small fire, throws her clothes back on, and goes back to the wagon. A few moments later, she's back with a pot. Dipping the pot into the water, she warms it over the fire, but not too much. Just enough to make it pleasant to use to wash up. Going back to her bathing cloths she cleans herself up and Crystal exits the water in her full glory. Penelope shakes her head and doesn't look up. "Some of us have this thing called 'modesty' you know?"

Crystal, taking her towel out of her bathing bag, dries her hair. "The grass is taller than me. Who's going to see?" She rings her hair out, then wraps the towel around her head.

"That's not the point, Mistress." Penelope adds more soap to her rag. "What if someone walks through that grass?"

Crystal, picking up a second towel from her bag, holds up her hand. "They will go to their death with a smile on their face." The flat tone of her voice as she dries off leaves much to interpret.

Penelope thinks about it. *She's not serious about that.* She speaks up, trying to tease Crystal. "What if it was William who saw you?"

Crystal doesn't hesitate. "Dead before he hits the ground."

"You would kill the Captain for looking at your naked body, knowing you should have at least a bathing suit on?"

"He should know better than to come over here knowing I'm bathing, regardless of what I am or am not wearing." She looks down as Penelope washes her elongated ears, trying to get the dirt from the tips. "And he knows what I'm doing. To come over here, knowing I'm bathing, means he's wanting to commit suicide by sorceress."

Penelope giggles a little, thinking about it. *He's not dumb enough to follow her here after last time.* She wraps up her own bathing as some of the female troopers walk through the grass. This prompts Crystal to dress. Penelope helps her get buttoned up in the back, as the troops set up. Crystal looks at herself, straightening the deep blue dress she picked out for the day. "Think he will like it?" Crystal looks at Penelope, holding her arms out.

Penelope, getting dressed, turns to her. "Who will think like what?"

"Do you think Captain Blakely will like the color of this dress?"

Several girls look up but don't speak. Penelope shrugs. "I don't know. Why don't you ask him?"

Crystal packs up her things and slings the bag over her shoulder. "Well, you're a lot of help! I'll see you back at the wagon." She then departs back into the tall grass.

CHAPTER 13
(Scared petrified)

They take a few hours, and the sun is high above them. The rain must have brought a warm front because the temperature is rising fast. Everyone has freshened up, and they're ready to take back to the road. They travel for several hours, and the sun is well on their left. Gelga calls a halt, as something isn't right on the road ahead. Penelope can see it too, but doesn't understand what exactly she's looking at.

Tia breaks the silence. "Why are we stopping?"

Crystal calls from one of her windows. "That's what I want to know!"

William walks by on his way up front. "I'll find out in a moment."

Getting up to Gelga, William asks about the problem. She points up the road. "There is someone up there, but they ain't mov'n." William looks to where she's pointing and sure enough, whoever that is, isn't moving, and not metaphorically. They are still like a statue.

"Could be a trap." He looks back to Gelga. "Let's proceed with caution. When we get closer, we will get a better idea about what we are dealing with." Gelga nods, and William heads back to his horse.

Penelope looks down as he passes. "I don't like this, Captain."

William agrees and keeps walking. "I don't either."

Getting up to the side of the wagon, Crystal stops him. "What is going on?"

"There is a person or persons just standing in the road, unmoving. We don't know what's happening, but we are going to check it out."

"Sounds like paralysis or petrification." She visibly bounces in excitement. "Might be something I was looking for."

William turns to her for a moment. "Well, let's find out first, before figuring out what to do, ok?" She nods and ducks back into her wagon.

Mounting back up, he whistles, and they set off again. A few minutes later and they are getting closer to the figure. Gelga calls for them to stop. William dismounts and Crystal already has the door open, with the stairs down. William, by reflex, holds out his hand and helps her down.

He looks down at her and her smile is wide. "Don't get your hopes up, this might be nothing."

As they walk to the front, she replies to him eagerly. "Captain, as I explained the other night, they live in this area. They have been spotted here so, I was expecting something like this."

Penelope and Tia overhear, and Tia asks the obvious question. "Who lives here, Ms. Hellstromm?"

She looks up. "I'll tell you in a moment. I want to be sure first."

Sure of what? Penelope wonders in her head. *That's a statue in the middle of the road.*

They continue walking past Gelga, who doesn't dismount, preferring to stay where she is. "That doesn't look natural."

Crystal and William walk up there, and he pulls his sword. The surrounding grasslands are quiet and the wind blowing through it makes green waves. He looks over at the statue and studies it. Muttering an incantation, he turns to her, and she looks around. "It's petrification alright. This person is, was, alive."

Sarcasm drips from his lips. "Great."

"It is great, Captain." He glances down at her and the fact she's very gleeful about this sends a shiver up his spine. "This means I'm one step closer to my goal." She continues to look around. "I see something." She points off into the grass to the northeast. Without waiting, she takes off; William hot on her heels.

"Crystal wait! It could be dangerous!" Gelga, still mounted, rides after her. Other troopers' years of training kick in, and they move into defensive positions. She runs only a few dozen feet and finds another statue broken in the grass.

"There is definitely a nest around here."

Gelga asks from the back of her mount, while glancing around. "A nest of what?"

William looks at her. "Cockatrice."

Gelga's eyes widen and sweat appears on her face. "So, we need to get going, right?"

"No, we aren't." Crystal snaps, bringing them both around. "They are making this part of the road dangerous, and we need to exterminate them for the people of the Rose Empire."

William knows that's not what she's up to, but it is, technically, in the job description. *She knows the law and is using it to her advantage. I'm not sure what to make of it.* He turns to Gelga. "You heard her. Let's start back, form a plan, and figure out how to proceed safely." They walk back, but Crystal is scanning the area again. She walks in a different direction, going after the next glimmer of magic she can see.

"Ms. Hellstromm, what should we be looking for?" When she doesn't answer right away, William turns around and she's not there. "MS. HELLSTROMM!" Penelope's ears twitch and Tia and her both stand.

She calls back from the tall grass. "WHAT!"

"Where did you go?" An ivory-white arm shoots up over the green grass and waves back and forth. He marches through the grass over to her. "Ma'am, please stay with us. If you are right, and there is a nest of these things nearby, you could end up very dead, very fast."

"Aww, you care."

"No, I don't want your father to cut me into small pieces with his latest power armor for letting you get killed on my watch." He waves her back to the rest of the group. She smiles and giggles but follows his instructions.

Penelope feels relieved, seeing they are walking back with Crystal. "Let's find out what's going on, Tia."

She hops down and Tia clambers down the ladder behind her. Taking a few steps, Tia stops. She searches the area, getting Penelope to stop too. "Do you hear that?" Penelope perks up and finally hears it too, drawing her daggers with a fluid motion, from wherever they were hidden.

The sound of a loud clucking noise is joined by others. Penelope calls out, "TO ARMS!" causing Gelga to ride hard and William to pick up Crystal and run at a full sprint back to the convoy. Out of the grass, flies a giant ugly chicken, knocking down one trooper before he even readies a weapon. Metal slides against leather and rifles

109

click as the soldiers react. Taoni knocks the cockatrice off with a shove, causing it to fall onto its side. More burst from the grasses, trying to take down their prey. A female voice screams but is cut short. A female trooper was bit on the neck and her body turned to stone from the origin point, cutting off her lungs before she could finish her cry.

William puts Crystal down and Gelga goes to engage when another one of the ugly birds takes Gelga right off her pony. It turns and attacks, biting the pony, and tearing off some flesh. The horse rears up and turns to stone within seconds, falling over. Crystal's eyes go wide as William turns and swings his long sword at the fowl, stabbing it in its flank. Still flopping and snapping its beak at whatever it can reach, Crystal mutters an incantation and points at the critter. Her hands glow red, like a ball of ice forms at her fingertips and launches at the foul beast. The impact causes the ball to shatter into splinters, piercing the beast's hide, freezing, and killing it.

Gelga gets to her feet and pulls her axe from her back. Penelope leaps into action, jumping onto the one trying to get up after Taoni knocked it over. She stabs it in the neck with both daggers and it snaps at her, tearing at her leather coat.

Tia, looking around, runs to the back of the wagon after Penelope. Seeing three more birds, she gets an idea. She picks up a few decent-sized stones and says a prayer, making them glow blue.

The cockatrices continue their attack, biting, clawing, and leaping through the air. Troopers counterattack, but another is turned to stone as the foul beast lands a telling blow. The formation breaks, as one runs into the tall grass, fleeing, with one of the ugly things giving chase. Sounds of screaming are cut short, but not the sound of the clucking and squawking. Penelope is desperately trying to hang on, but the one she has pinned is wildly bucking and snapping at her. The soldier on the ground next to her rolls and stabs the thing in the gut, causing them both to be sprayed with its blood.

Gelga runs into the fray. "Watch the crossfire! Use swords, no guns!" One trooper is holding one of them back with his scabbard in the thing's beak, wrestling with it on the ground. Gelga cleaves into it with her axe, knocking the other man free. William looks at Crystal and grabs her hand with his free hand and pulls her to the wagon. "Get under here and stay put."

He tries to pull away, but she holds fast. She chants an incantation and a light blue shimmer, which surrounds him for a fraction of a second. "Go kick their ass, William."

Crystal climbs up the wagon instead and gets on top of the Vardo. Looking down, she can see the one in the grass coming back. "LOOK OUT!" Out of the tall grass, the one who chased down the trooper comes flying out, colliding with William. The faint shimmer of her spell deflects the foul thing, causing it to stop in its tracks. William reacts instantly, driving his blade into its chest and it lets out a deafening squawk of pain.

Tia, taking her chance, throws one of her glowing rocks, homing in on the creature's head. Blood splatters across William's armor as the rock crushes its skull. William turns in her direction after seeing that and nods in approval. The last one continues to bite at them, but three of the other troops have it speared and pinned. It doesn't take long for them to finish it with a few well-placed thrusts.

The battlefield is quiet. Looking around, they take a count of what happened. William looks up at Crystal. "I thought I told you under the wagon."

"But those things were down there. So, I came up here instead."

"They have wings, they can fly." He lifts one up for emphasis.

Crystal is getting red-faced. "They are giant chickens. Chickens can't fly, even though they have wings."

They continue shouting at each other as Penelope wipes off her daggers and puts them away. Tia is visibly shaking but heals those who need it, as her strength allows. Troopers put weapons away and take stock. Four more dead, bringing their casualties to eight on this trip. William waves his hands in dismissal at Crystal and sits on a wagon edge, looking at the lists.

Crystal climbs down and walks over to him. "We aren't done yet, Captain."

William looks up at her. "Oh yes, I forgot about your special quest."

Crystal sits down next to him. "It's not just that. We have to get rid of that nest even if I didn't have a special quest." She encompasses the area with her hand. "As long as it exists, this can happen to regular citizens again."

William knows she is right and stands up. "You're right. I apologize for my outburst." She offers her hand, and he helps her stand.

"Apology accepted, Captain." She smiles up at him, knowing she won. "Now let's accomplish two goals at once."

William barks over the noise of the troops. "Ok, everyone. We can mourn later. Right now, we need to find that nest. Given the size of these birds, those eggs can't be that small. Use your swords to cut the grass away and start sweeping the area. If you find it, don't touch it. Yell for one of us to come to deal with it." Everyone acknowledges their orders and searches in a circular pattern. It gets into the evening before someone shouts, they found something. Crystal, William and the others come running. Peering down in the short hole, there look to be a few giant eggs of white with yellowish spots. "Is that a cockatrice nest?" Crystal, who brought her book along, flips through the pages. After a few minutes, she finds the entry and points it out to William. William looks at it, then back to her. "I can't read that." She looks at the book and realizes that he must not know Draconic.

"Yes, this is it. It matches the description. Wonder what these are worth back in Rose Harbor intact?"

"You only need the shell, though, right?"

"Yes, why do you—" she's interrupted as he smashes the eggs with his sword, and Crystal turns to look at him, face turning red with rage.

"Just following the law."

She fumes but calms down since others are around them. "Shadow, can you grab a large piece of eggshell for me?"

Penelope looks up at Crystal. "Uh, why?"

"Because I need a sample to take back to Rose Harbor, and I don't want to get dirty."

Penelope sighs and pulls a dagger out, crouches down, and picks up a chunk with the flat side of the blade. "Ok, where do you want it?"

"Back at the wagon, of course. I have a jar just for that."

Penelope glares up at her. "You brought your book, but not the jar?"

She shrugs. "I guess it slipped my mind, sorry."

Penelope takes the eggshell into her tiny hands and carries it back to the Vardo. Crystal follows, with William by her side. Everyone gets back to the wagons and William reviews his reports. Gelga looks up and says they still have maybe an hour of daylight.

Crystal looks over the troops that were petrified. "We should grab the statues." Everyone just turns to her like she's crazy. She states her case, "The petrification can be reversed if we can find someone who is strong enough to reverse it." She pulls out William's map of the area. "There is a monastery here." She points at it on the map. "It's maybe six hours away? Maybe they have someone who can reverse it, and if not, maybe they know someone who can?"

William looks at the map. "It's a long shot, but we must get to Black Rock. If it means getting four of ours returned to normal, then it's worth a shot."

They work as a team, carefully loading the four statue guards into the wagons. Breaking one could mean they might never be returned to normal. William orders they move out even though it will be dark soon. He doesn't feel it's safe, even with those things dead. They head out and the temperature is diving again, but not as low as it has been. Crystal secures her first component. *Five to go.*

CHAPTER 14
(The monastery)

They travel for hours, and a thick blanket of stars, joined by an almost full moon, greets them to the far right, as it rises overhead. Crystal is riding next to Penelope this time, as Tia is treating the wounded on the medic's wagon. Crystal stares at it as if expecting it to do something. "No matter how many times I see it, it's always an amazing sight." Penelope shivers as temps drop below the forty-degree mark.

Penelope responds through chattering teeth. "It is beautiful, but it's getting cold out here, Mistress."

Crystal looks at her tiny companion and lays a hand on her. Reciting an incantation, her hand glows blue, enveloping the Halfling. Within moments, she stops shivering altogether and looks comfortable.

"What was that you just did?"

"It's a spell that allows you to endure just about any temperature."

Penelope looks at her hands as the shivering has stopped. "How long does it last?"

Crystal shrugs, looking back up at the stars. "A while, I think. Like a few hours or so? Why?"

Penelope sits there nice and warm for a few minutes until it dawns on her. She turns and looks at Crystal. "That's how you're able to bathe in freezing cold water. You cast that spell on the way to the water before you jump in, so it doesn't bother you and leave the rest of us sitting on the shore heating water."

Crystal laughs and covers her mouth. This catches the attention of the point guard, causing him to turn around, but not enough to make him stop. She waves a hand in the air and calms a little, but the smile stays. "The only spell I use on the way to the water is the one that removes all my clothes, so I don't have to slow down getting in." She leans into Penelope, getting quiet. "I like the cold water. It's heat I have trouble with."

"I knew you liked the cold, but I have never seen you in water that was freezing before. Guess I haven't really thought about it."

Another twenty minutes go by, and the point guard signals a rest stop ahead. Crystal sees this and raises her right hand, utters an incantation, and snaps her fingers, causing some sparks to fly up like fireworks, signaling the others behind them that the point man spotted their destination. Pulling in, they set camp. They get down, and Penelope starts their dinner. The commander's tent goes up first and lamps are lit. The air is cool, about thirty-eight degrees. Fires are lit and food for the troops is distributed. Tia, exhausted from treating those who could be, sits down on a log and stretches.

Taoni brings her some warm tea and sits down next to her. "Thanks for all your help, Tia."

Sipping the hot tea drives the chill back for a moment. "Thanks for the tea, and it's my job as a priestess of Daniel." She sips her tea more. "I'm here to keep you all alive." Turning back to their petrified companions. "I really hope Ms. Hellstromm is right, that the monastery can help."

Taoni places an arm around Tia and the two medics lean on each other. Tia starts a little at the unexpected action but welcomes it. "We will pull through this somehow. Between Daniel and the Provider, we will overcome and accomplish our mission."

Gelga sits with the other two. "Too bad we couldn't bring my pony. These wagons are hard on my rear." This causes Taoni and Tia to laugh. Gelga looks at the two medics, not understanding the joke.

Crystal walks into the commander's tent, opening the flap. William looks up, and seeing it's her, he stands, but she raises her hand first, motioning him to stay seated. "It's ok, Captain" She then sits opposite him at his table.

"What do you need, princess?"

Her eyes lock with his, and a slight sigh comes from her. "Why do you keep calling me that?"

"Because I know it bugs you."

"What if I like it?"

"Then you would have ordered me to call you that from day one." He places both his hands on the table, lacing his fingers and leaning closer.

I can't fault his logic, but we both know it's a crime to call yourself royalty when you're not. She places her own elbows on the table, cradling her face and looking at him. They continue to talk about the trip and how they must delay getting to Black Rock, but it's for a good cause. This convinces William that despite the selfish things she pulls and some of the more questionable moral things she doesn't seem to have trouble pulling, she has a glimmer of a conscious in there somewhere. Penelope walks in with Tia, holding several dishes. They set the Captain's table and Tia takes a seat with them. Penelope bows and steps out.

The silence is broken by Tia first, which gets both William and Crystal to look surprised. "I was thinking about something." She takes a bite of food. "We need a morale booster. We've lost eight members of our team, almost got eaten by an animated plant, and attacked by a bunch of ugly chickens that turned things to stone."

Crystal drops her hands and looks away. "And I was almost kidnapped." She turns to her meal and the guilty pleasure it's about to bring. Taking a bite of her seasoned rare steak, Crystal moans in pleasure.

William pauses before taking his. "So, what are you suggesting?" He then takes a bite of his own steak and can't believe how good Penelope's cooking is.

Tia shrugs and finishes chewing. "Well, we need some kind of recreation, maybe?"

William drinks some water and glances in her direction. "So, what? Are we just supposed to delay the mission?" Crystal is uncommonly quiet, just enjoying her food, but looks at each as they continue.

"No, that's not what I'm saying. Maybe we can do something fun while we walk. Like a game or just talk to each other. The stoic silence, with just the marching of boots, is boring."

William, enjoying his entrée, nods and the answers. "Tia, I appreciate the suggestion, but these are soldiers. We are trained for months to be battle-hardened for these kinds of things. Yes, we lost a few and with luck, we will gain a few back tomorrow." He takes

116

another bite. "But every guard out here, including myself, knows that we could be dead tomorrow. And we accept that." Tia puts her head down and William extends a hand to put on her shoulder. "We signed up to protect the people of the Rose Empire. That includes you, Penelope, and Ms. Hellstromm on this trip."

Tia takes a bite of her steamed vegetables and Crystal finally pipes in. "Maybe we could do a traveling song?" She looks to Tia, and then William, gauging their reactions. "Just to help pass the time instead of just dead silence. Our talk on the wagon the other night really helped keep us going and awake. If it was dead silent, I don't think either of us could have made it overnight. I know I was bored sitting up there by myself driving after you passed out."

They continue to talk and enjoy their meal. Gelga sets the overnight rotations and makes sure they find plenty of things to keep the fires going. There aren't many trees out here, so keeping the fires burning will be tough. Crystal and Tia finally leave William's tent, and Penelope picks up the dishes to wash. The new morning breaks as the blues, reds, and yellows replace the blackness of the sky. Horses are fed and prayers are said, as they prepare for the long day ahead.

They get back onto the road with Tia and Penelope idly chattering to each other. Crystal is sitting with them for a change, but on the roof of the Vardo, with a blanket under her. Wearing a bright yellow sundress, she shines like the morning sun. The ocean wind catches her hair, blowing it to the east. William objected to her being up there like that as a sitting target, but she insisted it would be fine. Her would-be assailant was running for his life and wanted her alive, so they would try nothing with her up there. He didn't like that reasoning, but she was in charge, so he couldn't object. The sun creeps its way upward and a side road appears on the horizon. Crystal points at it and calls it out from on top of her perch. "There's the road to the monastery." This gets the point guard's attention. "Turn right when you get there!" He turns back with a nod and a wave of his hand.

At least she's taking her job of being in command more seriously and is being more active.

They make their turn onto the dirt and mud road. William has a concern this isn't the main road and there could be issues. The telltale signs of wagon travel are visible, so it is a used road. They can see the monastery from the turn, and it shouldn't take too long to get there.

They continue their approach, but it seems like it's taking longer to get there than it should. The sun clears over their heads and casts their shadows ahead of them. Trees become more common with a light forest, but the monastery is still visible, looming larger than expected, as they get closer.

The road changes from dirt to gravel and looks much better maintained. The grass is cut down and the trees are trimmed. Sounds of civilization can be heard, and the main building of the monastery is huge. Built on top of a large hill, it's surrounded by dark brown stained wooden walls. The gate is closed, but several men and women of several races are outside of it. The convoy pulls up to the gate and is halted by a Human male wearing a simple white button-up linen shirt and black pants. He carries an unusual-looking weapon on his belt with a long-curved blade. William looks around for others, but it's only one man. *He's the only guard? Either he is good, or they get little conflict around here.* They seem to keep busy with the landscaping around here, keeping the forest at bay.

The armed Asian Human walks up to the point guard and speaks to him. The point guard gestures back to the Vardo and up to Crystal. Crystal sits upright, observing the man now looking up at her. He casually walks in her direction and she hears the telltale sounds of William getting off his heavily armored mount. She keeps her seat on top of the wagon to keep an unobstructed view of her surroundings. William greets the man with an open hand and the strange-looking Human takes it and then bows.

The man speaks softly, but not in a whisper. "What is your business here? We are not a vacation spot."

"We aren't here for vacation. We had an incident with some cockatrice and four of my members were turned to stone. We hope your monastery has someone who can reverse the effects."

The man glances up at Crystal, who gives a casual wave and looks back at William. "Show me." William waves the man to the back. As they get to the wagon for medical, he introduces their medic. "Taoni, this guy wants to see our petrified companions." She dismounts and gets onto the wagon, lifting the sheet covering two of them.

The man looks and nods, then turns back to William. "Follow me and do not leave the path. I will take you to the main building." He looks down and notices William's sword is close to his hand. "Your weapons will not be needed here. If you would, please put them away. This is a holy place and violence isn't permitted here." He walks away, and William stops at his horse, to mount up, prompting the man to stop as well. He doesn't look at the knight as he speaks. "Also, do not judge here. Many are here because they are making a new life. Respect all, despite any prejudices you have."

William orders all weapons to be stowed and secured. "We are guests here and need their help. Respect their wishes."

As he walks by the Vardo, he stops and looks up and askew at Crystal. "This goes especially for you."

Penelope and Tia turn to Crystal, with visible anger in her face for be singled out like that. She crosses her arms, tilts her head, and rolls her eyes. "Excuse me? What is *that* supposed to mean?" They look at each other and dare not answer. The massive wooden gate to the monastery creaks open, echoing off the trees. The guy walks with his hands behind his back and the convoy follows as instructed.

Crystal, Tia, and Penelope all whistle in unison, seeing the beauty of the landscape inside. The paths are made of red brick, starting at the gate, with flowers and shrubbery lining them, giving the road accents. Sand, with intricate patterns drawn into them, with artistically placed stones of different colors and sizes, is scattered about. In the short grass, in the courtyard, easily a hundred people of every race and creed go through morning exercises, all dressed as the man who escorts them. They don't even turn to acknowledge the convoy. William's lips curl down and he gives a subtle nod. *That is some real discipline.*

Pulling up in front of the hill where the main building is located, he stops and turns, holding up one hand. Steps carved of stone lead their way up to the top, what looks to be a thousand feet up. "From here, only those who need to see the master may go." Crystal takes this as her cue that he means her and gets down off the roof.

William also dismounts and meets her at the bottom of the steps. Penelope stands, but Crystal waves her down. "I believe the Captain will be good enough. If they meant us harm, we would all be dead by now."

"Just be careful, Mistress."

Crystal notes the concern in her voice and waves a hand dismissively. "Don't worry. We will get our companions back and maybe even replace our stock of food, so make up a list of things we are needing. These people are much friendlier than the last." Penelope acknowledges with a nod and gets down.

William and Crystal make their way to the Human in the white cotton shirt. With that same flat, emotionless tone from earlier, he starts up the steps. "Follow me." At first, the duo has no trouble keeping up, but after two hundred steps, Crystal tires, and her breathing is becoming labored.

William stops a few steps ahead of her and looks back. "You alright?"

Crystal shakes her head. "Why are there so many steps?"

From ahead of them, the monk answers her. "To whittle out those unworthy of the Master."

Oh, he did not just call me unworthy! This lights a fire in her mind and she starts her climb, hiking her dress up and passing William.

I better stay behind her. She's motivated now, but if her body gives up first, it's a long way down. The sun starts its long journey back to the sea, casting long shadows to their right. Crystal stops and William almost runs into her.

"What gives?"

Crystal points to the west. "It's beautiful, isn't it?"

William looks west, and the sun is just above the water. The colors change shades from red to purple. It can be seen so clearly from up here. He nods in agreement, appreciating the view. "We need to continue, Ms. Hellstromm." He holds his hand out, palm up, as a prompt to keep moving.

She whispers to William. "My legs are killing me. I don't know how much longer I can keep this up."

"Well, we're about halfway. So, whether you go up or down, it's the same distance. Might as well continue, right?"

She looks down and can see just how small everyone is. Looking up, it doesn't look that far anymore. "One thing is for sure... I'm earning my dinner tonight." William covers his mouth, stifling a laugh.

Penelope and Tia stare up at them as they go. Tia nudges her as another member of the monastery approaches. A Dark Elf female bows. Long white hair is tied behind her, and is also wearing the same white cotton outfit. "If you all will come with me, we will get you quarters for your stay." She waves an open hand toward some buildings.

Gelga doesn't look happy. "Our stay?"

The woman smiles. "Yes. You are our guests and it's customary to treat anyone who comes here with hospitality. Please, if you come with me, we will get your horses fed and meals ready for you."

Penelope looks up as Crystal and William continue their climb. "And what about the wagons? Do we bring those with us?"

Her smile stays firm, and she places a hand on a horse, petting it soft. "No, please leave them parked there and they will be fine. Hitch your horses to the posts in front of the hill, and we will take excellent care of them."

Tia, Gelga, Taoni, and several others in the group look uneasy, but they are under orders from William not to cause a scene. A Dark Elf, in this monastery, is unsettling to them, but they were told not to judge. Penelope reacts first, by jumping down and hitching the Vardo.

The monk continues. "Also, if you have a change of clothes, we have a bathhouse if you need, and a laundry if anything needs cleaning."

Tia wonders if she is referring to her since she has only the one robe and hasn't had a proper bath in a few days, but they gather things and leave the rest behind.

Penelope glances back up and sees Crystal and William look to be past the halfway mark. "Think she will jump from the top when she finds out there is a bathhouse down here?" This causes Tia, Gelga, and Taoni all to laugh, picturing Crystal, like a naked swan, diving from up there into the water below. They make their way, following the lady monk, to another set of buildings. They can smell food cooking and the clattering of plates and utensils. A large hall is filled with many long tables, and hundreds of people eat and talk. Some glance in their direction, but more out of curiosity than anything else.

Stopping at a group of small, white-painted buildings all arranged in a grid pattern, the Dark Elf woman motions to encompass them. "These are our guest cabins. Fresh linens are inside, and enough beds for four people per cabin. Each has its own stove for heat and making of drinks or food if you rather eat there than with us." Across from them, and around the red brick path, she points to another large building, painted a faint yellow with a black-tiled roof. "That is the bathhouse. The water is kept warm and there are several pools at different temperatures, so you can pick from which one you think fits you best. Everyone has different tolerances, so we try to keep that in mind." She turns back to the group. "If you have questions, just ask for me," she points to herself, "Sioki."

Taoni and Gelga trade glances and assign cabins to troopers. Penelope stops Sioki and asks if they have a bathrobe or something Tia can wear while she washes up her clergy robes. Sioki smiles. "I can get her a change of clothes, sure, but I can't tell from here what size clothes she needs, so I'll take a guess. If it's not right, I can find something else."

Penelope points to the closest cabin. "Guess we are staying in this cabin here, then." Sioki bows and walks away. Penelope and Tia walk in and plain, and different from the grounds. Penelope tosses her pack down and lights the lantern inside. With the sun setting, it's getting dark and cold. Tia sets her things down and sits nearly at a bed.

Penelope changes into her bathing suit and looks at Tia. "Aren't you going to change?"

Tia stares blankly at the floor. "Into what?"

Penelope blinks, as if not understanding how she can miss her meaning. "Into your bathing suit?" She gathers her towel and soaps. "It's been five days that I know of, that you haven't bathed. That's not healthy."

"I don't have a bathing suit. I forgot to bring one."

"Well, want me to ask Sioki? I'm sure they have plenty of them around here. You could borrow one?" Tia nods yes and looks flushed, deep in thought, but says nothing. Penelope waits patiently, but Tia sits silently, still looking at the floor. "Well?"

"Well, what?"

"I need a size. It's not like anyone can tell anything under that robe. I get it, that's the point, but if I'm going to request a suit for you, I need to know something other than 'bed sheet'."

Tia shrugs. "I don't know. I know I'm bigger than most other girls."

Penelope's brow shoots up. "You barely eat, I doubt that!"

Tia turns almost red. "No, not big as in fat."

Both of Penelope's eyebrows come up and her eyes widen and she lets out a snort. "How big exactly? Let me see, and I can get a pretty good idea of what you will need."

Tia rubs her hands together and then removes the smelly robe and Penelope gets a good look at her. "Well, way bigger than Crystal's, that's for sure, but I can agree above average. I'll see what they have." Tia puts the old robe back on and sits quietly.

Penelope, with her towel wrapped around her, finds a monk and asks if he knows where Sioki is. The guy bows and tells her to wait at her cabin and he will send her. She doesn't wait long, and Sioki walks into view. Penelope explains to Sioki what they need, and she nods, informing her she will be back in a moment. A few minutes pass and she returns with a suit she hopes will fit and an extra towel to protect her modesty. She takes them inside and hands them to Tia, who is grateful. She changes and wraps herself up and the pair head to the bathhouse.

CHAPTER 15
(Growth of Wisdom)

Crystal and William crest the top and manage a few more steps when she collapses to the ground, clutching her leg. She screams in agony, getting the monk and William's attention. "What is it? What's wrong?"

"CRAMP!" She grabs at her leg and sobs. "I've been attacked by giant chickens, shot at by bandits, and almost turned into plant food, but I'm going to die from walking up a hill."

William kneels and rubs her calves, trying to massage the cramp out. The smoothness of her skin surprises him and the tightness of her muscle must put her into considerable pain. He notices the scars on her leg are all that's left of that plant attack. Crystal shoots daggers at him with her eyes, and William can guess she has killed him a dozen times in her head already. He continues to massage for several minutes and her breathing calms down. She lays back in the grass and the muscle relaxes in his hands. "It's going away finally."

William stands up, looking down at her. "You look like a giant sunflower, laying in the grass, with that dress." She sits up, and he offers his hand, pulling her back onto her feet.

"Not exactly the look I was going for."

She brushes off the grass and the monk interrupts. "Are we ready to proceed, then?" He pans to the temple with an open palm. "We are nearly there. You did well to make it up all one thousand steps. That is a feat few can claim to have done on their first try."

Crystal glances up at William and walks with a slight limp. *She won't even let pain slow her down when she's after something. Not sure how to take that.* They walk up to the main doors, which are much larger than a standard Human should be using. Easily ten to twelve feet high and a good eight feet wide. Sounds of people inside shouting in unison and in a timed manner can be heard, even from out here. The man turns to them as they get to the doors.

"Please stick close. It's easy to get lost in there if one doesn't know their way around." He points to their feet. "Also, you must leave your shoes here." They accept and kick off their shoes. The monk opens one of the large doors and inside, humanoids from all over the world are inside training. Punching, kicking, and weapons are all in motion with students learning from different masters, guiding them on each of their paths. Crystal notes there is a female Minotaur among them, shattering boards with each blow of her fist. Another Asian student, with a dirtier belt than her, is giving instructions.

The monk leads the duo to a chamber where there is a short Asian man, wearing a black shirt and pants designed much like the one the monk is wearing. His eyes are closed and he hums to himself. He faces away from them, towards the wall. Incense and candles line the room, giving off a pleasant fragrance. Several other older-looking humanoids are also in there, sitting, meditating like he is. The monk in the black shirt stops humming. Still sitting, he speaks, and the acoustics of the room seem to amplify his voice. "I feel two souls in this room. One of ice-cold, calculating, yet burning with desire, the other of commitment and honor, but troubled and burdened." Crystal and William exchange glances and the monk who brought them up bows. Crystal and William follow, parroting him.

The old man opens his eyes and stands up in a fluid motion. He turns, seeing the two strangers standing in the doorway. With a smile on his face, he approaches the two with open hands. Crystal and William smile and greet him. "I am Master Ravo Monzulo. You are both from Rose Harbor."

William shakes his hand. "That is correct, Master Monzulo."

"And you search for purpose, Sir Knight?"

"I have a purpose."

Master Monzulo smiles as if knowing something they don't. "But that's not the only purpose you want to have. You crave more, but settle for less." He scrutinizes the large man. "You are honorable. I can feel it in your soul. You will have a new purpose, and it will be exactly what you want, but you must be born anew, reforged by the fires of battle." William nods, as if understanding, but doesn't have a clue what he means. "And you Miss. You are cold to those around you, to keep them from being burned by the fires of desire in your heart. You cannot obtain those desires if you keep those around you at arm's length." He steps to the wall of candles and picks one up, and turns back. "You are both in the dark, searching for what you need, but to see in the dark, you need a light." He hands the candle to Crystal. "Be the flame to light the way." Then he turns to William. "And you be the candle. A vessel for the flame to shine."

Crystal and William exchange brief glances, and she gives a slight shrug, but William answers. "Thank you, but we are here because four of my troops were bitten by cockatrices and turned to stone. We hoped that you or someone here could help us turn them back to normal."

The old Master's smile doesn't fade. "I cannot help with that, but there is someone who stays here who can help you. I will have a student inform her you need her assistance with this problem, but in the morning, after breakfast." He holds a finger up. "For now, enjoy our hospitality and relax. You have a tough challenge ahead of you both." He motions for them to leave. "I have students that need my attention. If you would excuse me."

They bow to each other, and the monk who brought them up here escorts them out. Crystal sees the female Minotaur again, and she's talking to the Asian male from earlier. She stops, but William and the man escorting them walk on without her. She walks up to the strange pair and they stop as she approaches. The Asian man addresses her first. "Something you need, lady?"

Crystal smiles and puts on her friendliest voice. "I know this is going to sound very odd, but I need a lock of Minotaur fur for a project I'm working on." She turns to the Minotaur. "Could I possib—"

The deep feminine voice of the Minotaur interrupts. "I don't think so."

Crystal isn't deterred. "Just one little lock, though. I'll pay you for it."

The Minotaur turns and looks down on the short Human. "I said, No."

"But I really need it."

The woman bellows, stepping in close and bending down. "I said 'no'. You don't hear that word very often, do you, tiny one?" The hall grows silent as the towering Minotaur stands over the tiny ivory woman.

Crystal doesn't back down, craning her neck up at the towering monster. "Look, I just need a lock of fur. You wouldn't miss it and I'll give you five gold for your trouble."

The Asian male gets between them, pushing the Minotaur back. "Miss, you're about to get your face caved in. She said 'no' and take it at that."

William walks up and takes Crystal by the arm and leans down, breaking her staring contest with the beast woman. "I would take him at his word. We need to get back to the others and get ready for tomorrow." She looks back at the Asian man and decides William is probably right. He escorts her to the door.

"But I needed that fur."

"And she would probably kill you trying to get it."

They get to the front door and the Human tells them, when they can find everything, and Crystal gets excited about the bathhouse. She winks at William with a tease in her voice. "Well, you know where *I'll* be."

Stepping out of the building and into the cool night air, the new full moon starts its trek across the sky. Crystal stops before the stairs and looks up at just how big it is here. She reaches out. "It's almost like I can touch it." William looks up at her and agrees. They look down and dozens, if not hundreds, of torches are lit in the courtyard down below, casting dancing shadows as members of the monastery walkabout and prepare for the night. "That's beautiful too."

William opens his mouth to say something, stops, then starts again. "Well, let's be careful on the way down. I know you're tired and not used to all the exercise."

She looks up at him with an impish smirk. "So what? You want to hold my hand on the way down so I can't fall?" She offers her hand, causing him to blush.

He takes it with a smile growing on his face. "This doesn't mean anything. I just don't want you to fall to your death."

"Don't explain that to me. Explain that to everyone who sees."

"You're going to have to explain it to them too, you know."

"I will just tell them to ask you."

They take their time walking down, with the full moon lighting the stone white stairs well enough they have no trouble navigating. They get to the bottom and Crystal walks to her Vardo. William stands at the bottom of the steps, knowing she must grab her bathing stuff. She carries out a large bag and hands it to him. He goes to look at it and she grabs it. "That's personal."

"Then why did you give it to me?"

"Because you should always carry a lady's things. Isn't that what *honorable* men do?" William sighs and resigns himself to the fact he's carrying her stuff now. They get directions to where the rest of the troops went and where the bathhouse is located.

They pass by the dining hall and see most of the troops eating and talking to each other and even Gelga is in there. "They look happy." Crystal's smirk returns, knowing exactly what's going to make her happy in a few minutes.

While Crystal and William were speaking with Master Monzulo, Penelope, Tia, Taoni, and some of the other soldiers take the opportunity to get cleaned up. The bathhouses have several large pools to choose from. Other men and women are in them already, but they find one with few others around. Penelope drops her towel on a nearby rack and sticks her foot into the steaming water. She smiles, as it's warm and feels wonderful. She jumps in and finds it so soothing.

Taoni looks at Gelga as she enters the water. "How is it?"

"It's water." She walks in and settles down and lets out an audible moan of pleasure. Her shoulder-length brown hair splayed outwards on top of the water. "But it takes the aches out." Penelope can feel it, as the aches in her muscles just melt away too. "It's amazing."

Taoni looks at Tia, unwraps herself, and places her towel on the rack, revealing many scars on her body from several campaigns. She walks down into the water and a smile creeps across her face as she sits down, leaving just her head above the water. Bliss is on both ladies' faces and Penelope turns to Tia. "You getting in?"

Tia looks, as the other female troopers are following, with scars on their bodies from battles fought. She nods and takes her towel off, but she blushes in embarrassment. The bathing suit covers little, and she's so used to hiding behind her robe. She walks up to the edge, and climbs in, sinking as far as she can. She doesn't react verbally, but her face betrays her feelings.

Penelope swims up to her. "Feels good, doesn't it?"

"Yes, it does. Glad you dragged me along." She relaxes into the water. Tia looks up, and can see the full moon through the opening in the roof, above the water. "It's a beautiful moon out tonight" The others nod in agreement.

The four trade stories and Tia opens more and comes out of her shell. Time goes by as the moon crosses over them. Female monks come in and bring them drinks and make sure they are taken care of. Penelope is small enough she can swim in the water and glide around the warm pool. Crystal and William can be heard talking in the hallway as they finally made it back. Everyone turns to look at the door as Crystal, still in her bright yellow sundress, walks in with William beside her. He looks spins, and turns several shades of red, then hands Crystal her bag and darts out and calls from the hallway. "I'll be in the next room if you need anything, Ms. Hellstromm."

Crystal smirks and walks over to the edge of the water. She puts down her bag of all her fancy soaps and stands back up. Speaking an incantation, her dress just drops to the floor in an instant. She hops into the water and settles in, closing her eyes and inhales heavily. She reaches behind her head and fans out her hair, removing the ties and tosses them back up on the deck. Everyone in the pool is in stunned silence, as the bright ivory woman just lays there like it's nothing to just be naked in the water.

Penelope exchanges glances with the other girls who all shrug. "So, I guess I'll ask. Why are you naked?"

Crystal just leans back, closes her eyes, and enjoys the water running across her skin. "Because it feels better than having a suit on."

Taoni gets curious and asks further. "Don't you care others can see you?"

Crystal gives a slight shake of her head. "I didn't see any men in here, and since we are all girls here, it's not like we haven't seen ourselves naked. So, nothing special to see here."

Tia visibly changes a few more shades of red. "Not everyone here thinks as you do, Ms. Hellstromm."

Crystal doesn't open her eyes. "I have nothing to be embarrassed about with my body. Except for those scars on my leg, from that evil plant, it's perfect as is." She waves her hand, splashing some water. "Besides, the water feels better without the suit. It's so liberating to me." She tries her best to sum it up. "I don't know. I used to be like you." She sits up and opens her icy blue eyes. "I was so different, you know? I mean, look at me. My father is a black man, my mom is a Half-White Dragon, and instead of being a mix of color that's toned down like you, or my brother, I'm practically an animated snowflake." She leans back again. "For most of my early years, I was embarrassed to go outside because I was so wildly different." Crystal looks up at the moon and stars. "It wasn't until I was around fifteen or so and was in the magic academy that I finally understood why I was so different. I'm different because I'm stronger mentally and magically than others." She holds up an arm out of the water. "The Dragon blood flowing through my veins gives me an innate magical gift, and it shows in my body." She puts her arm down and glances at them all. "But seriously, being completely exposed and letting the water run across your skin feels amazing. You should try it, if you're brave enough." Crystal lays back, with her face just barely above the water. "So why did you become a cleric, Tia?"

Tia sinks down in the water more. "I was an orphan. Just a street urchin, if you will, when I was incredibly young." She closes her eyes, recalling her childhood. "I did things I wasn't proud of surviving. I stole from others so I could eat." She sits up as the water parts away from her, causing a ripple in the otherwise calm water. "One day, a member of the Church of Daniel caught me trying to steal from them. I thought I was in trouble, but the man bought me a meal, and while I ate, he talked about Daniel and how he brings fortune to those who believe in him. He heals all wounds and is as strong as the morning star." She opens her eyes and leans against the wall of the pool. "He talked and talked, telling me stories of Daniel and the Provider bringing prosperity. So, I went with him, back to the church, and didn't leave. I found a purpose."

"That's respectable. I'm glad you found yours." Crystal sloshes in the water a little. "I'm still working on mine." They all exchange stories for half the night. The moon disappears from overhead. Most troopers have left and went to their cabins to get some rest. Taoni gets out and picks up her towel, calling it a night. This prompts the rest that it might be a good idea, so they can start the new day early. Tia refuses to even look in Crystal's general direction. Crystal picks up one of her towels and dries her hair first, leaving it wrapped up. She then dries the rest of her body and realizes the scars on her leg are gone. It's smooth as ice to the touch. "That's odd."

Penelope looks at her but Tia keeps her eyes down. "What's the matter?"

"All the scars on my leg are gone." She runs her hands over it again and scrutinizes it. "It's like it never happened."

Penelope wraps herself up in her own towel and investigates herself. "Yeah, it's all gone. Now cover yourself before some man walks in here and you kill him."

Tia pipes in. "I feel great too, not like well-rested, but all the aches and pains are gone from the trip."

Penelope towels off and looks distant. "Now that I think about it, Taoni had a bunch of old scars on her body, but I don't recall seeing them when she got out."

Crystal wraps a towel around her and looks back at the water and mutters to herself. "I wonder."

"Wonder what?"

Crystal speaks an incantation and her eyes glow purple briefly. "That's why." She sees the yellow tint of alteration in the water. A telltale sign of magic. "The water has alteration properties." She turns to Tia and Penelope. "We need to get our wounded in these pools to soak up the magical healing."

William, seeing all the girls in their bathing suits, quickly darts back out of the room. He shakes his head. That was not right for him to do. He walks back to the cabins and enters. Stripping his armor off and changing clothes, he calls for one soldier to take the laundry and do it, since they can do so. He grabs a bar of soap and some linens. *It's been a while since I got to relax and why should the ice princess get to enjoy it all?* Joining several other troopers, he drops his towel on a rack. Scars on his body crisscross his chest and arms, each one he earned in combat with a foe. The muscles under his iron-like skin move like cable, flexing as he stretches before getting in. Years of training, reflected in his movements.

Testing the pool first, it feels perfect for him. Stepping the rest of the way in, he can feel all the tension in his muscles just melt away. He sits down as the water rises halfway up his barreled chest. He can hear Crystal and the others joking and laughing in the other room, trading stories. The other soldiers in the room sit quietly, in contemplation, also seeming to enjoy the time off, from the ordeals of the past few days, but keeping their problems to themselves.

He must have dozed off, because the moon is gone from overhead, and he can hear the girls getting out of the water. *Might be a good idea too. Early day tomorrow.* He gets out of the water and dries off when he notices the scars on his arms and chest are gone. He shakes his head in disbelief and looks back at the pool. Looking back to his chest, then back at his arms and legs, sure enough, all the scars are gone. *Where did my scars go?* He looks at the water. *Is it like a healing potion or something? That doesn't make sense. Healing doesn't erase scars. What is going on here?* Shrugging it off, he wraps his towel around his waist and walks out the door, almost running into Crystal.

She jumps back, not expecting him. She looks at his bare chest and the rippling muscles. *By the Provider, he is strong and handsome.* Instinctively she reaches out and touches his chest, feeling the muscles, and jerks her hand back and her heart skips. *This looks bad, think of something!* She takes a sharp breath, as if frightened. "Captain, you scared me."

"Sorry." He looks over at her standing in just a towel. "Tell me you have something on under that."

She twirls and saunters away. "I'll never tell, Captain." She smiles over her shoulder, looking back at him. "But I need to find Taoni. Those pools are magical baths of healing. We need to get the wounded into them."

William perks up at this and catches up to her. "Did you say magical healing pools?"

"Yes, I did. I figured it out because I'm just that amazing."

They walk up to the cabins and they find Taoni. She is wearing a simple shirt and shorts waiting for laundry to get done. William notices her scars are gone too and points that fact out to her, "I've lived with them so long, I stopped noticing them. Didn't realize they were gone."

"Where did you house the wounded?"

Taoni points to the cabin behind hers. "I wanted to keep them close."

William pats her on the shoulder. "Good idea. Let's get them into the bath."

They get the wounded troopers and carry them to the bathhouse, lowering them in. Taoni sits watch all night, as they lay in there, while everyone else gets some sleep. The next morning, William checks on them. Taoni is asleep in her chair, not looking comfortable, but someone was nice enough to put a blanket over her. The four soldiers are awake and moving around, but haven't gotten out yet. They all stand up at attention in their soaked clothing when he enters. "At ease." He shakes Taoni awake, and she comes around. She then stands up at attention. "At ease, Corporal." He turns to the troopers in the water. "How do you feel?" After they confirm they all feel well, he orders them back to the cabins to get ready to go.

William gets back to the rest of the guest cabins and can smell Penelope cooking breakfast already and troopers putting on armor and getting ready for the morning routine. The monks are out, doing their own exercises in the courtyard. Crystal is standing outside, taking in the morning rays. She wears a teal-colored dress, and has her hair in five long, skinny braids, hanging from different points around her head. She gets called back in, meaning Penelope has her breakfast ready, and William joins the rest of the troops in the dining hall.

CHAPTER 16
(Preparation)

Daylight comes, and the sun starts its way, casting long shadows of the early morning. The temperature picks up a little more, and the morning dew shines on the grass. William finishes his meal and heads back to the cabins. He sees the Asian male and dark brown and gold haired female Minotaur from yesterday, at Crystal's cabin. *What in Johnathan's name is going on now?*

The Asian man is speaking. "We were sent here by Master Monzulo's request."

William breaks into the conversation before Crystal can speak up. "And you are?"

He turns in William's direction and extends a hand. "You can call me Tom." William shakes it and Tom directs his thumb to the Minotaur. "And this mountain of fuzz behind me is Tyra."

Tyra snorts at the jab and holds her hand out in friendship. "Tyra Nightmare."

William shakes her hand. "I'm William Blakely, Captain of the Royal Guards." He then indicates to Crystal.

She tries to sound impressive. "I'm Crystal Hellstromm, daughter of Jack Hellstromm, of the Third House of Rose Harbor and magical prodigy."

Tom and Tyra look at her for a moment, then back to William. "Ok." Tom clasps his hands in front of him. "We were told that you need to see Mistress Olovira about a problem you have with your friends." He thumbs to Tyra. "And she was informed that it was some heavy lifting, and no one around here is stronger than her."

William points back to the wagons. "I have four members of my troop that are currently petrified and need to be restored somehow."

Tom turns to Tyra. "Shall we get going?" The three take off, heading to the wagons, still talking among themselves.

Crystal also follows along, as she has nothing better to do, and she is letting her curiosity get the better of her. *She might get snagged on something, and I'll get my tuft of fur.* Getting to the wagons, William notices the horses are unhitched from them but are being fed.

He points to the four statues in the wagon. "These are the soldiers I need to take to Mistress Olovira."

Tom and Tyra look and she shrugs. "No problem."

William glances at her a moment, then looks around. "I'll get a horse hooked up and follow you there."

"No need." Tyra backs into the wagon, grabbing the wooden poles on either side. With a grunt, she lifts the front off the ground and drags it, with the four statues and other supplies, along the brick path.

Tom smiles and shrugs, following behind. "Told you she's the strongest person here."

Crystal watches her walk by with the wagon in tow. "I'm so glad you got between us, Tom. I have no doubt in my mind now that she could have killed me with a single blow." *But that's not going to stop me from getting a tuft of that fur I need.*

William, Crystal, and Tom follow along and Tom asks them a few questions about what they are doing. Mostly friendly banter and small talk, but William knows he is trying to judge their character. Tyra huffs and drags the wagon over to another decent sized, but still plain-looking building. She sets the wagon down and points to the building. "Mistress Olovira is in there and she's waiting for you. We don't have permission to enter."

Crystal and William exchange glances, and William opens the door, letting Crystal go in first. He follows her in and the inside is not what either of them expected. Exotic looking items line the walls and lay on tables. Bubbling from heated flasks, brews concoctions of unknown origins. Crystal doesn't dare use her spell to detect magic. Out of fear, it could blind her. William looks through the stuff, wondering what it all could be. Crystal is fascinated by all the spell components. *Most of the stuff I need for the ritual is already here, but how do I get it from the lady who lives here? She might sell it or trade it for a good price?* She's almost giddy, looking through everything. *I can have the stuff for the ritual within a few weeks, instead of years.*

They make their way through, and Crystal must smack William's hand to stop him from messing with things he shouldn't be touching. Crystal hasn't seen a setup like this since the magic academy. A woman stands at a table, lined with all kinds of bubbling and gurgling things. A black clawed hand sticks out from under her fancy robe as she reaches for a bottle. *Oh, she's a Half-Dragon.* Crystal smiles and greets her. "Hello." The woman turns, revealing her elderly face and short dark gray curled horns wrapped around the back of her head. *Not Half-Dragon, but something else. Dragon born possibly? I haven't seen anyone like her before. Half-Dragon humanoids don't get all the Dragon features, bloodline is too impure.*

Shelves around the area have things labeled, making it easy to find what she needs. "I hear you have some troubles, yes?" Her voice is raspy with age, and they can both tell common is not her favored language.

Crystal and William stop short, keeping their distance. Crystal speaks first. "Yes, we were attacked by a flock of cockatrices and four of our members were petrified by their bite."

The Dragon lady turns slowly about. "They can be a nuisance, yes." She looks at the two. Crystal can't even guess at her age, but she looks ancient. William is being respectful and letting the two sorceresses talk it out.

Crystal speaks in Draconic to the elderly woman. "Is it easier for you to talk in our native tongue than common?"

Olovira's red eyes light up as she speaks. She chortles. Both William and Crystal notice it for but a moment, but he doesn't have a clue about what Crystal said. It must have been really something to catch the old woman by surprise. She nods and speaks back in Draconic. "You have a Dragon heritage?"

Crystal grins. "My mother is a Half-White Dragon, but she only has the scales, no horns or claws like yourself."

The elderly woman walks up to Crystal, but even in her old age, she's still a good six inches taller. She reaches out and touches her face with trembling, clawed hands. "You have Dragon's blood. That part is true, but you don't have the Dragon's power." She pulls her hand back and holds up a claw tipped finger. "But you aren't here for that, no." Crystal can see the wrinkles in the old woman's face, but her arms are scaled black with a graying along the edges. She limps back to her table.

Crystal steps forward. "We need to get our soldiers turned back to living flesh again, but after that, would you sell some of your spell components?"

Olovira looks back at her with a puzzled expression. "You're a sorceress, yes? What do you need with spell components? Unless you're brewing potions or crafting a magical item, you shouldn't need anything here."

William, still not understanding anything, then witnesses Crystal pull out a small Dragon figurine from her handbag. The old woman's eyes widen again as she looks at it. "I need those spell components to add to this, to take back to Rose Harbor. The elder pontiff said once I got all the components, he could cast a ritual to awaken my Dragon blood."

Olovira lets out a cackle the chills William's blood, and turns away, gathering items. "I know this ritual, yes. I have much of what you are looking for." She turns back with a grin. "I, too, can do this ritual. When I'm done helping your friends, I can help you with this too if that is your desire?"

Crystal beams and hugs the old woman, almost knocking her over. "Yes, let's help the others first, then we can perform the ritual." She looks around. "So, what do you need?"

Olovira responds calmly. "An assistant, to gather the stuff I need, yes."

Crystal looks around as if looking for space. She continues in Draconic. "Where do you want the petrified men at?"

"Leave them where they lay. Moving them could risk fracturing them. Then, they would be beyond fixing, yes."

Crystal turns to William and switches back to common. "She wants you to wait outside with the statues and make sure they aren't broken. If they get broken, then they cannot be turned back." William looks at the two women, nods, then exits. Crystal switches back to Draconic. "So, what do you need help with?"

William walks out and Tom and Tyra are standing there, but so are Gelga and Taoni, having made their way after breakfast. "What news do you have, Captain?"

"Crystal says Mistress Olovira can change them back and wants us to make sure no one moves them, so they don't get broken. If they are broken, then they are beyond help." William's manner gives them all pause, knowing how serious that is.

Gelga investigates the back of the wagon. "Well, they look intact. We could use more blankets to pad it a bit more, but if we don't move them, they should be ok."

They are interrupted by a giggle from Taoni, as they both look and see Tom is talking to her. Tyra stands there like a mountain and William has seen his fair share of Minotaur's but they have all been males. He didn't think the females were just as imposing.

"Taoni!" William barks.

Her smile and giggle die instantly as she snaps to attention. "Yes, Sir."

"We are working on the wounded and petrified here. Maybe, as the medic, you should participate?"

"Yes, sir."

Tom nods, understanding that discipline is needed. "I apologize for that. I was speaking with her while you were inside and didn't think I was causing a problem."

"She's free to fraternize all she wants, but only when she's off duty."

"It won't happen again, Sir."

"We need to get these secured. I don't know how long it will take for Ms. Olovira and Ms. Hellstromm to do whatever it is they are doing in there."

Gelga contributes her suggestion. "I say we just pad them real good with blankets. Let's go Taoni, and see what we can find."

Tom joins Taoni and gets underway. "I can show you where to find those if you want to follow me, Taoni."

William rubs the bridge of his nose. "Gelga, go with them and get as many as you think are necessary. I'll wait here for Ms. Hellstromm."

They walk off and it gets quiet. William can hear the monks training, birds chirping and the air rustling the trees. He sits down on the steps and Tyra speaks up. "Sometimes you have to quiet yourself to hear what's around you."

William looks up. "What?"

Tyra stands there stoically. "You need to clear your head if you're to take it all in." She closes her eyes and takes a deep inhale through her nostrils. "Smells good out here, doesn't it?"

William knows Minotaur's have a superior sense of smell and doesn't argue. "Yeah."

"If you don't mind, I need to go through my morning exercises, since we are waiting anyway." She points to an empty patch of grass. "I'll be over there."

Crystal is looking for the ingredients Olovira is asking for. They still speak Draconic. "I don't see a basilisk claw in here."

The elder Dragon lady points. "No, it's in the cabinet over there." Crystal worms her way around the apparatuses and artifacts to the cabinet. Opening the latch, sure enough, it's hanging in with many jars and bags of other things. She takes it out carefully and brings it to the older woman. She looks at it and nods, pointing to the small boiling pot.

"What else do we need?"

Olovira looks at her brewing book, then reaches over and grabs a small jar of white powder and adds in a small amount. "Well, that's it. Now we need to let it brew for an hour for potency."

Crystal looks around at the library of tomes here. Organized by type and element. Spells on fire, ice, force, transmutation, and enchantment. "The things I could learn in this room, along with the other stuff."

Olovira breaks into her thoughts. "What do you have already gathered for your awakening ritual, child?"

"Well, I have the trinket here. I managed to get the cockatrice eggshell, and I was able to buy the sail snake wing in Rose Harbor before we left. I know I wasn't supposed to, but those things are only found in jungles way south of here. So I still need a tuft of Minotaur fur, the basilisk eye, Lycanthrope blood, and adult White Dragon scale."

"I have the basilisk eye, and the Lycanthrope blood. I can get the White Dragon scale easily enough. Yes."

This turns Crystal's head. *How could she easily get a white Dragon scale? Doesn't seem possible.*

"Minotaur fur? That's a bit harder, yes?"

Crystal shakes her head. "Outside is a Minotaur, just standing there, but she won't give up any of her fur. I tried." Her hand flies outward toward the door in frustration. "I offered money, I asked nicely, I pleaded. Nothing worked."

Olovira chortles. "And you gave up so easily?"

"No! Just looking for an opportune moment to snag some without her noticing."

Olovira has a short and labored laugh. "Have you tried challenging her for it in combat?"

Crystal's eyes widen, and she tilts her head, looking back at the old woman. "You haven't seen this woman. She's huge and could punch *through* my face. I can't take her in combat."

The old lady continues with her chortle. "Not confident in your abilities, no?"

Crystal reddens and crosses her arms. "What is that supposed to mean?"

"Strength is subjective, yes?" Olovira grabs Crystal's arm. "Use yours and you can win. Smaller, faster, smarter you are. She's a monk here, yes? She will hold back out of hospitality. Use that to your advantage."

Crystal ponders that and thinks about it for a moment. "And what if she does punch me all the way back to Rose Harbor?"

Olovira chortles more. "Saved you a trip back, yes?"

"So if I get it, when can we do the ritual?"

"Tonight, at the peak of the full moon. If we don't do it tonight, another twenty-eight days you will have to wait," Olovira speaks in a foreboding tone. "Or you could keep looking for your items and take them to Rose Harbor, but they will know that you didn't gather these yourself and refuse till you do. If we have more, we won't need the moon, but for me and you, and a friend of mine, the full moon will be enough to bring the Dragon out of your blood."

Crystal steps out of the building and William is sitting there. He stands up. "So, how's it going in there?"

"It's brewing. Needs about an hour till it's ready."

William clasps his hands in front of him. "Good. If they get changed back, we can get going before noon."

Crystal turns to him, looks him in the eyes, and then away. "We can't leave yet. There is something I must do here before we go, and it must be tonight." She can see him already getting frustrated. "But, first thing tomorrow morning, no matter what, we will go. I won't delay us longer than that, ok?" She turns with a cocked head, looking back, with her icy blue eyes.

William sighs, but accepts it. "You're in charge. If you want to stay an extra day, then we will stay an extra day."

Crystal's mood changes and it's reflected in her words. "Can you run and get Tia for me real fast?"

"What for?"

She looks back at William, then at the hulking woman of fur and fury. "I need someone to pray for me."

William doesn't understand but accepts his orders. "As you command, Ms. Hellstromm."

He leaves, and it doesn't take too long for him to return with Tia, but Penelope is in tow. Tyra is going through her moves, with a grace betraying her size.

"Ms. Hellstromm?" Tia sounds tentative. "William says you need me to pray for you? Why?"

Crystal points to Tyra. "I need some of her fur, and it looks like the only way I'm going to get it is to fight her for it."

Penelope looks at the mountain of fur and back to Crystal and the sarcastic tone in her voice wasn't lost on anyone present. "There are easier and less painful ways to kill yourself."

"I know what it looks like and—"

William cuts her off. "I know I swore to protect you, but letting you pick a fight with a monster twice your size and weighing at least six times as much isn't my idea of keeping you safe."

She turns and places a hand on his chest. "I know. That's why, at this moment, I'm releasing you from that duty. Shadow, Tia, you're witnesses. So, if something happens, you can testify in Williams's defense, so he isn't executed for dereliction."

Penelope sounds desperate. "And what do I tell your parents?"

"I don't know, make something up. Just don't tell them I went plumb stupid and picked a fight with a Minotaur, but I need to get that fur."

"Why not let me fight her?"

She shakes her head. "Olovira says it's on me to get it. I guess it's part of the ritual. To prove I'm worthy of it."

William realizes what she's talking about. "That ritual you told me about that night we drove?"

"Look, I don't have all day and if I wait, I'll miss my opportunity." Crystal looks at the trio. "I have to do this."

Tia shakes her head, not understanding, but she does as she asked. She prays, holding Crystal's hands. Tia's hands glow as Daniel answers. She prays for guidance for her friend, to shield her in her battle. While Tia does this, Crystal utters a few incantations of her own and glows faintly of blue for but a moment all around her body and fades.

After a minute or two, Crystal nods that she's ready. She strolls out into the grass and stands in front of Tyra. "Tyra, I want a tuft of your fur. May I please get a sample?"

"I told you 'no' yesterday. What makes you think I would have changed my mind?"

"I need it for a ritual. I'll fight you for it if I must."

Tyra lets out a deep, bellowing laugh, that causes people from across the courtyard to turn and look. "You?" she points to the tiny girl. "Fight me?" Tyra laughs more. "You're so tiny and meek. Is the heat getting to you, snowflake girl?"

Crystal is sweating as the temperatures rise with the sun is beating down on them, but doesn't step back. "So, do you accept or yield? If I win, I get the fur I need."

Tyra looks down at her. "If you win, I'll happily give it to you." She cracks her knuckles, then points to William. "But when you lose, your boyfriend over there better not come over here and try to avenge you." William swallows at being called her 'boyfriend,' as Penelope and Tia turn to look at him. "You are asking for this."

Crystal nods in agreement. "When would you like this duel to start?"

Tyra looks at her. "Being you're about to be beaten into a coma, I'll be sporting about this. You can have the first shot."

Crystal smiles, remembering what the Emperor had told her before she left. *Overconfidence can get you killed.* Speaking a short incantation and pointing as Tyra's eyes widen, a black bolt of electricity flies out and strikes her square in the chest. Tyra is immediately fatigued and feels as if she was kicked by a mule.

"That's not fair." Stepping forward to take a swing, her arm feels like it's weighed down with lead. It's slow, but Crystal can't get out of the way. The magic shield around her body flares blue, absorbing the impact. "You didn't say you were going to use magic."

Crystal, stepping back, looks for another opportunity. "I didn't say I wasn't either. This is a duel. You use what is at your disposal." She starts a new incantation but doesn't get to finish it as Tyra gets down on all fours and rams into her with her head, knocking her to the ground. William, Penelope and Tia stand nearby looking at each other and to the fight, as both participants are now on the ground.

Tia's voice cracks on the verge of tears. "Should we stop this?"

Penelope shakes her head. "I've seen her this way only once before. Get in her way now, and you will regret it."

Tyra is panting hard, as her body feels so much heavier than it should, and Crystal is coughing up a little blood from the impact.

"Ok, that hurt." Gasping for air, she rolls over and stands up. "I'm going to stomp you straight to the Silvian Empire."

I believe it. Crystal speaks a new incantation. A ball of ice forms in front of her hand and darts out, catching Tyra right in the face, causing her to go back down. She shakes off the ice crystals and reaches up and feels her nose. Blood is flowing from the impact of the small girl's icy orb. Crystal gets back to her feet.

Tia looks at the blood on her hand and then stands back up. "That was a good one."

Crystal grins, trying to bluff. "I've got more where that came from." She is breathing harder. For all her power, she can only pull on the magic in her blood for so long, before it drains her.

"My turn." Tyra lances out with a kick. Crystal takes the hit and the shield flares again, taking the impact, but still knocking her back.

I need to end this fast or she will rearrange my insides. From the ground, she chants a short incantation and her hands glow red. A short ray of magical frost flies out from her fingertips, striking the

143

Minotaur, causing a small portion of her fur to frost over. Tyra looks down and back to Crystal. "I made a huge mistake."

Tyra grins in agreement and swings again, but is tiring fast from how heavy her body is. She misses the smaller woman who rolls. Tyra, not used to the extra weight, stumbles, allowing Crystal to get back to her feet once again. Thinking fast, she kicks Tyra in the leg, but yells out, looking at her foot as if she just kicked a tree. Tyra turns around, breathing hard, grin still plastered to her face.

"Had enough?" Crystal breathes hard, with dark crimson blood still leaking from her mouth. *I need to hit her with another draining ray, but I'm not getting any opportunities.*

Tyra sounds a little impressed. "For a puny little stick figure, you got spirit." Her breathing is labored. "Going to be a shame when I knock your teeth out. Your boyfriend isn't going to want you when I get done messing up that pretty face."

William sighs and mutters. "I'm her bodyguard and captain of the guards, not her lover."

"Yeah, can't mess up your face, can I? All I would do is make improvements." This makes Tyra rear up in anger. She looks down and stomps one of her feet, pumping herself up. Crystal, pulling the last of her power, starts another incantation. Tyra hears the words, and her eyes widen, and looks up. She starts her charge, but the second bolt of black lightning hits her square in the chest. The strength in her body drains away, and she collapses to the ground, unable to hold her mass up. Crystal, drained of magic and exhausted herself, also falls to the ground. She crawls across the ground, to the downed Tyra, who is barely holding herself up. "So, do you give up?" She crawls on top, adding her meager ninety-five pounds to Tyra's already six hundred plus, causing her to collapse, pinning her to the grass. Tyra lays there unable to move and snorts angrily. "I can't move."

"Do you yield, or do I need to hit you again?"

Tyra snorts, powerless to move. *She feels like a full-grown bear on my back.* She grunts and strains, hen gives in. "Fine, I yield. Get off me."

CHAPTER 17
(The Ritual)

The two lay in the grass and Crystal's magic wears off, granting Tyra her strength back. Crystal is sitting there as Tyra gets up, knowing that if Tyra wanted to, she could kill her and she would be powerless to stop her. Tyra looms over Crystal and smiles. She reaches down, offers her hand, and pulls Crystal to her feet. "You fought well."

Crystal is holding her ribs. "And you kick like a mule." She looks up at Tyra. "I meant that as a compliment. Please don't kill me."

Tyra laughs, swatting her on the back, and Crystal goes face-first into the dirt again. "Sorry about that." She helps her back up and Crystal brushes her off. "Come get your girlfriend before she gets herself into more trouble."

Tia beats William and Penelope to Crystal and Tyra. Looking at their injuries, Tia examines them both. "Doesn't look like any ribs are broken, Ms. Hellstromm." She turns to Tyra, "Nor does it look like your nose is broken, Ms. Nightmare, but that can't feel good. Let me heal you two." She says a prayer as William holds Crystal upright. Tia's hands glow blue and envelopes Crystal. The blood stops leaking from her mouth, but the dress is ruined.

"Thanks, doc." Crystal winces as she tries to move, so she motions to William to let her back down. "Still hurts, so I'll just sit here."

Tia says her prayers and does the same for Tyra, stopping her bloody nose. Taoni, Tom, and Gelga return with the blankets

Tom puts the blankets down. "Work out your differences, did ya?"

Tyra looks to Crystal. "Yeah, we did." She reaches over and takes a dagger from William and cuts a lock of fur from her side. "Here, you won it fairly." She hands the dagger back to William and the fur to Crystal.

145

Tyra goes over and rests, and Tom walks with her, talking in hushed tones. William sits next to Crystal on the ground. "I've seen you use that black bolt thing three times now. What is it?"

Crystal looks at her trophy. "It's a strength draining spell. It makes the target feeble. If Tyra hadn't offered to let me have the first shot, I'm sure she would have killed me on that ram attack."

Tyra looks over. "That's why it felt like someone poured lead into my veins?"

Crystal coughs, as the pain in her ribs is still hurting. "Yep. I drained your strength, letting your body's natural weight do the work for me."

Tyra shakes her head. "That is smart. I must look out for that in the future."

Crystal stands up, wincing as she goes. "All I need now is the White Dragon scale, but Olovira said she can get that easily. I don't see how by tonight."

"Tonight?" Penelope looks to William. "We aren't leaving?"

William shakes his head. "Crystal is doing some ritual tonight with Olovira, and needs to be here." He stands with her and escorts her to the door. The injury is gone, but the pain will remain for a while. "We are on R&R, but will still do some drills to keep up our training, just like you wanted, Tia."

"I'm going to go check on the potion to see if it's ready and give her this." She walks in, leaving them at the door, and makes her way up to the bubbling pot. It stinks, but she knows that's part of the process. Olovira, seeing the rips and stains in her dress, grins. She speaks in Draconic still. "You're alive, yes. You win, or did she beat you and let you live?"

Crystal holds up the fur. "It was a hard battle, but I outsmarted her."

Olovira chortles again. "See girl, you do have it in you. You are worthy of this ritual without having to get all the components yourself." Crystal smiles at the praise from someone who finally sees her capabilities.

Olovira walks over and stirs the pot. "This is ready." She gathers four empty vials, carefully pours the smelly liquid into each one, and stoppers them. Handing them to Crystal, she gives the young girl instructions. "Pour these on the source of the wounds. Then, come

146

back tonight, at one hour before the apex. I will have everything ready for us to proceed, then."

Crystal smiles and hugs the old woman. "This makes me very happy, Olovira"

"I know, child. I'm happy to grant you what it is you seek as well, yes."

She takes the vials and carefully walks out with them. Everyone turns, wondering what to expect. "Ok, carefully get them out, and stand them up so I can administer this." Gelga, William, and Taoni struggle with the first one, and Tyra snorts. Getting up, she walks over and picks up the first one. Crystal nods and finds the bite mark. Opening the vial, she applies the potion to the contact point, and the soldier returns to normal.

Looking around in a panic, "Where am I?"

William calms down the man. "You're safe. You had a nasty run-in with a giant chicken."

Crystal, happy this is working, proceeds with the other three. Once they are all up and moving about, William tells Taoni to take them to the healing pools. Crystal decides after her brief bout with Tyra is where she will spend her day. William gathers the troops and does drills. Penelope and Tia spend time with the monks, learning about them. The day passes, but Crystal never leaves the pool except to eat. She loves the water, and would never leave, but they won't let Penelope bring her food here.

The day goes by, and the sun sets. Crystal gets out of the pool and towels off. Walking back to her cabin, wearing only a towel, she runs into William. He stops her, complaining about what she's about to do. "So, this ritual." He starts and stops a few times. "What does it do exactly? You talked about all this stuff, but never explained what it's supposed to do."

"Well, it awakens my Dragon blood, allowing me to reach my magical potential."

"But what does 'awakening your Dragon blood' even mean?"

Crystal looks at him and pauses. "I believe it means that the magical potential in my blood will be released and I should gain more power."

"You believe, or you know?"

Crystal places a hand on his armor, remembering his appearance under it all. "It will be fine, William." She looks up into his eyes. "Now, I'm going to go get dressed." She pauses and her voice turns to tease. "Unless you're trying to keep me this way?"

William shakes his head and lets her pass. She walks away and turns back. "Are you going to come and watch?" Williams's mouth gapes a little and he blushes. She goes from a smile to a frown. "The ritual, you dirty-minded man." She huffs and walks away.

How was I supposed to know? You send all kinds of mixed signals. He just watches her go, shaking his head.

She gets back to her cabin and shuts the door. She takes her towel off and hangs it on a rack to dry. She looks through her dresses, trying to find one that will work best for this evening. Olovira didn't say what to wear, so she figures anything would work. She holds up different dresses of a variety of colors, comparing them to her skin. *The benefit to her bright white skin is just about everything works.* She picks a nice chartreuse-colored dress with some silver thread inlays. *This should look good tonight in the moonlight.*

Crystal gets dressed and has dinner with Penelope and Tia. William is eating with his troops. Crystal does her best to pass the time until the full moon gets to where it needs to be. *I wonder where Olovira will get the white Dragon scale for tonight. She hasn't left her house all day.* Standing outside, the temperature goes down and she watches the moon climb its way up and towards its zenith. She starts her walk, knowing she still has just over an hour till it's ready. William sprints up next to her after seeing her from the dining hall.

Penelope stands, but Tia talks her down. "This is a personal moment for Crystal, and we should only go if we were invited. Being William hasn't been shooed away. Maybe he was?"

Penelope looks to Tia for answers. "Do you know anything about this ritual?"

Tia shakes her head. "Not much. All I know is it has something to do with her heritage, her magical potential, and it's personal to her."

Penelope looks back in the other direction, back into the dining hall, and points. "I think Taoni and Tom might become a thing."

Tia's voice lowers and moves closer to Penelope. "Do you think William and Crystal are dating?"

She lets out a long sigh, giving her time to formulate her thoughts. "Not yet, but I think there is something there. She teases him way too much, I think. It's like she's daring him to make a move, but he's trained to be so proper that he is not taking the bait, or he's clueless."

Tia looks at her. "How do you know this?"

She smiles. "I see it in her mannerisms. Crystal is strong-willed, and she's trying to maneuver him into finally taking that step first. I think she's afraid if she makes the first move, it will make her look weak to him."

"So, do you think he's interested in her?"

She shrugs. "His training makes it hard, but I notice he gets embarrassed by her flirting. I would tell her to stop, but I think that would make me the target of her ire. Besides, I think he is honorable enough."

Crystal and William travel back to Olovira's place and she has everything set out and is ready to go into the yard. Another person is also standing there. A Human male that looks to be in his mid-fifties. Looking up, the full moon is getting close to its peak, and she asks Olovira where she should be.

"Your place is here, in the center of the circle. I have placed each of the items you need in each of the smaller circles around you, yes."

Crystal notes that two of the circles are empty. "You're missing the Lycanthrope blood and the White Dragon scale?"

Olovira laughs, pointing to her friend. "You have what I need for the young girl here? She seems to be concerned, yes?"

The old man nods and speaks an incantation. Crystal knows some of those words but can't piece it all together. In the end, he changes shape and reveals himself as an old White Dragon. He speaks to Olovira in Draconic. "With this, my debt is paid, by the way." Reaching down and yanking off a small scale with a wince, he then repeats the incantation to return to being an old man.

William and Crystal just stare in shock, as this happens so quickly. Olovira nods in agreement, holding out her hand. "Are you staying to help with the ritual, or will you be on your way?"

Looking at Crystal, he hands over the blood-covered scale, and then a vial of blood. "I'll stay and help. It's only a few more minutes away." He turns and looks at Crystal with a warm grin. "Plus, I'll be helping a fellow White Dragon, right?"

Olovira places the blood-stained scale and the vial in their places and then hands the trinket to Crystal, directing her to sit in the center of the transmutation circle. "Hold this for the entire time and don't let it go." She walks over and sits in front of Crystal, but outside the circle. "It is time, yes."

The old man sits behind Crystal and all three of them start their incantations in sync. William watches from the building, and Penelope and Tia watch in the distance, curious but respectful. A few minutes into their chant, the circle glows a dim yellow. The sounds of the night fade away as the trio chants nonstop. The wind picks up, but only locally around the circle, and the spell components rise and orbit her. Thirty minutes of the trio chanting, and the moon approaches its zenith. The circle's glow intensifies, making it almost painful to look at. It catches the attention of everyone in the monastery as they all look on at the phenomenon.

William can still see the three as the spell components evaporate and absorb into Crystal's body, leaving only empty vials and containers behind. The moon reaches its apex, and the wind lifts Crystal from the ground a few feet into the air. Wind is blowing her dress and hair about, but she holds fast, not losing her place in the incantation. The glow intensifies so much it's almost golden. The moon moves on and the circle of light fades. Crystal's eyes roll back and she collapses to the ground, unconscious.

William runs over to where she lies. The Dragon trinket is laying on the ground close to where she crumpled. Her eyes flutter as if she was coming out of a trance, and focus on William. She wraps her arms around him as he lifts her off the ground, but then loses consciousness again. Penelope and Tia, along with several others, come running to figure out if everything is all right. William looks down at Olovira as she and the old man stand up and brush the grass off themselves.

"Is she going to be alright?"

Olovira walks up and looks at her. "She got what she wanted, yes. Her Dragon blood has awakened."

"What does that mean?" William looks down at Crystal's unconscious form.

"She will go through." She pauses as if searching for words. "Changes. Stronger she will become. Her Dragon side will make her much stronger, yes."

William continues to press, not sounding any happier. "What kind of changes?"

"Hard to say." She shrugs. "I went through this myself and I changed. Became much stronger, you will see. Effects each person differently, yes." She looks at the girl, who twitches a little. "And it could take several days to fully manifest, but I can tell already that it worked." William doesn't look amused, but is concerned about Crystal.

The older man waves and says his own incantation, and with a flash, is gone from sight. William carries her back to her cabin with Penelope and Tia right behind. Penelope opens the door, letting William inside. He places Crystal on a bed, but she is out cold. Grabbing a blanket, he covers her up and calls for Taoni.

Tia starts a prayer and her hands glow purple, laying her hands on Crystal.

Taoni comes running in and sees Crystal. "What happened?"

Tia informs Taoni. "She's not sick, no diseases, no poisons. I don't know. She's clean, but alteration magic is flowing through her body."

Taoni looks at William, expecting him to answer. "She went through with that ritual and it did this to her."

Taoni checks her pulse, "It's elevated, but so is her breathing, but not dangerously. Her temperature is cooler than I expected, however." Taoni shrugs. "I agree with Tia. Guess we just need to watch her overnight."

"I'll do it." William grabs a chair and sits at the table. "I promised to protect her, so I'll be here." He looks at Penelope. "I'm going to need some coffee."

CHAPTER 18
(Changes)

Morning comes, and the dawn breaks over the mountains. Crystal stirs, wakes up, and stretches. *How did I get here?* Looking around, she notices she's still wearing her dress from last night and swings her legs over the edge of the bed. The last thing she remembers is passing out in William's arms. *He must have brought me here.* She looks over herself and doesn't see any changes. She can feel something has happened to her but sees nothing. Looking around the room, she notices William asleep at the table. She smiles. *He takes his duty seriously. So much so that he watched over me all night. Very admirable in a man. It's too bad he's married to his job.*

She opens the door and the creak of it causes him to awaken. She stands at the door, with the sunlight shining in. Her hourglass silhouette is visible through the dress as he opens his eyes. *She is rather beautiful, but she is so full of herself and selfish. It just pushes people away. If she could get past that, she would make a wonderful woman, but it's my job to guard her, and I take my job seriously.* His movement causes the chair and table to squeak, causing her to twist in the doorway. William looks down in embarrassment, getting to see more than she realizes.

"So, you waited for me this whole time?"

"It's my job. If you got further ill, I would have tried to get you back to Rose Harbor. It seems that ritual didn't work."

She shrugs and notes his relief if it hadn't. "Maybe she was wrong and couldn't do it. At least I know how the ritual goes, and when we get back home, I can try again." Holding her left arm up, looking at it. "But I do feel different. Maybe it just takes time?" She sits down at the table across from William and places her hands on his. "Well, I said we would get going first thing in the morning. Let's get the troops ready and head out, Captain."

William smiles, looking up at her. "We have time for breakfast first, don't we?"

Crystal smiles in return, leaning on the table, making herself closer to him. "Always."

They have breakfast and assemble the troops. Master Monzulo comes down to the assembled guests and greets everyone. "Thank you for staying at our humble monastery. I hope you had a warm welcome."

William greets him. "Yes, we did. This place is delightful, and we are grateful for you letting us use your healing pools to get our men back on their feet."

Crystal also chimes in. "And the food here was wonderful. I hope I can return someday and visit." Crystal is helping William get his armor on; since everyone else is busy, she takes it upon herself.

Master Monzulo speaks up, addressing them both. "I have some parting wisdom for you both." They both turn to him as he speaks. "Protection and power are not as important as happiness and love." Crystal and William exchange glances, causing the Master to smile. "Also, a gift for you. I replaced your lost horses and loaded your wagons with fresh supplies. Penelope was nice enough to give us some of her recipes for our dinner service." He chuckles happily, rubbing his belly. "I found it fitting that since you improved our lives, I should do the same." They thank him, but he says he has one other thing to ask. "Tom and Tyra have asked if they could join you on your trip, and I believe it would be an excellent experience for them."

Crystal smiles, cinching up the leather straps on William's armor. "We would be happy to have them along, as long as they follow orders." Tom and Tyra bow, being respectful. "But we don't have any extra horses, however."

Tom speaks up. "That's ok, we would rather walk."

They get underway, letting the monastery fade in the distance. The morning sun is approaching close to eleven as they begin the last leg of their journey. The temperature is rising as springtime goes on. Crystal sits on top of her Vardo, taking in the sun. She doesn't tan and is so bright that she's hard to look at. She looks down at William, who is happily back at the point of the column. Tom walks alongside Taoni and the two talk and laugh, and Tyra walks with Gelga. The two seem to hit it off, talking about how much they like to break stuff.

As the sun hits the water to the west, Crystal remarks how beautiful it is, as the colors transition into night. The stars emerge and

153

the last night of the full moon is rising above their heads. Reds and yellows fade to purple and then black as the night comes. It's not as cold as it was the day before, a trend Crystal knows means she must use her magic to protect herself from the heat. Night falls, and in the distance, the streetlamps of Black Rock, from across the bridge, are visible. Crystal whistles to William and he pulls back alongside the Vardo, and looks up at Crystal.

"You need something, Ms. Hellstromm?"

"Yes, I need to get down now. It wouldn't look right for me to ride into town on top of my house, would it?"

William shakes his head. "No, no, it wouldn't." He calls for the convoy to halt so she can get back into her wagon and if anyone needs to use the bushes. After a few minutes, they get to cross the giant bridge, entering Black Rock. The town is big enough to have a very nice inn and some decent restaurants. It also has its own guard presence and is a good working town, so it's very prosperous. They pull up in front of the Onyx Hotel and Bathhouse. Crystal can't wait to try this place, since she got reviews on it before they left. William dismounts and then opens the door to the Vardo, helping Crystal out. She walks down the steps, holding William's hand, and they walk in together.

The main lobby is very spacious. Decorative plants and fine black leather furniture are set to maximize how upscale the place is. It's three stories high inside, with some looping stairs that lead upwards to the second and third floors. Crystal and William walk up to the main desk, and a female Half-Elven lady greets them. "Welcome to the Onyx Hotel and Bathhouse. How may I help you tonight?"

Crystal, putting on her most regal voice, speaks to her. "We are interested in renting some rooms for a few days"

"Rooms?" She looks from one to the other, confused. "You two aren't going to share one?"

Crystal turns red, and William notices her smile fade. William speaks up before she can speak again. "No, we aren't together. I'm staying at the local barracks. She needs a room; her companions need separate rooms."

"My apologies. The way you two walked in here, I must have misread the situation." The smile never leaves her face.

Crystal is already plotting how to end her.

Crystal's regality evaporates. "We just need three rooms all next to each other, if possible."

"Of course, Ms., I can accommodate you and your party." She writes up the receipt. "For two days and three rooms, that will be thirty gold." Crystal nods and pulls out thirty gold worth of notes and hands it to her. She hands Crystal the keys and a receipt and places the notes in a safe. William realizes he forgot to take the money back from her and almost laughs.

"Where are your stables, so I can park my wagon?"

"We will take care of that, ma'am. In our hotel, everything is full service." Crystal and William watch as Penelope, Tia, and a few troopers help take Crystal's things up to her room. It doesn't take him long before he notes she has so many clothes and bath items.

"Before I get settled in, let's run by the city hall. It's not too late, so the mayor could still be there. We should say hi to them if possible."

William thinks about it. "I guess it can't hurt. They're going to find out we are here first thing in the morning when the morning shift reports forty-six extra guards and a captain."

They walk out front, but the Vardo is already gone. "I'll have them pull your wagon around, Ms. Hellstromm."

She waves frivolously. "That's unnecessary, Captain. I'll just ride with you on your horse."

William looks at her and smiles. "You're in charge, ma'am." He mounts up and leans down, extending his arm.

Penelope is watching from their room as William yanks Crystal up onto his horse and she wraps her arms around him and rides off. "Did Crystal and William tell you they were going out for a moonlit horse ride?"

"No, why?"

Penelope just shakes her head. "No reason." She turns away. "Let's go check out the bathhouse before Ms. Hellstromm gets back."

William and Crystal arrive at city hall, and the lights are still on. William dismounts first, then picks Crystal right off the back and sets her down. He hitches his horse and the two stroll in. They talk to the guard, who is standing watch, and he points them to the mayor's office, on the second floor. Making their way through the building, they see that most officials have gone home. They admire the stonework of the building built by Dwarves.

Crystal walks alone into the mayor's office, with William standing outside guarding. The male Halfling receptionist is sitting there and greets her, "Can I help you Ms.?"

Crystal gives the aide a simple smile, trying to be polite. "Is the mayor in? I need to discuss a few things with her."

"No, I'm sorry Ms., she's already gone home for the night. Want me to leave a message?"

Crystal shakes her head. "What time will she be here in the morning?"

"Eight a.m. Ms. I can book you an appointment for tomorrow if you would like?"

"That won't be necessary." Crystal stands upright and turns a leg towards the door. "She will see me when I get here. I don't need an appointment." She turns the rest of the way and exits. "Let's go, Captain."

William and Crystal head back outside, and he mounts up and then pulls her onto the back. She wraps her arms around him, and he turns to head back to the hotel, when she speaks up, "Before you take me home, let's look around town a bit. Might be a good idea to get the layout?"

He turns to look back at her. "Why exactly? Are you looking for an excuse to keep your arms around me?"

She leans back and blushes, making him smile. "We are here to investigate on behalf of the Emperor, remember? So, looking around and getting the layout is important, isn't it?"

He nods, smile not fading. "You're in charge. If you want to ride around and look at the town, then that's what we will do."

Penelope and Tia enjoy the water for some time, but William hasn't returned with Crystal. She brings up her concern with Tia, who

156

lays in the water, enjoying it. "They have been gone for a few hours and it's getting late."

"You think they are doing something they shouldn't?"

"I don't like the idea that they took off and didn't tell anyone where they were going. The Captain and Ms. Hellstromm, who oversee this whole thing, are gone together, and we don't know where the Black Rose guy went." She slams her fist into the water. "They could both be dead for all we know."

This brings Tia upright. "What should we do? If we go looking for them and they are connecting and are on a date or something, we could ruin it by showing up."

"Or, if they are under attack, we could save them. That's the problem." She clambers out of the warm water and grabs her towel. "Well, I'll split the difference with you." She looks at Tia, who is also getting up. "I'll go look for them. If they are fine and just enjoying each other's company for once instead of fighting, then they will never know I was there." She looks back as Tia grabs her own towel. "And if they are in trouble, I'll sound the alarm." She exits and goes up to their room and gets her black leathers on, and stows her daggers in their hidden locations. Tia walks in as Penelope turns to her, sitting in the window. "Be back as soon as I know something." She leaps out, tumbling as she hits the ground, avoiding the injuries normally associated with a fall from that distance. She looks around, trying to spot anyone who could have seen her, but the shadows are her friends. With the night covering her even existence, she heads the same direction she saw them leave last.

William and Crystal casually stroll around the town. The old oil-fed fire lamps, burning in the open, are reminiscent of Rose Harbors' own lamps of just twenty-five years ago, before both were born. They cast flickering shadows as they ride under them, and the sounds of the night are overwritten by the clopping of the heavy warhorse. Crystal swears she sees movement and jumps occasionally, but William shows no fear of anything. "Where is the obsidian mine?"

William shakes his head. "Probably outside of town, closer to the mountains. We aren't going out there tonight. If you want to go tomorrow, we can bring Gelga with us. Being she's a Dwarf, and would know what to look for."

Crystal finishes his thought. "And she would know if we were being fed a load of crap by the mining foreman if he is covering for the mayor."

William turns to look back at his passenger. "So where to from here, Ms. Hellstromm?"

"Take me back to the hotel... Unless you have any suggestions?"

"Not this late at night. If we are going to visit the mines, I need to get Gelga informed, so she has time to gather maps and reports."

"Then back to the hotel, please. There is a spa with my name on it." She smiles at the prospect of laying in the water for hours.

William kicks the steed to speed up, causing Crystal to tighten her grip on him. He smiles, knowing she can't see his face, and she buries her head into his back.

Penelope follows the road, sticking to the dark and avoiding the streetlamps. It's late and there is almost no one awake, but she sees movement occasionally. *I'm not the only one prowling tonight.* Moving from point to point, she figures that if they took this road, it would have to be to go to city hall. It leads to the center of town, and only makes sense this is where they would go. *They are both here on the emperor's orders. Maybe they were hoping to find something before morning? Would make sense, but there are also a lot of businesses down here.* Restaurants, shops, and entertainment are all open this late. *If she went shopping, he could be begging for help.*

She checks for the Captain's horse. It's hard to miss with all that steel and red and gold trim. Looking around buildings and moving along the different roads, she doesn't spot it anywhere. She moves into the alleyways when she notices something behind one shop. A black rose is scrawled on the wall. *Not good.* Looking around, she spots no one else in the alleyway. *Wonder if there are any other of these markings around here?* She investigates further. Making her way up the alley behind other businesses, she sees the same scrawling repeatedly. She notes that one of them is on a basement entrance to one restaurant. *Odd placement, very telling.* She will be back later to investigate that, as she has an idea about what that means.

She makes her way to the city hall, and most lights are off, except for the ones on the main floor. There is a guard inside she can see, but there is usually one other that would do patrol. She has to be careful not to be caught, not that she's in any real danger here. She makes her way around the building, and there is no sign of William's steed. Finding a place along the wall, and climbs up to the second floor. The decorative pattern to the brickwork makes it easy to find handholds for someone of her stature. Whipping out a dagger, she slowly pries open a window and worms her way inside. Looking around in the dark, her eyes had already acclimated from the trip around town, searching for anything that could be useful. *I have to be careful here. Move something too much and someone will know I was here.*

She picks the lock on the door leading to the main hallway and grins. *Child's play.* Slowly opening the door, to keep it from making a sound, she peeks out, looking for trouble. The hall is lit by a single lamp in the middle, casting just enough light to see the whole thing dimly. She walks slowly and carefully like a shadow of her namesake and picks the door on the records office. She shakes her head in disbelief. *They need to invest in better locks.* Closing the door behind her, with the faintest of clicks, she looks through the files.

Using the moonlight to her advantage, she does what she was paid to do and searches for information. She knows she can take nothing, so she notes the file name and locations, so Crystal knows where to look. Parts of the shipments are being diverted to New Haven. *That's on the east coast and outside of the Rose Empires influence.* She continues to dig around, finding other deals with the city state and puts everything back where she found it. *New Haven is three-month travel by horse from here. Why would they bother dealing with them when Rose Harbor is only five days away?* Making her way back to her exit, she scans for the other guard. Not seeing or hearing any signs of him, she makes her way out, closing the window behind her.

William and Crystal make their way back to the hotel and spa. He dismounts first, then lifts her off the horse, as if she were weightless. His large hands can almost wrap all the way around her tiny waist. He gently sets her down on the ground and escorts her back to her room. She unlocks the door and enters, but he stands in the hallway. She turns around and tosses the key on the dresser. "I want you to be here by seven in the morning. We will have breakfast with Gelga, Shadow, and Tia and get our plans in order. Understood, Captain?"

"Seven a.m. I'll be here as ordered, Ms. Hellstromm." He slowly closes the door, trying to keep things quiet.

Time to enjoy the bath. Wonder if Tia and Shadow are waiting for me down there? Crystal gathers her bathing items.

William mounts up and heads to the garrison with little left to do tonight, and he needs to get his rest. Making his way unimpeded, he notes that as he passes through the center of town, where still busy. *I see no other guards. There should be several, for this many people, to keep the law. What is going on around here?* The people looking at him as if he doesn't belong don't help matters. It reminds him of the look from Mossy Fields. Kicking his steed, so he doesn't waste time. Making it to the garrison and checks in with the watch commander. He gets the run-down of the place and perks up when told that they have their own bathhouse below the main building. "Don't tell Crystal, or we will never get her out of here."

"Don't tell who, Sir?"

"Ms. Hellstromm. She's a representative, placed in charge of this mission by Emperor Marcus himself."

"We will do our best to accommodate you and her, sir."

"Why are there no guards on duty protecting the town?"

"The mayor asked for them to be pulled. We had some unrest here and people were getting hurt, so she thought pulling the guard and letting things calm down would help the situation."

"How has that worked out?"

"We get a lot of reports of thefts and break-ins at night, but the conflicts died down. We investigate what we can."

"Starting tomorrow, I don't care what the mayor says. We will have guards on the streets. Understood?"

"Yes, sir!"

William finds Gelga and lets her know to be up early. "Crystal says to be there at seven, but I want them there earlier than that." Gelga understands and goes to her rack and beds down for the night. William, taking this cue, does the same thing.

CHAPTER 19
(Hidden Danger)

Penelope doubles back to the alley where she spotted the Black Rose scrawled on the basement access door. With the night in full swing now, most people have gone home, and only people like her are out this late. Picking the lock on the door was easy for such a new lock. Opening the door, it creaks a little, but not enough to have given her away. She quietly descends the stairs and into the basement. If this were a common eatery's basement, she would expect jars and food, and other food-related items. That's how her own storeroom is stocked, but this place is different. It's not pitch dark as it should be. There are lamps on down here and she can hear people talking.

A familiar deep voice speaks. "Yes, I'm sure it's her. There is no mistake. If her dress hadn't had torn, I would have had her here days ago."

Another male voice speaks. "So, what do we do now?"

A third male voice adds to the conversation. "We must get rid of them. You saw her and that Captain bodyguard. She's here on official business and went into city hall."

A feminine voice speaks. "Look, we have way more here than they brought with them, but we need to figure out where they are going. They are much better armed and armored than us, so we need an advantage."

The first male voice speaks up again. "Maybe we can get her from her room at the spa?"

A second feminine voice speaks up and sounds familiar. "I was there when she and her party checked into the Onyx Hotel and Spa. She has three bodyguards and a priestess watching her back. You would get nowhere near her. One of them is a female Minotaur. She dwarfs all of us."

The deep voice cuts in. "The Minotaur is new. She wasn't part of her party in Mossy Fields. But I agree Minotaur would smell us coming before we could do anything." Penelope moves around trying to get a look at the people talking, but the door behind her opens, causing her to hide under a shelf.

A new female voice enters the conversation, sounding older. "I got word that the Emperor has sent an envoy and there are many new troops in the garrison."

Penelope hears none speak. *They must fear this lady.* Looking at the exit, he pans around for any other people. *I need to get out of here and warn Mistress Crystal of the danger here.* With her training, exiting is easy. *They won't ever suspect a thing.* She opens the door to the alley and steps out, but is surprised by someone standing there. They reach for her, but her tiny size and speed make her hard to grab. The man in the alley shouts a warning into the basement and she can hear them coming. Grabbing a handful of rotted food from the ground, she throws it into the man's face and then runs.

They give chase, but she only needs a moment of them losing sight of her to vanish. She runs just to see another person step out into the alleyway's entrance, ready to grab her. Thinking fast, she pulls her hidden daggers and slides under the figure, slashing both inner thighs. She hops up before the figure hits the ground. He screams in pain, grabbing himself and dropping to the ground. She darts to the left into the darkness. The people chasing her stop to help their friend and give up their pursuit, realizing they will never find her out there. She owns the darkness.

The older lady speaks. "We're going to need a new plan. They know about the other one now."

Penelope makes her way back to the hotel and makes sure she's not spotted coming in. She climbs up the wall and back through the window she had leaped from earlier. Tia is asleep, half uncovered in her nightgown. She closes and then traps the window. *If I can get in that way, someone else can too.* She goes out her door and checks the hallway, and doesn't see anyone. *It's well lit, so there is no way to hide out here.* She picks the door to Crystal's room and sneaks in. It's dark in the room, but she can hear Crystal sleeping in her bed. *She must have been enjoying the pool, because her wet towels are lying next to the bed, on the floor.* Walking up to the window, she secures it so the window must be broken, alerting everyone that is danger. She then adds bells to the door, to trigger if it's opened by someone larger than herself. She then exits, giving Crystal her privacy, locking the door behind her.

William and Gelga arrive at the hotel at six a.m. and take a seat in the restaurant. William knows it's a full hour before the meet time, but he wants to get some fresh coffee and go over things with Gelga, before Ms. Hellstromm steps all over them and puts her own plans over what's reasonable. About six-thirty hits and there is a scream from upstairs of pure terror. William looks at Gelga as they both jump up and say, "Crystal," simultaneously.

They fly up the stairs, metal armor clanging against swords as William and Gelga pull their weapons, expecting an assailant. Penelope and Tom are both already at Crystal's door and she is picking it open as fast as she can. The lock clicks and William barges in first, shoving the Halfling aside, ready to kill whoever is attacking her. The alarm, triggered by opening the door, also goes off. Crystal turns from a mirror she was looking at, to the intrusion, and screams again, grabbing the blanket off the bed. William turns as red as his armor, having seen more than he bargained for, and turns around as quickly as he can. *I'm dead.* He waits for the deadly bolt of magical energy, but he hears her sit down on the bed, and she sobs. "Are you ok, Ms. Hellstromm?" Giving a dirty look and waving away those in the hallway trying to get a peek, he mouths, "Shut the door and leave." Penelope nods, disarms the alarm, and slowly closes the door.

"Something is wrong with me."

William stands like he was bit by a cockatrice. "What do you mean, Ma'am?"

She pounds her fists on the mattress. "Just *LOOK* at me."

William slowly turns around and notices she has wrapped herself, but she is different physically. She now has small Dragon-like horns protruding from her temples, not more than an inch or two long. The skin below each elbow has some small, glossy white, Dragon-like scales and her fingertips have become pointed like claws. He sits down next to her and rubs her back, noticing that he can feel the scales along her spine, more defined and larger. She continues to sob, then leans over onto his chest. He doesn't know what to do, feeling powerless.

He gets a bigger surprise when she looks up at him with those tear-filled eyes and sees her pupils have changed. They are still the icy blue, but they too have taken on a Dragon-like appearance. "I'm hideous."

William wraps his arm all around her, rubbing her left shoulder. "No, you're not. You're different, but you've always been different." He can feel she feels a little cooler to the touch. "You awakened your Dragon blood, and maybe that means you're going to have some Dragon-like appearances?" He looks down at her. "And your mother is a Half-White Dragon, right? She's beautiful, isn't she?" William is trying his best to comfort her.

"You think so?" She looks at herself in the mirror and points to her new horns. "But she doesn't have these." Then she holds up her clawed fingers. "Or these."

"Yes, I do think so." He slides his hand along the scales of her lifted arm. "And these look like they can take a beating. You might be a little tougher now." Shock replaces her sadness, and she shoves him, but with more force than yesterday, causing him to move. "You've grown in strength, too." He rubs his arm. "You don't look any stronger, but that had more behind it than yesterday."

She looks at him with that icy stare, but it melts within a moment. "There is more." Moving the blanket aside just enough, she reveals her legs from mid-thigh to her feet are also covered in small, glossy white scales and her toes have also turned into claws. "I'm going to need new shoes."

He smiles and holds her close. "We will go get you new shoes on the way to the mayor's office, ok? Now, let's get you dressed." Standing up, she looks back at William, who turns his head away, turning a little pink. She looks through her clothes and can't decide on what to wear. She looks back at William and walks back over to him. She sits with her head down and waves depressively to the closet. "Why don't you pick one? I just don't know what would look good on me now."

William stands up and walks to the closet, not knowing what to pick. He sorts through the dresses and picks a black sleeveless one, with gold and silver threads sewn into it, making intricate flower-like patterns. He walks over to it and places it on the bed. "I'll leave you to get dressed, but I will be right outside. Ok, Ms. Hellstromm?"

165

She stands. "I won't be long." He places a hand on her shoulder, reassuring her, and walks outside, closing the door behind him.

Tia asks first. "What happened, Captain?"

He looks back at the door. "Crystal is going through some… 'changes'." He looks at her. "She's going to need some adjustment time, so just be there for her. I think the ritual worked, but not in a way that she was prepared for."

Penelope speaks up. "Captain, I heard some things last night. There are Black Rose scrawls at some businesses here."

William addresses Penelope, motioning for her to follow. "Come to breakfast with us and you can tell us all what's happening." He looks at Tom. "That goes for you and Tyra as well. I think we are all going to need to talk about plans."

Tom partially shrugs. "I'll get her and meet you downstairs." Tyra and Tom go by and William is the only one standing in the hallway directly in front of Crystal's door. William steps out of the way as she exits. *She is still as beautiful, if not more so now, being very exotic looking, and she's a little more grown-up than when we started.* She walks along barefoot and down the stairs, but not used to her new clawed toes, keeps getting hung up on the carpeted floor, agitating her.

William and Crystal make it to the table, and everyone goes silent as they look at her. She looks away, but Tia gets up and places a hand on her shoulder. "It's ok. We are still your friends, and we don't think of you any differently."

"You don't think I'm grotesque?"

Tia embraces her. "No, we would never think that. You're just more Dragon-like." She lets go quickly, looking down. "But those horns are pointy."

William pulls Crystal's chair out. "Penelope indicated she had some news for us." He pushes her up to the table and motions for a waiter to come to take their order. Penelope tells them everything she found last night and of her close encounter. When the food comes and is all spread out, Tia stops Crystal from eating, till she can see if it's poisoned. Tia speaks a prayer, and her eyes glow with a light purple and she looks about the table. She believes everything is good and to proceed. Whoever Penelope was talking about isn't here or isn't trying to make a move now with them all here.

Crystal finishes her meal and leans back, patting her belly, getting Tom to pipe up. "Keep that up and you will start to look pregnant." Crystal isn't amused, as a bolt of frost strikes his coffee cup, freezing it solidly in his hand. He tries to shrink into his chair. "Withdrawn."

Tyra snorts. "If you had said that to me, I would have pounded you into the ground. I think you got off light."

Tom looks back at her. "But you have anger issues. That's why I'm trying to help you overcome them."

Tyra looks down at the tiny man, but Crystal interrupts. "Why don't you two do some snooping around? Shadow, you watch our backs at city hall. Stay hidden, but if you see a threat, I authorize you to eliminate it." Penelope nods. "Tia, you come with us. You're a cleric of Daniel, so you should be able to tell if someone is lying, right?"

"I can pray to him and force people to be truthful in my presence, but it's not a sure thing. Those who are strong enough willed can still be deceitful and I wouldn't know."

"It's all I ask that you try. Now let's go get me some new shoes."

The group gets up and goes to their assigned areas for the day. Crystal insists on riding with William. Tia rides her own horse she borrowed from the hotel. *She enjoys riding with him.* Arriving at the town hall, William dismounts and lifts Crystal right off the back, like he always has. This brings a smile to her face. *She needs it at this moment.*

They walk in and the daytime guard stands up. William, in his full battle dress, glowers him down and the others walk past unimpeded. Walking upstairs to the mayor's office, Crystal can clearly see she's in. The receptionist stands up to object, but she just says "SIT!," cutting him off and making him cower back in his chair.

The female Elven mayor stands up. "Can I be of assistance?"

Crystal stands in front of her desk. "Yes, you can. I'm Crystal Hellstromm, of the Third House and on official business from the Emperor himself, Marcus Rose." She pulls the official documents from her handbag, handing them to her.

She looks at it with scrutiny. "What is it you need, Ms. Hellstromm?"

"I want to know why the shipments of Obsidian and taxes have been cut to Rose Harbor." Crystal sits down in a chair, her arrogance on full display.

The mayor sits down herself. "The mine hasn't been as productive. We've had some setbacks."

Penelope knows her voice. *She was at that meeting last night, but I can't say anything right now.*

Crystal leans forward, locking eyes with the mayor. "I see. So, if we were to question your mining boss, he can confirm this with documentation?"

The mayor waves to the document with her left hand. "He can vouch for this, yes."

"Look, I want access to your records, all of them. I'm going to scour through them and find out everything."

"You don't have that authori—"

Crystal cuts her off, coming out of her chair and slamming her clawed fingers with a crack on the oak desk. "Don't you presume what I do and do not have authority over! I am here at the behest of our emperor to find out what is going on here, and I will rip this place down to the foundations if I have to." The Elven woman's eyes widen and she holds her hands up in front of her, leaning back against her chair. Tia and William, in the other room, jumped when she slammed into that desk. She stands upright, leaving eight deep scratches on the wood from her fingertips.

The Elven woman's lips quiver. "David, give her access to everything and don't get in their way."

Crystal walks to the door and turns back, looking at the woman. "Thank you for your cooperation."

She steps around William and he comments under his breath. "You mean coercion?" She looks up with those icy blue Dragon eyes and he puts his hands up. "My mistake."

Tia watches Crystal go to the records room with Penelope, then speaks to William. "Is it me, or is she more aggressive?"

Crystal and Penelope enter the room, with William and Tia right behind them. Penelope shows Crystal all the stuff she found last night, pointing at stacks and drawers. "Captain." Crystal doesn't look up at him as she digests the information. "Go ahead and take Gelga and Tia to the mines and start your investigation there. We need to find the corruption and how deep it goes around here."

"Ms. Hellstromm, my place is here with you, as your protector."

"Yes, yes, I know." She stops what she is doing. "I have Shadow here and if anyone comes through that door, they will have an extra reason to hate me."

William stands firm. "Still, I feel it best to stay here. Gelga is a capable officer and can get the job done."

With a sigh, Crystal goes back to rifling through the paperwork. Her clawed fingers make it frustrating to search them and it's visible on her face as her forehead wrinkles and face reddens. "If that's how you feel, then I have faith in your judgment."

William turns and walks out and informs Gelga and Tia. "Take a squad down to the obsidian mines with you. Find out if they know about the corruption and shipments." He turns to Tia. "And pray to Daniel for us to keep them honest, if you wouldn't mind?"

Gelga salutes, but Tia looks nervous. "I don't know a thing about mining."

"You don't have to. Gelga is a Dwarf, and it's in her nature to know these things. All you have to do is make sure that all the answers are truthful."

"I will do my best, sir."

Gelga and Tia ride back to the barracks, and pick up a squad on the way out to the mines, as ordered. They travel a good thirty minutes to get there. The ground goes from pleasant grass and trees to very rocky and upturned from the digging efforts. Dwarven men with their long beards work busting up rocks. Female Dwarves take baskets of those busted rocks to some Gnomes, who continue the refinement process. Tia watches in awe. *It looks very efficient.* The ground is very uneven, with large rocks and holes pockmarking the entire area along with ruts caused by wagons coming and going. Gelga has no trouble navigating the area, and they arrive at a building that's directly carved into the side of the mountain.

They dismount their horses, and Gelga addresses the troops. "Spread out and look for anything suspicious. If you find anything, report it immediately." They salute and get to their tasks.

Walking in, a very corpulent Dwarf, with a charcoal-colored beard, is sitting at the desk as two other Dwarves and a Gnome stand nearby. They all stop talking as Gelga and Tia enter. "Well, what do we have here?" The fat Dwarf looks at them both. "A beautiful lass and an Elf." They all laugh. He leans back in his chair. "What can I do for you girls?"

Gelga doesn't look amused and starts in immediately. "I'm here on the authority of the crown Emperor Marcus Rose." This brings the laughing to a dead halt.

He leans back forward, placing his hands on the table. "And what exactly are you here for?"

"Are you the foremen here, Mr.?"

"Ironrod," he finishes for her. "Yes, I'm in charge here."

Gelga looks at the others in the room. "Get out."

The other Dwarves and the Gnome clear out in a hurry, having no doubt she is serious. He stands up. "What is this about, officer?"

"I'm here to inspect your mine, go through your paperwork, and pretty much anything else I can think of."

Ironrod's smile returns, motioning with one arm back to the door. "Of course, I would love to give the pretty lass a tour."

They walk the mines and Tia feels uneasy being underground, and must stoop from being so much taller. *Everyone is working together. There is almost a musical harmony to it.* He shows them everything and sounds like he's trying to impress her. They walk for hours before getting back to his office.

"Everything looks in order here, but I have some questions you need to answer." Gelga turns to Tia. "Do your thing, priestess."

Tia nods and says her prayer to Daniel to keep those around her truthful. The floor glows a faint green for but a moment, and fades.

Gelga walks up to his desk. "The shipments here have been arriving short of their usual load capacity. About twenty percent short, to be more exact." She looks over his desk, picking at things. "Is there a problem with the mine?"

He speaks, then closes his mouth, starts again and pauses. "There is nothing wrong with the mine. It's running at capacity."

"What do you know about the shipments being diverted away from Rose Harbor?"

Anger creeps across his face, but he is compelled. "I know we are putting part of the shipment into other containers."

Gelga can tell he's not forthcoming with everything. "Do you know why you're putting those shipments into other containers? Where is it going?"

He looks uneasy and breaks down, unable to fight the enchantment. "I do. The mayor approached me with a deal. I would get a five percent pay increase if I did, and for doing so, we would have more income for the city." He stands up. "Rose Harbor hasn't increased our pay in months and, frankly, doesn't seem to appreciate our work here." His smile creeps the two girls out. "Mayor Shaenyla and I don't see eye to eye on a lot of things, but the glimmer of gold makes all the difference." He shrugs. "Other than that, I don't know where it's going. All I know is we are making more for them than from Rose Harbor." He steps around the desk, walking up to her. "And that's good enough for me."

"Fine. What do you know about the Black Rose?" He smiles at the question.

Crystal, with Penelope's help, finds the documentation of the diverted shipments. They are there for hours and the evening is setting in. *They started off small, it appears, and the pay for those shipments was better by selling to New Haven. Going by the dates, they got increasingly emboldened as Rose Harbor failed to notice the shipments decreasing. They decreased the taxes sent to Rose Harbor in proportion to the decrease in shipments and were pocketing it in the city coffers.* She can't believe it. *This is very bold for being so close to the capital city.*

She takes the ledgers, shows the payments, and walks back into the Mayor's office. The mayor turns in her chair, looking out onto the street below. "I take it you found what it was you were looking for?" Shaenyla seems uninterested.

Crystal tosses the papers down on the desk. "You're stealing from Rose Harbor. Why?" William and Penelope wait in the office with the secretary but can hear everything going on in the office with Crystal and Shaenyla.

She stands up fluidly from her chair; her voice changes from indifferent to indignant in a fluid motion. "Stealing? You call getting paid what you're worth 'stealing'?"

Crystal's ice-blue eyes lock with Shaenyla's golden ones. She drives a clawed finger into the desk. "You're selling to another city-state outside the empire, when you know that's not lawful. So yes, it's stealing."

"We don't want to answer to your empire anymore." The mayor's anger and raising voice are heard even down the streets. "You don't pay us enough to stay when others will pay more. We don't want hostilities. That's why we kept selling to you, even though it wasn't beneficial for us to do so."

Crystal's blood boils, ready to escalate the confrontation, as it occurs to Penelope where she has heard that voice before. "Ms. Hellstromm! She was at that meeting last night. She's a member of the Black Rose!"

Surprise crosses Shaenyla's face as she is being ratted out. "What of it?!"

Crystal snaps. "Did you order your man to kidnap me in Mossy Fields?"

She shakes her head. "I had nothing to do with that, but he said you were coming." She is still getting louder. "And when you didn't show up on schedule, I had hoped the cockatrices got you and your little group and we were home free."

William strolls in, hearing everything. "I'll take it from here, Ms. Hellstromm." Turning to the Elven lady. "I hereby place you under arrest, on the charge of embezzlement and treason against the Crown."

Crystal walks out of the room stuffing the papers into her purse, just to be blindsided by the secretary, hitting her in the head with the glass ink vial from his desk. Black ink, blood, and glass run down the right side of her face as she collapses to the floor. William turns to the commotion and Penelope pulls her hidden daggers in reaction. Shaenyla pulls a dagger hidden under her desk, and thrusts at William, catching him unaware and plunging it under the breastplate's protection. He reacts instantly, punching her with the hilt of his sword, knocking her out as she is flung against the wall in a slump.

Penelope jumps into action, climbing over the desk. The Human secretary must have forgotten she was there because his reaction of surprise is evident all over his face. She leaps from the desk and plants her daggers into his chest, riding his body to the ground. William helps Crystal up and the ink stains her perfectly white skin. "What just happened?"

"You were attacked by the secretary and the mayor attacked me." Crystal examines him, finding blood oozing from under his breastplate.

"Are you going to be ok?"

He turns and looks at the blood. "I've had worse from bigger." He smiles, turning back to her, hoping it put her at ease. "I'm not going to fall to some Elven girl."

Penelope scouts the hallway as Crystal grabs the evidence, stuffing it into her handbag. They make their way downstairs and the guard is standing in front of the exit. "What's going on? I heard a lot of commotion up there."

William walks up to him, sword still in hand. "The mayor is a traitor and tried to kill Ms. Hellstromm and me. Get your cuffs and detain her." The guard nods and takes off up the stairs. William looks at Penelope. "How long will it take you to get her wagon so we can get to the garrison?"

Penelope thinks for a moment. "Ten minutes, less than that if I'm allowed to commandeer a horse." William nods, giving her the go ahead.

CHAPTER 20
(Battle of Black Rock)

Ironrod spells out everything he knows about the Black Rose. "They are a group of people who think that the Rose Empire has been doing them dirty." He leans against his desk. "They don't want to be part of the Rose Empire and are working on splitting off." Gelga and Tia exchange glances. "It was going to be simple. Just decrease the shipments and when a messenger came in, explain that the mine was drying up and soon it would close."

Gelga understands. "And you and the mayor keep the profits from selling out to New Haven instead?"

"Exactly. It was a good plan, and no one had to get hurt."

Gelga steps back. "What do you mean?"

"Well, you're not a simple messenger and neither is the snow-white girl I heard about whom you're taking orders from. One person we could pay off or convince to be quiet, but your little contingent complicates matters."

The sounds of metal bashing against metal filter into the room and Gelga's face contorts. "If it has to come to this, then I have to place you under arrest."

He grins evilly. "You don't have that authority here, I'm afraid." He pulls a short sword out from behind him, but Gelga senses this coming and pulls her axe instantly. Tia, wide-eyed in surprise, realizes they walked into a trap.

Ironrod thrusts, but being that he's so overweight, throws himself off balance. Gelga responds by knocking the sword from his hand with her axe and brings it back around, pinning him to the wall. Tia reacts by chanting a prayer to Daniel and blesses Gelga, as both are momentarily encased in a green glow. The sounds of gunfire and clashing of metal outside increases, causing Gelga and Tia to turn to each other. "You realize that you're not getting out of here alive, right?"

Gelga looks back to Ironrod. "Well, in that case." She then cuts him down.

"Was that necessary?"

"One less enemy to fight, and it increases our odds of survival." Opening the door, the squad she brought with her, are in a dire battle with the workers. Pickaxes are effective against armor, as both workers and her troops lay dead about the area. A pickaxe swings at her head, but she catches it with her hand axe and punches the assailant with her other hand. Tia says a prayer to Daniel and fans her hands, catching two of their attackers on fire. They scream and drop to the ground, allowing Gelga to dispatch them.

"Get to your horse. This is a losing battle!" Tia nods, mounting up as Gelga continues her fight. "GO, I'll be right behind ya." Tia takes off riding as fast as she can as Gelga continues her fight. Tia rides for a few minutes and waits for Gelga to show. Time goes by, and after several long minutes, the reports of gunfire cease. Tia is fearful that Gelga didn't make it and speaks prayer for her Dwarven ally that Daniel will protect her.

Tom and Tyra are walking around the town, taking it all in. They both feel something isn't right, but can't place it. Tyra mentions they are being watched and scrutinized by several members of the crowd.

Tom nods and continues in oriental. "We know there is something wrong here, but we need to find out what. They went to the mayor's office hours ago, but we should have heard something by now."

Tyra agrees and responds in oriental. "I can smell the intent out there. The fear and anger is palpable to me." Tyra follows Penelope's trail from the other night and comes across the scrawl she said she found.

"Her scent is all over this place."

Tom looks down at the lock on the door. "You have a key?"

"Always." She reaches down and rips the latch and all off the wood.

Tom goes in first and Tyra stands outside, noting she is way too tall, so go into such a cramped place. Tom searches the basement and can tell Penelope was correct. He finds a few things, including a piece of a torn lime dress. He also notices that something in the back of the room had been moved by the scratch marks on the floor. Investigating, he finds a section of the wall is fake. Pushing it in, there are small lockboxes. He takes one out and there is a Black Rose inscription. *Interesting.*

Noises from the restaurant above his head keep him looking over his shoulder, but he gets the box open. Inside are details of a planned attack on the capital. *They can't be serious. There are thousands of troops in the capital. It would be suicide. I have to get this back to Crystal.* Returning up the stairs, Tyra has her massive arms crossed, as three men wearing black cloaks are standing there.

"About time you got up here. I didn't want to have all the fun alone."

"What are you doing down there?"

Tom looks at them and holds up the message talking about the attack. He speaks in common. "Looking for this."

They draw pistols from under their cloaks, but Tom is much faster than they expected. He steps forward and lashes out with a kick, sending one sliding across the ground a few feet back; his gun clattering to the stone street. The other two exchange glances, stunned by his speed. Tyra takes this opportunity to throw a punch herself. Blood sprays over the third man, as the second one's head collapses from the blow. Fear grips the last man, causing him to drop his weapon in panic, and flees down the alley.

Tom smiles and runs him down, knocking him to the ground with a kick to the back of the leg. Tyra walks up calmly and picks him off the ground like a child. "I have some questions."

Penelope runs out of the building and grabs a Dwarven pony. Riding through town at lightning speed, she makes her way back to the hotel. Not waiting for the staff, she goes around back and takes the Vardo.

William and Crystal are standing outside the door, waiting for Penelope to get back, when from the upper floor, they hear Shaenyla shouting. "They know, stop them!" On the street, everyone stops to look, and several pull weapons and approach the duo.

"Get behind me, Ms. Hellstromm." William pushes her behind him, blocking the assailants with his body. Gunfire comes from the street, but his armor deflects a few shots as he takes cover. She steps back and speaks out an incantation touching him. He glows blue for a moment as her armor spell envelops him. "You think you can take this many?"

"I have before, and you have my back, right?"

"Give me an opening and there won't be anything left to identify."

He pushes back into the doorway as men with swords make their way. This keeps the attackers to stay at his front and unable to flank him. He can see a few guards responding, but they themselves get attacked by random people in the street. A sword swings in and he parries it with ease. *My superior training against these amateurs will make this easy.*

Taking a second blow, he turns it into the first attacker, making him back up. William returns with a thrust of his own, stabbing the second man in the shoulder, forcing him to drop his weapon. Crystal speaks an incantation, then holds her hands out, emitting a small cone of ice and snow that envelops the attackers. Both men have dozens of ice shards sticking out of them, and the second man falls back with an ice shard sticking out of his throat.

Bleeding from several locations and seeing his buddy drop causes the first man to pause and back up, but more assailants arrive. Crystal backs up a step as the two attack William and look for an opening. The shield flares as a sword and small arms fire hit the armor. William, for as skilled as he is, cannot block everything coming at him. He counters with a shoulder ram, knocking the second guy off his feet and losing teeth. Crystal takes another step back and starts an incantation. A ball of solid ice forms and flies out at incredible speeds, hitting the third attacker in the face and breaking her nose. She can feel the power in her blood. *I should be getting tired after using this much, but I feel I can pull more. I feel incredible.*

Penelope pulls up with the Vardo, hitting a man firing at the building with a rifle. William seizing the opportunity; grabs Crystal, tossing her over his shoulder, and dashes out the door. Guards are fighting people in the street, smoke from exchanging rifle fire, and others in melee fighting with swords and spears. Penelope is already down and running for the back door. She opens it and William helps Crystal get in with a slight shove. He then grabs the tiny Halfling and tosses her in, slamming the door shut behind them.

He takes a shot from behind, putting a dent in his helm, but it doesn't knock him out. He spins in a fluid motion and stabs a male assailant through the gut and out the other side. *I better get moving. This armor isn't meant to take this many hits.* Running to the front and taking control of the Vardo. He hates leaving his horse here, but his charge is to keep Ms. Hellstromm alive. *Horses can be replaced, she cannot.* He doesn't stop for anything, covering his face with an is arm to deflect incoming fire. Arriving at the gate of the garrison with the sun setting, the guards open it just long enough to get them in. Tia had arrived earlier, giving them a warning of what was happening at the mine. "Report?"

The watch commander looks down. "None of the guards have returned from their rotation yet, Sir."

"How many are out right now?"

"Roughly forty. That's one-third our complement."

Tia cries, unable to hold back anymore. "Gelga and the squad are dead, too. I was a coward and ran off instead of staying to help."

William shakes his head and places a hand on her shoulder. "I know her. She told you to go. She was protecting you, so you could inform us of what happened there. If you had stayed, we would have gone there and would have gotten killed too." Tia looks up at him, her eyes puffy from sobbing so much. William embraces her. "She was a soldier of the Empire and died protecting its citizens."

Tom and Tyra come up to the gate and are let in. "Well, we found some stuff out, but it looks like you already know."

Taoni is doing her best to patch up William, but he won't sit still. Tia offers to heal him, but he refuses. "Save it for the wounded coming in that is critical."

Tia's mouth gapes. "But you've been shot and stabbed! Doesn't that hurt?"

"It stings, but I'll dress it later."

Taoni shakes her head in defiance. "Sir, as squad doctor, I'm ordering you to get looked at. You're too important to die from pride."

William sighs. "Fine then. Do it here."

Crystal approaches Tom. "What do you have?"

He hands it over to her and then points to the black stuff all over her face. "You have black ink all over your face. Did you try to get a tattoo?"

She shoots daggers at him, but Taoni giggles. Crystal looks at the papers. "Whoever these Black Rose people are, they are ambitious. We need more answers."

Tom puts his hands out. "How exactly are we going to do that? The whole town is hostile to us."

Taoni helps William get his armor off, and he winces as each blood soaked piece is peeled from his skin. Penelope examines the holes in it and glances back up at the large man. *This guy is inhuman.*

Crystal turns to William. "Well, we know the mayor is at the top of all this. Let's get her in here to answer some questions."

William removes his gauntlets, letting them clatter to the ground. Taoni dresses the wounds and Tia cleans up the blood. "And how do you expect us to get her?" He winces as she puts on some peroxide. "We can't exactly get out."

Crystal turns back to Tom and Tyra. "You two aren't widely known to be part of our group, and she hasn't seen either of you two."

Tom looks up at Tyra, who crosses her arms. "We aren't ninjas, but you're right. The only three people to see us aren't talking to anyone."

Crystal looks at them both. "Are you two up to it?"

Tom scratches his goatee. "Well, it's a matter of the Empire, so yeah, we will do it." His voice tells her he doesn't like the idea. In a few hours, it's dark enough and the two monks dress in black and hop over the walls. They make their way through town and follow the directions to the mayor's house on record at the garrison. They dodge almost everyone and arrive within thirty minutes. Checking out the house, it is well-lit and guarded. "Well, you're too big to sneak in, so wait here in case I get into trouble." He looks up at her and she gives a subtle nod and hunkers down, trying to hide. "Just be ready to carry a kicking and screaming woman all the way back to base." Making his way up to the house, he can see several servants working in the building. He waits for an hour, till she finally appears where he wants her. Using the trick Penelope showed him to pop open window locks, he easily gets inside. Making his move, he grabs her and drags her towards his exit. She bites him, getting him to let go. Letting her scream, he drags her outside, silencing her with a quick knockout blow and hiding nearby. A man comes running out and in their direction. *If I'm right, I can get two for the price of one here.* He runs up to

179

Shaenyla, who's laying on the ground unconscious. He checks on her and looks up to speak, but never gets the chance, as he too is introduced to the darkness. Tyra comes over with him waving her on and scoops up the two bodies. "Why are there two?"

"He looks like her butler. He could know something, too. Can't hurt to bring them both." They make their way back to the garrison. Guards fire into the darkness after them, but hit nothing. Dragging them back and rushing through the gates, the night guards slam them shut as a mob of people clash with them. They fix bayonets and shove them through the bars, warding the enemy back. The mob takes a few steps back from the gate, and the guard stands at their post.

Tom and Tyra bring the two in and William places them in separate cells. "Where is Crystal? She wanted these two."

"She's down in the wash getting that ink off her face." As if punctuating the thought, he can hear her calling from below, asking for her dinner. "Good job, you two. I'll let her know."

"How's the bullet holes?"

William points at the fresh scars. "Nothing a well-trained medic and some light healing from a cleric can't handle."

William travels down to the basement and then averts his eyes. Crystal is sitting in her towel, at a table brought down to the pool, and is enjoying her meal.

"Is this really appropriate?"

Crystal looks up at him between bites. "You see anything you want to eat?" She swallows. "I'll have Shadow whip it up for you, and you can have dinner with me."

William shakes his head. "Tom and Tyra are back with two prisoners. They snagged the Mayor and they are guessing her butler."

This gets her attention. "Do we have an interrogation room?"

"Of course. It's adjacent to the cells. Why?"

She waves for one of the female guards to come over. "Grab this table and chair. I'm changing locations. Show me to the interrogation room."

"But you're only in a towel."

She saunters past him. "Well, either carry something or step out of the way. I'm off to get answers."

William grabs the table and the female guard grabs the chair, following Crystal up past the cells.

She looks in at the mayor, who is sitting there defiantly. Shaenyla sneers at her. "You haven't won."

Crystal puts her face to the bars and grips them with her talons. "In two minutes, you're going to be begging me to kill you." Crystal sneers back and Shaenyla's vanishes, seeing the exposed fangs. Crystal walks into the large room, has her table set in the corner, and sits down with her meal. "Bring Shaenyla in here and begin the interrogation, Captain."

William nods and he drags her into the room, bound with her hands behind her back, and sits her down.

"Now..." Crystal chews her food slowly. "Tell me everything about the Black Rose." The Elven lady sits there quietly. "Captain, loosen her lips a bit, if you don't mind."

William stands there and objects. "We don't have to do this. We have the papers already. It's enough."

The anger in Crystal's eyes becomes evident to William. This isn't just about getting information. "I gave you an order, Captain." The hardness in her voice tells him he has no choice.

He sighs and turns around. "Tell her what she wants to know. I really don't want to do this."

Shaenyla looks up at him and rolls her eyes. "Bad cop, good cop? Isn't this a bit cliché?"

An incantation from behind William causes him to turn around, and he dodges as a ball of ice strikes the Elf in the face, knocking her backward out of the chair and onto the floor. Blood flows from her misshapen nose and William can see teeth missing. She screams in pain writhing on the floor. He turns and Crystal puts her glowing red hand down and takes another bite of her steak. "Shadow really outdid herself this time."

William's mouth goes agape, looking at the blood. He turns to her. *I know she gets angry, but this is just ruthless. What has gotten into her?* "That was uncalled for!"

She looks up at him calmly, but coldly. "William, you're a soldier of the Empire." She points her steak knife at the crying woman on the ground. "This bitch is planning to attack our emperor. Is it not your duty to stop any assault on the Empire before it happens if you get a chance?"

She's right. I have an oath to uphold. He glances back to the poor Elven girl still screaming on the floor, spewing blood. Tia comes running in, reacting to the tortured noise of the poor woman. William concedes. "Yes, Ma'am."

"And is it not also permissible to use any means necessary to gain the information needed to prevent such an attack from occurring or making sure the Empire is prepared?" She holds a hand out, stopping Tia from doing anything.

Tia protests. "She needs medical attention."

Crystal nods, taking another bite and moaning in response to how good it is. "Hey, Shaenyla, I would offer you a bite, but I don't think you can."

Letting Tia go, she runs over and gasps at the blood. Saying a prayer, her hands glow blue, summoning the healing magic and fixing the poor woman's face. She's still in agony as the pain stays with her for the moment, but she's better. She looks at Crystal with blood still on her teeth. "I won't tell you anything. You can go to hell." She spits at Crystal with blood. Crystal raises her hand, but William reacts first, backhanding the woman with his gauntlet back onto the floor.

Tia is dismayed at the violence. "Why?" The woman's nose was now broken again and bleeding anew.

"Answer Ms. Hellstromm's question, Shaenyla."

She looks up at him from the floor, believing he would be the one to save her. With blood still oozing from her nose, she stays defiant. "No."

Crystal pipes in with unsolicited suggestions. "Could start breaking fingers. Or I could just flay your skin off with these claws of mine." She demonstrates by stabbing a veggie with a sharp fingertip. "I never really thought about doing the dirty work myself, but I think I would enjoy it." William and Tia glance at each other and back at Crystal, not knowing if she's serious or not.

William drags her back to the chair, sitting her down. She purses her lips. "I don't believe you would take it that far."

Crystal's eyes flair as she stands up from her table. Flexing her fingers, her towel hits the ground, showing she's not dressed under it. William diverts his attention away and sidesteps, trying not to look. *She did that on purpose, knowing my honor won't let me look upon her.* Crystal reaches back and takes a swipe across Shaenyla's chest, leaving four bloody scratches on her white evening dress. She screams, but the man in the other cell yells he will tell them everything if she just stops.

Crystal rears her hand back to take another swipe, but Tia stops her, grabbing her wrist. "You made your point, Ms. Hellstromm." She cries. "You're scaring everyone here, not just your prisoners."

Crystal smiles and lowers her hand. "Heal her then, and put her back in her cell. Bring him in here." She reaches down, picks up her towel, and wraps herself back up. "I'm decent again, Captain." Picking her fork back up, she glances at the Elf. Tia heals the poor woman, but the pain is still with her, and she winces as she is taken back to her cell. As she leaves the room, Crystal speaks up. "If he doesn't give us what I want, you're going to be right back in here."

He walks in with no resistance. He lays it all out, confirming everything in the letters, and how they were setting everything up. "I think it's all propaganda. No one really believes there could be an attack on Rose Harbor. It would be suicide." He takes a deep breath and Crystal leans in. "It is just recruitment talk for these Black Rose people. People are fed up with the stagnant wages."

"What about the shipments to New Haven? What's that about?"

"People, mostly the upper class, feel that since Black Rock is technically on another continent, we shouldn't be part of the Rose Empire. So, they started selling to New Haven for a better price."

He talks for an hour at least, and Crystal finishes her dinner. She stands up. "Thank you for your cooperation. Glad we had a productive conversation." Looking at William. "I'm sorry if I scared you and Tia, but these people only know one thing: violence. So, you must show them who's the better woman by force." She points to the cages. "Words won't work on people like this." They go upstairs planning to retire for the night. They perk up as sounds coming from the outside sound like a battle.

"I'll check it out. Stay here." Crystal puts on her evening wear and the sounds continue and get louder. When William doesn't return, she gets curious and ventures upstairs into the front office. Looking out the window, there is a full-scale battle going on outside.

Crystal's eyes widen as William, with no armor on, is out there assisting the other guards. Blood runs down his body from several cuts and gunshots. She runs back to her room and throws on anything and grabs Penelope from the kitchen. "What is going on, mistress?" Crystal points out the window as they get upfront. Her eyes go wide as people are just bashing their way through the gate. Others are climbing over the walls and guards are fighting. Penelope turns to run. "I'll sound the alarm."

Tia can't believe what she is seeing. "We need to get out of here."

Crystal turns to her and then back outside. "No argument from me." William and the watch commander are back-to-back, fighting off attackers. Crystal opens the door and calls out an incantation as a ray of solid ice lances out from her red glowing fingertips, blasting one man into frozen pieces.

William looks over and sees her standing in the doorway. "Thanks!" He catches another sword on his, then punches the man to the ground.

Crystal looks a little fatigued after that. Tia glances down at her. "What was that? I've never seen you use that one before."

"It's an icy version of the fire ray. I can feel it in my blood. The new possibilities waiting for me to unlock." She falters but stays upright. "That takes a lot out of me, but it's effective."

Penelope gets back, and the sound of the entire garrison coming means the day can be won. They advance into the courtyard, engaging the enemies as they are encountered. The main gate buckles, allowing more to come through. The battle rages and William is taking hit after hit. He's bleeding from several places now and has a dagger sticking from his flank. The watch commander and the other guards are doing their best to hold the line, but it's just an onslaught of enemies.

William observes the numbers coming in. "Are we fighting the whole town?"

"It looks like it, Captain." The front gate finally comes down and there is nothing stopping the flood.

William sees an opportunity for Crystal to escape. He turns and yells at her. "Get in your wagon and go. We will hold them here while you escape." Seeing her hesitation, William punches another man down. "Penelope, Tia, grab her and go." Crystal is at odds with this request. *I know I must save myself, but not like this. I can't leave him.*

Fear creeps into her chest for the first time as Penelope and Tia grab her. Tom and Tyra are busting heads as fast as they can, but even the mighty Minotaur cannot take on this many. Gunfire and blades clashing fill the air. They usher her into the wagon as Tom, Tyra and William start a fighting retreat, trying to cover her escape. Penelope urges the horses forward, trying to steer away from the masses, but bullets strike the wagon close to where she sits. The gate is clear, as the attacking army is all inside. William and the troopers turn the fight so the gate is behind them as the wagon departs.

Crystal is watching from the back door as Tom takes a few steps in her direction and leaps onto the wagon. Tyra does the same, landing on the roof. "Get out of here, GO." He catches another man's sword arm and snaps it with his bare strength alone. She cries, knowing he's fighting a losing battle for her. She starts an incantation, and another ray of solid ice lances out, destroying another aggressor. This takes the energy out of her, but before Penelope gets up to speed, William turns to look at her one last time. A woman fires point-blank, hitting him in the chest, causing him to look down at the fatal wound.

Crystal screams. "NOOOO!" Kicking open the back door, she leaps from the wagon. Before anyone can react, she races back to William's body. The female assailant raises the weapon, but Crystal can feel the Dragon's rage inside her. Letting it out as a small but powerful breath weapon, ice and snow spew from her mouth, catching three in the blast. The woman dodges with minimal exposure and takes a shot at Crystal. She puts her arms up and her new scales deflect the shot, hitting another assailant.

Tom and Tyra both leap back into action to save the suicidal woman. Crystal grabs the murderer by her gun hand and swipes, rending her chest open with her claws, blood spewing into the chilly night air. Tom grabs her from behind. "Ma'am, we really need to go."

She looks at Tom and his blood chills. "Not without William."

Tom, lashing out with a kick to another man. "We must leave him. He died to protect you."

Crystal's anger gives way to sorrow as tears flow. "I know, but we can't leave him here for these butchers."

Tom punches a Dwarven man, knocking him out clean. "Tyra, you heard the lady. Grab him and let's go before we are overrun."

"But he's dead. We should leave." Tyra grabs another guy and tosses him thirty feet through the air.

Crystal lets out another incantation and a cone of snow and ice flash out, catching two more as she stands over William's body.

"I have a feeling she's not leaving without him." Tyra snorts and grabs William's body, and Tom grabs Crystal as they take off for the wagon. Tyra puts him inside and Crystal climbs in, dragging him in the rest of the way. Tom slams the door and punches two more guys while Tyra kicks one guy several dozen feet, hearing the shattering of bone.

Fire lights up the area as the garrison is set alight by the rioters. Grabbing onto the back, Tom shouts, "GO, GO, GO!" and Penelope kicks the team into motion. Rifle rounds hit the lead horse and wagon, but Penelope refuses to slow down. She pushes the horses hard as they hit the bridge. They were being chased up to that point, but their pursuers stop there, giving up. She doesn't let up, pushing the horses until they can't take it anymore. With the town fading behind them, the only sounds they can hear are the horses' labored breathing and the anguish of Crystal from her wagon.

CHAPTER 21
(The Sacrifice)

The dawn comes, gray and heavily overcast, punctuating the feelings of everyone on the Vardo. Penelope had fallen asleep, and Tia took over, using prayer to keep her motivated. Tom and Tyra lay on the roof talking to Tia all night, trying to figure out what they could have done differently. They pushed those poor horses all night, but they dared not to stop out of fear they are being pursued. The horse that was shot died during the night and had to be cut loose to keep going. Tom hops down next to Tia. "We should head back home to the monastery, see what Master Monzulo thinks, and get a better perspective."

Crystal wakes from her bed, still wearing the same clothes from last night. Covered in the dry blood of both hers and William's, she doesn't change. *I deserve to be covered in blood after my failure.* She doesn't bother sitting up or even move, just stares at the ceiling, listening to the others talk. *I wasn't strong enough, powerful enough to stop the attack.* She fights back more tears. *I lost all my soldiers, including William, who had sworn to protect me.* This causes her to cry again. *I went through so much to gain power, but in the end, it wasn't enough.*

She raises her hands to cover her face and realizes that the scales on her arms are more defined now, still flexible and moving with her, but tougher, more ridged. That's when she notices there is something blocking the top part of her view and she reaches for it. The horns on her head grew out and around the crown of her head and turned upward a little and even bit thickened. Her hands collapse back to her side in despair. *How many more changes am I going to go through?* She musters the strength to turn over and look at Williams's lifeless body. *So strong, so honorable, so handsome, and he gave his life to save mine. It's the least I can do to keep those savages from desecrating his body and delivering it to his parents back in Rose Harbor for a proper burial.* She wipes away her tears. The Vardo comes to a halt and she can hear Tyra talking to someone. The vehicle shakes as she and Tom jump down. Crystal doesn't care. *I guess we are under attack again. If I die, I die. I don't care anymore. Maybe I'll meet William in the afterlife.* The Vardo moves again and she can see the large gate of the monastery go by in the window. She lays back on her back. *At least they got home. We still have four days to make it back to ours.* The Vardo pulls up in front of the stone steps just as it did a few days ago. Tom and Tyra walk by the window but say nothing to Crystal. Tia and Penelope dismount the carriage and make their way to the back. Penelope opens the door carefully and looks inside just to see it's dark. Crystal still laying in her bed, looking up at the ceiling, not even acknowledging their presence.

Penelope takes on a soft tone. "Would you like breakfast, Ms. Hellstromm?" Only silence greets the poor Halfling. Penelope waits a moment, then quietly closed the door. *There are two dead people in there. One in body, the other in spirit.* Tia is sitting on the steps of the monastery and Penelope joins her.

"What are we going to do, Ms. Penelope?" She buries her face in her hands. "Ms. Hellstromm is our leader, but she's in no condition to lead anyone."

Penelope stares at the Vardo. "I don't know Tia. In the years I've known her, she's always been so gung-ho and always having to show she's the best at everything she is put to. This defeat and losing William have hit her hard."

A voice from behind them interrupts their thoughts. "Life can be like a dark tunnel. You might not see your way, but if you keep moving forward, you will eventually come to a place of light. Only if you stop will the darkness be with you forever."

Penelope and Tia turn around to see Master Monzulo standing there and Tom and Tyra bow respectfully. "Master Monzulo."

He bows in return. "I could feel the troubled souls enter this place from all the way up there and had to come and see what had happened." He turns and looks at the Vardo. "And the most troubled soul is hiding in the darkness."

"Crystal is in a state of shock and grief, Master." Tia glances at him and back to the Vardo. "Last night, Captain Blakely died saving our lives."

He stands there a moment, taking in the morning air. "I feel there is more to this."

Tia tries holding back her tears but can't. "She rushed into the fray to retrieve his body, refusing to leave him behind. We almost lost her, too. All our soldiers died, buying us time to escape."

He closes his eyes and takes a deep breath. "There is much work to do." Tia and Penelope look up at him and then at each other, not understanding. "I will speak with Crystal. You four should go and get breakfast. I know where I am needed." Tom and Tyra bow to Master Monzulo and the four walk away, leaving him with Crystal. He walks to the back of the Vardo and respectfully opens the door. Looking inside, he can see William's body on the floor surrounded by his own blood, with Crystal laying in the bed next to him as if dead herself.

Her voice carries from the darkness. "I'm a failure." She holds her scaled arm up, feeling the blood pump through it. "For all the power I had, I couldn't stop them."

"Failure just means you can begin again, wiser and more knowledgeable for the future."

She sits up, anger boiling inside. "And what knowledge do I gain from this?" She motions to Williams's body and grief makes her voice crack. "That there is no hope for me?"

Master Monzulo shakes his head. "No. Giving in to despair only means giving into the darkness in your heart. Hope is the light that wards off the darkness. Only with hope will you light your way."

"Hope he says." She flings her arms up and lets them fall. She turns to Williams's body. "What hope is for him?" Anger growing inside her turns into pure rage and places her hands on her head and snags her horns. "UUUUGGGHHH." She grips them in anger, pulling at them, trying to rip them off. "Olovira did this to me. She didn't tell me this would…" She trails off a second as an idea comes to her. "Change my body." Her eyes widen and turn to the old master.

He smiles. "You found your light." He steps aside as she comes down the steps, running across the grass.

Penelope, Tia, Tyra, and Tom watch Crystal running through the courtyard, wind racing past her blowing her hair back. "It is me, or have those horns gotten larger and is she glossier?" The rest look and wonder how she can see that detail from this distance.

Tia looks to her companions. "Should we see what she is up to?"

"No." Tom shakes his head. "Master Monzulo was speaking to her. It's obvious he has guided her to something, and she is after it." He takes a bite of his rice. "Unless she asks, her path is for her alone."

Crystal races through the grass, tearing at the ground with her clawed feet. The thunder crackles above her head as it rains lightly at first. The chilly dampness of it mixing with her and Williams's blood and running down her body being washed away. It turns heavier as she reaches Olovira's door. She tries to open it but it's locked, resulting in frustration and rapping on the door hard. Only a mere moment goes by, but the old Half-Dragon opens the door looking at Crystal.

"I see the ritual worked. Your Dragon blood is awakening, yes."

Crystal frowns and can't keep the sarcasm from her voice. "Yeah, it worked."

"Don't be angry, child, no." Olovira smiles and turns away, heading inside. "Stronger you are, more powerful and beautiful, yes?"

"I'm not here for me."

Olovira's face wrinkles more as her smile increases and she glances back. "What is it I can do for you?"

"William is dead. He died protecting me. I want him back. Restored as if nothing happened." She does her best to sound defiant, but thinking about it makes her voice pop.

"You ask much. Not a simple task to perform. Defiant of the gods is such a request, yes."

"My family is wealthy. I'll pay you whatever you want, just do something to bring him back."

"It's not about money, child, no." She waves Crystal inside, going back to her lectern. Crystal follows her in. "What you ask is difficult."

"But can you do it?"

Olovira looks thoughtful and takes a black tome off the shelf. "Yes, I know a spell that can bring him back, but it carries a heavy price."

"I'll pay anything, whatever you want, just name it."

"It is not material cost that is in question, no." She lays the book out with the markings of necromancy all over it. A skull dominates its face along with necromantic symbols and is bound in humanoid, tanned leather. Crystal can feel the power radiating from the book through her blood. Olovira unlocks the tome with a special key, opening it. The pages are filled with all kinds of draconic scripts of spells she's never heard of.

Olovira places a wrinkled hand on the book and turns to her. "Have you heard of resurrection?"

Crystal's eyebrows shoot up. "I've heard of it, but it's supposed to be taboo. No one is allowed to take a soul back from the gods. They won't permit it."

"In here is a form of the ritualistic spell that is the one you heard of. It does not take the gods' permission to use."

Crystal is intrigued, looking at the pages. "So, how does it work?"

Olovira reads from the book. "This is a life exchange spell. To give one back life, a life must be taken from another." She looks at Crystal and their eyes meet. "And it must be a willing exchange. The willing soul is replaced by the other keeping the gods…" She taps her clawed fingers on the spell. "Unaware."

"I'll do it." She looks at the book, knowing full well what is being asked of her. "He's the honorable one, always doing everything right. All I am is a spoiled rich girl who had everything handed to her then failed in the end." Looking away from Olovira. "His life is worth more than mine."

Olovira looks at her and turns back to the tome. "I have a special room in my basement for special rituals. Ones that require lots of time to prepare for and should not be interrupted by the elements." She closes the book. "I have much to prepare for. Yes. Bring him tonight, two hours before midnight."

"What should I do?"

The older Half-Dragon looks at her and touches her shoulder. "Go and be happy for the rest of your life, yes."

Crystal walks outside, and the rain is pouring down. Still stricken with grief, the rain is hiding her tears. She needs to prepare a letter for her family telling them this was her idea. She casually walks through the rain, letting the water soak her clothes. *I won't need them after tonight*. She climbs into the Vardo and sits on her bed. Looking down at William, and cries more. Wiping her hands dry, she grabs some parchment and pens a letter. She looks over everything and wants to take one last bath. She looks around and realizes that she left everything behind. Her soaps, her clothes, her towels, everything. She laughs in irony. "Will, you're going to find this funny, but I don't have anything left. Everything I have is gone, just the clothes on my back and whatever food is left in the fridge." She opens it and pulls out an apple, peeling it with a clawed finger. "I'll leave you one in the fridge for later."

She looks down and cries again. "I'm sorry I teased you so much. I just thought that you could never go away. You were my knight, my protector. That no matter what I did, you would always be there, and I could just get away with anything." She smiles. "Watching you get embarrassed around me always made me laugh inside." She drops the apple on the floor. "But like always, my selfishness got the better of me." She sniffles, wipes the tears away, and swallows. "But this time, this time, I'm not teasing. I'm not being selfish." She sniffles again. "In order to bring you back to us, I'm sacrificing myself. I have to take your place in the afterlife to give you back yours." She looks down at his bloody and sliced up body. "I won't embarrass you anymore." She stands up. "Well, I'm going to go and get cleaned up and enjoy the rest of my life, and the best way I know how is with a long bath."

She exits the Vardo; the rain is lessening, but she cares little. She calmly walks to the bathhouse. It's devoid of anyone else. *Good. I want to be left in peace.* She drops her wet and torn dress to the floor.

The rest of the group waits out the rain in the dining hall, watching it fall outside. The crack of thunder overhead punctuates the mood. Penelope and Tia knew William for only a few days, but he was honorable. "Crystal is taking it the hardest."

Penelope drinks some tea, nodding in agreement. "I think she genuinely liked him more than she let on." She looks down into her glass. "And I think, in part, he really liked her too. Despite what they both said, they spent a lot of time together and finding reasons to be around the other. He was a man of honor, but I think if it was anyone else, they wouldn't have put up with her shenanigans, in charge or not."

Tia looks down into her own glass, looking at the water inside. "I'm going to have to write a letter to William's parents explaining everything. I don't think I have it in me to speak to them face to face about what happened." She looks out over the downpour that picks up again, making the trees vanish in front of them in the fog. "But after the rain calms down."

The rain lets up a little and they see Crystal walk by. She's heading in the bathhouse's direction, but she's not carrying anything with her. Tom blinks a few times, wondering what he is seeing. "Is she going to take a bath?"

Penelope sighs. "That sounds like her. Water always makes her happy."

"But she's not carrying anything with her."

"We technically left everything behind and lack of clothing hasn't stopped her in the past." She turns to Tia. "But let's go, Tia."

"Go where?"

"To be with Ms. Hellstromm." Penelope swallows the last of her tea. "She's hurting right now, and we should be there for her."

Crystal lays in the water sunk to her neck. The water feels different on her scales but still enjoyable. Flowing between them, it almost tickles her, making it pleasant. She closes her eyes and just enjoys the water. Several minutes go by and she can hear Tia coming. She doesn't have a light step for an Elf. Penelope and Tia walk in and see the tattered and blood-stained dress laying on the floor. Crystal lays in the water with a smile on her face.

Tia walks up next to where Crystal is. "I'm glad you're feeling better."

"I was wondering when you two would show up. Please join me?"

Tia shakes her head. "Our bathing suits were lost, remember? I can't get in there."

Crystal opens one icy blue eye, then reaches out, grabbing Tia's leg. She says a quick incantation and Tia's robe and undergarments drop to the floor, exposing her. "Better jump in before someone sees you, priestess." Tia's mouth is agape, but they can all hear footsteps coming. She hurriedly makes her way into the water and sinks as far as she can go. "That's better."

Tia turns red, placing her arms over her chest. "How did you do that?"

"It's just a simple cantrip I know. Usually, it doesn't work on others, but I guess I caught you off-guard." A grin creeps across her face and she closes her eyes again. "Or you secretly wanted it to happen." Tia shakes her head and sinks further. "You getting in Shadow?"

She sighs. "If it makes you feel better. Just don't hit me with that spell of yours." She strips down herself and gets in. *Crystal looks happier. Glad she's feeling better.* The trio sits in there and talks all day and well into the night. Getting things off their mind.

"What are we doing tomorrow?"

"Back to Rose Harbor." Crystal cranes her head back, looking up at the rain coming down. "We have a duty to fulfill to the Emperor." She smiles to herself. *Not long left. I guess the rest of my life was pretty good.* She gets out of the water and picks up her tattered dress, and puts it back on. This catches the other two ladies off guard.

Tia takes note first. "Are you done, Ms. Hellstromm?"

Crystal's voice is flat and emotionless. "Yeah." This gets Tia and Penelope to exchange glances, knowing something isn't right. "You two go wait in the dining hall with dinner, ok?"

Penelope stands up. "Where are you going to be, mistress?"

"I'll be along for a midnight snack. I'm sure you can make something excellent with the foodstuffs here."

Penelope shakes her head, knowing her too long to be fooled so easily. "You're up to something."

Crystal sighs, realizing Penelope isn't wrong. "Just do as I ask, Penelope."

Her long ears twitch and her blood feels cold. *Crystal has rarely called me by my real name.* She points a finger at Crystal. "I want to know what you're up to."

Crystal reaches down and gathers Tia's and Penelope's clothing as they both look on in horror. "Should have just done as I asked." She exits taking their clothes with her.

Tia and Penelope exchange glances, both knowing neither has Crystal's lack of modesty to just walk out naked. They are stuck there till someone finds them. "What is going on, Ms. Penelope?" Tia sinks down as far as she can in the water.

Penelope shakes her head, still standing in the waist-deep water. "I don't know, but whatever it is, it's something she doesn't want us

194

involved in." She glances out the door. "And that has me more scared than my modesty."

"In that case, can you bring me some clothes? There is no way I'm going out there like this."

Crystal hurries through the rain back to the Vardo. She opens the door, throws their clothing in, and pulls William out. He doesn't feel as heavy as yesterday, but she has a hard time believing she should have been able to move him. *Must be part of this transformation I'm going through.* She drags his body as quickly as she can to Olovira's and knocks on the door.

She motions for Crystal to enter. "Let's take him downstairs and prepare, yes." Crystal does as she is told and Olovira turns to the door uttering an incantation.

Penelope uses her legendary sneaking skills and slowly makes her way around till she finds clothes to steal that fit. The monastery is busy, so she takes time to move about. "White cotton isn't going to work well in the rain, but it's better than nothing." She also grabs a few towels she can find and heads back. Penelope walks in and hands Tia a towel so she can get up.

"What took you so long?"

Penelope glowers at her. "I'm stark naked, walking around a bunch of monks that would get really offended that a naked Halfling is desecrating their monastery. So I had to be extremely careful."

Tia is doing her best to get dressed, but the monk's top isn't fitting too well. It looks silly with it just draped over her front. "I think I was better off in the water. I look like a streetwalker."

"Then wrap yourself in the towel and let's go. Crystal has a huge head start on us for whatever she's doing." They walk out and head towards the Vardo. "Let's check to see if she ran away first." They hurry through the rain, taking a direct path instead of following the brickwork. Tom sees them from a dojo where he and Tyra are exercising. He taps her on the elbow. "Tyra!" Pointing outside, she follows his finger. "Something looks off with those two?"

Tyra nods. "Those are not her cleric robes."

"We better check this out."

Penelope and Tia make their way to the Vardo and the back door is open. Penelope climbs inside and turns on a lamp over the table. Inside are their clothes and Tia notices William's body is missing.

Penelope spots a folded piece of parchment sitting on the table and opens it. She reads it and her eyes go wide. "This is worse than I expected."

"What is it?" Tia throws her robe on. Penelope hands her the letter and Tia gasps and places her hand over her mouth. "What are we going to do, Ms. Penelope?"

"I don't know."

Tom is outside. "What's the problem?"

Penelope lays it all out that Crystal took William somewhere and she plans on ending her life. Tyra looks around and sees the drag marks in the wet grass. Her nose picks up William and Crystal's scents. "She went that way."

"What's in that direction?" Penelope peers in that direction but she can see nothing in the dark and rain.

Tom answers, coldly. "Olovira's place."

Tia's face turns to shock in realization. "It must be ritual or spell. She's not dying to be with William. She's dying to bring him back with her help."

"We better go. For all we know, she could be dead already." Penelope doesn't wait and runs at a full sprint. Tyra grabs Tia and lifts her off the ground. They run through the rain, taking several minutes to get to Olovira's door. The drag marks lead all the way here and into the door.

They can hear muffled chanting of an incantation coming from within. Penelope pulls out her picks and works on the old lady's door lock. She frowns in frustration. "This lock isn't that complicated. Why am I not getting through?"

"How important is it we get in there?".

"Life and death."

Tyra nods and reaches back and punches with everything she has, but a blue flare comes up and a magical ward appears for a second and goes away. Tyra brings her hand up and yelps. "That was like punching a tree."

Tia looks at her hand. "It's broken." She performs a prayer healing the damage.

Penelope looks around and sees a small window, but it's up high. "Tyra up there! Get me to that window." Tyra lifts her up, and it's not protected like the door is. She easily gets in and can hear the incantation much better. *Sounds like it's about to get serious.* She walks up to the door and unlocks it, but it still won't open. She shouts through the door. "It's magically barred shut. I can't open it from in here." Turning to the sound of the chanting. "I'm going to stop this."

She looks around, looking for the source of the sound, but is careful not to touch anything because she doesn't know how things will react if messed with. Finding another door, she opens it leading downward into the basement. She sneaks around and reaches the bottom where William and Crystal both lay in some magic circle alongside each other. Olovira is on her knees above them and centered, holding a dagger made of bone. She raises the dagger as the incantation reaches a crescendo. Penelope moves forward to stop the ritual, but bounces off another barrier placed at the basement's entrance. She hammers the invisible wall, screaming as Olovira brings the dagger down, causing Penelope to turn away. The chanting is replaced by the sound of the dagger piercing flesh.

CHAPTER 22
(Home is where the Heart is)

Penelope collapses in frustration and tears, unable to lookup. She couldn't stop Crystal from her sacrifice. She falls to her knees and then hears a thud of a body hitting the ground. The barrier she was leaning against suddenly disappears and she falls backwards to the floor. She can hear the door upstairs open as heavy hooved feet step onto the floor above. She picks herself up and looks over to see Olovira laying on the floor with blood pooling on the floor. It follows the magic circle, and it glows black. The blood races around and when the circle is complete, there is a flash, and it vanishes.

William takes a deep breath and sits upright, feeling his chest and looking around in a panic, not knowing where he is. Crystal opens her eyes, hearing him, not understanding how she is still alive herself. She sits upright and looks down to see Olovira dead on the floor with the sacrificial dagger sticking from her chest, her hand still wrapped around it. Crystal hugs William with a tackle that knocks him back to the floor as Tia and Tom make their way down. Crystal is crying harder than ever before, but Penelope rushes to the ritual site.

Tom looks at Crystal holding William, who is alive and well, but the old woman lying on the floor. "What just happened here?"

Crystal looks at Olovira, still crying. "Thank you."

"I believe that's my question?"

Crystal can see the smile on Olovira's face fade as her soul leaves for the afterlife. "You planned this from the start, didn't you, you old crone?"

Everyone but Crystal looks confused. William looks around, then back down at Crystal, who is still on top of him. "Are you going to explain anything, or am I going to guess?" She glances up at him. "Not that I'm complaining."

She moves quickly, kissing him fully on the lips for several moments. Everyone there gazes at her actions but stays quiet. "Don't you ever leave me again, or next time it's going to be me coming into the afterlife after you." She uprights herself. "And I will burn the heavens and freeze the hells till I get you back."

Tia looks shocked and trades glances with Penelope. "I can't tell if she's kidding or not."

Penelope also crying. "No, she's completely serious. I feel sorry for any god who messes with her." Crystal gets up and offers her clawed hand to William. He takes it and she pulls him to his feet.

"So, are you going to explain what happened?"

Crystal gives everyone the run-down of the ritual, and what Olovira said about the spell. "When she told me it had to be a life for a life to keep the gods happy, or fooled at least. I volunteered immediately."

Tia crosses an arm across her front and looks away, grabbing her other elbow. "So that's why you wrote that letter and took our clothes from the pool?"

Crystal looks away at the floor. "I knew if you found out, you two would try to stop me, but I had decided and was at peace with my decision."

"You were really going to sacrifice yourself for me?"

"You did for me. I only felt it was right to return the favor."

William looks shocked by that. "So how long was I gone? You have larger horns and almost yanked my arm off, pulling me up."

"According to Olovira, I won't change much more, but the Dragon blood in my system is magically enhancing my physical body. I won't look like Tyra with muscle mass, but I'll be physically stronger. The scales will harden a little more as well and the horns aren't fully grown in." She shrugs. "Guess I will end up looking like her." She looks up at him and then away, but William lifts her chin up with his hand. "I think they make you more beautiful." He leans down and kisses her back, wrapping his arms around her.

"Let's go, Tyra. We need to inform Master Monzulo about what happened here." Tom sighs, clearing the area. They can faintly hear him yell, "get a room," from upstairs.

They all walk upstairs, and Crystal has another look around. On the lectern, where Olovira had the book of necromancy, is a note. Crystal opens it and reads.

Young Crystal, you reminded me of that age. I see how you volunteered to be the sacrifice to give young William another chance. You did what I could not. I go now to be with my husband. Been too long and will be nice to see him again. I hereby leave you my lab and its contents and secrets. Think of it as an early wedding present. Use them wisely as I did and heed their warnings. Tell Master Monzulo thanks for giving me a place to stay.
Ondra Olovira

She shows it to William, and he reads it. He smiles at her. "Does she know something I don't?"

Crystal shrugs with a spring in her step he hasn't seen before. "I don't know about that. I can't predict the future." She scans the place, then looks down at her tattered clothing. "But what I do know is I lost all my clothes in that garrison fire and when we get back, we are going shopping for new ones." She turns off the lamps and locks the doors while William stands on the front porch. She looks at him up and down, standing in his own tattered clothing. "And we need to find you some new clothes too and a bath"

Penelope and Tia follow Tom and Tyra back in the rain with flashes of light above their heads. Crystal, arm in arm with William, follows them with a smile on her face, not minding the rain. They get to the cabins that the monks let them have last time they were here. Sioki brings them fresh clothes and linens for the night. The three women bunk up together and William takes the other cabin.

The morning dawn comes and most of the clouds are gone. Morning sounds of the birds are in the air. Tia wakes up first as usual to start her morning prayers and finds Crystal is nowhere to be seen. She wakes Penelope up immediately in a panic showing her the missing bunk. She gets up and gazes at the empty bunk. "Teenagers."

Tia shakes her head. "I don't understand."

Penelope motions for her to follow, and they walk over to Williams's cabin. Sure enough, she's in there. She's in a separate bunk, but she's in there. "At least I don't have to kill him... Again."

"Now what?"

She thumbs at the cabin. "Now you go say your prayers and add a few for them. I'm going to get breakfast going."

Tia nods, turns and shrugs, then heads out.

Within thirty minutes, William awakens, sits up, and stretches. He looks up from the floor and across the room to find Crystal laying in the bunk still asleep. William turns red but sees she's wearing the monk's robes from last night. *At least she's dressed, and her horns are larger and even more pronounced. She can hurt someone with those if not careful... Like me.* He gauges them better, getting an idea about them. *They must be at least three inches thick at the base, and the way they sweep around her crown and taper up and to a point above her eyes means she could use them as weapons.* He notices the scales on her arms thickened more. *I don't know what Olovira did. I just hope it doesn't hurt her.* A knock at the door wakes her from her sleep.

William answers it as Crystal stretches in the background. Sioki looks tired with bags under her eyes, as if she was up all night. She looks past William at Crystal and raises a platinum blond eyebrow. William shakes his head. "Nothing happened, I swear. I have no idea how she got in here."

Even though he is being honest, she doesn't look convinced. "Breakfast is served, and after you have eaten, Master Monzulo would like to speak to you both." She spins and walks away onward to her next task.

Crystal shrugs while stretching and bending backward and William can hear the Dragon scales on her spine pop. She stands up and walks over to him, placing a hand on his bare chest. "We should get to breakfast" Her eyes meet his. "And we need to talk about what's going to happen when we get to Rose Harbor."

They step out and walk to the dining hall. Hundreds of monks are standing in the muddy grass doing their morning routines. "What do you mean, Ms. Hellstromm?"

She looks up at him with those icy blue eyes, but they aren't as cold as he remembers. "Crystal." She looks back at the path. "I think we evolved past formalities when it's just us, don't you think, Will?"

It brings a smile to his face when she calls him that. "What do you mean when we get back to Rose Harbor?"

They walk into the dining hall and Tia is already at a table with Penelope, Tom, and Tyra. They sit down opposite each other and Penelope gets them some food. "We failed at Black Rock, and the Emperor doesn't tolerate failure. Once we report that failure, our lives are forfeit." She takes a bite of food and it's heavenly to her.

201

William bites into his own food, savoring it. "He might not be tolerant of failure, but he's also wise. Once he hears what happened, there is no way we would be executed."

"Will you two stop talking about death all the time?" Tia interrupts, dropping her spoon. "I've had enough heartache in the past two days to last the rest of my days."

Crystal doesn't look up from her plate and points to Penelope and Tia. "You two are clear. You're just underlings as far as the Emperor is concerned."

William chuckles. "You just brought me back so this time so I will die at your side?"

Crystal smiles up at him. "Would you want it any other way?"

Penelope interrupts with a slap to the table. "No one is going to die. You didn't fail on purpose, and we still got the documentation. Your handbag is in the wagon where you dropped it in our escape. We technically fulfilled the mission, didn't we?"

Crystal shrugs, going back to her breakfast. "It's all on the Emperor and how he feels."

They finish and head back to the Vardo. Crystal tells them to get ready to go when they get back. Master Monzulo wants a word with them. They climb the one thousand steps to the front doors of the main building. Walking in, William takes off his shoes, getting Crystal to laugh to herself being her shoes were burned up with the rest of her clothes.

Being escorted to Master Monzulo, they find him as they have before, meditating on the floor, facing away from the door. "I sense two souls that are more in harmony now than they were days ago." He stands up, opens his eyes, and faces them. "You two have come a long way in a short time. And you have a long time to improve." He places a hand on each of their shoulders. "Do not go where others have already made a path, go where no one else has gone, and leave your own trail for others to follow." He lowers his hands to his sides. "I have ordered Tom and Tyra to go with you. They are getting extra horses and a wagon of supplies for your trip to Rose Harbor." He raises a hand to stop any objections. "And if you ever need some wisdom, I'm here, but don't just take wisdom from me. Take it from many sources to balance yourselves out and find what works best for your future."

Crystal and William bow to the wise old man. "I'm sorry about Olovira."

Master Monzulo grins. "Don't be. She chose her own path, and where it was to end. We should all be so lucky to make such a positive difference in others' lives." He waves his hand towards the door. "You have a long way to go, so I won't keep you, but I am glad you both began again."

They make their way down to the steps, and everyone is waiting. Tom and Tyra are on the second wagon, a horse is ready for William, and the Vardo is ready to go with a replacement horse. They start their way out and William rubs his face. "I'm going to need a shave when I get back to Rose Harbor." Crystal leans out her window. "I like it, Will. Makes you look older, more gallant."

He muses, rubbing his stubble. "I'll keep that in mind since we have a long way home." The days go by. They pass Mossy Fields, but they don't stop giving the last incident. The wagons of the caravan they met sit outside the general store. They continue along, not stopping but to sleep, and soon the dome and gates of Rose Harbor are in the distance. It's late afternoon when they finally make it to the check-in gate. Guards check them and a cursory glance over the wagons. Penelope smirks. *After all these years. They still don't do a good job.*

They go straight to the palace knowing that they report to the Emperor. The Vardo comes to a halt out front and William helps Crystal out. She is still wearing that torn and tattered black dress with gold and silver patterns. She had put perfume on it and had Penelope wash it as best she could.

William looks at her and he sighs. "It's the only dress I have left." She faces the palace and foreboding hits her gut. "And I refuse to wear the peasants' clothes the monks gave us, as much as I appreciated it."

"That's not what I was sighing about."

"Then what is it then?"

"That no matter what happens, this dress won't be around much longer. It has character now."

She peers into his eyes. "I'm nervous too." She looks down. "And if this is our last moments, I'm glad I'm spending them standing with you. The last two weeks together have felt like a lifetime." He lifts her chin, getting her to look up at him once more. She takes his hands and steps close to him.

"For once, I can agree with you." He leans in and kisses her passionately. "Let's go, destiny awaits."

They walk with guards escorting them up into the palace. They cross the map of all precious metals and stones and into the great hall of the Emperor himself. The guards stop on either side of them as they both kneel in front of the Emperor. His voice booms throughout the room. Echoing as it should for a room this size. "Ah, Ms. Hellstromm and Sir Blakely, you both have finally returned to me."

They speak in unison. "Yes, Your Highness."

"You kneel here before me without your armor, Sir Blakely." His eyes fall upon Crystal. "And you, Ms. Hellstromm, come before me in a torn dress and your form has changed." They both hang their heads in disgrace. "The troops I sent with you did not return?" He stands and stalks around them, his footfalls echo. "So, what news from Black Rock, Ms. Hellstromm? Why are the shipments short?"

She can feel his presence without even looking at him. She knows he doesn't like bad news, but he hates being lied to more. "Black Rock has revolted against the Empire. They are selling their ores to the city of New Haven on the eastern shore instead of you." She swallows, finding her words carefully. "We were able to get documentation from their records as proof that they were dealing under the table to another City State." She swallows again, feeling her throat dry. She continues, not daring to look up from the black marble floor. "They revolted because they felt they weren't getting paid fairly and New Haven offered them better terms."

"And you Sir Blakely?" The Emperor's presence presses down on him. "How is it you returned without the men you swore to lead?"

William speaks clearly, without fear in his voice. "In Black Rock, members of a faction calling themselves 'The Black Rose' assaulted the garrison in mass and by surprise. We fought to the last man defending it, including me. Ms. Hellstromm risked her life pulling my body from the battle before escaping."

"Pulled your body? As in, you died defending it?" The disbelief in his voice is palpable in the air. "So how is it you kneel before me now?"

Crystal responds, causing him to turn his head toward her. "That was my doing, Your Highness. In my grief of failing, you and losing him, I consorted with an old Half-Dragon woman who had a ritual that could return those to life, but only if the sacrifice was willing." She clenches her jaw and tears well up. "I was going to give my life to bring him back. William is honorable and I felt-"

The Emperor cuts her off mid-thought. "Spells like those are forbidden, Ms. Hellstromm!" He steps over to her. That presence of his presses down on her like a heavy burden. She places both hands on the floor, doing all she can to hold herself up. "So why are you kneeling here with him if you were to be the sacrifice?"

She is trying her best to check her emotions, but the tears won't stop. "Olovira." She sniffles as the tears flow unchecked. "The old lady sacrificed herself instead to give us both hope of a future." Her tears hit the black marble floor, but she doesn't dare raise a hand to wipe them away.

Marcus reaches down and takes her handbag, digging the parchments out with all the evidence, and looks through them. For long moments, there is utter silence in the hall but for her sobbing. Scaring her out of her introspection, the Emperor's voice thunders across the throne room again. "And I take it this same lady helped you with your transformation?"

"Yes, Your Highness."

"Tell me, Ms. Hellstromm." The emperor speaks, but the oppressive force is gone. She can breathe again and the weight has been lifted. "Do you believe you and Sir Blakely have failed me?"

Crystal checked her emotions as best she could and nodded her head. "Yes, Your Highness, we failed you. We lost everything on our trip."

Marcus passes in front of William. "And you, Sir Blakely, share this assessment with Ms. Hellstromm?"

William speaks with the courage he can muster. "Yes, Your Highness."

Marcus speaks to them more softly than before. "In the end, it is I who decides to pass or fail when it comes to your mission, and one day, you will gain the wisdom to see the difference. You brought me the proof I asked for." He holds the paperwork up. "And I can assign a new garrison, and now that I know what they are upset about, we can negotiate with the workers and bring them back to our side." He continues stepping away. "This was all crucial information that I was needing. You did not fail me."

They reply in chorus. "Thank you, Your Highness."

"On the other hand, there is the matter of the forbidden spell usage." The Emperor continues. Dread fills them both, knowing they might have dodged one bullet to just catch another. "Do you know why such magic is forbidden, Ms. Hellstromm?"

Her face is still pointed at the marble floor. "It's not right to take souls from the gods once they depart."

"That is correct, Ms. Hellstromm." The Emperor steps away with his back turned. "And do you know the punishment for such a crime?"

"I do, Your Highness." The pain in her voice from her heart causes her voice to crack.

"And why did you do it knowing what the punishment is?" He turns back to look at her. The oppressive weight returns. "And please be truthful."

Tears flow from her eyes and they both turn their heads slightly to see each other. She sobs. "Because I couldn't live without him." She turns back to the floor. "He's honorable, strong, well mannered, and is caring." The tears flow unchecked, now knowing these are her last words. "I couldn't go on without him."

Marcus stands there for a long moment and then crouches down between them. Once again, the force vanishes. In a low, soft tone, he speaks to them. "Passion, sacrifice, and honor. These things separate the common folk from the nobility." Standing up, he continues. "You were willing to sacrifice yourself for another. You have passion for each other and what you represent, and there is no greater honor than admitting your mistakes, especially when facing certain death." He takes a few steps away and sits back upon his thrown.

"Rise you two." They both stand, knees hurting from the black marble floor, but neither shows any sign of their pain. "I must confer with my advisers about Black Rock and I want a full report on who these 'Black Rose' people are." He looks back at them after a pause. "On Monday." He stands. "Spend time with your families and friends. But I expect both of you here Monday morning by nine a.m. with your reports ready." He walks out to his side chamber with his guards falling in step. "And Sir William." Marcus turns his head, addressing the young knight.

William snaps to attention. "Yes, Your Highness."

"Get Ms. Hellstromm some new clothing. She shouldn't be dressed in such rags." Marcus waves as he walks out, dismissing them. They turn and walk out with a guard escorting them along the way.

Marcus watches them go and Skylar turns to him. "Uncharacteristically nice of you to let someone break one of our most sacred laws and live, my love. Are you getting soft after two hundred years?"

"Who am I to stand in the way of love?" He turns to her. "Especially since that's what the family is lacking." He turns his attention to the fading couple. "They have proven themselves that they are who we need." He turns back to his wife and leans over, kissing her. "Now to see if she's worthy of such responsibility."

Coming outside, the sun setting casts long shadows from the towering buildings. The city's tone changes from that of working to that of entertainment and joyfulness as another day is coming to a close. Penelope and Tia are visibly relieved to see they survived. William helps Crystal into her Vardo, but before he can close the door, she reaches out and pulls him into her, giving him one last kiss before they depart. He closes the door and mounts his horse, taking point.

"I'll escort you home."

Tom speaks up from the back wagon. "And where do you recommend we stay? Know any good inns around here?"

Penelope speaks up. "I know the one I can recommend."

William gives his attention to the monks. "I have a place for you and Tyra at my manor."

Tom ribs Tyra with his elbow. "He's got a manor. This should be interesting." They ride through town, making their way to the Third House district. Steam cars are more prevalent here than in any other district, but horses are still present. They ride to the Hellstromm manor, and the guards recognize Penelope and the Hellstromm crest on the Vardo and immediately open the gates.

Entering the grounds, Penelope looks around at the familiar sight. *It's nice to be home.* News of Crystal and Penelope's return spreads through the house like wildfire. Jack and Jasmine come out of the house as William is helping Crystal out of the back of the Vardo. Jasmine, seeing her daughter so disheveled in a torn-up dress, comes running as fast as she can muster. She collides with Crystal and gives her an enthusiastic embrace. She holds her daughter there for long moments. Jack walks up to the towering knight and looks up at him. William cannot believe how short her father is. *He isn't much taller than Crystal, but he radiates strength and power like the emperor.*

Jack holds out his hand and takes Williams' and shakes it vigorously. "Thank you for protecting my daughter. Going by how everyone looks, I say it wasn't a simple task."

William places his free hand behind his head and looks away from the older man. "It's a long story and will have to wait for another day. I just wanted to finish my duty before heading home myself."

Jack grips his hand more tightly. "Tell me tomorrow then."

"Tomorrow sir?"

"Yes, I want you here, along with the rest of you, for dinner. I want to hear all about what happened." Jack lets go of the man's hand. "It's been a long time since I did any adventuring. I would like to hear yours."

William looks uncomfortable but agrees. "What time should I be here, sir?"

"The feast will be at six, but be here early, and extend the invite to your parents. I would like to meet those who raised you." Jack asks politely and in a friendly manner, but William knows there is more to it than that.

Holding her daughter at arm's length, Jasmine looks Crystal over. William notes they look a lot, but Jasmine is a full half foot taller than Crystal and Jack. She reaches up, touching Crystal's horns. "You've changed so much. What happened?"

"Remember that ritual we were supposed to do when I got home?" Crystal explains as the two walk out of hearing distance.

Tia gets down from the Vardo and Tom calls out to her, watching her head for the gate. "Hey, where are you running off to?"

"I need to report to my church."

"Ride with us. We can take you there."

She shakes her head, refusing. "It's alright. I'm used to walking in the city. It will be nice to take it all in again. Thank you for the offer, though." She then strolls out into the street with a smile.

Jack orders Penelope to park the Vardo and he will have repairs made to it and restocked if Crystal takes it out again. She nods and sets the horses in motion. William mounts up and Jack walks up to the two mysterious monks. "That invite goes for you two as well for dinner tomorrow. I want to hear everything that happened." He looks at each. "And in return, I'll tell you all some of the crazy stuff I pulled when I was your age." He laughs hard and waves them on. William shows them the way out and onward to his own home in the Seventh district.

CHAPTER 23
(Day out on the town)

Evening sets as William takes Tom and Tyra to his home. The monks take in the sights as shops and all the people coming and going. An assemblage of smells fills the air as the dinner service of hundreds of different restaurants proceeds. Tyra looks uncomfortable and finally bursts. "It's been twelve hours since we ate, and this city is making it torture. Can we stop and eat something?"

William laughs. "We will eat when we get to my home, I promise, and you can have whatever you wish."

Tyra's stomach growls loud enough for those around them to even hear. Tom looks at her, then at William. "Sir, I hope we get there soon. I'm starting to wonder if she's looking at us as snacks."

Tyra punches him lightly on the arm, but it still causes a lot of pain, causing him to winch from the impact. Tyra continues to grumble, and Tom finally breaks the awkwardness. "Remember what Master Monzulo says about this?" Tyra shakes her head. "Yeah, me neither."

William shakes his head with a grin. "We should be at my humble home in a few minutes, don't eat anyone."

The sun hits the ocean to the west, casting an array of colors from red to orange to yellow and fades into purples with the scattered clouds being wisps of flames racing across the sky. They pull into the Seventh House's manor. Guards take the horses and wagon. "Not as big as Crystal's place." Tom scans the area and Tyra just shakes her head in response.

Williams's mother, Muriel, wearing a white dress of the finest silk, sees them walk in and she barrels right into him, wrapping her arms tightly around his body. "You're home, Will."

He smiles down at the old woman with her head in his chest and embraces her for the moment. He pointed to his two guests. "Yes, I'm home, and we are hungry."

"Who are these people, Will? They don't look like members of the Royal Guard."

Stepping back, he keeps her in his arms. "They aren't, mother. These are my guests for now till I can find them a place to settle." He starts the introductions, motioning to the Asian man first. "This is Tom." Tom bows in respect and William indicates next to the eight-and-a-half-foot-tall Minotaur. "And this mountain of muscle is Tyra." She bows in respect. "They are both from a monastery north of here. They helped us finish our mission and fought at my side. I owe them a lot."

She holds her hand out and shakes their hand, not understanding why they are bowing. "Welcome to our home. Sally will make sure you're taken care of and have accommodations made."

"So how long till dinner, Mother?"

She turns back to him. "Dinner was an hour ago, but I'll have the chef make you whatever you three want. Go ahead and wait in the dining hall."

"Oh, and mother. One other thing." She looks back with a look of concern. "You might want to clear our schedule tomorrow from around five to nine tomorrow night."

"Why is that, dear?" She cocks her head a little when he doesn't answer right away. "What did you do?"

William looks down for a moment, then back to her. *After all, I've been through, she still scares me.* "We have been formally invited to the Third House for dinner and entertainment."

"The... Hellstromm's?"

"Let's not disappoint them, please?" She looks at him and see's he's slightly flushed and nods her head in agreement, heading to the kitchen lost in thought.

Will shows them where everything is and they run into his father. William explains to him what happened as they are sitting at the dining table with Tom and Tyra throwing in parts of their own story into the mix. The night sets in as the artificial flames of the lamps are the only source of light.

"So, I hope you're not busy tomorrow. I need to get new armor made myself. Tomorrow is going to be a long day." William stretches, feeling his body ache.

"All in good time, son. You three should get some rest." They all agree and settle for the night. Tom and Tyra are taken by Sally, their Elven estate steward, to their rooms. She summons the tailor to get their measurements so she can get their formal wear ordered for tomorrow night. They don't enjoy being all fancy, but understood that it was a formal dinner.

The next morning Will eats breakfast, and then he and the two monks join Gerald in the back courtyard. They appreciate he has all this equipment for training William his whole life. The sun is well above the mountains to the east when he receives a note from Sally closed with the Third House's seal. He breaks the seal, knowing it can only be from one person.

Come to the front gate.
Crystal

Front gate? Did she leave something there for me? He clears his front door and pauses. The armored steam car she's always carried in is sitting there. He walks up to it and she opens the door. He finds this as odd as usually, the driver would do that, so she must have told him to wait. She holds her hand out and William takes it to steady her. She steps out in a gold silk dragon scale pattern dress that is form-fitting, barely covering her bosom but allowing her arms and upper body to be exposed. Her jet-black hair is braided and is wrapped once over her horns on either side, framing her face. She looks up at him with those ice blue Dragon eyes and his heart rate increases.

She steps into him, placing a clawed finger on his chest and craning her head back to look up at him. "I believe Emperor Marcus gave you an order."

She knows how to present herself. She's gorgeous and frightening all simultaneously. "What order was that, exactly?"

"He ordered you to help me get some new clothes…" she leans into him and her voice is almost a purr. "Remember."

"I don't think that's-"

She cuts him off and turns back to the car. "Orders are orders, Will. Now get in." She lowers herself into the car with his help and she glances up at him. Her voice is both soft and ominous. "Or I'll have to use force."

William turns back to the house to say something, but a clawed hand grabs him by the belt and drags him down into the car. He is surprised by the strength she has, but she looks so frail. *She hasn't changed any further on the outside, so the awakening must be over.* He sits in the car and she barks at the driver to take them to Asorin's in the Second house district. The car takes off and William isn't prepared for it and almost falls onto Crystal.

She looks at him askance through the gaps in the braids hanging from her horns. He takes notice but says nothing. "I'm disappointed in you, Will." She looks back to the road.

"About what?"

That blue eye of hers turns and looks at him again. "It's been fifteen seconds and you haven't kissed me yet."

He smiles and leans in, pausing just inches away. "What about the driver knowing?"

She cradles his jaw with her clawed hand. Her voice was barely above a whisper, bringing him in. "If he says a word, they will never find his body." Their lips meet, and he revels in the feeling of their softness.

I'm not sure if she was serious about that or not, and that's frightening.

After a short passionate embrace, they separate to breathe, and William straightens up. "What if someone is looking for me? They might get upset I'm missing."

"Your 'Housekeeper' knows I took you. I told her that we had important business to take care of before dinner tonight."

"Is shopping for new clothes important?"

"It is to me, and that's good enough. Besides, I want you to look your best at dinner tonight. I would hate for my father to get a poor impression of you." She glances over at him and all emotion drains from her speech. "My last boyfriend barely survived."

Again, he can't tell if she's being serious or not. He's seen her brutality and her compassion both firsthand, so she's full of surprises. They make their way through the streets and *The Church of Daniel* can be seen coming up. Crystal yells at the driver. "Stop here first. I want to see Andrew and Tia." He nods, but doesn't speak. They pull in, and William gets out and extends his hand, helping her to get out. They contrast differently; she looks like royalty and he's dressed simply.

She hooks her arm into his and they walk into the church together. They are greeted at the door by Lyndis. "Ms. Hellstromm, Sir Blakely, how can the church of Daniel be of service?"

"I'm looking for Andrew and Tia." Crystal doesn't mince words and speaks with the confidence and authority he is used to. "Are they available?"

"They are helping with chores around here, but I think I can spare them."

Earlier that day, dawn comes, and Lyndis awakens her clergy to get things going for the day. The sun's rays strike the top of the tower and the mirrors filters sunlight down into the main chamber. Tia starts with breakfast, sitting next to Andrew. They are eating the same as everyone else at the table. A dozen clerics and priestesses all gathered, talking to each other.

"So, you and my sister had trouble on the road?"

Tia nods, chewing her oatmeal, but sounds excited to talk about it. "It was quite the ordeal. First, we were attacked by a giant plant, then we came to this little town and these guys tried to kidnap her, and then these giant chickens tried to eat us…"

Andrew laughs. "So, it wasn't all bad?"

Tia grows somber, putting her spoon down. "No, it was bad. A lot of people died and I couldn't save them." She looks at him. "And your sister has a mean streak in her."

Andrew chuckles as if amused. "She's always had a mean streak." He takes another bite. "But she's also very loving. Once she latches onto someone and considers them an ally, she will protect them."

Tia's eyes widen and she tilts her head with a nod. "I've seen it firsthand. She teased poor Sir Blakey the whole time, knowing he had to take her every order. I could see he didn't like it much, but he stood by his honor and did it, anyway." She picks her spoon back up and digs in again. "But when it really came down to it, she was ready to die to protect him, even breaking one of the most serious laws in our kingdom for it." She looks out over the room, staring at nothing. "I wonder why the Emperor didn't execute them both for it?"

Andrew shrugs. "The only people that know are the Emperor, Crystal, and William." He takes another bite.

Tia breaks from her introspective. "Daniel protected them. I was praying to him the whole time they were in there. Maybe he protected them from punishment?"

Andrew smiles, nudging her. "Yes, he did. Thanks for saving my sister."

They get to their chores. Andrew and Tia talk and laugh and joke about Andrew's old life and Tia speaks in-depth about her two-week adventure. Mid-day is approaching when Lyndis walks in on them, playing more than working. She clears her throat, bringing them both around, and flushed with embarrassment. "Disappointing. You're clerics of the church, but acting like children."

Andrew answers. "Sorry priestess, just trying to make the work less tedious."

Lyndis raises an eyebrow as Tia bows her head down. "It won't happen again."

"You two both have guests."

Andrew and Tia exchange glances and reply in unison. "Guests?".

The three walk into the main chamber and Crystal and William are standing there. Andrew runs up to his sister and gives her a big hug, lifting her off the ground, and when her feet hit the ground, Tia does it too. Crystal lets out a pitiful gurgled squeak of, "help me."

Tia finally let's go and Crystal straightens out her dress. "Thanks. Would be a shame to die of asphyxiation after surviving all the other things that were thrown at us." William fares better since he's so much bigger than Tia is.

"What brings you to the church, you two?" Andrew points to Crystal's head. "And what's with the braided horns?"

She glances upwards at them, barely within her peripheral vision she dismisses it with a wave. "I'll tell you later about those. I was going to send a messenger, but I decided to stop by since we were on our way out to go shopping. Dad is having a feast tonight to celebrate our first adventure and returning alive. He wants you and Tia to come as well."

Andrew looks at them. "I don't know if we can make it. We have duties around here."

Lyndis speaks up from behind them. "What time?"

"He wants the guests to assemble by five this evening. That gives you five and a half hours to get your chores done."

Lyndis gives them both a stern look. "I'll make sure they make it, Ms. Hellstromm."

They lower their heads but Crystal, being so short, can see them both smirking. "Thank you, Lyndis. I will hold you to that." Crystal turns about to face the doors. "Let's go, Will. We have much to do still before the party." She hooks her arm back into his and walks out.

Andrew watches them walk out and then turns to Tia. "You left part of your story out."

Getting back into the car, she tells the driver to proceed to Asorin's. The car makes its way through town and pulls up in front of the large shop. They go inside, and William takes it all in and feels so out of place. Suits and dresses of impeccable quality and as varied as the colors of the rainbow are shown around the store. William is in awe. "Is this where you get all your dresses from?"

Crystal shakes her head as she pulls a suit out to look at it. "No, this is a lower quality place than I'm used to."

William's mouth ceases to function trying to find words and he can't believe what he just heard. "So, if this isn't where you buy your dresses from, then why are we here?" She drags him around the store, eventually getting to the back.

"Because this is where daddy gets his suits from, and they look good on him. So, they should look good on you." She holds one up to him, then shakes her head and puts it back. "Besides, daddy doesn't like expensive suits. With his work, they get dirty and hard to clean."

They get to the service desk and a Halfling male is sitting there wearing glasses. He looks up and sees the couple and smiles. "Welcome to my humble boutique. How may I serve you two?"

"He needs a formal suit for a dinner party at my home that will impress my father."

Asorin stands up and walks over to the much larger man, barely standing above his waist. "If you will follow me, sir, I must take your measurements and see what I can do." He leads William over to an odd-looking contraption with different levels built into it. Climbing up and down, he clambers over the large man getting the information

216

he needs. Clambering down, he looks to Crystal. "So, have a material picked out, or maybe a pattern in mind? And how soon do you need it?"

"I need him in it by five tonight."

"I can't throw anything good together in such a short time, but I can alter something I already made to fit if it's close enough." They take this time to look around for several minutes, looking at patterns and styles.

William looks at one that is black with some gold-threaded runic patterns sown in. "This looks nice." She looks at it, then at him, then shakes her head with a smirk. He shrugs and puts it back. She finds something in a nice red and royal purple and holds it up for him to see. "Looks too much like my guard uniform, don't you think?"

She looks at it again and then puts it back. "Now that you mention it." They continue to look around. He finds a nice navy-blue tunic and pants combination with gold patterns running down from both shoulders along the front and back. He holds it up and shows her.

She walks over and takes hold of it, feeling the material. "That I think would look good on you. Let's take it to Asorin and see if he can work with it."

They present it to him, and he measures it. "It's small for the large lad, but I can make the alterations. I'll have to contact my supplier for this material, and I could have it ready in three hours." He looks it over and then at her. "You will have to pay in advance. Once I make alterations to this, I won't be able to sell it to someone else."

"And how much is that, Asorin?"

"Thirty-five." He looks up at William, then at her. "Your friend here has an eye for the expensive."

"Thirty-five gold is a bit much, honey."

"Gold?" He turns to William, confused. "Platinum, you mean?"

William's eyes widen. "Platinum? As in three hundred and fifty gold?"

The Halfling nods. "This stuff is imported from Titania. A very special type of woven cotton that only grows on that continent. Not to mention the dye to make this color."

Crystal smiles and pulls out some banknotes from her handbag. "Here you go. Get to work on it right away and have it delivered to the Seventh House estate no later than four."

"Yes, Ms. Hellstromm." He takes the money and places it in a magical safe.

She hooks William's arm and walks outside to the waiting car. "Time to find some superior quality dresses for me." William spends the day with Crystal traveling around the city. They talk about all kinds of different things, from politics to business, to their trip to Black Rock. She asks his opinion on many things and seems to value everything he has to say. She laughs as he tells her some of the crude jokes he heard in the military academy, and she must explain her jokes from the magic academy, as it seems beyond him to understand. She eventually drops him back off at his house so he can prepare for dinner. "Just don't shave. I like the rugged look on you." He kisses her one last time before exiting the vehicle, allowing her to be on her way.

CHAPTER 24
(Dinner with the Hellstromm's)

Andrew is busy with his chores, scrubbing melted wax from the floors under each chandelier in the main hall when Tia bumps into him carrying an armful of new candles, dropping them. They both say "sorry" simultaneously and gather the runaway wax sticks. They continuously bump into each other under the pews or grab each other's hands, reaching for the same thing. Tia blushes several times, trying to keep her composure. Andrew gets a quick count and says he has twelve. Tia counts through hers. "I think that's all of them." He carefully places them into her crossed arms, making sure she has a handle on them.

Her face is visibly flushed, and Andrew takes notice. *She's very beautiful.* He shakes the thought away. *I'm married to my god. Such things are no longer my concern.* She carries the candles to the altar where they belong and sets them up.

"So… your sister, Crystal." She replaces old candles with new. "What is she like behind the scenes?"

"What do you mean?"

"I spent two weeks with her, but I get a feeling that she isn't the narcissistic woman she displays to keep people at a distance." Tia fumbles with one but catches it before it hits the ground. "But she plays it very convincingly. There were times I thought she was cruel just to get information from prisoners."

Andrew continues to scrape up wax off the floor. "That depends really." Andrew peels a sizeable chunk up. "Get on her bad side, and she can be vindictive. She almost got expelled from the magic academy over it."

This brings Tia's head around. "What do you mean?"

"There was a boy at her school, a Kobold named 'Qheg'." Another chunk comes up. "He was a special kind of Kobold that was a type of Dragon descendent or something. He had wings unlike other Kobolds and a natural gift for magic like Crystal." He sits on the floor

219

breathing hard, putting the chunks into a bucket to be reused. "He was jealous of her gifts, being she was just a 'hooman' and would tease her almost daily. That her white skin and frailty meant there is no way she would ever be 'strong like Dragons. Strong like him'."

"That's horrible."

Andrew nods in agreement. "But what Qheg didn't know was she's just as conniving as our White Dragon heritage." He starts on a new part of the floor. "She kept all this stuff hidden from us, from everyone, really."

"What do you mean?"

"She had to prove a point; I believe. To herself and to others that just because she was physically meek doesn't mean she would be pushed around." Andrew stands up and wipes his brow. "I was always a 'forgive and let it go' kind of person, believing that fighting over such inconsequential matters to not be worth it." He looks at Tia standing in the light that accentuates her angelical face. "But then again, I'm physically more imposing than her."

"So, what happened?" Tia is facing him now. "She didn't kill him, did she?"

Andres laughs lightly at the thought. "No, she didn't take it that far. She researched a new spell that was simple yet effective." Walks over and stands next to her. "Qheg was always wearing the best of the best clothing and jewelry. Really showing off how prominent he was among the other Kobolds and the other students." Andrew takes a drink of water placed next to the altar. "She researched it so much and practiced it to the point that it fused into her blood, no longer needing material components or even much of a verbal one." He puts his cup down and goes back to work. He scrapes the stone floor harshly pealing up the built-up wax from overnight. "She waited for her time to strike. There was an assembly where he was to give some kind of speech and he was dressed as if he thought he was the Emperor himself."

Tia walks over to him. "Then what?"

Andrew continues his story. "We were all in attendance. Every family that had a kid in that academy was there. That's when Crystal struck. She managed somehow to be in the front row, and I would guess she threatened someone for their seat." A smile creeps across his face. "I'll never forget what happened next. She leaned forward and grabbed his foot and said a short incantation that none of us heard, but she had to of said something because Qheg looked down with his jaws wide open in shock. Then, in front of several hundred people, he was stark naked. Everything he was wearing hit the floor as if it was made of lead and afraid of him."

Tia's eyes grow wide. "She did that to me at the monastery, then stole my clothes." Her face reddens thinking about it and surprises Andrew. He didn't think she was capable of anger.

"So, she got you with it, too?"

"Too? As in she's done this to others?"

Andrew laughs. "Yeah. Crystal got into a lot of trouble over that, but Qheg was so embarrassed that not only was he nude in front of hundreds of people, but he was shown up by the 'frail ivory white girl' at the same time." Andrew starts on the floor again. "He dropped out of the academy in disgrace and went to another one in the eighth house district." Andrew finishes and gets up to start on a new section and Tia joins him. "That day, we all learned that when Crystal is being vocal, that's when you're safe. When she gets quiet around you, worry about your safety. When she gets angry, she gets real quiet about it, and that's when she's plotting to end your very existence."

He looks at Tia with a thoughtful look on her face, then laughs. "I'm just kidding. I don't think she's capable of outright murder." Tia's eyes widen a little and tilts her head but didn't look at him. Andrew glances up at the clock. "Think we can get this done in thirty minutes? We're both going to need to get cleaned up before we head back to my house for dinner."

Tia looks up at the clock and back to Andrew. "Yea, if I chip in, we should easily get that done."

"Let's get to it. I've never brought a girl home to dad before." He returns to his work on the floor, and Tia's face flushes bright red.

William hears a knock on his bedroom door as he prepares for the night. His estate steward Sally is standing with a large gold inlaid darkwood box. "This just came for you, Master William."

"Thank you, Sally. It's my outfit for dinner tonight." He turns around, placing it on the bed.

"That's why you were out with Ms. Hellstromm, to get a new suit?" He nods affirmative, pulling it out of the box. She whistles appreciatively. "You're going to look amazing in that. I didn't know you had such impeccable taste."

William chuckles at the thought. "I've been around Crystal for over two weeks nonstop and seeing what she wears, I guess, is rubbing off on me." He holds it up to his chest and shows her. "What do you think? She wears stuff better than this all the time."

"It looks wonderful. Is there anything else you need?"

"Yeah, make sure the two monks have dressed appropriately, as we need to get going if we are going to make it in time."

"Yes, sir." She bows her head, closing the door as she leaves.

Tom and Tyra are in the back courtyard with Gerald training. They are laughing and trading stories and techniques for fighting. Tom spars with the old man as Tyra does one-armed pushups with almost a quarter ton of weights on her back.

Tom throws out punches Gerald easily blocks and counters with a punch of his own, hitting Tom square in the nose. He backpedals and the two circle each other. "For an old man, you hit like a battering ram." Blood flows from his left nostril.

Gerald grins, feeling his heart pump from the excitement of sparring with someone new. "I've been a military man my whole life. Experience can make up for physical shortcomings. Strength is good, but all the strength in the world won't matter if your opponent is craftier than you are."

A snort from Tyra punctuates his statement. "I think you hit a sore spot with her." Tom lashes out with a spin kick, catching the old man in the waist. Gerald takes the blow and brings down his elbow into Tom's knee, bringing him down.

"Why do you say that, Tom?" Gerald offers his hand to help the younger man up.

Tom looks at Tyra, then back to Gerald. Taking his hand and standing up, he continues. "She lost to Crystal." Gerald looks at Tyra, confused

"Lost to Crystal?" He looks back at Tom. "Wait, did they fight over William?"

This brings another snort of frustration from Tyra, but Tom just busts out laughing. He's trying to catch his breath while picturing that in the back of his head, of Tyra lifting William off the ground and licking him all over his face in some weird Minotaur kissing ritual.

Gerald shakes his head, not understanding. "What is so funny?"

"Crystal and I didn't fight over your son. We fought over some of my fur." She flexes her arms. "She needed it for some ritual thing." She's pumped as ever, with muscles larger than Gerald's head.

"And... she won?"

"Yeah. Just as you said she would. She was smarter, and I was arrogant. Taught me a valuable lesson that day."

"And what lesson is that?"

"Don't give a sorceress a free shot." Tom is still laughing, unable to get the picture out of his head of William's head wrapped with her huge cow like tongue. Tyra punches him in the shoulder. "Care to share? What's so funny?"

Tom explains what he's thinking between breaths and Gerald laughs too, but Tyra doesn't look amused. "Gives new meaning to the term 'cowlick' doesn't it?"

Tyra fumes, then thinks about it and laughs too. "It wouldn't work out between us, anyway. I would break the poor boy in half on the wedding night." This starts a new cacophony of laughter from the three.

Sally walks into the back courtyard and raises an eyebrow. "Master Gerald, Master William asked me to make sure everyone gets ready to go. It's just after four and you must be at Mr. Hellstromm's by five."

Gerald, Muriel, William, Tom, and Tyra all arrive at the Hellstromm's manor just before five in their carriage. Tyra had to ride with the driver, being too tall to fit inside. Cline, wearing his typical blue and white tux, walks out and greets them with two household guards. Muriel gets out first, her flowing white dress looks as if it was made of liquid pearl. She takes Cline's hand, but she has a look of uneasiness as she does. The sensation goes away after letting go, which she finds odd. Gerald gets out next and steps down. He's wearing a formal-looking suit and doesn't look comfortable in it.

Tyra and Tom exit next wearing simple white and brown leather tunics. Keeping it simple is their way, and they would wear nothing fancier. Crystal comes from the house and everyone's attention turns to her. Her sapphire blue dragon scale pattern dress flows with her. It covered her body but looks skintight. Her arms from the shoulders down and her head are the only parts of her free of the dress. Multiple long thin braids with gold spun wire bind them, and hang from her around the horns. Tom whistles but is cut off by Tyra slapping him in the back of the head with her hand. She walks up as William in his navy blue and gold pattern tunic steps out last. She extends a clawed hand to his parents. "You must be Mr. and Mrs. Blakely." She's only chest high to them both, but she figures as big as William is, it's being expected.

Gerald beams with a smile as he takes her hand. "You must be Crystal; I've heard so much about you".

She returns the smile. "Yes sir, I am."

"He didn't tell us you were so stunningly beautiful. If I had a daughter like you, she wouldn't go anywhere without an entire complement of guards."

She motions to her right, pointing to Cline. "That's ok. I don't need a bunch of Guards. I have Cline." Her eyes shift to William. "But now I have someone better in mind."

She steps over to him, and he smiles and lifts a hand, touching her braids hanging from her horns. "This is the third time you hung your hair from your horns." He runs his hands along her braids. "I like it."

Her smile grows. "I do it so if anyone wants to see my beauty, they have to look at me directly. Plus, no one else can, so it's kind of like a personal aesthetic trend I'm trying to start."

Cline pipes up, breaking into the conversation. "Dinner will be ready soon."

Crystal reaches around and hooks her arm into William's, putting him into motion. "Best not to keep daddy waiting." Cline raises an eyebrow and waves them on. Gerald offers his arm and Muriel smiles, taking it and walking behind Crystal and William.

Tom shrugs and hooks his arm through Tyra's and tries to walk with her, but she is having none of it and stands firm, jerking him backward. "What are you doing?"

Tom points to the others. "They're doing it, so I thought it was a thing."

She shakes him free. "Grow up." They walk into the house behind the others.

Cline stands there and pulls out his pocket watch. As if expecting them, Andrew and Tia arrive wearing their plain clergy robes. They are laughing and talking as they get to the gate. "Ah, Master Andrew, priestess Tia, dinner is about ready. You've arrived just in time." Cline sounds stiff as ever. "If you will come with me."

"I missed you too, Cline."

"It's good to have you back, sir. Even if it's only for an evening."

William and Crystal walk in first. Jack, sitting in a plush red leather chair, is wearing a crimson red suit with adamantine wire threads making intricate patterns that almost look magical. Jasmine sits next to him in a similar chair wearing a crimson red evening dress with adamantine wire embroidery patterns sewn in like his. They get up and welcome their guests as they walk in and shake hands. First William, then Gerald and Muriel, and Tom and Tyra. They are talking and exchanging pleasantries as Andrew and Tia walk in. Jasmine launches herself at her son and hugs him tightly. "Glad you could make it, Andrew." She turns to Tia, giving her a big hug, squeezing her with a strength she shouldn't possess.

Tia looks at Crystal and squeaks. "You set me up."

Crystal smiles. "No, she's naturally a hugger, like you."

Jack is over-animated and already talking. His short stature contains large amounts of energy. William and Gerald trying to keep up with him as he talks about the military tech he's developing in his back shop. Jasmine shoots him dirty looks every time he mentions lightning coils and augmented battle suits. Cline walks in, interrupting politely as possible. "Dinner is ready in the grand hall." He bows, gesturing to the room to the left. "If you have any special requests, Penelope and I will get them to you."

They walk in and Cline and the other staff help to arrange everyone. Jack and Gerald sit at the table end with Jasmine and Muriel sitting each to their respective right. Followed by Andrew and Tia, then William and Crystal, and Tom and Tyra, all sitting opposite of each other. Drinks are poured and stories told. The kids tell their tale of the trip with Penelope, getting in a word or two as she brings in fresh food and drinks.

They retire to the main hall, where they continue to laugh and tell jokes. Crystal sits with William on a red leather two-person couch, and she leans on him, smiling and laughing as Jack tells the story of him, Jasmine, and Cline.

"So, get this." Jack leans forward with his glass of wine. He points to Jasmine. "Me and Frost, that was her code name at the time, are standing in the desert with this army of animated plants assaulting the city of… uh." He looks at Jasmine. "What was the name of that city with the scorpion people?"

"I don't remember that was sixty or seventy years ago."

Gerald, Muriel, and William exchange glances. *If they were in their late teens sixty years ago, that would put them into their eighties or nineties, but none look older than thirty. Must be an inside joke.*

Jack continues with a dismissive gesture. "Anyway, this demigod guy was attacking the city with this army of plants, and Jasmine and I managed to sneak behind him. So, as I was about to ambush him." He motions to cline. "And Cline over here pops out of nowhere." He makes a popping motion with his fingers. "And he's standing possibly no more than thirty feet from me."

"Yes, I just teleported to my half-brother also intent on stopping him but for different reasons, but I was hunting Jack as well." He raises a single eyebrow in his direction. "He had caused me a lot of pain and suffering."

"Yeah, that's true, but neither one of them saw me nor Frost standing right between them in the damn desert because of our invisibility." Jack cackles and Jasmine leans on him.

Cline sighs, sounding disappointed. "As usual, I wasn't expecting you to be there."

"So then what?" Tom prompts as Penelope brings in more drinks.

"Well, we were dead. Like dead, dead." Jack gestures with his hand. "Like we could maybe take one of them on and with an ice cube's chance in hell maybe survive, but not with both standing there. So, I was ready to lay it all on the line and told Jasmine here that I have one final trick but it was going to cost us our lives, and told her what I was going to do. I had made a device that was set up to snap wands." They exchange glances again and Jack picks up on it. "When you snap a wand, it releases all its stored energy on that spot. The upside is I had a timer built into it." He takes another drink of his wine. "So, there we were, in a no-win situation, and all I had was a magical bomb with three wands in it, one of them with maxed out meta magic stuff thrown into it." As he gets animated with his story, and sloshes his drink that causes Penelope to sigh. "I set the timer and was about to hit the button when Frost says, 'I can teleport us out of here but I need a few seconds for a distraction'." He laughs even harder, pointing to himself. "Distraction? Both of these guys have been hunting me all over the damn continent. I know how to distract them. So, she starts her incantation and I rip the bomb off my arm and throw it on the ground, making me visible again. They both stop their monologues as the one person whose ass they wanted most just materialized right in front of them."

Cline shakes his head and rolls his eyes. "Here it comes."

"So, I say 'looking for me? Well, too bad, byeee', and Frost teleports us out of there. Seconds later, in the distance, the night turned into day and the sound of the blast was nuts."

They all turn to Cline, with his hand on the bridge of his nose. "Yes, he teleported away and left that thing ticking on the ground. I didn't know what it was or why he left it, so I picked it up and the damn thing detonated in my face." Jack, Crystal, Andrew, and Jasmine are laughing and even Cline snickers recalling the tail. Everyone else is hung in suspense. "If you're wondering how I survived, I didn't. It vaporized me, my half-brother, and half the city Jack and his friends were trying to protect." He glances back at Jack and Jasmine. "Four days later I wake up and Jack is standing there holding my phylactery and says, 'we should talk.' Ever since then, I've been in his employment. He's treated me very well and I've come to think of him as a friend."

Muriel speaks up, fear clear in her tone. "You're a Lich?"

Cline shrugs, not knowing how to answer, turning back to her. "Yes, and no. I *was* a Lich, but I no longer hold those ideals. I may be undead, but I now serve to protect Jack's children and make sure his house runs smoothly." He looks at Jack. "You could say he saved my soul, and I'm grateful."

Crystal settles in more, leaning against William, and looks content. They trade more stories, and they laugh. Crystal tells a few, and Tia talks about her life growing up on the streets. Tom and Tyra tell their story of how he found her when she was just a tiny calf in a field when he was a boy and brought her back to the monastery. Crystal gets up, dragging William outside, leaving the others behind. She looks up at the stars, noticing she can't see as many here as she could in the woods. "So, are you going to run away?"

He looks down at her. "Why would I do that?"

"Because my father has the capacity to level this city, and he's best friends with a Lich who is also my butler, bodyguard, and babysitter."

William chuckles at her being straight-faced. "That's just a funny story. It wasn't real." She stands in silence, looking up at the stars. "It's not true, is it?" She only moves her eyes to look at him, then looks back at the stars. But in his mind, that confirms that it's not a folk tale nor embellished. "Guess I better treat you right then. I don't want to be launched into space next." His grin can't be muted as he looks down at her and she smiles too, but then looks around.

"Kiss me, you fool, before someone sees us."

He leans down, wrapping their arms around each other, and makes his move when Cline steps outside looking for them. They are in their moment when Cline clears his throat. As if expecting it, he puts out a hand and catches Crystal's frost ray, dissipating harmlessly. "Really, Mistress?"

She breaks her kiss with William but does not break eye contact, as if looking into Williams's soul. "Sorry, reflex action. Don't tell daddy, I really like him."

"Yes, well, if you like him, that means your father will, too, but I understand and will not inform him of your affection." He turns to leave. "Even if it's so self-evident that a blind Dwarf could see it. I believe you're hiding it over nothing."

CHAPTER 25
(Young Love)

Crystal comes down in her nightgown as she has often. Jack is sitting at the table eating when she walks in. Sitting down, Penelope gets her a fresh glass of orange juice.

"What would you like to eat for breakfast, Mistress Hellstromm?"

Crystal thinks about it for a moment. "Just an omelet today."

Jack speaks from behind his paper. "So… you like this William guy, huh?"

Crystal fears little, but her father sends chills through her with his tone. She drinks some O.J. "Yes, I do." She looks at him through his paper and swallows. "Why? Do you not like him?" She's doing her best to hide the fear in her voice. *I don't know how I could hide this behind his back.*

"I've been reading his file from the Royal Guard." Crystal picks up her glass, hiding behind it best she can. Putting his paper down, he reveals the report is still in his hands, hidden by the paper. He speaks as if reading from the file. "He graduated top of his class and was at the top of his class in the junior corps. He's been in the military life since he was able to walk." Jack places the file on the table and glances at her.

"I know, and I've seen him in action on the battlefield. He's very good."

"And he laid his life down to save you?" Jack places his hands on the table and leans forward. She fiddles with her glass, putting it back on the table, and staring at it. The pain from the incident comes back and Jack can see that. "Your mother saved me on multiple occasions and I her." She looks up at him and they lock eyes. "Neither of us were soldiers, but we were willing to make those sacrifices."

Crystal investigates the orange liquid, avoiding eye contact with her father. "So, you're saying he only did it because he was trained too?"

Jack shakes his head and reaches out, taking her clawed hand. "No, actually. Self-sacrifice for others is personal. I've seen soldiers dive into danger and seen them run at the mere sign of death."

Crystal looks at his hand and then up at him. "What are you saying, daddy?"

"I'm saying he reminds me of myself. I wouldn't risk my life for anyone but for those I truly hold dear, and I believe he's no different. You have that same spark, being you did the same for him."

Crystal smiles. "You're saying he can court me officially?"

Jack smiles in return, patting her hand. "Yes. He shows great honor, and I believe I can trust him." She squeals and jumps up joyfully and circles the table, giving him an enormous hug. "Just promise me he will keep you honest."

She looks at her father, puzzled. "You mean to keep him honest?"

"No, I've seen him firsthand, and your mother prepared several spells. With this report, it confirms he's the honest one. You're the one who does things behind everyone's back and then acts innocent."

Crystal's jaw drops. "I've never lied to you or mother."

"I know, but you can't say the same for anyone else, can you?"

Crystal looks at the clock. "Well, we must make reports for Emperor Marcus. We should get those going, so they are ready Monday morning."

Jack tilts his head in her direction. "Sounds like you're making an excuse to be with him. If you want to go out, then go out, but make sure you get that report done."

Penelope walks in with her breakfast and she starts in. *I hope William is eating well. He's going to need the energy today.*

"Cline!"

"Yes, sir?" Cline appears from the kitchen. "Go to Asorin's for me and get William's measurements. I know his handy work when I see it." He drinks his own orange juice. "I want them."

"As you wish, sir."

William, Tom, and Tyra spar in the back courtyard, improving their fighting techniques. Tom is smaller and faster, but William is battle-hardened and puts a real hurting on. Gerald joins them after he's

230

down with his breakfast. "Crystal and her family are something else, aren't they?"

Tom muses drinking some water. "A man capable of that kind of destruction. No wonder he's the Third House."

Gerald laughs, waving a hand away. "I think that's a bit embellished, but still, I've seen his steam creations in action. They can be scary. He loves supporting our military efforts." He picks up a towel. "I remember years ago he was only the Fifth. He's made a lot of money and connections in the last decade."

Tyra flexes, curling a four-hundred-pound bar. "Machines don't have anything on the might of a Minotaur."

William towels his face and laps around the yard. "What do you think of her father?"

"Crystal? Well, she's prim and proper, well-adjusted, and seems very nice." Gerald reflects on the thought and turns to his son. "Not that I have anything to really say about it. Yesterday she was practically advertising that you two are an item." He shrugs and tosses the towel onto the rack. "But if you really like her and want to court her, you have my permission to ask Mr. Hellstromm."

William stops to answer, but Sally walks in. "I have a message for Master William from Ms. Hellstromm."

William takes it and thanks her, opens it and reads. "She's wanting to meet to discuss the reports we need to write for Marcus. Says we don't have long to get it done and want to make a good impression on him."

Gerald nods approvingly. "She knows what's important. I like that. Better get cleaned up and get that done. Don't want to disappoint the Emperor."

Tom puts his cup down. "What time does she want to meet?"

William looks at him. "She wants to meet *me* in an hour."

Tyra's nostrils flare. "Well, *you* need a bath."

"Is it that bad?"

She nods her head. "You're meeting one of the most beautiful women in the kingdom, and you're going to go stinking?"

William looks down at the sweat stains and nods in agreement. "Yes, you're right, I better do that." He collects his things and walks inside.

Tyra shouts after him. "And put on some nice cologne!"

William arrives at Crystal's home and the guard lets him in, escorting him to the door where Cline greets him. "Ah yes, Master William, you're here to pick up Mistress Crystal, yes?" He steps aside, letting William in.

"Sort of. She wanted to work on our report for Emperor Marcus, and being that's rather important, I came over to proceed with getting it done."

Cline raises an eyebrow. "I will fetch her for you, but first Master Jack would prefer to see you in his workshop in the back first. You need me to escort you there, or do you think you can find it?"

William's hands get a little sweaty. "I believe I can find it. Thank you, Cline." Cline turns on his heel and walks upstairs.

William heads outback and can easily see the workshop. As he approaches, he can hear the banging of hammer and steel. Walking into the open door, he trips over a small ladder laying on the floor. "Come in and have a seat, young William. I see you found my step ladder." Jack sounds serious. "I never knew my real one."

William lets out a belly laugh and shakes his head, scanning the area with all kinds of different contraptions Jack has built over the years. Plans for different armors and exotic materials from around the globe are stacked neatly in bins. "Cline told me you wanted to see me."

Jack puts the hot metal sheet down in some sand and slips off his goggles. "Yes, I did." He puts his hammer down on the anvil and walks up to the much larger man craning to look up at him. "You said last night that you lost your armor back in Black Rock."

"That's correct, sir. I didn't have time to don it when the battle started."

"Have you commissioned new armor to be built yet?"

"Not yet, sir. I was going to do that after my meeting with Emperor Marcus. No need for armor if he decides to kick me from the guard."

Jack closes to inches of him. "Your file says you figure things out quickly."

"What do you mean?"

Jack places a finger in William's chest and William swallows. "Marcus would have killed you outright if he thought you failed him.

So, he's keeping you, and you're going to need new armor if you're going to be protecting my daughter." Jack walks away, picks up some plans off a nearby desk, brings them on over, and shows them to William. "This is one of my newest designs. It's not mechanically enhanced, but I've been working on a new alloy to strengthen it but also to lighten it. In this, you would be practically invincible. It's a mix of mithril, adamantium, and star metal." Jack looks up at him. "It gives it a teal hue, but if you want, I can paint it to your house colors." Turning back and indicating on the paper. "It doesn't weigh much less, but with that weight reduction, I can cover the joints better. This eliminates some of the soft spots in conventional armor." He grins, putting a hand on his hip. "It's bullet and sword proof. Short of being thrown off a roof, you should live through anything."

William is shocked at what something like this would cost. "What do I owe you for something like this?"

Jack places his hand on the boy's shoulder. "Use it to protect my daughter and I'll call us even. I'll be at least a month even with my advanced machines. The smelting of the alloy takes several days to make the ingots for forging."

William continues looking over the armor. Functional and aesthetically intimidating. "That's understandable."

"Don't worry, I'll let Marcus know what I'm doing." He glances out a window back towards the house. "Now I can see from here that Crystal is waiting for you. So, you guys get that paperwork done and have some fun."

William shakes Jack's hand. "I would like to ask your permission to court Crystal, sir."

Jack glances at her and back at William. "You have it. Even though you were already doing it without my permission but I appreciate the thought."

"It wasn't my idea, Crystal—"

Jack cuts him off. "Yes, I know. She can be forceful when she wants something." Jack looks and Crystal is still standing there looking at them. "You better go before she thinks I'm setting you against her."

William takes off across the rear courtyard where Crystal is standing in her signature hairstyle and a black evening dress with gold wire embroidery decorations. William goes to embrace her, and she steps back, holding her hands away from him. The look of confusion is all over his face. "Hold your hands out." He does, and they are covered in grease and soot. She recites an incantation, and in an instant, they are clean. "That's better. Ready to go up to my room and write that report?"

Cline not standing far away is looking in their direction. William thinks better of it. "Uh, we should do that down here where Cline can get us fresh supplies if we need it."

She shrugs. "Fine, I guess. We can work in the dining hall. That way, we can keep the snacks and drinks coming."

They work on the report of everything from Mossy Fields to Black Rock, the Black Rose, and what they learned about New Haven. They take hours and it's getting late when they finish. Penelope walks in getting ready for dinner service. "Oh Sir Blakely, are you dining with us again tonight?"

Crystal gets up, interrupting before he can speak. "Nope. We are going out tonight."

"Very good Mistress. When will you return so I can tell Master Jack?"

"I don't know yet. I'll have to think about it." Penelope stares daggers at William, letting him know she's not happy. Crystal seals up the reports. "I would like to go ahead and deliver these so they don't get lost. I'm sure the emperor attendants will accept it."

"That's not a bad idea. He didn't say not to deliver it early and will be one less thing to go wrong Monday morning."

"Then let's go then, and after that, we can have an enjoyable meal somewhere." They walk out and William mounts his horse and pulls her up onto it. She smiles and wraps her arms around him. They make their way to the palace and the sun is still just above the sea. The colors changing with the setting sun make it look so much more majestic. "I want one."

William dismounts. "You want one what?"

William lifts her from her horse. "My own palace, or a castle. I dream of living in a place like this someday."

"You sure dream big, don't you?"

"You have to dream big to give yourself a goal in life."

They walk in with their escort and Marcus is sitting on his throne as if he expected them. They both take a knee and Marcus' voice booms through the room. "You're three days early. Is there some urgency I should know about?"

Crystal dares not look up from the floor. "No, Your Highness. We got our reports done early and thought it would be prudent for us to bring it in so it wouldn't get lost."

Marcus stands up. "Present it to me then, Ms. Hellstromm."

She stands and walks up to him, handing him the document.

He opens it and reads. "I'll go over this and make some decisions. You two may go and enjoy the rest of your date. Be back here Monday as ordered."

William stands and they leave together. They cross the precious metal map when William speaks up. "Did you catch the part where he said 'date'?"

Crystal says with a smile. "If anyone would know it would be him. I did pronounce my love for you crying on his floor, after admitting to using a spell that should have cost me my life."

They go out on their date and have a wonderful evening of food and entertainment. They spend the weekend with each other's parents, getting to know them and interacting. Monday morning rolls around and they arrive at the palace that morning a little early. William is wearing his dress officer's uniform and Crystal has on an ice blue dress with gold and adamantine lace that matches her eyes. They walk into the throne room, but Marcus isn't there. They patiently wait a few minutes, and Marcus comes out of his office on the side where they originally planned everything. "In here, you two."

Walking in, Marcus sits behind his desk and gestures to the chairs. They take their seats, and Marcus starts with his meeting. "After analyzing your report and having sent a representative to Black Rock. I decided that what I needed there was a Baron to do official business on our behalf. I'm sending a new garrison and they are getting their pay raises, so everything should calm down."

William sits forward. "What about the 'Black Rose' cult that was present?"

"Thinking of the tactical situation? Good man. I like that." He waves dismissively, looking through some parchments on his desk. "Most of them seemed to have dropped it, but I had to make a mass arrest and execution for those involved with the killing of my men and the destruction of my garrison."

Crystal speaks up next. "Do you have anyone in mind for being your new Baron of Black Rock?"

Marcus smiles as he looks at her. "Actually, I do."

Her heart races and she can barely contain herself. *I'm going to be a baroness?*

He continues pulling up a file and handing it to her. "A Gnome that's been with me for a long time, named Jabari. He's my leading expert on Obsidian, so he will know if anything is wrong." Crystal continues to smile, but her heart sinks. "But that's old business. I have a new use for you two. I'm going to put your skills to the test on a new trip. Being we have this problem with the Black Rose and New Haven, I need someone to investigate. New Haven is a large city. Not as big as Rose Harbor, but vastly larger than Black Rock." He laces his fingers and leans down on his desk. "And I have reason to believe that this Black Rose was started in New Haven. That's why they were trying to take Black Rock. It's relatively close to our home here."

Crystal agrees, desperately hiding her disappointment that she wasn't promoted. "That makes sense, but it would be suicidal to take on Rose Harbor. We have the most advanced military in the world. My father's weapons and battle suits would destroy them. They would have to know that."

William builds on her statement. "It's not like we don't advertise our strength. That's why we have so many peace and trade treaties. Why would they provoke us like this?"

Marcus lets out a belly laugh. "Those are the kinds of questions I expect from you two. So, this is what I'm ordering you two to do." He pulls out a map of the northern continent and lays everything out. "I'm sending you to this city-state called Portstown. As you can see, it's south of New Haven and we have an embassy there. We are on friendly terms, so my airship can land there without provocation. I'm assigning you a larger contingent of guards than the last time. A full company. They will travel with you from Portstown on the road to New Haven."

William points to the mountains along the way and notes the distance. "That's about two weeks or more walking one way. Why not just use a ship from Portstown to New Haven? It's shorter since we can go straight across the gulf here."

"Spoken like a true military commander. They have their own navy and if they see a fleet of Rose Harbor aliened ships, they might think it's an invasion. I want to be on friendly terms with them. That's a secondary objective for you." This gets them both to look up. "So, you're going to take my airship to Portstown. While you're there, talk to their government and see if they would consider joining the empire by choice. We are friendly with each other, but I think we could work better as one unified government. Less red tape and all that. Then travel by foot to just outside New Haven. Find out who oversees the Black Rose and eliminate them and anyone associated. I don't care how messy you make it. Then make peace with the government of New Haven themselves unless they are behind the Black Rose. If they aren't, pursue a trade agreement with them so they won't have to steal our workers."

Crystal looks up with her eyes. "And if they are?"

"I'll send them one of your father's... specialties." William's eyebrows move up a little now, understanding that tale Jack spun was most definitely a real thing. "Anything else?"

Crystal speaks up. "If I'm acting in your stead, I'm going to need some kind of official documents allowing me to speak on your behalf, won't I?" She looks him in the eyes with more bravery than she feels. "I can't make deals in your name; they won't hold up legally."

Marcus looks at her in appreciation. *She knows a lot about these things.* "That is correct, Ms. Hellstromm. Very astute observation. That's why I'm granting you a temporary position of countess." Crystal's jaw drops a moment but catches herself. She can barely hold her excitement at her promotion. "Now this title is conditional on two things. One, you seal the deal and bring Portstown into the fold and bring them under my flag." He stands up. "And two, you neutralize and seal a trade deal with New Haven. If you pull off both objectives and these troops come back, I'll make it permanent, and you will be the Countess of the Northern Continent with all the rights and privileges associated with it." He pulls something from his desk drawer and hands her a new signet with the official seal of the First House. "Congratulations Countess Hellstromm."

She bows her head and places the new First House signet on. "What is the time set for our new mission?"

"Doing negotiations for entry into an empire and trade agreements can take some time. So up to three years? Depends on how hard you work and they feel about things." He motions them to rise and they walk out with him. "Now I understand that Captain Blakely here lost his armor in Black Rock. Well, my scouts found it and you're not going to want it back." He circles his desk, sitting on it between them. "But I was informed by Mr. Hellstromm that he is personally building you a new suit of armor. You should feel very privileged he likes you that much, William. He doesn't do custom personal orders for very many. You must have made a good impression on him. The same you did on me for your self-sacrifice." He motions to them to stand up and they walk out into the main hall. "Normally I would have been pushing you two onto the ship already, but he claims to need a month to get your armor ready, and I want you fully armed to protect the countess here." He places a hand on them both. "Plus, it will give you two time to bond. Enjoy the next thirty or so days. Whenever Jack finishes, then you will be off." He lets go, showing them to leave, but as they are about to exit, Emperor Marcus booms from across the room. "And make sure you have your Vardo stocked and ready to go, Countess. It's going to serve as your mobile command post!"

They walk out of the palace and Crystal still can't believe it. *Countess at my age isn't unheard of, but still quite the accomplishment. I'm going to have to study and prepare myself if I'm going to be an ambassador and really earn this permanently. I will make sure he is one hundred percent satisfied with my performance.* They walk up to the horse, and she pulls on William, causing him to turn around.

He can see she's beaming as a newborn star in the artificial lamplight. She wraps her arms around his neck. "Did you ever think you would be kissing a countess?" Before he can reply, she pulls him down, kissing him. "Let's go eat."

CHAPTER 26
(Onwards and upwards)

The weeks go by as they all prepare for the next task. Crystal and William get reports back from Black Rock, and with Gerald and Jack's help, formulate different ideas about what could happen and how to proceed. Crystal, with Tia's help, works on her diplomatic skills and gets more information about Portstown. Their major economy is the culture of the people. Andrew has never seen Crystal try so hard for something. Tia talks about how she's trying since she was offered the countess position.

Jack is having William come over almost every day, to Crystal's delight, so he can fit the new armor. Crystal is constantly trying to get more decorative patterns to make the armor look better, but Jack is having none of it. Several days before Jack is finished, a new report comes in, and Crystal, Tia, and William are all summoned to the Palace. They arrive as soon as they could, based on the urgency of the message. They make their way into the throne room and Marcus is standing with several other advisers. "Ah, Countess Hellstromm and her council have arrived finally." He waves them over and hands her the report. "Good. This just came in from Black Rock."

She reads it over and can't believe it. "This is more than a labor dispute, after all. The other reports say the workers were happy with the new contract."

She hands it to William so he can go over it. "Black Rose forces launched and failed to take the garrison in Black Rock a second time." He looks up to the Emperor. "That's at least good news, but if they are coming from New Haven, how are they making that four-month trip so fast unless they have a powerful magic user helping them?"

Marcus agrees with Williams' assessment. "This is why I have people like you to deal with this. It's good to see young people coming into their own. You must learn if someday you're going to lead where we go in the future."

Tia speaks up, glancing up at him. "And we have the best teacher for that future, Your Highness himself."

Marcus smiles back and wraps his arm around her. "Thank you for saying so, Tia, but right now, we have more pressing issues." He steps away, patting her on the back as he goes, and turns to William. "How long until your armor is ready? It's been over thirty days and Jack hasn't sent me an update."

"It's close, maybe a day or two. We can rush it and have it done tomorrow, perhaps?"

"No, don't do that. Rushing the armoring process could cause some problems overall." He tilts his head in Crystal's direction. "And I don't want Crystal committing any more sins against the gods." This causes Crystal to change a few shades of pink, putting her head down. "I'm going to have to change the plan a little. We can't go in with a full company of guards or we will never figure out who oversees the Black Rose group. It's just going to be who you select to go with you." He turns to Crystal and then William. "I'll toss in two squads of guards, but they won't be wearing Rose Harbor colors. Think of them as part of your personal retinue, Crystal." He places his left hand on her and points at her with the right. "But remember our goals. Find the Black Rose leadership and eliminate them. Get New Haven on our side and bring Portstown into the empire."

Crystal looks at him. "Yes, Your Highness."

One of Marcus' advisers flags him over, but he holds a hand up, silencing them. "Tia, give these two counsel on the journey. I've heard great things about you from Priestess Lyndis. I hope you keep up the excellent work." Marcus returns to his advisers. "I'm getting the airship loaded up right now with supply wagons and anything you might need. Have your Vardo brought to me so it can be loaded." He waves his hand, dismissing them.

Tia and William walk away, but Crystal is steadfast. Marcus notices she is standing alone. "Is there something else, Countess?"

She looks down, takes a deep breath, and looks back up at him. "Not to be presumptuous, but about the negotiations with Portstown, I had some thoughts that I wanted to run by you, if I may?"

Marcus' eyebrow raises. He silences his advisors with a hand chop. His voice booms over the room. "Well, let's hear it, Countess."

She rubs her hands on her legs. "I was wondering if as part of the negotiation we could gift them something as a show of good faith?" She places her hands behind her back and stands up straighter. "As a gesture or example of what we could do for them if they joined the empire, I was thinking maybe five or so of our older outdated power armors that are no longer in service? Maybe even some rifles and handguns?" She does her best to keep eye contact, judging his expressions. "Reports say they don't have advanced weaponry."

Marcus looks at her for a long moment goes by and then he moves, crossing the area swiftly towards Crystal, causing Tia to flinch, but stand her ground with uncharacteristic bravery. Marcus reaches out and places his large hand over Crystal's horned head, covering it almost completely, and ruffles it a bit with a smile on his face. "That right there is a great idea. Spoken like a true negotiator. Very well." He turns to his military adviser. "Make sure five of our older models are loaded on board as well, along with instructions for their use as a gift to the Baron of Portstown, with two crates of rifles and pistols with ammo." The other man nods and writes it down on tomorrow's schedule. He looks back at her and winks. Then sends her on her way.

She turns with a smile on her face and joins William and Tia and they are quiet till they exit the palace. Tia glances at her, exhaling hard. "Bold move."

Crystal lets out a nervous giggle. "I'm going to be honest. I was scared out of my mind, but if I'm going to earn this countess position permanently, I'm going to have to take some risks."

William looks at her as the stable hand brings his mount. "I'm starting to rub off on you finally. Only took a month and a half."

She mutters under her breath. "I'm ok with the rubbing." This causes William to snort and flush a little, but Tia stands there looking at them both. The sun hides behind the tall towers of the city, casting long shadows and the sky starts its colorful change from day to night. Walking up to his armored steed, William turns to Tia. "You know you don't have to walk everywhere; I can get you a ride back to your church, especially with it getting dark."

Tia looks at the couple. "It's ok, Andrew is supposed to meet me here anytime and we are going to walk together. He had an assignment up the road doing last rites for a burial at the Second house. So, when he's finished, we will walk back together." Her voice seems

241

very excited about this, causing Crystal and William to glance at each other.

"You two have fun." William mounts up and reaches down and plucks Crystal right off the ground and pulls her on back. "She's supposed to be picking up some magic bracelets, and then we going out to dinner at the Sugar Rose if you and Andrew want to stop by, my treat."

Tia looks up the road for Andrew, hoping to spot him. "I'll ask him if he wants to go, but I don't want to intrude on your date night."

From the back of the horse, Crystal interrupts. "Nonsense. I order you two to come. We could count it as a double date."

Tia laughs, concealing her mouth. "You're such a joker now."

Crystal's face goes from mirthful to emotionless, and the tone changes. "I'm serious about coming to dinner. As your Countess, I want you two there and I don't want any excuses." William and Tia both turn to face her. "This is our last day before the new mission starts. I think we should spend it having fun since it's going to be possibly years of sweating my ass off in a desert." William laughs, cutting her off. "What's so funny, Will?" She looks at him with an evil eye.

He shakes his head and places a hand up in surrender. "Not a lot of places to take a bath in the desert. How ever will you survive?"

"I'm going to be sweaty and icky." She looks at him and an impish grin crosses her face. "Guess I'm going to have to have someone bathe me along the way."

Tia looks in wonderment. "Why would someone else bathe you?"

Crystal holds a hand up in a half shrug. "Why would I do it myself when I can order someone else? What's the point of being royalty if you have to do things on your own?"

Tia blinks. *I don't know how to answer that.*

William interrupts. "We have things to do, Countess." Crystal blushes when he calls her that. He knows how much she loves her new title.

She waves him onward. "Yes, let's get going. Captain. I want my new jewelry."

They wave to Tia and ride off. Slowly making their way through town, she grins feeling her sky blue dress flowing behind her in the wind. They come to the *Bloodstones and Runes* in the Third House district. William dismounts and plucks Crystal off his horse with her, letting off a little giggle. The shop is brightly lit with magical flame and wares of all kinds. Exotic items hanging in the windows that William can't fathom what they do. He holds the door for Crystal and she walks regally with many years of practice. She approaches the counter and is greeted by an older Gnome with a typical long white beard and a wide-brimmed hat with a few unlit candles in it. Wearing a royal purple robe, he doesn't look too out of the ordinary to Crystal, but she knows he's very gifted in the ways of magic and enchantment.

"Hello Barnett, do you have my order ready? I got here as soon as I could."

He smiles and is very animated. "AhyesCountess." His speech is fast and spoken with a single swift breath and climbs down off his perch, "I'llgogetthemifyouwillwaitamoment."

William crouches down and whispers. "Does he always talk that fast?"

"He wasn't born here. He's from 'downunderquartz' east of here. So he is still adapting to talking slow enough for regular people to understand."

"But you understand him?"

"Of course. I've been coming to him for all kinds of things over the years, for my parents and such. And he teaches at the academy a few times a week. You get used to it."

The tiny Gnome returns with a small wooden box and hands it to her. "Hereyougoaspromisedhopeyouenjoy."

She opens the box and inside are two bracelets made of gold, with sapphire and emerald gems inlaid in an alternating pattern around the outside, with a prominent diamond at the center. She gets giddy as she slips them on and the magic does its thing. Her clawed hands and feet reform back into her normal Human ones as if nothing happened.

William is amazed. "Those only change your hands and feet? Nothing else?"

"Yes. I've grown to like the other changes. It makes me..." She tilts her head, looking up at him. "Exotic?" She fiddles with them more, so they fit right. "Besides, without my horns, what would I hang my braids from?" She points to the diamonds. "And I can turn them off by hitting the diamonds so I can get my claws back if I need them see?" She taps the diamond on one and her claws come back sharp as ever, then tapping it again gives her normal hands again. "It's just a minor polymorph effect."

William doesn't have a clue what she's talking about, but nods along. "So does that mean you won't be scratching me up anymore when we ride together?"

"That's why I wanted them. I felt bad about that." She looks at the clock. "I believe we have dinner to go to?"

From the moment they arrive at the Sugar Rose and they are the center of attention. He dismounts and plucks her off the back, locking arms, and walks in. *He's been practicing his walk to match mine. He works so hard.* Once inside, she shows the maître d her new signet, giving them a table right away. *It's good to be the countess.* They get a place not too far from the band that's playing, and it allows them to make requests from the minstrels. William and Crystal smile and talk over their appetizers when William spots Andrew and Tia walking up to the restaurant. The maître d' doesn't look like he will let them in at first, but when he turns to see Crystal and William waving them over, he relents and leads them to the table.

"Here you go, ma'am and sir. What will you be drinking tonight?"

Andrew and Tia speak simultaneously, "water." They exchange glances and laugh, looking over the menu.

William looks at them both. "Order what you want. I'm paying for it."

Crystal holds up her wineglass. "Just the way I like it."

The waitress arrives and they order simple meals, a stark contrast to William and Crystal's dinners. Crystal takes a drink from her goblet and sets it down, swallowing. "So, are you excited about getting to fly on the emperor's new airship, uh the...?" She looks to William for help. "What's it called again?"

"The R.H.A.S. Bastion." Then takes another bite of his steak.

She shrugs. "I can't wait myself. It's going to be great being able to claim we got to ride in an actual airship."

Tia looks about the table but says nothing. Andrew speaks up, however. "I'm so excited for you, sis. You've worked hard and getting to realize your dream. You might not be an empress someday like you wanted, but countess isn't too bad at your age. Emperor Marcus must see something in you he likes."

Crystal shrugs her shoulders. "I am superb at this, but I had help from all of you along the way. I could have done it myself, but it would have taken much longer. I'm lucky to have you all helping me."

"That was almost a compliment."

Crystal shoots him a glance, and Tia speaks up finally. "I see you have your normal hands again."

She holds one up, for example. "Yep. These magic bracelets can change them back so I don't have any fear of leaving scratch marks on things I grab too hard. This Dragon awakening thing has been an ordeal to adapt to. It's like everything I touch is fragile now and made of paper." She takes another bite. "I put so many new scratches on dad's table just reaching for things, and my bed is torn to shreds."

This gets a snicker from William as a wide smile appears, but says nothing. She shoots him a dirty look, causing him to chuckle more. Tia doesn't understand, and Andrew just shakes his head in disapproval. They continue their dinner, planning out the next few days. Crystal tries to convince Andrew to come along, but he refuses, stating he has commitments here in Rose Harbor. "Daniel chose Tia for this calling. She's a wonderful person once you get her out of that turtle shell of hers." He reaches out and takes Crystal's hand, getting her full attention. "Heed her council, sis. She won't let you down."

The evening sets in and it's getting late. Andrew and Tia say their goodbyes and head back to the church. Crystal sighs in disappointment. "What's wrong, honey?" She smiles when he calls her that, knowing that he's so ridged in public to never show that affection.

"I feel so sorry for those two."

"Why do you say that? They look content to me."

"Neither one is happy." She places a hand on his arm. "I've always been good at reading people." She turns back to her dessert. "They are both very good at hiding it, but they *like* each other. Just their commitment to the church and Daniel forbids them from what we have. It must be torture."

William thinks about it and how it would affect him if he couldn't be with her now. "Yeah. A vow of celibacy and being around someone you find attractive all the time would be so horrible."

Crystal shoots him a knowing look. "Neither of us took any such vow."

"I know, but I fear your dad more than you." This gets him to let out a deep belly laugh, getting her to join in too.

"Yea, he can be scary, but the real danger is Cline." Her voice gets dark. "Daddy can only *kill* you. Cline is the one who can trap your soul forever."

This doesn't make William any less fearful. *Her family wields a lot of power, and she knows it.*

"Let's take an evening stroll around the city before you drop me off at the house. Take one good last look at our home before we leave it all behind."

They stroll through town and the streets are empty this late at night. The magical firelight casts its glow, causing shadows to dance about. The riffraff of the city keeps their distance from the couple. William still carries his bastard sword on his horse and the heavy armor of its barding tells all those around that he's not an untrained peasant. They make their way back to the Hellstromm Manor and William escorts her to the front door. "I will see you in the morning."

She lays her hands on his chest, leaning in close. "You could stay here in the guest bedroom. Daddy should have your armor ready in the morning. You could get up and have breakfast with us."

William cocks his head slightly, looking down into her ice-colored eyes. "I would take you up on that offer, but I have a feeling that you, or Cline, or possibly both, will end up in there with me and I would be in more trouble than I could reasonably talk my way out of."

She wraps her arms around his neck, pulling him closer, their lips almost touching. Her voice is a purr, pulling his face closer to hers. "Are you saying I'm more trouble than I'm worth?"

He stammers, getting her to give him that impish grin once again. "I didn't say that it's just we shouldn't be doing something like that. It's not honorable."

She kisses him for several long minutes, with him wrapping his own arms around her petite frame. She finally pulls back. "That's what I love about you. You're so honorable." After a long embrace, they finally step away from each other. "See you in the morning, darling." Then she mouths the words, "I love you," so no one can hear.

He does the same in return, wondering why they have to be quiet about it. "See you in the morning, honey." He turns and walks back to his horse. She closes the door and goes upstairs to her bedroom. *Two to three years plus flying there and back. I will have to bring along a lot of clothes.*

CHAPTER 27
(Call of Adventure)

Sally knocks on William's door, and he answers it with a simple razer in his hands. He invites her in and continues trimming up. "Are the monks ready to go?"

"Yes, master William. All preparations are done." She snickers as he tries his best in the mirror. "Careful. The countess has particular tastes." He glances at her momentarily.

"I'm supposed to pick up my new armor today. You should see it, Sally. It's a masterpiece." He cleans up and turns for the door.

"I'm sure it's wonderful if it's made by Mr. Hellstromm himself." She watches him go. "Just stay safe."

William arrives at the Hellstromm house as requested. Cline lets him in and takes him out to the workshop where Jack is still working. He is finishing the last details of getting the leather straps for the helm riveted in. He places it on the armor stand holding the rest of the massive armor when William and Cline arrive.

"Ah, William my boy. Come take a look, it's finished." He drags William over to it. "It's my best non-mechanical work yet."

The sunlight reflects off the red-tinted armor. Shoulder pauldrons angle upward to deflect sword blows away from the head and protect the neck. Joints in the armor are covered by mithril chain backed by leather. The armor is thickened along the forearms and thighs to protect from enemy blows. And the gold trim to make it pop out and be seen. "Let's get it on you, Will. If I did my calculations correctly, it should only feel about ten percent heavier than normal full plate armor, but will protect you so much better." William runs his hands over the smoothness of it, the rivets, and the grooves of the armor. "Stop caressing the thing and put it on. I want to see how you get around to it. The last test of any armor is the person wearing it."

William looks at his reflection in the helm. "Let's do this." Jack and William strap the armor on one piece at a time. Each piece overlaps and fastens the next, interlacing its protection.

Crystal watches from her bedroom window, as William is being encased in the new alloy her father made. *The finest armor ever constructed, and my William is the first to wear it.* She is so proud of that fact. *And they get along so well, as I had hoped they would. I've been dropping hints to William to take it another step forward, but his honor keeps him stationary.* She runs her hand along her neck. *No matter. I always get what I want. It's not a matter of if, but when.* She looks down at her nightgown. *I better get dressed. We might leave today, and I need to look my best.*

She comes down in a very elegant form-fitting plum purple dress with gold thread embroidery, giving accents to her feminine form. Diamonds are sewn into the collar and cuffs, giving a sharp contrast and glimmer as the sunlight hits them, giving off a prismatic effect. She steps out back with William, Jack, and Cline as the last pieces are strapped to him. He's a golem of adamantium, mithril, and this new star metal that was found. He looks implacable in the armor as he flexes and moves around, leaving small indentations in the grass. Every part of the armor deflects incoming blows and absorbs shock from small arms. Jack pins the red and gold-colored cape for the 7rd house's crest to his back breastplate, finishing the ensemble.

Jack gives him a cursory inspection. "So how does it feel?"

William flexes and walks around in it. The metal sliding against metal sounds different from the old steel armor he had when they first met, sounding deeper, more solid sounding. "It feels good. It is heavier, but I feel like I can take a storm of hits in this thing. Hope it doesn't spoil me and I forget how to block or take cover."

Cline catches her attention with his use of her new title. "Countess Crystal, are you wanting breakfast?"

Crystal shakes her head. "I need to get the Vardo loaded up and taken to the palace. I was wondering if my 'personal protector' would escort me there, then take me out for breakfast."

Clines makes his way back to the house. "I'll notify Penelope that you're ready to go."

Jack walks around William as he goes through his motions. "I have something else for you, William." He walks back into his shop and brings out a new bastard sword with a star metal and Mithril scale Damascus pattern to it, a brass guard, and a pommel with a shadow leather wrapped handle. He hands it to William, who is amazed by the craftsmanship.

William grips the new sword and swings it about. "It's light." He hefts it, rolling it around in his hand. "And very well balanced." He walks over to some of the practice dummies and takes a few slashes and swings as it cuts cleanly. "And it's *really* sharp."

Jack smirks. "Just don't drop it on your foot."

William returns and Jack hands him the scabbard for it, also decorated to match his armor in color. William sheaths the sword and attaches it to his old sword's place. He turns to Crystal and holds his arms out. "How do I look?"

She beams and walks up to him, feeling around the armor. "Like my knight in shining armor, ready to sweep me off my feet."

Jack grumbles. "I'm standing right here, you know." She giggles and Jack huffs. "Be glad I like you."

Cline comes back out and informs Crystal her Vardo is ready. Crystal's smile continues to grow in anticipation of the new adventure. Looking at it, Penelope is still driving a team of horses. "I thought you would have upgraded this to steam, daddy."

Jack shakes his head. "If I had installed a boiler and all the other things to get something that heavy to move, you wouldn't have a place to sleep. I would have to design and build one from the ground up and that would take way more than a month." He thumbs at William. "Besides, his armor was taking up all my time."

She gives him a hug. "We should go. Emperor Marcus told us to report when your armor was done and he wanted to get my Vardo loaded. Best not to keep him waiting."

They go to walk away and Jack places a hand on Williams's huge, armored shoulder, stopping him. Crystal doesn't notice and keeps walking. "Normally I would be very protective of Crystal. She's headstrong, arrogant, and very sure of her abilities, but she's still my daughter. You two go well together. I won't deny it. She's had other boyfriends, but you are different."

William turns to look at Jack towering over the much smaller black man. "I will protect her with my life, sir. You have nothing to worry about."

Jack shakes his head. "I know you will, William. That's why I built this marvel of modern armor and weapons, so you can protect her in a way no other man could dream." He clears his throat. "But that's not what I'm talking about. The other relationships she's had barely lasted hours. She's just too…" He motions with his hand, trying to find the word.

"Uncontrollable?"

Jack nods in somewhat agreement. "Yea, that's one way to put it, but somehow, you managed to calm her down. You're just as headstrong as she is, and that keeps her in check." He turns and gets them both walking through the house. "I'm glad she's latched onto you. Just be careful. She has real claws now and once she's gotten a hold of something; she doesn't let go." They walk out front, and Penelope has the Vardo ready, but Crystal isn't in it.

"Waiting for me to help you get inside?"

She shakes her head no. "I'm riding with you; I've gotten used to it." William turns to Jack, and he has a half-smirk on his face of *told you so* and shrugs. "Besides, I want everyone to see me with the most handsome knight in the kingdom and let the ladies be green with envy."

"As you wish, Countess." He mounts up on the heavy warhorse with its own heavy barding. He reaches down, and she takes his hand, pulling her up onto the back of the horse as done often in the past. Her dress and long coal-black braids wrapped in gold flowing behind her. He nods to Penelope and Crystal waves to her father as they take off.

They make their way through town and heads turn at the red and gold knight with his white, purple, and gold passenger hanging onto him. The metal clangs as the warhorse trots along and the Vardo follows. They head to the palace and pull in and the guards recognize them and the Vardo and allow them to pass. Penelope elects to stay there as Crystal and William make their way inside. William's new armor echoes off the walls as they cross the great map in the foyer and cross into the throne room and Marcus sits with his second wife at his side. They both kneel in front of Marcus, but he commands them to rise right away.

Marcus stands, making his way over to the knight walking around him. "This is very impressive armor. This is Jack's best work, no doubt." Marcus goes through the same motions as Jack, asking about how it fits and its flexibility. "That's amazing. Too bad that star metal is so rare of I would have several of these commissioned. It's still missing something, though."

"What would that be, Your Highness?"

"Your rank insignia. Can't be a captain if you don't have the insignia."

"I'm sorry, Your Highness, I'll get one right away."

"Don't bother. I have on right here." Marcus attaches it to the right pauldron.

Crystal has a look of surprise on her face. *That was not in his hand when he walked over here.*

Marcus stands back. "Are you ready to load up? Every moment you're here is a moment not figuring out this Black Rose thing."

William nods in the affirmative. "We brought Vardo to load up. I will gather the others if the troops are ready to go, your highness."

"They are Captain. Please be on your way and get Tia and whoever else you think needs to come along." He motions them along. "But be quick about it." Crystal and William turn to leave, but Marcus' voice booms. "Countess, where are you rushing off to?" This causes them both to stop.

"I'm sorry, Your Highness. I thought you were dismissing both of us. My apologies."

"I figured while Captain Blakely here was out gathering the others, you would like a tour of your ship." Marcus plays on her curiosity and she notes the word *your* in that statement.

Her voice shakes a little. "My ship?"

"It's the ship you're taking to Portstown, so that makes it 'your' ship." He grins, knowing he got her to think he was giving it to her. "You didn't think I'm *giving* it to you, do you?"

Crystal bows her head, hiding her embarrassment. "No, Your Highness. I was temporarily confused. It won't happen again."

"Ambition is good, Countess, but don't let it get out of control. Burn too hot and you will burn out instead of glowing for ages." He turns to William, who is still standing there. "You need to do better at coaching her, Captain Blakely."

"Yes sir. I will help her with that on the trip."

Marcus looks at him quizzically. "Aren't you supposed to be going somewhere?"

William bows his head. "Yes, Your Highness." He leaves with the sound of the armor echoing in the distance.

"Where were we?"

"The ship 'R.H.A.S. Bastion' sire. You were offering me a tour?"

"Ah yes. Follow me." Marcus's second wife, a tall black woman, waves them on.

She bows her head. "I'll hold things here. You two have fun."

They walk and Crystal looks up at the Emperor. "So how many wives do you have if I may ask, Your Highness?"

Marcus doesn't miss a beat. "I have five. My first wife, Skylar, I married out of love, like you and William."

She smiles and flushes a dark pink. "Will and I aren't married, sire." *But I wouldn't say no to the idea.*

Marcus sounds puzzled. "Oh. As much as you enjoy each other's company, I thought you two were in love."

"We are, sire. We just aren't married."

Marcus looks at her with a small smirk. "All you need is love. The other stuff comes later."

"So, about your other four wives? Do you love them all?"

Marcus looks thoughtful, as if composing his answer. "I grew to love them. They are all amazing women in their own rights, but they are of arranged marriages based on peace treaties and empire mergers. There are many cultures out there and some of them are stranger than others." He looks onward. "You can marry whomever you want for any reason, but you need love and compromise to make them work. Just like running an Empire."

Crystal smiles, knowing Marcus is teaching her a life lesson as her own father would. *He might be big and scary, but he's a father and looks to us all as his children.* They come to the back door of the palace leading into the massive rear courtyard and Crystal is almost floored by the size of the Bastion. It's easily the size of a frigate sailing ship. It just has no masts and is made of metal. *It's shaped a little strange, but it's not meant to go into the water, so maybe they based it more off a bird?* They walk up to it and the Vardo is being brought around the side. Crystal can see that Penelope is also boggling at the size of it. "Can my servant Shadow be part of the tour, Your

Highness? She's my personal chef and is coming with me on the trip. If not, I won't press the issue."

Marcus looks over at the Halfling. "Sure. If you trust her, then I do too, wave her over."

Crystal smiles and raises one ivory white arm and waves at Penelope, motioning her over. She dismounts as a guard takes over, bringing it into the ship, and makes her way to Crystal and Marcus. And she kneels before him. "You summoned me, Mistress?"

Marcus chuckles. "Rise child. I asked her to wave you here."

She stands up slowly. "I am honored, Your Highness."

"I was about to have Crystal be given a tour of the ship and she asked for you to come along, little one."

"Thank you for thinking of me, Mistress."

Marcus corrects her with a stern look. "Countess."

She swallows hard and bows her head again. "Countess. Forgive my error."

Marcus waves them to follow. "It's a modern-day wonder. Everything has been updated with the highest qualities..." Marcus talks for long minutes about what he knows of the ship and boasts about it as anyone would. He turns to Crystal. "Speaking of modern marvels. Have you heard of this telegraph thing the Empire of Naerth invented?"

"No, sire."

"I'll tell you about it when you get back." He looks at the time. "You best be going."

They arrive at Crystal's private cabin. It's very luxurious, with several windows on the port side. It has a private bath and kitchen for personal staff. There is a second door that leads to the next cabin, which is designated for her personal guard or staff member, like a servant, to stay. Each cabin has an exit that leads to another cabin and to the main hallway. Marcus explains that it's his room when using it, but since she's the ranking official, it's hers to use as she pleases.

He shows them the bridge and all the fancy gadgets with polished copper and brass fittings and pressure gauges. Dwarves, Gnomes, and a handful of Humans operate everything. Marcus puts his hands on one. "This fine lass is Captain Kala Zylra." He points to a stout four-foot female Dwarf. She has long pulled-back hair of spun

254

copper the length of her back, and she wears the blue and purple uniform of the Royal Navy. "She knows this ship from bow to stern and to the keel with every nut and bolt of this ship, so I'll let her give you the tour. I must get back to my second wife before she misses me."

Crystal and Penelope both shake the captain's hand as Marcus exits. "So, you must be Countess Crystal?"

"I am." She introduces Penelope. "And this is my personal chef, Shadow." She glances around the bridge. "It's a beautiful ship. I can't wait to see the rest of it."

They walk the boat and Captain Zylra shows them everything. The galley, the holds, the guns. They work their way down to the engine room and it gets more cramped. Crystal is thankful for once she is so small and petite. *Will would be hard-pressed to be in an area like this.* Kala brings them to the "heart" of the ship.

"This ship has eight boilers that run everything from the weapons to propulsion and even maneuverability. The compartments on the older ships were way larger, but thanks to Jack Hellstromm's newest designs, they are more compact. By binding a fire elemental inside the boiler, we no longer need to carry tons and tons of coal. We just need a water tank that we can recycle the water from for an infinite energy supply." She looks back at them. "And I know, how do we 'fly'? The ship's individual armor plates have mass reduction magic cast on them, making them weigh less, so we only need to adjust the ballast to float into the air. By letting the hot air in the steam expand between the hulls, we float, and by redirecting it to the radiators it cools faster, bringing us down."

She continues her techno-jargon. Crystal having grown up with the man who built everything here knows more about it than the Dwarf does. But she's trying her best not to speak over her. She's the Captain of the ship and it wouldn't be right to embarrass her. Crystal is biting her tongue, but she wants to set a good example to show Will she can change.

They finish the tour and get back to her estate cabin. "Captain, with this ship, how long will it take to get to Portstown by air?"

"About eight days, Countess, barring any unforeseen turbulence."

"Could you have one of your men go down to the hold with Shadow here and bring up my clothing, then? Since I'm bunking here a few days, I'm going to enjoy myself."

Zylra bows her head. "At once Countess."

Crystal walks into her cabin and sees the silken sheets on the canopy bed, and places a hand on it. *It's as soft as a cloud.* Checking the refrigerator, there is fresh water and an arrangement of juices. "I could get used to this." There are books on the entertainment shelf mostly referring to sailing, but Marcus had books about Portstown and New Haven stocked for her to read about their cultures. She can hear the clanging of metal on the deck plates, and she knows that means William is coming. Her smile grows at his approach and knocks on the cabin door. She bids him enter as she sits on the bed, legs crossed and leaning back slightly, looking as seductive as possible.

William hasn't removed his helm yet, and he's glad for it. His jaw unhinges, and he turns several shades of pink, fighting the dishonorable thoughts trying to enter his mind. *Jack is trusting you*, repeats in his head as he looks upon her. "Everyone is here and being assigned to their cabins, Countess."

She slowly stands up and speaks a short incantation and flicks her wrist, shutting the door behind him. She saunters over to him and reaches up, removing his helm. "I made sure to save you the next cabin over joining mine. I wouldn't want my *bodyguard* to be too far away, would I?" She wraps her arms around his neck, pulling him down. They kiss passionately for a few moments, only pulling away when there is a knock on the door. She tosses his helm back to him and he slides it on with a fluid motion.

"It's open!" Crystal calls, her voice cracking a little. Penelope and a sailor walk in with her clothing. "Where would you like this stuff, Countess?"

"In the closet?"

Penelope motions with her head at the sailor and they get to work. William turns back to Crystal. "I'm going to my cabin and get my own things set up." They both exit through the joining door and close it, hearing the sailors move her stuff in.

"It's getting harder and harder, isn't it?"

William knows how she likes to play on words. "What is?"

She gives him an impish grin. "Getting private time for just us."

He takes his helm off and sets it on the desk that's in the room. Walking over to her, he wraps his enormous arms around her. "We've got private time. We ride all over the town together."

"That's still public. I mean, just you, me, and no one else."

"You do have your own private cabin. Why don't we have dinner tonight, just us then?"

Crystal's grin grows, exposing her new fangs that are almost predatory, and cranes her neck to look up at him. "I would like that very much"

"But first, I need to remove this armor. I won't need it while on the ship. I can just wear my normal uniform."

Her eyebrow shoots up and holds up a finger. "I can help you with that."

He backpedals, causing her to snicker. "Oh, no. No way. I've seen what that spell can do. Just what we don't need is sixty pounds of metal slamming into the deck plates to make a sound that your father could probably hear."

She looks at him with her head turned and tilted down but glancing up at him all innocent looking. "Is that the real reason, or are you afraid I won't be able to control myself?"

"Both." He steps back and sits down at the table and unbuckles his armor. She walks over to him and helps, pulling the armor plates and chain-mail from his body carefully. Penelope enters with Crystal standing behind William, getting the buckles for his breastplate. "Everything alright?"

Crystal groans, pulling on the leather straps. "Daddy really knew how to keep this stuff on. You might have to sleep in it."

Penelope turns away and leaves back through the door she came in, closing it back behind her. William gets the last of the buckles for the greaves and takes them off. She finishes the last buckle for the breastplate and removes it, setting it on the bed. "What do you want for dinner, darling?" Crystal wraps her hands around him from the back and plays with his chest hair.

William thinks about it. "Not sure. Do you have any suggestions?"

She places her head on his shoulders. "It's been a while since we had salmon. Think they have any onboard?"

He turns his to her. "That, I don't know."

Marcus watches his ship fly away, then turns to Skylar. "The second test has begun. She's very driven to earn her place, even though she is clueless about what her place is going to be."

"She suspects nothing?"

Marcus turns and joins Skylar on the bed. "Not a thing, but I have to wonder if Jack knows what's happening. I need to speak with him soon about this."

"He raised her quite well, as if anticipating this. He's probably expecting your summons at any time."

CHAPTER 28
(The Bastion)

Tia sets down her altar on the desk and lays out her candles in her own cabin. Andrew is helping her with the bags of stuff she bought. "Hope you didn't forget anything."

"Just toss that on the floor." He has no problem doing as he is told, and she digs into one. "I'm just making sure I'm prepared this time. We could be gone for a full two and a half to three years and I don't know what we might run into." She holds up some herbs and vials. "I was not prepared for the first trip and people were dying. I couldn't do anything about it, so I brought some healing salves and some powerful elixirs for every situation."

"That first trip gave you a lot of experience."

She turns with a somber look. "I wish you were coming with us. I could use the help here, but I know how awkward it would be with your sister in charge."

"Yeah, she might be focused on me if bad things happen instead of doing the right thing. I've never been good at the combat thing. Crystal is the fighter."

"Well, I think you're great." Tia puts the stuff down on her desk. "I'm glad you answered your calling and came to the church to me." Surprise crosses her face for a second and gets frustrated. "Us. I mean us. You know what I meant. My mind is all over the place with this stuff. I've never flown before."

Tyra comes in hunched over with a handful of her own items. "This isn't fun for me either." Tossing them to the side, she walks over and sits on her cot, which creaks under her weight. "Oh yeah, I see this going well."

Tom chuckles from the doorway. "Should I just have them bring you a bunch of pillows to throw on the floor to sleep on?"

Tyra looks up at him and squints her eyes. "Would you?"

Tom laughs, holding his hands up. "I was being serious. I've seen you angry and sleep-deprived. This ship wouldn't survive one of your rage attacks."

Tyra looks at him and sighs. "Well, they sure didn't have someone like me in mind when they designed it."

Tom shrugs. "Have you seen the crew? They are shorter than Crystal, and that's saying something." This caused a chuckle from everyone in the room but Andrew. "But seriously, I'll see if I can make you a bed, sis. Give me a few minutes while I drop off my stuff."

Tom exits and goes to his own cabin assignment. Entering the room, Tom notices Penelope changing and averts his eyes. She screams, grabbing a blanket to cover herself.

"So sorry." Tom spins fast away from her. "I was assigned these quarters. I didn't know I would be bunking with a woman, or I would have knocked. I swear I didn't see anything."

She hurriedly gets dressed. "Yea, that's odd that they would do that. They must be short on space."

"We could hang up a blanket or something to split the room for your privacy."

"That's a good idea. I would hate to have to kill you in your sleep."

Tom chuckles, putting his stuff down. "You wouldn't do that."

"You're right, I would stab you right in the chest so you knew it was me as your life drained away."

Tom glances at her and the look she is giving him sends a shiver up his spine. *Note to self, knock before entering to stay alive.* He looks around. "Do you know where some extra linens are? Tyra can't sleep on the cot provided, so I'm hoping to make her a decent makeshift bed out of something."

"Well, we are still on the ground. If you're fast, you might be able to requisition some from the quartermaster on duty before we leave. Better hurry, we are lifting off soon."

"I'll be back in a flash." He gets down the ramp and Dwarves and Humans are finishing the preparations for liftoff, and he grabs one's attention. "Where's the quartermaster's office and how long till departure?"

The Dwarven man points. "He's in that building way over there and about thirty minutes if you're leaving with them."

Tom dashes across the distance in only a few minutes. His speed was enhanced from years of training and running from Tyra's anger. *Nothing makes you fast, like an angry Minotaur chasing you.*

He gets to the building the Dwarf pointed him to and knocks on the door. A mid-sized Human answers. Tom explains what he's after and that he's a member of Countess Hellstromm's retinue. The quartermaster nods and hands him extra blankets and many pillows as he can reasonably carry.

He dashes back as the mooring lines are being cast. The boarding ramp is retracting and he leaps. Running along the ramp, the door on the side of the ship opens with Penelope standing there. "You almost missed the boat."

He pats her on the shoulder. "It was worth it." He knocks on the girls' door and Tia allows him inside. "I did what I could. Hope this helps."

Tyra takes the pillows and other items and moves the cot. "I will make it work. Thank you." She returns to him and picks him up, giving him a hug. "Thanks for looking out for me, as always."

Tom returns to his cabin and opens the door, and stops. He knocks and gets no answer. He peeks in, ready to catch a thrown dagger, but none comes. *Oh good, she's not here.* He unpacks and makes himself comfortable. They have eight days before the work begins, according to Crystal. He sits on the floor crossed-legged and meditates.

The ship takes to the sky and Crystal can see everything from her windows. Penelope is in the kitchen preparing her and William's meal. She's disappointed there is no salmon on board, so they settled on duck instead. A knock at the door causes her to fling the door open with a minor spell, letting William inside. He joins her and gazes out the window, watching the city shrink under them as they make their way to the eastern mountain range. She was informed by the captain that going through the one to the east first would be difficult, but it's a shorter route than going around to the north. So best to just go through here first and shorten the travel time.

She wraps her arm around his waist. "It's amazing from up here. You can see where the two ranges meet up by Black Rock from here."

"Yeah, you can."

"Shadow?"

Penelope calls from the other room. "Yes, Countess."

"How long till dinner is served?"

"About thirty minutes Countess."

Crystal looks up at William. "You want to take a stroll around the upper deck?" He looks down at her and knows the only answer is yes. They walk out and Tia is standing out there, her cleric robes blowing in the wind as she leans on the railing.

"Be careful." William glances over the side. "That's a long fall to think about all your mistakes before you hit the ground."

Tia nods but says nothing. Crystal looks up and whispers to him. "Remember what I said at dinner the other day?" He looks at her, then back at Tia.

Crystal pats him on the arm and goes to stand next to Tia. She looks out, and it's one hell of a view. The sun is almost right above them, casting the ship's shadow down on the trees below. Birds fly past them and they can see the river's winding course and a large lake. The rush of the wind blows past them, making it chilly out on the deck.

Crystal leans on the railing with her. "What troubles you, Tia?"

Tia looks over, her blond hair blowing past her face. "What makes you think I'm troubled?"

"A hunch."

"I've never gone so far from home. I know this is an important mission, but I'm going to miss Rose Harbor."

"Homesick already?" Crystal's tone shifts a little lighter. "Or do you miss someone in particular?"

"Just homesick, Countess."

Crystal turns and looks at her. "If you want to tell me anything, you can. I know I don't look like it, but I'm good at keeping secrets. I would probably only tell William, and that would only be to get his advice because I'm not good at this whole life lesson thing."

Tia shakes her head negatively. "I'm just homesick. I promise, that's all." Crystal can tell she's lying but doesn't press the issue, knowing all too well the truth.

"If you want to talk, I'm available for you. William and I are going on a short walk to see the sights, then go eat dinner."

Four days go by, and they are halfway there. The shimmer of the Quartz Desert passing beneath them reminds them of the stars at night. It's warmer than usual here, but the breeze from the ship's movement keeps Crystal from having too much trouble. She spends a lot of time out on the deck, sitting in a lounge chair with the rest of the group. Being cooped up in the cabin would drive them all crazy. William and Tom do some light sparring, keeping to the center of the ship so as not to fall off by accident. Crystal watches William flex and move those wire-like muscles moving under his skin.

Tia sits down next to her on the deck. "Now you're the one who looks troubled."

"I guess so." Crystal gazes at the man. "He's incredible, isn't he?" She scrunches her nose. "The perfect warrior. Noble, honorable, truthful, strong in force, but gentle in touch."

"And completely loyal to you." Tia sounds almost jealous, getting Crystal to look askance at her. She looks away, putting her head down. "You have something many look for their whole lives."

Crystal turns fully to her and becomes more assertive in her tone. "You found it too, didn't you?"

Her head comes up, but she doesn't face Crystal. "Found what?"

"Love, of course."

Tia blushes, trying to push the feelings away. "I don't know what you're talking about. I love my god and that's, that."

"We are both in the same boat, no pun intended." Crystal turns her gaze back to look at William.

"How so? You can act on your love. I made a vow. We both did. To go against it would mean losing our connection to our god."

"So, I was right all along. You have feelings for my brother." Tia turns a brighter red, but Crystal calms her down. "It's ok. I won't tell anyone."

"You don't understand. I'm not allowed to have these feelings." Tia looks up at the sky. "Not for anyone but Daniel."

"I don't know much about gods, but I know they do some weird stuff with us sometimes. Maybe it's a sign that he wants the church to change? Something to pray to him about to get an answer?" Crystal contemplates. "I might have to pray to him, too."

"For what?"

"Guidance. How do I get that man, a man I know, loves me beyond life itself, to make the next move?" Crystal sounds frustrated.

"He adores you. What next move are you saying? Marriage?"

Crystal shrugs, glancing at her for a moment. "Maybe someday. I wouldn't say no if he proposed." She sighs, closing her eyes for a moment. "I don't know what I want. Maybe it's best if he stays so chivalrous. Provider knows what I would be doing to the poor guy."

Tia blushes more. "That's not something you should think about before marriage, Countess."

"And that's the problem we both share. We both want something. Neither of us can get it." Crystal opens her eyes again and tilts her head to Tia. "It's infuriating and frustrating."

"That it is." Tia shrugs. "That's just how destiny works, I'm afraid."

Tia watches as Crystal grins big, exposing some of her new short Dragon fangs. The first time Tia ever saw them like that and it frightens her a little. "I shape my own fate and I refuse to be led around by the nose by 'destiny'." She gets up and looks down at the blond woman. "Thanks for the council, Tia."

Crystal knows more spells as her connection to her Dragon blood grows. Ideas come to her and stay and she will put them to good use. She and William have dinner that night, and they talk, but she plans to get what she desires. No one will stop her from what she wants. Night falls and everyone retires to their rooms. Crystal lays in her bed in her nightgown gazing out into the darkness. The moon will be full again tomorrow and it casts enough light now she can see.

She climbs out of bed standing up. Concentrating on the blood in her veins, she pulls the magic and starts an incantation. She knows the spell because her mom knew the spell as well when she was her age. Feeling nervous as she finishes, then vanishes from sight. Using her master key to unlock the door to William's room, she slowly opens it. It squeaks a little, but the other noises of the ship mask it well. She closes it as softly as she can, then walks over to the sleeping man.

He has a regular bed, not as fancy as hers, but at least it's not a cot. *What am I doing?* Her mind is a whirlwind of confusion, not knowing what she's about to do. *I so want this, but what if he gets upset? When if he rejects me for being so forward?* She closes her distance with the sleeping man getting up next to him. *For all I know, he wants this to happen too, but his honor is keeping him away. No, I*

264

shouldn't do this. I could ruin that honor. She reaches up and grabs her own horns in frustration. *What is wrong with me? I had a plan but now look at me cower. I should just do it and accept the consequences?*

She steps back to flee and trips over a table, knocking it over and scattering its contents. This causes her fragile invisibility to break and for William to sit up fast, scanning for enemies but only the silhouette of Crystal in her nightgown lit by moonlight. "Crystal, why are you in here?"

She sits down in a chair and puts her face in her hands. "How do I say this without offending you?"

William sits nearly at the bed, placing his hand on her. "Did I do something wrong?"

She shakes her head. "I came in here intending to seduce you. To force you to take our relationship to the next stage." She glances up at him. "But I just couldn't do it. I know your honor means a lot to you." She looks down, not knowing what else to say.

He understands with all the hints she's dropped. "You're the most beautiful woman I've ever laid eyes on, and I've had a really hard time keeping myself in check." He lifts her chin up to gaze into her eyes. "And honestly, had you climbed into bed with me, I don't think I could've stopped myself."

"So, you do feel as I do?"

"I do. I just couldn't believe you wanted into my bed, of all things. I thought it was just teasing." He scratches the back of his head. "I appreciate you thinking about my honor and you're right, it wouldn't look well on either of us."

She smiles and stands up. "Then let's compromise then." He looks confused as she pulls him to his feet. "Climb into mine, and damn anyone who denies our love."

The next morning William awakens with Crystal laying on top of him. She's been using him as her personal pillow all night. He's not sure if he did the right thing or not, but the smile on her face, even while sleeping, is good enough for him. The sounds of staff and getting up and starting their morning routines reminds him of where he is. He nudges Crystal awake, and she looks up at him smiling, then gives him a good morning kiss. "I need to get back to my room before someone realizes I'm missing."

They get up and she gathers up her clothes and walks over and drops them in the hamper. He's glad he can finally look upon her and not be completely embarrassed over it because she walks around with no modesty in mind. *She seems much happier now that she can ask me about her clothing options.* Both of their heads come around as someone knocks on his door. He puts his pants on and gives her a quick kiss before exiting to his room. Crystal quietly closes the adjoining room door and stands there, listening in.

He opens it, and Tia is standing there. "Captain William, you're not dressed?"

William looks down. "I'm wearing my bed shorts. I'm not naked."

"Can I come in?" Not waiting for an answer, she barges past him.

"Uh, sure." He closes the door after the fact. "What's on your mind, Tia?"

"I have a problem, and I think you might be the most qualified to help me with it." She sits down. "What happened in here? The table is turned over."

William freezes. *What do I say to that? I can't tell her the truth, but I can't lie either.*

Tia doesn't bother for an answer continuing. Her speech is faster than normal, catching him off-guard. "Anyway, I talked to Crystal, and I think that it might have been a mistake. I should have talked to you."

"I think you've had too much coffee this morning, but what do you want to know?" He sits on his bed facing her.

"You love Crystal, right? Like, no question in your mind."

"No question. I would lay my life down on the line for her again, knowing that there was no chance at all coming back."

She looks him in the eyes. "So why do you let your honor stop you from bedding with her?"

William sweats a little, trying to formulate a thought. Crystal covers her mouth, stopping herself from bursting. "I don't think it's a matter of honor completely. It's certainly a large part of it. We love

266

each other and that's a natural function of love, but we are both building our careers and it's being respectful of her father." He leans back and glances at the joining door. "But I believe if the conditions were right, maybe we could." He turns back to her, placing a hand on her shoulder. "Why are you wanting to know?"

Tia looks down. "I've had some impure thoughts and I have no one to confess to and you're so honorable, so I figure I could confide in you."

"Slow down, tiger." He takes a deep breath. *I'm completely over my head here.* "Take a deep breath and carefully explain the problem."

"I-think-I'm-in-love-with-Andrew-but-his-and-my-commitment-to-our-god-means-I-can't-act-on-it-and-it's-driving-me-crazy." She speaks so fast that William has a flashback of the Gnome.

"Well…" William glances back at the door and can only imagine Crystal rolling right now. "That's, uh. I'm not a scholar of religion. I'm sure this ship has a chapel, you can ask." He looks down. "I'm not one—"

She cuts him off. "How do you keep resisting, Crystal? What's your secret?"

He puts his hands up. "Resisting Crystal?" He lets off a nervous chuckle. "I don't think that's possible. Not over long-term."

Damn straight. I always win, and I always get what I want.

"Look, the only advice I can give you is to do what you feel is right." He puts his hands down, gripping the bed lightly. "But since this isn't a matter of honor, but religion, I can't help you. I really wish I could. If this was a matter of honor, you would just have to speak with him about it and get an understanding between you." William clasps his hands in front of him. "But this is a religious matter and is beyond my expertise." After a long pause, he heads to the door, grabbing a shirt along the way. She stands up, still looking at the floor, and makes her way to the exit. He opens the door for her but she exclaims, getting his attention once more.

"Captain, you're injured!"

He raises an eyebrow. "Injured?" He looks around himself and sees no wound. "What do you mean?"

"You have a bunch of scratches on your ba—" She stops speaking and glows red. William and Crystal both panic with the fear of being caught. "Never mind. I'm sure it's nothing." She races out the door. "I'm going to go do my prayers and you and the countess have a nice breakfast."

He closes the door and Crystal opens the one, joining their rooms. "That could have gone better."

William grins and puts his shirt on. "Speaking of breakfast, what would you like to eat?"

CHAPTER 29
(Portstown)

Tia has been avoiding Crystal and William, turning red with embarrassment every time she runs into them. Crystal finally corners her on the bow of the ship so she can talk to her. Tia looks down, holding her hands in front of her. "I said nothing to anyone, Countess."

Crystal sighs. "Look, I want to talk to you about that woman to woman. Could you give me a moment here so you will stop fleeing? You can't be a very good counsel and source of wisdom if you can't look me in the eye." Tia gives a subtle nod of her head but still doesn't lookup. Crystal crouches down, getting under her face. "Up here please, don't want to stab you with my horns."

This gets Tia to giggle. "I didn't know you and he took it that far. I'm sorry if I ruined anything."

"Look." Tia continues to look down. Crystal pulls her head up enough to see her making eye contact. "Look what Will and I did. We talked about it first and decided to take that leap together. I didn't cast a spell on him or throw myself onto him, although to be honest, I was really considering it." She looks away a moment. "But we talked about it and our feelings for each other. We know we must hide it because it will interfere with our business and make our families angry."

"I didn't mean to find out."

"I know that. That's why I'm not tossing you off the side right now." Tia's eyes go wide, causing Crystal to sigh. "It's a joke." She shakes her head. "Will has been trying to get me to be more humorous, but I take it my punch line needs more work." She waves flippantly. "But I took control of my destiny. You should too." Crystal walks over to the side and looks out, and can see a city in the distance. "If you have a chance to be happy, take it." Turning back at the poor Half-Elf. "Make your own way, but now it seems we need to get ready for the big day."

Crystal informs everyone to look their best as this is a diplomatic mission as soon as they land, and she will not tolerate screw-ups. The ship lands outside the walls, far enough as to not be seen as a threat. A yellow and white-furred Catfolk, that could be easily mistaken as an upright tabby cat, approaches the airship with a detachment of guards. He is wearing purple and white robes with a small, white round hat, looking important. The guards are a mix of Catfolk and other races Crystal hasn't seen. The guards carry the standard of Portstown in the same colors as the tall Catfolk. Crystal wears a full dress and train of red and purple, the Rose Empire colors, that sparkles with rubies and purple diamonds. Penelope wears a dress with a similar color pattern and William, in his full armor, walks to her side, closing the gap. Tia wears her traditional brown robes of her faith but is already regretting it as the temperatures here are higher.

They meet halfway and Crystal extends her ivory white hand and the large yellow and white Catfolk man takes it in return. Speaking at regally as she can, she introduces herself and her retinue. "I am Countess Crystal Hellstromm of the Rose Empire, here on official business on behalf of His Highness, Emperor Marcus Rose." Indicating her hand to the tall red knight. "This is my personal bodyguard, as well as the captain of the troops I brought with me, Sir William Blakely."

The tall Catfolk stands just taller than William, smiles with his fangs exposed but doesn't look menacing in the least. "I am Karasharr Raaoun of Portstown, adjutant to Baron Murau Tenishar." He motions to his left to a black furred Catfolk with streaks of silver wearing a steel breastplate, and chain-mail. "This is our Captain of the Guard Zaros Motsana." Crystal and William shake hands with him, showing friendliness. "We saw the airship fly overhead and gave us a small scare till our spotter recognized the Rose Harbor Standard." He looks back at his squad, then returns to Crystal, spreading his hands wide. "None of us knew such wonders were possible."

"That's why I'm here Adjutant Raaoun." Crystal pronounces his name as a native, having practiced on the flight there. "I wish to speak with Baron Tenishar about our relationship with each other. We, the Rose Empire, are hoping to improve our relations further." The clanking of metal on metal in a steady rhythm gets Karasharr to look up at the ship and see large suits of armor belching out black smoke and fire from their backs. Huge swords attached to the arms with monstrous shields make them look like giant fire-breathing knights.

His face changes from happiness to shock, and Crystal picks up on it. "Adjutant Raaoun, on behalf of the Rose Empire, I present gifts to the Baron and the people of Portstown. I would like to present these to Baron Tenishar himself." She grins largely, showing fangs herself, returning his gesture from earlier.

There are dozens, if not hundreds, of citizens walking out of the inner walls of the city to speculate and gaze upon the flying ship and the mechanical marvels. The adjutant's smile returns. "Well Countess Crystal, I will happily escort you and your personal bodyguard to see the Baron, and the rest may stay in town and partake of our humble city and enjoy our hospitality. Welcome to Portstown."

They turn and she falls in step with him, William and Captain Motsana falling in step behind them. William is only a head taller than Motsana, but the Catfolk are displaying nervousness. He chalks it up to the difference in armor. William is encased in the best alloy known to the Rose Empire, and Motsana is only wearing a breastplate-covered chain. *I'm clearly the superior warrior.*

Just as Crystal is doing, William follows by starting small talk, with Motsana trying to put him at ease. It seems to work as they get to the gates; he's chattier. William notes the difference between the two nation-states. *The Rose Empire troops are heavily armed and armored, but not wearing the colors of the empire. Portstown's guards are lightly armored but armed with curved swords known as a Talwar. A select few walks with Patas known as gauntlet swords. Very unusual weapons.* William notes other things. *Glad I studied the information Crystal gave me.* William, while talking to Motsana, also notes he has a Moplah hanging on his back. A light, double-edged sword with a curved blade that got larger as it got longer, putting all the weight into the striking edge. William is sure it could be devastating in combat against even armored opponents.

The crowd parts as they approach, and hushed whispers and comments in several tongues are spoken. Crystal looks at them as she continues to talk. *This place might not be as big as Rose Harbor, but it's just as diverse.* The buildings are white, with large timbers holding them together. More official buildings look to be of hewed stone, but the common ones look to be made of plaster, clay, and wood. The procession continues and the newness of their presence wears off to some, but others are curious. A small Catfolk girl of copper and white fur runs up to Crystal, causing her to stop. The tiny girl, who couldn't be over five or six in Human terms, holds up a white lily-like flower. Crystal crouches down, putting herself closer to the tiny Catfolk. In a kind voice, she reaches out. "Is that for me?"

The girl holds it out with a wide smile. "A white flower for you, white lady of the sky."

Crystal takes the flower and kisses the young girl on the head. "Thank you so much, little one. It's beautiful." She adds it to the top of her braids hanging from her horns. "I'll cherish it, thank you." She stands up and the little girl runs back to her mother. She turns to look at William and he is just amazed how she can just incorporate anything into her outfit, and make it look like it belonged there all along.

They come to a large keep close to the shore and William guesses it was a port side fortress before being converted into a government building. They pass through its gates, and there are hundreds of Catfolk along with Dwarves, Centaurs, Sand Elves, and dark-colored Humans training together. William can appreciate such things. *Working together, building off each other's strengths, just like we do in Rose Harbor.* They come to a halt as Adjutant Raaoun turns. "Please enjoy our city. From here, only the countess and her personal bodyguard may continue." He indicates to another building. "But please have some food from our mess hall and feel free to train with others here."

Crystal and William follow Karasharr and Zaros up some stone steps to the third floor. The metal clangs against stone resounding through the long hallways. Traveling down a long hallway that ends in a pair of heavy double red doors, the guards on either side open them with a creaking noise. Inside are several more Catfolk, a Sand Elf, and a few Humans, all working on different minor projects. Beyond this chamber is another set of red doors. Crystal assumes is where the Baron himself is.

"This is far as your bodyguard may go. Baron Tenishar is waiting for you to enter. As soon as it was confirmed it was a Rose Harbor ship, he wanted to meet the one in charge. You will have your privacy with him." Adjutant Raaoun steps aside and opens the door.

"Thank you, Adjutant Raaoun. You serve the Baron well."

He closes it behind her and looks at William. "Captain Blakely, you can post yourself next to the door as your duty demands, but please do not enter unless you absolutely must. Captain Motsana will stand opposite you, also on guard. I hope you understand."

William takes his place next to the door. "I do, and thank you for the courtesy." He stands there unmoving for the long hours Crystal is in there, stoic in his duty.

Crystal enters the large chamber. Paintings and tapestries line the walls and wall sconces are attached to the pillars holding up the tall ceiling. At the far end is a large oak wooden desk covered in papers, figurines, and other trinkets. Behind the desk is a large Catfolk, easily standing close to seven feet tall. His fur is smoke gray and black striped, and wearing white cotton clothing with a purple belt and assents, his golden yellow eyes seem to glow.

He steps around his desk and towers over the much smaller Crystal. He's very fit, but you couldn't tell under all that fur. He extends a hand in friendship, and she takes it while dipping into a curtsy, bowing her head in respect. His voice is deep like Marcus's but lacks the booming weight of the same authority. "I am Baron Marou Tenishar, and you are?"

She keeps her regal tone. "Countess Crystal Hellstromm. I'm here on behalf of his Highness Emperor Marcus Rose. I have his authority to conduct business and negotiation." She shows him the signet crest of the first house.

He smiles, showing his fangs, and she returns the gesture. She learned that in their culture, showing fangs if you had them, was to acknowledge the other as a fellow survivor and apex predator. He points to a large plush chair with an open palm and returns to his own chair. Crystal waits to let him sit first, showing he's in the place of authority over her.

"What brings you to my humble city?"

"I'm here to negotiate terms of including your town under the banner of the Rose Empire. As a gesture of goodwill and mutual support, I offer as a gift of five steam-powered armors along with instructions for their use, maintenance, and capabilities, as well as several crates of advanced weapons."

"We already have a trade agreement with Rose Harbor and a non-aggression pact. Why should we agree to be part of your empire?"

"There is more to the world. We must band together. Rose Harbor is powerful, but even the mightiest of empires can fall from outside influences." She folds her hand in her lap. "And we've learned of a recent threat coming from New Haven to the north. So, this had concerns you might be under threat too. We felt we should come to your aid before it was too late."

"There are some who say that Rose Harbor is the threat. That you will eventually bring your armies here to conquer us." He leans forward, resting his elbows on the desk. "Why shouldn't I believe them over you?"

"Baron, we are offering you some of the most destructive military pieces of hardware for free." She places a hand on her chest. "If we wanted to conquer you, it wouldn't be necessary. But conquest only leads to death, resentment, and oppression. We don't want that. If we came in here, destroyed your walls, killed your troops, and destroyed the buildings in a bloody war, neither side would come out ahead no matter who won." She crosses her legs and leans back, getting comfortable. "But if we were under one banner, more of these battle suits and a well-armed garrison armed with the latest technology would be at your disposal. What I'm offering is you get to keep this place and run it how you feel. You will still be Baron here. The troops we send to reinforce your borders will be yours to command, and you can request additional help. Plus, you will have the full might of our industry to help build up yours."

He sits up but doesn't remove his elbows. "So, what's in it for Rose Harbor? You can't make me believe that all this is free in exchange for loyalty for a crown thirty-seven hundred miles away."

"No, of course not. In exchange, there will be a new tax that will go to maintaining those troops. This allows us to dock our ships here without suspicion and stop the smuggling of goods into our empire from here. The trade will be better since there won't be any import/export taxes bringing more business for both of us."

He leans back all the way. "So, you tax us, we get better, more advanced military equipment and better trade?"

"Not just military equipment. We have advanced farming tools to help increase crop yields, better methods of transportation, advanced metallurgy, and teaching. We have much to offer you."

They talk back and forth, negotiating for hours, hammering out minor details, and establishing a rule of law under the agreement. Both take notes for later, but the sunsets to the west, disappearing into the savanna. They laugh and joke and share stories and anecdotes. As the meeting ends, Baron Tenishar reveals something that shakes Crystal's confidence.

"About a month ago, I had someone in here who was a member of something called the Black Rose. They claimed they were representing Rose Harbor and threatened us if we didn't give them money and supplies, that the Rose Empire would crush us and just take it. Do these people work for Emperor Marcus?"

Crystal's face betrays her feelings of anger from what they did to her. "No, they do not. They are wanted fugitives and terrorists. I have a personal grudge against them myself for poisoning me and attempting to assassinate me. They use false pretenses to cause good citizens to rebel and it gets people hurt and killed." She turns to the floor as tears well up in thought. "They even killed the one I love."

Marou nods his fluffy head. "That I believe. You're an excellent negotiator, but you can't completely control your genuine feelings. Therefore, I'm going to believe you about the Black Rose. We can continue these negotiations in the morning. I am looking forward to your beauty gracing my office again." He smiles with fangs bared and she returns the gesture.

William and Motsana turn to face them as they exit the chamber. "Captain Motsana, make sure these two find their way home." They travel down and out, reaching the courtyard. Crystal stumbles having William catch her. She looks up at him, not speaking, and shakes her head. As it gets darker, they notice the streetlamps are spaced much farther apart, keeping the streets dim. The full moon is starting its climb, casting its own shadows over the city. Crystal can't decide if it looks romantic or frightening.

CHAPTER 30
(Water of Life)

It doesn't take long for them to get to the embassy. Captain Motsana leaves them as they enter the gates. Crystal and William can smell Penelope's cooking from there. The red and gold Vardo is parked inside the gates, along with William's heavy warhorse and several wagons of supplies. The clanking of William's armor alerts the guards to their presence, causing them to drop what they are doing and salute.

They enter the central hall where others have gathered and William removes his helmet, taking a deep breath, sweat pouring off his face. Crystal flops unceremoniously onto the couch and he notices Crystal isn't sweating. Tia hands them some water, and he just guzzles the whole thing. A maid walks by, and William has her go get more water. "It's hot in this suit. It has to be the humidity from the ocean and the fact that summer is right around the corner."

Her words labored as she breathes hard, getting his attention to Crystal. "You think that's bad? I'm feeling like a broiled chicken in Shadow's oven. If I don't get out of these clothes soon, I'm going to lose it." Her normal ivory white has changed to a pinkish color he notices under the better lighting, and she starts a very recognizable incantation.

Will and Tia both jump to stop her. Tia places her hand on Crystals. "Now is not a good place for this."

Crystal looks at her and Tia can tell there is something wrong. Her words are labored. "I'll take any other suggestions. I'm burning up."

Tia asks in a panic, looking around. "There must be a bathhouse or pool around here, right? Where do they go to get cleaned up?".

Crystal's eyes widen. *The heat must be getting to me. I should have thought of that.* She stands up so suddenly that it causes everyone to jump. She shouts at a random woman. "YOU, MAID!" The young girl turns around and locks eyes with Crystal. "Where is the bathhouse in this embassy?" The girl looks frightened and stammers. "Tell me now!" Crystal barks, grabbing her by the shirt and breathing harder and sounding almost drunk.

"Take the stairs down. Turn left for the women's bathhouse. Why? What's the matter?"

Crystal doesn't answer. Letting go, she starts but stumbles, colliding with the girl, trying to get to the stairwell. Everyone exchanges looks, and William and Tia take off after her. Tom looks at Tyra. "What was that all about?" Tyra just shakes her head in confusion.

Crystal makes her way down the stairs, almost falling. William catches her and she looks up at him, but she doesn't look like she's all there. Her eyes are glassy, almost unresponsive. Tia looks at her, feels her head, and checks her pulse. "I see it, but I don't believe it." She looks at William. "This looks like severe heatstroke, but that rarely happens till it's way above one hundred degrees."

"In Humans." She goes limp as he lifts her. "She awakened her Dragon blood, remember?" He huffs, moving as fast as he can in the heavy armor, Tia hot on his heels. "She's from a White Dragon lineage. They are cold-based Dragons." He leaps the last portion of the stairs. The thunder of his armor hitting the carved stone floor echoes throughout the embassy, causing people to duck and wonder if they were under siege. "Don't worry Crystal. The water is right up here. I'll cool you off."

She opens one eye, partially having a hard time keeping conscious. She lets off a pathetic croaked laugh. "Fat chance of that happening."

Tia rushes around William, grabbing the door. "We're here Crystal, I'll help you in the water."

Tia, standing at the door, is praying to Daniel to get her healing magic together. Crystal barely opens an eye and looks up at him. Hearing the water and having started her incantation, she murmurs the rest, releasing the power she pulled. His armor hits the stone floor, and some tumbles into the water.

Tia spins in place, red as an apple, unable to react to the situation, ruining her prayer. Crystal falls unconscious as her eyes roll back with that little taking what's left out of her. William lowers her and himself into the water, cradling her in his arms. Cupping one of his hands, he takes up water, pouring it over her head to bring her temperature down. "Tia, I need you over here. Swallow your pride a moment and get her some medical aid. She looks serious here." He continues to cup water and pour it over her forehead. *How long has she been hiding this in the meeting with the Baron?* Tia closes the door and crosses the gap quickly. *She must have been dying in there, but pressed on and walked out, hoping she could keep it together for the negotiations.*

Tia starts her prayer again, trying not to look at the naked couple in the pool. Her hands glow purple, and it envelops Crystal's body. The magic is feeding Tia information about her condition. "Her status is stabilizing. She's unconscious, but no longer dying. She really pushed herself today." William is still cupping water with his hand and pouring it over her head, hoping to disperse the heat. "All we can do now is get her temperature down, but she's going to make it."

William sits in the water with her across his lap, and her head held out of the water. He's glad they got over their minor bump in the road. "Tia, do me a favor. Get her clothes and my armor out of the water. Then bring us some towels. I'll sit here with her till she comes back to me. Even if I have to wait all night."

Tia does as she's told, picking up the heavy armor out of the water and placing it to the side. "I'll bring a cup back as well for you as well, so you can move the water better." She leaves, closing the door behind her, and heads back upstairs.

Tom asks first as she crests the top. "What happened? We heard William fall twice and then silence. Are they ok?"

Tia looks somber. "She's stable. William is taking care of her needs down in the bathhouse. I'm getting them some towels for when she finally wakes up, they can dry off."

"Want me and Tyra to go down and stay with them?"

Tia's face flushes, and she waves her hands frantically. "No, I think they will be ok, and they should have some privacy. She just needs to cool down, and I'll check up on them as a medical professional."

Penelope walks in with dinner and glances about the area. "I was bringing dinner to the countess. Where is she?"

"She's down in the pool right now, cooling off."

"OK, I'll take it down there then. Won't be the first time she's eaten by the pool." Penelope turns to head downstairs.

Tom steps in front of her and blocks her path, trying to gather the words without panicking her. "Crystal had an accident. William is down there with her. Somehow, she's suffering from heatstroke, so you might want to wait for them to return up here."

"Heatstroke?" Penelope thinks back. *She mentioned on their wagon ride she couldn't stand the heat.*

"It's true. She did everything but vomit, and I only think she didn't because she hadn't eaten today." Tia looks away. "William figured it out, or at least came up with a reasonable explanation about how she's suffering when the rest of us don't mind." She lays it out in terms everyone can follow along with. And they all agree it's reasonable.

"So, what do I do with her dinner?" Tia shrugs and doesn't give an answer. "Fine, I'll take it back to the kitchen. You better check on her."

Tia comes in with the towels and William is still there, cradling her in his arms. She hands him the cup, and he continues to pour water over her head. "Is she still alright, Tia?" The hurt and worry in his voice reflect her own in her heart.

"Yes sir. The spell I cast earlier is showing that her temp is coming down and her pulse is returning to normal. It's still elevated but the cool water is doing its job. She will recover. It's just a matter of time. I have your towels for you." He nods, not saying a word, keeping his eyes on Crystal. Tia places them on a nearby chair. "I'll leave you two, but I won't be far. If you need me, just yell. I promise to stay that close."

She exits, walking back up the steps. Hours go by and Crystal wakes up, naked in the pool, not remembering how she got there. She blinks and can see Williams's enormous arms holding her from behind. She slowly turns her head and see's he's asleep, but he's holding fast to her. Her movement wakes him, and he looks down at her and smiles. "Morning sleeping beauty."

She smiles, reaching up to rub his gruff beard. "What happened? How did we get here?"

"What's the last thing you remember?"

"You and Tia stopping me from removing my clothes in the grand hall." She looks down at them both. "Looks like I got a 'two for one' that time."

He smiles and leans down and kisses her. "I should alert Tia that you're awake. She's probably sitting in a chair outside asleep in it waiting for you to wake up."

He turns, but Crystal stops him, turning around herself to face him. She utters another incantation, and she glows white for a moment. She leans in, cradling his face. "Let's let Tia sleep."

Penelope makes her way downstairs, finding Tia asleep in a chair outside of the bathroom. She can hear Crystal and William talking in the next room and some splashing. She knocks on the door, and it instantly goes silent. "WHAT!" Crystal yells angrily from behind the door.

Penelope exhales a sigh of relief. *She's fine.* "It's three a.m. Countess. You haven't eaten today, and you have your meeting in the morning with the Baron."

"FIIINE!" comes from the door, followed by some giggling and the splashing of water.

"Should I come in?"

"No, I have everything handled in here, Shadow. You can go."

Penelope wakes up Tia and she blinks and stretches. "Did I miss anything?"

She just turns and looks at her. "A good night's rest. Go to bed."

An hour goes by, and Crystal peeks out the door and can see that it's clear. "Ok let's go." Crystal is carrying her clothes and William clanking loudly from his armor loosely fitting. They make their way through the embassy, but people are awakening from the noise. She stops William. "I can't stop the noise, but I can stop anyone from seeing us."

William just shrugs and takes in a hushed tone. "I can't believe I'm sneaking around like some thief in the night."

She speaks low herself. "Sneaking doesn't mean 'walking around sounding like an angry toddler banging garbage can lids' my love." She speaks her invisibility incantation twice, one for her and one for him.

They both vanish and William is tugged along by Crystal up another set of stairs to her room. People look out their doors listing to the clanking of metal, but see nothing. Penelope knows exactly what's going on and wishes that Crystal had a silence spell so she could get some sleep. Entering her room, she breaks the enchantment and they both reappear. "Now I know how mom and dad felt when they were sneaking past Cline's lackeys." She giggles in thought and kisses him goodnight. "You better get to your chambers before you're caught."

CHAPTER 31
(Moonlit Festival)

Crystal is awakened by a knock at the door. She stretches and can already feel the heat of the day creeping up on her. Answering, Tia is standing there with her breakfast. "Ms. Penelope made you a high-calorie meal, both because you barely ate yesterday and because of your close call." Crystal steps aside and Tia sets the tray on her table in the center of the room.

Crystal sits down and picks up her fork, stabbing a piece of sliced fruit and chewing on it, and waves for Tia to sit down. "Will saved my life a second time. It's becoming a habit with him." She looks up at her. "Am I really that prone to those situations?"

Tia places her hands on the table. "You push yourself too hard, Countess." She leans forward. "I understand these negotiations are important, but you could have died if they lasted much longer."

Crystal leans back and swallows. "I must get this done. This is going to take months, if not years, and every minute shouldn't be wasted. Especially if I want to keep my title."

Crystal's eyes widen hearing anger in Tia's voice for the first time. "What good does that do you if you kill yourself in the process? You might not luck out a second time."

"You don't understand—"

"Think about William." Tia grabs her hands. "Think about how devastated he and the rest of us would be if you died." Crystal looks at her with a frown and Tia realizes she's making headway. "I know you have access to a spell for temperature resistance. Penelope mentioned to me last night that you used it on her back in the woods months ago when it was freezing. Why aren't you using it?"

"I was using it, but it wore off too soon, and I'm not just going to cast a spell in the middle of talking to the Baron. That could make him suspicious and blow the whole deal." Tia looks at her and Crystal's face changes from anger to defeat. "I understand." She sits upright. "And you're right. I'll see if he's willing to schedule breaks in the talks so I can reapply the spell every four hours. I should have enough in me to keep it going a few times."

"Is it finally getting easier to cast your spells?" Crystal can sense more curiosity in that tone than she has herself.

Crystal nods happily. "It feels like I'm adapting as the situations arise. The harder I'm pushed, the more I seem to be able to unlock and access." She picks up her fork and takes another bite of fruit, moaning about how good it is. "Spells that would have normally exhausted me months ago are almost trivial to what new spells I've been able to access and learn."

"It's like physical conditioning. You're pushing your body to contain more magic and use them more often. This is a good thing."

"How about you? Are you feeling the increased possibilities?" Crystal continues to eat.

Tia thinks about it. "I feel closer to Daniel every day. He is revealing more possibilities to use to aid you and the others on our journey. New prayers and how to use them is an amazing feeling." Her grin dies as she contemplates it all. "But I don't feel that I deserve them."

"Why not? You've been instrumental in our journey." Crystal comforts her, reaching out and placing a hand on her arm. "He's rewarding you for fulfilling your purpose."

Tia shakes her head and pulls away. "You know why. I don't know why he continues to have me with my feelings betraying him."

"Maybe because he knows, and doesn't mind. I'm not a religious scholar. So don't take my word for it, but as an observer."

The two talk and enjoy each other's company and Tia finally settles into her role as Crystal's counsel. They break so she can get dressed and she and William see Baron Tenishar start the day's negotiation. She informs him of her condition and he agrees he too would like breaks for drink and food as needed. The negotiations go well for Crystal on the second day. Each side makes offers and counteroffers and details are written down. She displays the new battle suits and their function in combat for the Baron. "Very impressive." He walks around the towering marvels. "And you would send more of these as part of the unification?"

"The taxes provided will go to build more of these units, or more upgraded models in the future, along with improving your infrastructure. As part of that, all records of the taxes, and its use, will be at your disposal so you can audit them." She can feel the headache coming on with the telltale signs of nausea that will make things worse since she has been eating. *The spell must have worn off. It's ok, the day is almost over, just fight it for the last few moments. You can do this.*

"You make a tempting offer, Countess." He turns to her with fangs bared in a wide grin. "We must talk more about this at another time, as it is getting late, and we must feast together tonight." He lets off a hearty laugh. "I would like for you and your bodyguard here to join us and taste some of our delicacies as we celebrate the full moon tonight."

Crystal smiles the best she can, trying to hold it together. "I would like that, Baron Tenishar." William keeps turning his head in her direction, meaning he's noticing her changing colors.

"Good, we shall dine in five hours, then."

She opens her arms. "If I may ask Baron Tenishar, I would like to invite my friends to this feast as well, if it's not overstepping. I don't mean to offend if I have."

He gives off another hearty laugh. "By all means. How many will you be bringing total so I can make sure the chefs are prepared?"

She smiles, baring her fangs. "Six, including myself."

"Very well Countess. Make sure they are hungry." He takes his leave with Captain Motsana falling in step. "I look forward to meeting your friends. You can tell a lot about someone by the company they keep."

Crystal keeps smiling, but dread fills her gut. *I might have just shot the whole deal down by trying to be nice for once.* She hides her fright on her face, clenching her jaw. *Good job, idiot. Your entire future is based on a group of people who don't even know what forks go with what plates.* William takes up his place beside her as she waves to the baron. *Won't be making that mistake ever again.*

William leans down, getting quiet, his voice muffled by the helm. "How are you holding up, honey?"

She's sweating as it pools upon her dress. "I'm going to need a bath and a change of clothes." She knocks on his breastplate with her knuckles. "And I'm sure you're not doing much better in that oven you're wearing."

"I'll survive. You, on the other hand…"

"I will always be fine with you at my side. I can feel it." They walk back to the embassy and make their way to the grand hall and sit down wondering where everyone is at. Minutes later, as Penelope gets Crystal some water, the monks and Tia walk in from their adventure.

Tom is getting bored just sitting in the embassy all day. *Sure, it has a pleasant view of the ocean, but I yearn for more. I didn't fly clear across a continent to sit inside all day.* He swings by Tyra's room and see's she's working out. *She's always working out. He needs to break up her monotony, too.*

"What do you need, Tom?"

"I'm going sightseeing, you wanna come?"

"Sightseeing?" She puts the heavyweights down with a thunk. "What for?"

"Because I'm bored, and Crystal is going to be out all day. So, we should take this opportunity to learn more about the people."

She stands up and brushes off. "Ok."

This worries Tom. "Just, ok?"

"Yep, just 'ok'."

They walk downstairs to the Grand Hall, and Tia is in there sitting and reading. "Where are you two off to?"

"Sightseeing. Tom is getting cabin fever and wants to walk the city."

Tom puts his finger on her book, pushing it down. "Wanna come along?"

"Yes, actually." She places the book down on the table. "It will do me some good and expand my horizons a bit." The day is hitting its high mark, with temperatures rising above ninety. Tia smiles, feeling the warm breeze in the air rushing past her white robes. "I'm so glad I went with these over my old brown ones. The sun is brutal out here." Seeing others in the city wearing light colors to reflect the heat was a good sign she picked up on. The streets are filled with noise with street vendors selling many wares, hanging from canopies and the smells of exotic foods. None of the three understand felinese which seems to be the dominant language here.

Tia takes a moment to pray for 'understanding' and in moments their speech becomes clear to her. They continue to walk and look at wares with Tia translating for the group. Settling at a seaside eatery to have a late lunch and the food arrives, smelling divine. They can't believe how good it is.

Tia laughs, something Tom nor Tyra have seen her do in some time. "I'm going to get fat. There is so much good food here." She pats her belly, leaning back.

"Yeah, I agree." Tom takes another bite. "These Catfolk love their seafood delicacies. I would have never thought there were six ways to prepare sea bass."

Tyra rubs her own belly. "I'm so glad you dragged me out today. Barring Penelope, this food is way better than the stuff the chefs make at the embassy." Tia glances at Tyra. "No disrespect to Penelope. Her cooking is still better, but the other chefs need to take some lessons from here."

"So, how long do you think we will be here?" Tom pokes at his food. "Few more days?" He takes another bite of his sea bass. Tia looks up at him askance. Tom tries again. "A few weeks, maybe?" He hopes she will respond. She quietly eats her shrimp. Tom's mirthful smile evaporates. "Just tell me already."

"You shouldn't ask questions if you're not prepared for the answer."

This causes Tyra and Tom to trade glances and stop eating altogether. Realizing she must give them something and they deserve to know, she lays it all out on how these things go. Their faces change as she explains it all and goes through some of the greater details. "This is just the initial stages of the negotiation. It will take a minimum of a few weeks possibly to hammer out some of the larger details. Once those are in place, the finer details are laid out and this could take a few months to years, depending on the complexity."

Tom just stares in disbelief. "A few *years*?"

"I don't think it will be that bad, but we should get comfortable. At the minimum, we are looking at several months, possibly not earlier than mid-winter before returning." She looks at them both. "Most of it is going to be the paperwork flying to Rose Harbor and back as each side presents offers and counteroffers for Crystal to negotiate on." Tom and Tyra exchange glances for long moments, and Tia can almost hear what they are thinking. "Look, I know this isn't what you signed up for. If you two want to go home to the monastery, you can board the ship and head home. No one will blame you if you did."

Tom sits back and rubs his belly. "And miss out on all this delicious food? No way." Tyra nods in agreement with this assessment.

Tia's smile returns. "Glad to know you're staying." They continue walking through the town, working off their large lunch and overindulgence. They talk to the people and get an estimate of the culture as the sun dips below the walls and the sky turns colors.

As they make their way back to the embassy when Tyra speaks up about something that's been bothering her. "I think we are being followed. There is a scent that's been with us for well over an hour now and is keeping pace with us as we walk back."

"Have you spotted anyone?" Tia looks around with her eyes but doesn't turn her head.

"No, but I can smell them. Could just be a coincidence, but all the same, I figured I would warn you two."

"Crystal should be done for the day soon, anyway. Once we get back, we can figure out what to do next." *Whoever is trailing them is worthy of Penelope's skills. This is a very terrifying experience.*

They make their way to the grand hall and Crystal is sitting there drinking some water, with Penelope and William standing close to her.

Crystal looks overheated, but she stands up. "I've been looking for the three T's. You have a good day in the city?"

They talk for a few minutes, but Crystal halts the chatter. "Every one of us needs a bath and to get cleaned up for tonight. Barron Tenishar has invited all of us to a feast tonight for the full moon at its zenith." She locks eyes with Tom. "It's a cultural thing for their people, so be on your best behavior."

Tom looks back. "What?" Crystal continues to stare into his soul. "Fine, I'll behave."

"Good, because if you mess this up for me, all my hard work goes out the window." Her eyes turn hard as she stares at him. "And

I'll be very… unhappy." Then, as if turning a switch, she sounds chipper. "So, let's go hit the bath and cool off before I hurt someone."

They all sit in the pool together as a comradery. Crystal cuddles against a very uncomfortable-looking William as he washes her hair. Tia stays sunken as far into the water as she can. Penelope and Tom are wrestling Tyra as they try to shampoo her from top to bottom, but she's not having any of it. They laugh and talk about their days. Crystal doesn't react, concerned with the person following them. "Probably working for the government to see if you're spies or something. You did nothing suspicious; we should be ok."

The time for the feast gets closer. William is adorned in his dress uniform. Crystal is wearing a black dress with sequins, gold embroidery around the neck, and cuffs. Gold lace binds her braids in her signature style of hanging them from her horns. Tia is wearing her white robes and the monks have on some nice dress clothes matching Rose Harbor colors. Crystal looks over at the Minotaur. "You clean up really well, Tyra." Captain Motsana arrives at the Embassy gates in a yellow cloth garment that looks like a toga but has a brass sash with a silver or other highly polished reflective metal discs attached to it. "Good evening, Captain Motsana."

"Good evening, Countess. It is my honor to escort you and your party to our festivity." He waves them on to follow him.

The full moon lights up the whole town, with all the buildings being white. "Your town is amazing, Captain. There are no lights on anywhere, but it's so well lit. A true marvel of beauty." The captain nods but says nothing. He moves without making a sound that makes Penelope perk up.

They are taken back to the courtyard where she met with the Baron earlier, but this time there is a large, elongated table set in the middle of the moonlit yard. Servants come out and set the table with much food, from seafood to wild game found in the area outside the gates. Baron Tenishar walks up wearing a white toga-like garment with a gold sash with silver polished discs. Crystal's black dress with her ivory skin makes her look ghostly in the bright moonlight, and the sequins cause her to twinkle as if made of stars.

"You look wonderful Countess. We will start soon. Please take your seats. There are cards marked out for everyone. You will sit opposite me on the table ends." He walks with her with William and the others one step behind them. "Before we feast, we pray to the Goddess of the moon, Tatiana. For she lights our way in the darkest of nights." Crystal tilts her head in a slight bow in understanding and turns to make sure the others are listening. "Once the prayer is complete, we shall eat till we can't anymore, talk and sing. Let us have fun tonight and forget about all the other pleasantries."

They sit down at the table piled high with many foods. Crystal looks at the plates. *Where are the utensils?* Many other Catfolk are at the table, all dressed similarly. Large fish like marline to crab and shrimp. Wild boar, deer, and other large game tops the massive table. Another Catfolk you could swear was just a tabby in a toga stand while the others sit. She starts the prayer and speaks in Felinese. Being guests and none knowing what they are saying, they stay silent as she goes along. Crystal nor Tia dare cast a spell of understanding, as it might be rude. She goes on for several moments, and when it ends, all the Catfolk shout out a single word at the end. Then, to the people of Rose Harbor's surprise, just grabs food and tossing on their plates with bare paws and claws.

"Eat, eat my guests. Tatiana had brought us many good bounties this time and new friendships. Let the festivities begin." He grabs a leg of a large fowl. Tyra doesn't hesitate to grab a slab of boar and ripping into it similar to the natives.

Tom laughs. "As Master Monzulo would say, 'do as the natives, to best understand them'." He takes a handful of shrimp.

They all eat and trade stories of their homelands and families. Telling jokes and singing different folk songs with the others, trying to at least hum along. The band is playing music of different speeds and styles. William and Crystal dance together and Tom drags one of the female Catfolk to show him some dance moves from their culture. Tyra and one of the larger Catfolk that looks more like an upright tiger arm wrestle across the table. She wins with a heavy slam and he stands up, grabbing his goblet and offering it to her in a toast of respect. Tia and the Catfolk that lead the prayer sit to back and talk to each other. Penelope entertains by juggling some of the food and letting it land in her minuscule mouth as the Catfolk cheer her on. As the night goes on, the Baron asks to dance with Crystal and William respectfully bows out of the way.

Crystal is surprised by the grace of the large Catfolk. "Are you enjoying yourself, Countess?"

She laughs and nods her head yes. "This is not at all what I expected. You have a wonderful culture here and a fine people. I look forward to many more of these festivities." Her smile bares her fangs.

"That's good to hear, and I would like to say you keep excellent company. A very well-rounded group of companions." He twirls her around, kicking up some grass. "I'm glad you suggested bringing them along. You might be all prim and proper, but the company you keep is not. This shows me you understand the common folk. A sign of a good leader."

"Why thank you, Baron Tenishar. I appreciate the compliment."

The song ends and they bow to each other and Baron Tenishar hands her back to William. "You, sir, are a very lucky man. Cherish this rare jewel." The moonlight is being replaced with the dawn. As the stars fade from the sky, they are replaced with the morning's glow of reds, yellows, and oranges. The festivities wrap up as the moon sets under the savanna to the east.

Crystal and William walk up to the Baron before departing. "What time shall we meet today?" Crystal asks politely, fighting the exhaustion of being up all night.

He grins at the tiny girl. "Your dedication is admirable, Countess, but the day after the full moon is a day of rest. So go and get some sleep and I will see you again tomorrow morning. Enjoy your rest." He exits, walking away with the female Catfolk priestess.

Crystal looks at William, feeling tipsy from all the alcohol. "Carry me?" William nods in agreement, unable to say no to those pattering eyelashes. William gets the rest of them in order, Tyra is still standing having out drank the larger Catfolk that would make a Dwarf approve. Tom is still slow dancing with the female Catfolk he started with, but being the band is packing up, they part ways. Penelope is trying to wake Tia who didn't realize the drinks were alcoholic and fell asleep.

They start their procession back with Tom helping by carrying Tia and Penelope riding on Tyra's shoulder, giving her drunken directions. William carries Crystal up to her bed and lays her down. *For a rich prim girl, you sure know how to party like a Dwarf when you have to.* He then retires to his own chamber, letting the darkness take him.

CHAPTER 32
(Nightmare)

Crystal wakes up and cannot see with her hands and feet bound, unable to move. It's hot, and she reflexively tries to use her magic to cool herself, but she's gagged and can't utter the incantation. She can hear the turning of wagon wheels and the clod of a horse. She panics and pulls against her restraints. A deep male voice speaks up that she doesn't recognize. "You're awake finally."

He won't be amused when I get a hold of him. She continues to struggle. *My jewelry is missing so my claws are out, but how to use that as an advantage?*

"If you're plotting something, stop while you're behind." A moment passes as if he was thinking. "I was only told to bring you in alive. My client didn't say how much of you could be missing. So don't do anything that will reduce your value."

Crystal stops moving. *He sounds serious. I don't know where I am or what's happening, but it's obvious I'm a prisoner.* She is sweating heavily and can feel the heat sapping her life away. She tried talking normally with the gag to at least alert the man she was trying to be reasonable.

"What's the matter, Countess? Trying to plead for your freedom? Don't bother. I'm getting paid well for you." She keeps trying, and he gets a little angry. "If you don't quiet down, I'll give you a reason to be loud." She feels him grab one of her fingers and twist it, causing extreme pain. "I'll break a finger if you don't stop."

I have no doubt he's willing, but I must try something. She lays there trying to breathe and focus on something. She doesn't know how long goes by, but he speaks up again.

"I'm going to remove your gag so I can give you some water. If you try anything at all, you will regret it. Nod your head if you understand." She nods, knowing she needs that water. He sits her up and pulls the gag from her mouth. He puts a vessel to her mouth. The water is foul-tasting, but she knows it's the only thing saving her life right now.

He takes it from her mouth, but before he can gag her again; she speaks up, knowing it might cost her. "I'm suffering from heatstroke. I'm sensitive to heat and I'll die if I don't get cooled down." She doesn't struggle, and she's expecting the man to strike her at any moment.

"I'm sorry, girl, but there are no pools or spas out here."

"I get that. I know a spell that can adapt my body to the heat for a few hours. I used it while in Portstown. If you let me use it, I promise not to cause you any trouble. I just don't want to die out here."

The voice is silent and all she can hear is the wagon and the horse or other large animal. "I'll let you do it because you're worth more alive than dead." She feels the warm edge of a blade on her neck. "But if you pull any kind of stunt, and I'll know because I understand magic, you won't be casting spells ever again. Do you understand?"

She gives a subtle nod and utters her incantation and the protective white glow to protect her from the heat envelops her. She's about halfway through saying thank you when he gags her again and lays her back down. They go through this pattern for what Crystal thinks is forever. She fades in and out of consciousness from the heat.

William wakes and stretches. Its midafternoon but he expected as much for not going to bed till the sun was already up. *It's this hot already? I can only imagine what Crystal is going through. Better check on her. She probably has a raging headache from last night.* He walks down to her door and knocks on it. There is no answer after a few moments. *Is she still asleep?* He tries again, knocking a little harder, knowing it should be enough to rouse her. When she still doesn't answer, he panics. He tries to open the door, but it's locked and he knows better than to break it down.

"GUARDS, GUARDS!" Armored soldiers come running. "Who has the key to his door? I fear the countess could be in danger from the heat." One of them takes off and the Man at Arms arrives, carrying a large key ring. By this time, everyone knows about the growing emergency. He unlocks the door and William barges in, motioning for them to wait. He can see her bed is empty. The sheets are dragged onto the floor and the window is open. Looking out, he can see distinctive marks of climbing gear used to get in and out. Penelope and Tia barge in past the guards and see William looking out the window.

Tia scans the room and looks at him and the muscles in her back tense up. "Will?"

"She's gone. Someone took her!" He brings his fist down on a nearby table, splintering it to pieces. Tia flinches back, not knowing how to react. "We need to find her." Tia wraps her arm around William and he shakes her off. "I will find who did this and bring them to justice." News spreads fast and Captain Motsana and Baron Tenishar arrive as William and the others are investigating what happened. William reports what is happening to the Baron "Penelope is studying how the intruder could have gotten in and got her while Tom and Tyra are tracking her scent, hoping she's still in town somewhere."

The baron sounds fearful. "This is a tragedy. The entire weight of the Portstown authority is at your disposal, Captain William. Anything at all you want or need, just ask. We will find who took the countess, and they will bear the full weight of the Portstown legal system."

"I'm going to need your best trackers. Every single person in this embassy is going to be interviewed, and every movement scrutinized."

"You shall have them. Anything else you require?"

William glances at the Baron, giving him pause. "I need a soundproof room to do my interrogations in."

She's unsure how long goes by, but it feels like days. She is picked up unceremoniously and she can hear him walking on stone. The echo changes, meaning they entered a room, but then she is dropped on the floor with little care. "Where would you like her?"

A female voice echoes. "Up there, where I can see her properly." She feels herself hoisted up and hung from her wrist restraints. Eons pass as silence dominates the room. Then a feminine voice is heard from right next to her right ear, but sounds unimpressed. "So, this is Countess Crystal Hellstromm?" The woman places her hands on her waist, twisting her around on her binds, and causing her

294

shoulders to wretch. The gag is pulled from her mouth and she can speak now. "Go ahead and scream if you want. No one will hear you down here."

"What do you want with me?" She wheezes. *I can't even pull myself up. The heat from the trip has drained me.*

"I want to know things, Countess, and you're going to tell me those things as I ask about them. If you don't, well..." a crack of a whip across her back causes her to scream as it rips her skin and clothing. The scales along her spine are the only part of her unharmed. She jerks in her bindings but doesn't come free. She can feel the blood running down her back from the strike. "I want to know what Rose Harbor wants with Portstown." Crystal is silent, not saying a word. Another crack and she screams again as the whip crosses her back a second time, ripping through her clothes. "I can play with you all I want. You're defiant now, but you won't be for long." Crystal can tell by the sounds she's moving about the room. "What does Rose Harbor want with Portstown?"

I can't tell her anything. The second I do; my life is forfeit. The whip cracks again but this time across her stretched torso, ripping her dress and skin. The pain is excruciating as Crystal cries.

The woman grabs Crystal's face. "Oh, don't start crying now, you won't have enough for later" She lets go and lets out a cachinnation. "I'm going to enjoy making you suffer." She scratches Crystal's face with her nails.

"What did I do to you?"

"You're with the Rose Empire, and a member of the royal family. That's good enough." Crystal takes a punch to the gut where the whip had crossed earlier. This causes her to cry out in pain again.

"You want me to go easier on you, then tell me what I want to know."

"Go to hell, bitch. I won't tell you anything."

The woman continues to beat on Crystal for what she felt was an eternity. Long hours of nothing, just silence, punctuated by the mysterious woman's anger and rage. She doesn't know how long she's been hanging there like a slab of meat. Crystal drifts in and out of lucidity and the mysterious woman just keeps hitting her, trying to get information. She spends her time hanging there thinking of how to get away. She's been dangling there so long that she no longer has the strength to pull herself up. Her shoulders hurt too much, and all the lashings make her body burn across every surface.

"You look thirsty." Crystal's face is turned up and pungent water is forced into her mouth, causing her to gag and cough. "What's the matter, Countess? Is our water not good enough for you?" The woman scratches her face on the other side as she pulls away.

Crystal's voice is hoarse from hours or days of screaming. "If I were you," her breathing is labored. "I would kill me and flee for your life. When they find you, and see what you did to me, they will make an example of you that will be retold in horror stories." This earns another punch to her kidneys, and she cries out.

"You will die, but not until I get what I want."

Tia stands with William in a small room along with Captain Motsana. Tia prays to Daniel to keep everyone truthful who enters, and the floor glows green for a moment. Tyra drags in person after person who works in or around the embassy. Anyone whose scent even gets close. She's particularly pissed after losing the scent when she entered the desert. The shifting sands scattered the scent, making her unable to continue tracking with her nose.

Anyone whose scent also has Crystal's on them is brought in for questioning. She drags in the first one, plopping them down in a chair. William grills each one of them for hours. One after another as the hours go by with Tia's divine ward, making them tell their every truth. After twelve to thirteen hours, they must have interviewed every member of the staff in the compound. Tia, worn out from praying for the same ward repeatedly as they wear off, is ready to fall over from exhaustion.

After the last person leaves, Tyra shrugs helplessly and William's rage overtakes him and he smashes the wooden table with his fist, causing everyone to jump, even Tyra. "Damn it."

"Captain."

He interrupts her. "No, I will not rest, I will not stop, and I will rip this world asunder to find her." He gets in her face and points angrily, his face a deep red. "And Daniel have pity for the poor fool who took her, for I will not." She shirks away and William understands he needs to walk away. "Sorry Tia, I didn't mean to frighten you."

Stepping out of the room, Baron Tenishar waits for him and takes in step with the large knight. "Your anger goes beyond that of a failed officer."

William doesn't hold back the bite in his voice. "Is that a problem?"

Tenishar shakes his head and raises his hands in surrender. "You love her. You two share a special bond the others don't know about." William turns and looks at him, but they keep walking. "I understand. I too would feel the same as you in this same situation if my wife was taken from me."

William calms down. "We aren't married." The Catfolk man's whiskers twitch, but William doesn't know enough about them to understand the expression.

"Could have fooled me, based on your reaction. You have deep feelings for her. We will do everything in our power to get her back. I feel just as responsible as you. It happened in my town. A town I was hoping was a relatively crime-free city, of at least this kind." He turns to William, stopping them both. "Get some rest. Tomorrow we will start planning how to search the desert. We know of several places out there that someone can hide that are a few days away. Right now, I can send scouts to all of them and check for activity."

"I want to go with them and bring Tyra. If Crystal is even close by, Tyra will know." William stops at the gate and Captain Motsana is waiting there. "I want to say how much I appreciate all that you've done and are doing."

CHAPTER 33
(Discovery)

Crystal awakens with cold and noxious water thrown in her face. *I must have passed out. How long have I been here? Days?* Her body and face have been cut up, bruised, and battered from the abuse. The water stings as it crosses the open wounds from the lashings, but the pain is so familiar to her now that she doesn't react.

"You're a tough one, Half-Dragon thing, aren't you?" The woman's voice sounds more insidious today. "Looks like I need to try something new."

Crystal can hear a fire being started in the corner and within a few minutes, the temperature of the room rises. "I hear on good authority that you don't care much for heat. Tell me what I want to know, and all of this will end."

"I already told you everything you need to know. Let me go, and I'll spare your execution. You will only rot in a cell for the rest of your life, but if they find me, I promise to make your death a thing of nightmares."

"Is that so?" The voice speaks from directly in front of her. "How about I counter that offer with one of my own?" Crystal can hear the ring of metal sliding on the stone. "Tell me why Portstown is so important or…" Crystal screams as the hot iron is pressed against her chest, charring her flesh. "We'll see how much heat you can actually handle." Crystal breathes hard and cries again. "I'm waiting." The hot iron is pressed into the back of her thigh. Crystal can't scream anymore as her voice is gone, only silence comes from her mouth. "Uh oh. You can't talk anymore? I'll come back later and maybe you will talk to me then."

William and the rest go out into the desert with Captain Motsana and some well-trained trackers and maps of the different caves and abandoned structures out there. There are a lot of rocky outcroppings and sharp stones sticking up from the sands. "Not all deserts are just big piles of sand. These are the badlands that separate us from New Haven. They go on for several hundred miles. Works as a natural barrier between us." They head out at night with the cool night air of the desert. The moon is still full, being only one day, and waned so they all can see well. They travel and search the closest caves first and head north along the road. They agree on a search pattern and split into groups, but stay close enough that they can contact each other.

William and his group, including a few of the Catfolk trackers, are checking out the third cave in the badlands. Tyra doesn't smell Crystal, but detects the familiar scent from the other day tracking them. "That person must be nearby. It can't be more than a day old."

"Really?" William looks at her for direction. "Let's root this guy out." They continue their search and walk through a carved stone canyon that's not wide. Could fit a wagon, but it would be close on both sides.

They get a few hundred feet in and Penelope shouts a warning as one guard triggers a trap and a boulder falls from above, crushing him. "Nobody move. I saw the tripwire at the last second. We could be in real trouble here." She slithers through the ranks, slowly disarming every tripwire she can find. "Someone doesn't want us back here."

William looks around his feet. "Can you find them all?"

"I'll try. It's not just falling rocks we need to be worried about." She crouches down. "The ground looks different here." She pokes at the ground with her dragger and finds a catch, causing it to collapse into some sharpened sticks. "We may have to go around." She stands looking around. "There is no way we are getting through here." She makes her way back to the back of the line. "I'll check this way as we leave, just in case we aren't as lucky leaving as entering."

She works her way along, disabling everything she can find. *Some of these are very insidious and designed not to go off the first few times they are triggered.* She disables another one when a hole in the rock wall opens and a spear comes out of it, pinning her to the far side. She cries out in pain as it went through her right shoulder, bone, and all. William crouches down and tries to pull it out, but she cries out again. "I'm bleeding pretty badly here." Her body is trembling from the pain and blood loss. Tia pushes her way through and looks as if the tiny Halfling can't even fall.

"Tia's here, and she's going to help you, but I need to get this spear out of you before she can do anything."

"Careful Captain. Pulling it free might cause more shock and possibly kill her."

"She's going to die if we leave her here, so what choice do we have?" William reaches up and takes hold of the spear. "It doesn't help that it's dark in here." He ponders a moment as blood pools under her feet. "I have an idea. Start your prayer to heal, and when you're ready, I'll pull the spear out and you heal at the same time. It's not perfect, but what else can we do?"

Penelope's eyes close and her voice trembles. "You could just kill me. That sounds less painful." Tia starts her prayer, asking Daniel to heal Penelope. Her hands glow blue and she lays them on Penelope at the same time William yanks the spear out. Penelope screams in agony and passes out, but her body is encompassed in blue magical light as the wound closes.

Tyra carries the poor Halfling, and they make their way around and up. They look and the canyon goes on for miles. William turns to Tyra. "Can you still smell the trail from up here?"

"Not very well, but yes."

"Let's keep an eye out for caves in the area. According to this map, there is one close to here. Maybe we will get lucky with this one." Half an hour later and the sun is replacing the mostly full, waning moon. Tyra confirms he can smell the same person down below. "We aren't going to be quiet, so let's go fast."

Tom peers over the side. "Tyra and I can get down there faster than you guys." William looks at him like he's crazy. "There is a technique we know that allows us to fall along walls that keeps us from hitting the ground too hard. We can go in and slow the guy down or, if anything, get an idea of the area while you climb down."

"Do it." William stakes the ground with ropes and starts their own descent. It's little more than seventy feet, but still will take several minutes to descend safely. Tom and Tyra leap and slide down the cliff face using handholds and imperfections to slow their way down until hitting the ground. As predicted, the guy comes out of the cave to see what is happening and runs back into the cave and Tom and Tyra take chase.

Tyra takes a shot from a crossbow by surprise in the thigh. She reaches down and yanks it out in more anger than pain. A second shot from the dark turns from anger to concern as they both take cover outside the cave. Tyra peeks, seeing in the dark, and does a quick count to go along with the footsteps. She speaks to Tom in oriental. "We really need to wait for the others. I count nine or more in there."

"Only nine? This is going to be a quick fight." He looks in and snatches a bolt out of the air. "They really don't want us here."

Tyra doesn't disagree with him. A few minutes go by and William and the rest arrive. "What's the situation?"

"At least nine I saw, can't look in too long without getting shot by a crossbow."

William nods. *Crossbows again? These people are behind in the times.* He decides to check himself and a bolt careens off his armor. He ducks back behind the wall. "We know Jack was right about this armor, at least." He turns to the soldiers. "Get your guns ready. I'm going to step out and prop up my shield and take their shots. While they are reloading, you step out and shoot them. Then we charge. You got that?" He gets everyone to acknowledge and pulls his sword and readies his shield. "Fix bayonets."

He steps out, holding up his shield, and moves forward. Bolts ricochet off his armor and stick to his shield. Troops come around the corner and fire, picking off two of the assailants with precision shots. The bolts from the enemy stop as they reload. "CHARGE!" William rushes, plowing into them. They pile into the dark cave with just a hand full of torches for light. William smashes into one with his shield, knocking a bandit off his feet. He then takes his chance and stabs him through the chest with his sword.

He catches a sword strike on his right from another bandit. Tyra comes out of the darkness like a nightmare, caving the guy's head in with a single strike.

Knights and bandits clash with the sounds of echoing metal. Tom lets out several sudden strikes, knocking another out. More bandits arrive from further back in the cave to join in the fray.

Swords and armor clash in a fury. Bandits fall as William's sword separates limb from body. Crossbow bolts stick out of his armor and blood escapes from gaps, but he fights on, rage building as the pain grows. Blood and death stack up as the unarmored bandits realize this isn't a battle they can win. They surrender and drop their weapons. Tia treats injuries on both sides, showing compassion for the combatants. She dresses wounds on the soldiers first, as Tom and Tyra claim they will be fine. They know rudimentary first aid and can handle it themselves.

They round everyone up who's still alive and William points at them. "Tyra, which one is it?" She walks among them and grabs one who looks better off than the others. A Catfolk with red and white fur, but he's short for his race. She plucks him off the ground by his shirt and holds him so William can talk to him face to face.

"This one was the one who followed us and his scent was in the countess's chamber. I can still smell her on him. He carried her for a while."

"Really?" William punches the poor guy with his heavily gauntleted fist, rocking his head back and breaking his short nose. He cries in pain and blood pours out. "Tell me where you took the Countess, who hired you, and for what purpose, and I won't kill any of these other people."

The Catfolk guy looks around and realizes he's not able to argue. Penelope walks in, waking up from her small nap and feeling awful for missing all the fun. "Some weird pale-skinned chick, almost gray, I guess. She had a black rose tattoo on her arm." William growls, getting him to flinch. "There is an old ruin about a day's travel north of here, maybe less. She's got an army up there of all these weirdo followers. I hung around up there a bit and they are some kind of weird fanatics that think the Emperor of Rose Harbor is some kind of demon who has to be stopped. She's been recruiting for her boss who's in New Haven. From some of the gossip, I heard they fear this deal with Portstown would cause problems."

William is angry and presses close to his face. "WHAT ELSE!"

The Catfolk man wets himself. "I was kind to her. Gave her water and let her cast her protection spell thing. I was told to bring her alive and unharmed, so I was doing my best to keep her most comfortable."

William looks at Tia, and she nods her head, confirming he's not lying. "Being we are outside the Rose Empire's territories; I don't have the authority to execute you where you stand, but given you were at least kind enough to her; I'll extend that same kindness. If I see you or if she smells you ever again, there is no law that will save you. I suggest you find a new place to go." Tyra drops him to the floor and William turns to the troops. "Take their weapons so they can't be a danger to anyone else."

"Then how are we supposed to defend ourselves from the wilds out here?"

William turns to him and a chill runs up the Catfolk's spine. "Should have thought about that before you took the countess."

Crystal hangs in the dark, beaten, bruised, branded, and lashed. *Provider, let me die. I can't take this anymore.* The heat in the room is unbearable. She has stopped sweating some time ago and knows her time is limited finally. *Just let William find love again and protect him. Maybe I deserve this, but he doesn't.* She can't even cry anymore, being so dehydrated. She hears the footsteps of her captor come in.

"Are you still alive?" Crystal just hangs there, unable to speak, unable to move anymore. She pokes at some of Crystal's festering wounds that cause her to twitch and groan. "It looks like our fun is going to come to an end soon. You don't look like you're going to make it. Too bad too. All you had to do was tell me about Portstown and all this could have been averted."

The sounds of cannonade can be heard and the structure shakes. Her voice chokes. "It looks like your hidey-hole was found." She lets off a weak chortle. "I told you, I would have just killed me and ran. Now you can't run anymore."

"You know, you're right Countess." Crystal can hear metal being freed from leather. More cannon fire rocks the structure and the sounds of armored troops fighting fill her ears. Dust and small stones pelt her skin. She can hear William shouting orders. The voice gets close to her and Crystal can feel the sharp steel against her flesh. The blindfold comes off and Crystal's eyes sting in the light, but she can finally see her torturer. "I wanted you to get a good look at my face before you died, so you know who sent you to the afterlife. When the others join you, you can have something in common to talk about." She slides the dagger into Crystal's chest.

Crystal groans and blood spills from her mouth, but rage builds inside her. *This close to freedom and now I die? If I'm going, I'm taking her with me.* She looks down at the gray-skinned woman. "You first." Summoning the last little strength she has, Crystal opens her mouth and a blast of ice spews forth, encasing the woman's head. The gray-skinned woman reels back from the sudden blast to the face, pulling the dagger from Crystal's body, and blood pours out. The gray woman flails on the ground, punching her cocooned head, slowly suffocating, as fear is permanently frozen to her face. Crystal can feel her life running out of her body, along her legs, and onto the floor. As the door to the chamber is being rocked, she slips into the void.

William, Penelope, Tom, and Tyra are fighting through the hallways as the airship continues to pound the area with cannon fire. Baron Tenishar is on board the ship, watching from above as Portstown troops clash with the Black Rose fanatics on the ground. Tia stays behind them, healing as they go. "Her scent is powerful here. She must be just beyond that door ahead." William stops being defensive altogether and takes hit after hit as he is just a whirling blade of death. He gives no quarter as his rage fuels him. Running to the heavy door, he tramples down the last of the Black Rose guards. He can hear a struggle behind the door but isn't able to open it. He looks at Tyra, who is already in motion, kicking the door and almost comes off its hinges.

William sees the gray-skinned girl laying on the ground, her head sheathed in ice. William looks up and sees Crystal hanging by her wrists on the other side of the room. Shock, pain, and grief hit him all at once as he drops his sword and shield with a large clang. Tears stream from his eyes as he rushes across the room. Tossing his helm away, he wraps his arms around her, bringing her down to the floor, and cradles her limp body. His grief overtakes him, looking upon her as his tears flow unchecked. She's cut up and bruised, her face is covered in welts. Blood from her lashings looks old and dried blood on her swollen chin shows they put her through hell before she died. Tia rushes in and sees the carnage covering her mouth to stifle a scream of her own. Her own tears start as she walks over to William and kneels with him.

Her hand twitches from his touch, forcing both William and Tia to give pause. Tia, reacting with tears still in her eyes, starts her healing prayers. Glowing blue, Crystal's body is enveloped by the healing magic.

"Hang on Crystal." He looks to the sky. "Provider, don't take her yet, I forbid you." Tia's prayer closes a few of Crystal's wounds and the bleeding stops. "I'm here Crystal. We're all here." He embraces her carefully as Tia summons more healing energy, trying to keep her stable. More of her wounds close, but she still has many scars. William looks up at Tia as she continues. "Can we move her?" She prays to Daniel. "She's stabilizing, but it's touch and go. I'm going to be working on healing her for a while. She has several broken bones still, but the bleeding has stopped and the infections have been taken care of. I just don't have enough in me now to treat everything."

William stands carefully and carries her out. Penelope, Tom, and Tyra grab his dropped arms and armor and Tia continues to treat Crystal as they go along. Cannon fire is still echoing, and the sound of battle is still occurring. Tyra, Penelope, and Tom clear the path as they make their way out into the desert where the forces of Portstown and Rose Harbor work together slaying the Black Rose. Baron Tenishar spots them and instructs the Bastion to land and withdraw forces. They climb on board and the troops mount a fighting withdrawal under the cover of the airship's guns.

William takes her to her estate cabin and Baron Tenishar meets them there. William sits there holding her mutilated hand and looks at all the disfigurements. Tia is sweating and exhausted, but presses on healing her fractures. Laying a hand on his blood-soaked armor causes William to look up at the Baron, "Don't worry, Captain William. Our healers and shamans will do everything they can to repair the damage. That is my promise from one man to another."

"Thank you, sir. I'm in your debt."

"Not at all, Captain. It's the honorable thing to do."

CHAPTER 34
(Darkness)

Crystal awakens, her whole-body screams in agony, and moving at all is a chore. *This is good. Pain means I haven't died yet. Unless I'm in hell. Very possible given my life choices.* She turns her head slowly to the right and opens her swollen eyes. The room is dark and lit with a single lamp. William sits next to her in a chair, face down in her bed. His hand holding hers. She smiles, and that hurts too. *He came for me.* She scans the room and Tia and Penelope are also there on her couch, sleeping, braced against each other. William's white shirt is stained with old blood, showing he went through hell looking for her.

She raises her left arm; the muscles and bones screaming in protest the whole time and she looks at it. Covered in scars and burns, the disfigurement is revolting to her. *If my whole body looks like this, then who's going to want me? I'm a grotesque monster now.* She lets gravity take her arm back down. The shaking of the bed awakens William as he takes in a deep breath and looks up at her.

She slowly turns her head back towards him, and they make eye contact. William smiles as tears well up in his eyes. "You're awake." She opens her mouth to talk but finds she can't, so she nods instead. "Don't move around too much. Tia and the other doctors have been working to put you back together." He moves to sit next to her on the bed. She flexes her right claw weakly, showing William she understands. "You've been out for three days. You can't take much more healing magic, so it's been slow going, but your major injuries have been taken care of."

She cries and winces in pain in doing so. Holding up her left arm again a little, just enough for William to notice, and she drops it again. She mouths something and he tries to understand the best he can. "Are you asking about your injuries?" She closes her eyes and flexes her right hand again. "You're going to be fine and will be back to normal soon."

He sighs. As her eyes lock with his. "I understand. Your injuries were very extensive and none of us know how you survived. In fact, when we got there, we thought you had already passed on, but you twitched and Tia took a chance that your soul was still with us and tried her strongest healing magic to keep you with us." Her cries intensify. "Don't cry, honey, please. You're alive, you should be happy."

Despair turns to anger on her face and she holds her arm up again as it quakes in pain, then lets it drop again. She mouths something and William puts his head down in understanding. "They are doing what they can about the scarring, but being you're young, they will fade with time." Her anger goes away, and the despair returns. Tears flowed unchecked down her face. She mouths something again, causing her sobs to worsen. "No, no, you're not. Please don't think like that." She turns her face away from him, closing her eyes.

"I will never leave your side. We will get through this." He gets up and sits back in his chair, but doesn't let go of her hand. "I'll be here at your side, always."

She can feel her energy fading, but she can't face him. *I know I'm horribly disfigured, and one day you will be gone from my life, leaving me and my ugly face behind.* She continues to cry till the void takes her again.

Morning comes, and Tia awakens and her moving causes Penelope to fall over and wake up. The morning sun shines through the off-white curtains. The alarm traps Penelope set along with the newly installed bars show no sign of being messed with. Tia notices William is still asleep with his hands still holding hers. Looking over the bed, she realizes the sheets need to be changed again. The wounds must have reopened a little, causing some seepage by the look at the fresh bloodstains. She's glad that it's a lot less than in previous days, as a positive sign of progress. She lifts Crystal's left wrist and checks her vitals, feeling her heartbeat is getting stronger.

Lifting her hand causes Crystal to stir and Tia gets excited to see her finally awake. She opens her eyes a little and turns them to look at Tia. "Good morning, sleeping beauty." Crystal frowns and looks angry, then turns away from her. William, stoic as ever, sleeps in his chair, never once letting go of her. "It's been several days. I'm glad you're awake."

Penelope climbs onto the bed shaking it, awakening William. "What would you like for breakfast, Countess?" She fakes a smile. "Anything you desire, I'll bring you." Crystal turns back and looks down at her Halfling friend.

Her voice cracks and is hoarse, but she is using everything she can to speak. "Water."

"Yes, Ma'am." She spins and darts off.

William looks up at Tia. "You going to pray for more healing magic?"

"Yeah, but she won't absorb all of it. Her body needs to do some natural healing or else healing her in the future with prayer won't take. A body can only take so much before it can't anymore." Tia starts her prayer, and her hands glow blue along with Crystal's body. Some of the pain goes away and she can feel some of the heaviness leave as well. She raises her arm, but the scars and burns are still there. She reaches up and touches her face and can feel the scars there, too. She weeps as Tia grabs her left hand.

"Don't cry, Countess. Now that we are sure you will make it, we will send word back to Rose Harbor. We can get the best healers here and I'm sure your parents will want to see you." Tia winces in pain and Crystal flexes her left hand and realizes her strength is slowly coming back. Penelope comes in with some fresh water and climbs back up onto the bed. Crystal struggles to sit up as the lashes on her back and torso scream, reopening and oozing blood again. William helps hold her upright, placing his hand at the base of the back of her neck, the only place that hasn't seen any kind of trauma because of the thick scales.

Tia grabs bandages and redresses her injuries. Taking the water, she drinks, but some spills from her still swollen lips. Putting it down, she can see bloodstains in the water. She looks at Penelope. "Mirror." Penelope's smile vanishes as she looks to Tia and William for guidance. "MIRROR!" Her voice cracks in anger, causing Penelope to flinch away from the wounded woman.

"Countess… Crystal, please you don't—"

"I want a mirror!" Crystal's eyes scare Penelope. "Don't make me ask again." She slowly backs off, wondering how a woman who can barely move can still illicit fear of this magnitude. She walks over to get it.

Tia looks to Will, scared out of her mind, but still changing Crystal's bandages. "Crystal, honey, you should really rest and not worr—"

Crystal cuts him off with her voice still croaking. "I want to see." Penelope walks up with the hand mirror and she can't hold her tears back. She just can't bring herself to hand it to her. Turning her icy blue gaze to Penelope, she holds out her left hand as William is still holding her right. She says nothing, but shakes her head in defiance. She knows deep down what this will do. "Give it to me, Penelope." She has only heard her use her real name one other time, but this time it scares her more than anything else.

She hands it over and steps back to the far side of the room. Crystal holds it up and her tears start all over again, staring at her mutilated face. A sneer crosses her face as she throws the hand mirror across the room, shattering it into thousands of shards. Tia reflexively backs off as she tries to stand up. William speaks up in worry. "Crystal please, you need your rest. You're going to hurt yourself more."

"I don't care. Either you can help me stand or you can leave." She puts her clawed feet on the floor. Her night gown is stained with blood as she looks down at it. She can see the scars through the material, causing more anger. William stands with her and she takes a few steps across the room. William can see she's heading towards the large full body mirror.

"Please Crystal, you don't want to do this. Go back to bed and wait till you're better."

She shoots him an icy glare. "I have to know." Taking short and very painful steps as her legs burn as she steps in front of the mirror. She can see the scars and brands on her arms and lower legs. She utters an incantation and William tries to stop her, but her mere glance causes him to stop long enough for it to finish. Her gown drops to the floor, along with all her bandages. William closes his eyes and Tia and Penelope look away.

She takes in everything that was done to her. Every brand, every scar, every lashing. She can't bear to look at herself and how hideous she has become. She touches her body and face, unable to believe what her swollen eyes are telling her. Despair fills her. *I can't live like this. I can't end up like Olovira.* She reaches out and takes William's knife from his belt. She brings it up to stab herself, but William grabs for it, holding it away from her. "LET ME DIE! I REFUSE TO LIVE LIKE THIS!" She is trying everything she can to plunge it into her chest. Wounds reopen on her back and torso as William struggles to pull the dagger from her hands. Her tears flow unchecked once again and she claws at it to get it back. "I want to die, I told you. Give that back, that's an order!"

William tosses the knife away and embraces her in his arms, holding her, but not hard enough to cause more injury. "You don't want to die; we are trying to help you." She pounds and scratches at him in pain and anguish.

"Just let me end it already." He can feel the blood running down his back from her claws. "I'm a freak. My beauty is gone, my life is over." She continues to claw her way out, blood oozing from her own back and legs.

"You need to stop this, Crystal." He holds her tight, ignoring the wounds she's inflicting on him with horns and claws. "You're just hurting yourself more."

"I don't care. I want my life to end." Her body goes limp and William holds her up. "I should have given up in that room." William lifts her up and takes her back to the bed. Tia redresses her open wounds, stopping the bleeding. Using some of the healing salves she brought with her on the trip to close the wounds. Crystal looks up at William. "If you love me, then help me end my pitiful existence."

This strikes pain deep in Williams's heart. "You don't mean that." He takes her hand. "You need to recover, and we will contact Rose Harbor and send for the best healers they have. I love you for who you are, and will always look beautiful to me."

William forces her to lie back down, and tears fall back onto her pillow. "I'm not a fool Will, we both know that healing magic, even the high-level stuff, doesn't remove scars. I'm going to be a hideous freak forever. How long till you leave me for some other girl who doesn't look like a monster?"

This pains him more, but he knows she's lashing out in anger because of her plight and doesn't mean it. He pats her hand. "Never, I will never leave your side."

Tia finishes wrapping her legs and stands back. "Please Countess, refrain from moving any more than you have to. You will just hurt yourself some more."

"I don't care anymore." She looks at the three in order. "You can't stop me forever."

A knock at the door brings their attention to Tom, who is standing there. "If I may offer some assistance, Countess, I'm willing to help you."

"Well, at least one person in this room understands how I feel finally." She turns her attention to him. "Are you going to kick everyone's ass in this room and leave me with the dagger?"

He steps forward and William stands up, ready to take the monk on. *This guy can fight toe to toe with my dad, so he's able to take on guys as big as me. I don't know how this will turn out.* He walks over with his hands behind his back and William observes him. "Not at all Countess. Do you not recall the pools at the monastery?"

She sits upright, groaning and once again reopening her wounds, to Tia's dismay. Her eyes widen in realization. "Yes, I do. They removed scars if you soaked in them long enough. They have some odd healing capability." Hope finally comes to her voice. "Take me there right away." She tries to get up, but William grabs her and forces her back down to the bed.

"How about instead of risking your life again, we just import the water and fill a large tub for you to soak in?" William doesn't take his eyes from Tom. "That way you can continue your negotiations and heal at the same time." She lunges at him, wrapping her arms around him, opening her wounds back up yet again.

Tia is exasperated. "For Daniels's sake, stop moving!"

Tom smiles, having resolved this issue with wisdom. "It might take more than a tub full, but I'll go right away. If I have permission to use the airship, I can land right there and get some water tanks. I'm sure Master Monzulo will be happy to give it to you for your recovery."

She smiles even though it hurts. "I'll write the permissions up." She looks at Tom. "In my jewelry box is a key to Olovira's old place. She gave it to me before she passed. I want you to bring me a book back from inside."

Tom walks over and opens the jewelry box and finds the key. He holds it up. "This one Countess?"

"Yes, Tom. When you're there, go into Olovira's house, my house, and bring me back a leather-bound tome that's on the lectern there. It has a lock on it but the key for it should be laying on that lectern too, so bring both. If I'm going to be stuck here and not allowed to do anything, I might as well study. I'm not going to get stronger if I don't keep learning."

CHAPTER 35
(Power Corrupts)

Two weeks go by, and Crystal does not try to end her life. She seems happy that Tom remembered something they have all forgotten a lifetime ago. William has been helping her learn how to walk again on her own and Tia helps her get dressed and helps with washing up. With Tia's instructions, Penelope makes sure that the meals have high protein counts to promote healing and get her strength back up. She still can't look at herself in the mirror, but every day she's in less pain. The Catfolk shamans bring pain-killing herbs and salves, along with some of their own healing medicines courtesy of Baron Tenishar. This helps her get around better and heal the wounds.

Crystal is lying in bed when Tom returns. He's holding the brown leather book in his hands and presents it to her with the key used to unlock the large tome. "Thank you, Tom." She pats the book, running a clawed hand over it. "And the healing water?"

"They are bringing it now. Master Monzulo says he hopes for your full recovery and, if you need more, to drop by."

"Good, let's start filling my tub. I can't wait to get back to normal." She struggles to stand up. Tia gives her a hand and Crystal must put the book down to accomplish this. Tia gets a look at the book and dread fills her. Something about it repels her very presence. Tyra walks in carrying a large cask and empties it into the tub in the bathroom.

William picks Crystal up. "I'll help her into the bath, Tia. I promised not to leave her side, and I mean it."

They take a few steps and Crystal turns her head toward Tia. "Can you get my book and bring it in here for me?"

Tia turns and looks at the book and goes to reach for it but can't bring herself to get any closer to it. She feels as if her very soul is in danger if she picks it up and backs away. Tom looks confused. "You ok, Tia?"

"I can't touch it." The fear in her voice gives Tom pause. "I don't know why, but there is something wrong with that book."

Tom gives her an odd look. "Ok, I can do it then."

Tom sets it down next to the tub with the key, causing Crystal to look at him, puzzled. "Why didn't Tia bring it to me? I could have been naked by now."

"She's spooked by it." He shrugs as if that explained everything and walks out of the room.

She's going to get suspicious. Better keep it away from her. Crystal, with William's help, gets her clothes off and lowers her into the tub. The water stings her body where her wounds are but the painkilling herbs the Catfolk shamans brought to keep it bearable.

"Put that tray across here and hand me my book, please, William."

William grabs the tub tray and lays it across and picks up the book. He feels uneasy touching it and sees the skull prominently across its face. "What is this, honey?"

"It's a book of magic spells and information. If I'm going to continue to improve my abilities, I need to see what possibilities are out there."

"But there is a large skull on the front of that book. What does that mean?"

She speaks with arrogance to disguise her lie. "It's a ward. Anyone who tries to open the book without the key is killed. It's meant to keep these magical secrets just that, secret."

"Why would you need to ward a book with something that can kill? What's in there?"

"Magical power, my love. The answers to many things that will help me make a difference in the future." She turns to him. "Could you get me some vegetable juice? I'm thirsty darling." She turns the page. He looks at the book, but it's unreadable to him. "Sure, honey. I'll send Tia in to watch you."

"That won't be necessary. I will be fine here alone." She looks at him. "I will be the woman you fell in love with before this happened again."

"You are the woman I fell in love with." William kisses her, then exits.

When I'm done studying this book, I will wreck the Black Rose and give them someone else to fear more than Emperor Marcus. She soaks in the water every day for a few hours at a time. Weeks pass, and the scars fade and disappear, restoring her pristine white ivory skin. She gets out of the bath of healing water and walks to the standing mirror and smiles that all of her beauty has returned. Everything they did to her is a distant nightmare. She turns and looks at the leather-bound tome. "But theirs has only just started."

Tia speaks from the other room. "What was that, Countess?"

"We need to go back to where they were hiding at. Where you found me. We must get answers to what they were up to."

"Baron Tenishar already sent troops there. They are gone. They found nothing useful."

Still looking at her tome. "I'm sure I can find things they missed." Crystal turns around and Tia is looking at the floor. "Could you bring me my dress?" Tia picks up the dress off the bed and takes it to Crystal, not looking up.

Crystal frowns. "Is there a problem with looking at me now? When I was a brutalized monstrosity, you had no problem with looking upon my body, but now that I'm back to being my normal self, you can't look at me?"

"I'm sorry Countess, but when I was treating you, I had to look, but I can go back to my old shy self. I didn't think it would make you mad for me not to look at your naked body." Tia's face reddens, looking away from Crystal.

Crystal calms down and understands situations change things. She embraces the poor Half-Elf with her naked body just to tease her more. "Thank you for saving my life and not letting me kill myself." She gets dressed and calls for William, who comes in.

"Get your armor on. We are taking a trip."

"Uh, to where, honey?"

"Back to where I was found. Bring as many troops as you think we will need, but I want to look around there myself and find out what we can about these Black Rose people."

"But Countess, Baron—"

"As I told Tia, I know all that, but I want to look around." She points at him. "And you said you won't leave my side, and I'm going there, so are you going to keep your word?"

She's changed. She's getting meaner. William tilts his head, giving in. "Are you feeling alright?"

"I'm feeling top notch and I'm pissed off. I want to get the bastards who did this to me." She looks at him. "Don't you feel the same?" She puts on a silver bracelet with some onyx gems arranged around them. "And I hope to find my good jewelry there, too."

He smiles at seeing the fire in her reignite. "Yes, I do, let's go."

The Bastion lands at the old fortification in the desert. Bodies of Black Rose thugs litter the ground. *It appears they don't care about their dead as much as we care about ours.* She walks into the area. *Good, this is going to make it easier.* She speaks aloud with an air of authority that makes no one doubt her intentions. "Take me to the room you found me in. I want to see if there is anything lying around that might contain information."

William leads the group and troops fan around the area and check the old building for holdouts. William gets to the room first and stops. "Are you sure you want to look in here?"

Crystal pushes him aside without an answer and walks in. The decaying corpse of her captor lies on the floor. She can see the pool of dried blood under a hook and knows that's where she hung for several days as the woman on the ground tortured her. Speaking an incantation, and her eyes glow a light purple. She glances around the room again and finds something on the body. She picks out an ordinary-looking object from her pockets and looks it over.

"What's that?"

"I don't know." Crystal looks ominously back at the body. "But I know someone who does."

She reaches over to one of her bracelets and pulls out a few of the onyx gems from them. "What are you doing? Why did you destroy your jewelry?"

This commotion causes Tia to look through the door as Crystal sticks the gems into the corpse's eye sockets. *She's shoving onyx into the corpse's eyes? Wait, I've heard of a spell that uses those.* She turns to look at Crystal. *She can't be serious!* Then her eyes widen and Crystal utters the dark incantation and her claws glow black as night touching the body encompassing it in darkness. Tia screams in horror as the body animates and stands. William draws his sword and pulls Crystal back, and Tom rushes through the broken door.

"STOP!" Crystal shouts as an order to all. The newly formed zombie stands upright and doesn't move, but William, Tom and Tia look at her, wondering why they were stopped. A sinister grin crosses her face. "It worked."

"This is an abomination, Countess." Tia gasps, taking a step back. "When the Emperor finds out, he will execute you."

Crystal shakes her head. "No, he won't. It's only punishable by death if I take a soul from the Gods. The soul is still wherever it went. It's only the husk of the body that stands before me now." She turns and even Tom gets goosebumps. "By the letter of the law, I did nothing wrong." She gazes up at William. "Isn't that right, Captain?"

He looks at her, dumbfounded. "By the letter of the law, you're right, but that doesn't make it any less heinous, Countess."

Tia doesn't give in. "Necromancy is forbidden in the Rose Empire."

Crystal turns to Tia. "We are far outside of those jurisdictions. So technically, there are no laws out here to break." She turns back to her creation. "Don't worry, Tia. I'm not going to make it a habit, nor am I going to raise an army of the dead unless I have to." Tia still looks horrified. "Ok, I still need to work on those punchlines. Got it."

"But why?" She swallows. "Why did you do this?"

Crystal speaks with more joy in her voice than she should have. "It can't refuse any order I give it. Which means it will answer any question I have. It's completely loyal to me. Anything it knew in life is mine to know."

"Promise me you will destroy it when you're done."

"You honestly think I'm going to keep a rotting corpse as a pet? That's just gross." She turns to the zombie. "Who was the person who told you to kidnap me?"

The corpse answers, gurgling from the decay. "Her name is Zaleria Pyrewind."

"And who is that?"

"Leader of the Black Rose."

"What do they want with me?"

"To stop the joining of Portstown and Rose Harbor."

"For what reason?"

"I don't know."

"Where is the Black Rose leadership located?"

"Old Haven."

Crystal looks confused. *Old Haven was destroyed a century ago. Why would she be there?* "Is New Haven plotting a war?"

"No, Zaleria is trying to push them into war."

Crystal looks at William. "That's good. We aren't going against New Haven themselves."

"What's the Black Rose's next plan?"

"To attack the City of Portstown disguised as New Haven troops at the next full moon festival to start the war."

She looks at William, Tom, and Tia. "Aren't you glad I did this now?" Tia, still petrified in fear, shakes her head negatively and clutches her holy symbol.

Crystal holds up the odd object. "What does this do, or go to?"

"It's a magical key used to unlock the safe hidden in this room."

This perks up everyone present. "Show me."

The animated corpse walks over to the wall behind where she hung and presses one block, causing the wall to slide over. Inside is a safe in the ground. She dismisses the corpse, and it collapses lifelessly once again to the floor. Lining up the key in the safe, the locking mechanism turns, and it opens. Inside are her bracelets for her hands, a coded map and letter, and some chain mail that glows green to Crystal. She pulls it out and looks at it. It's light and flexible. She looks at Tia. "Present for you."

Tia looks at it and it doesn't look big enough, holding it up to her body. "Countess, this is too small for me."

"It's magical." Crystal takes it back, flipping it around. "If I guess correctly, it should change to fit your ample form, regardless. You should put it on, now."

Tia turns red, nodding to Tom and William. "Countess, I can't just disrobe here"

"They won't look. If they do, well, they know what I'm capable of. Now put it on. You can put your robes back on over it. I just don't want you to take a dagger to the back and die."

"But Countess."

"Fine. Try it on when we get back to the ship then. I got what I wanted." She slips her bracelets back on. "Let's get back to Portstown and warn them. We don't have long to prepare."

318

CHAPTER 36
(Preparation)

They gather their troops and get back aboard the ship. Crystal gives orders to return to Portstown and then retires to her cabin. She's not in there long when William and Tia come knocking. "Enter." William steps in first and his face tells her he is troubled, and Tia follows with her head down, looking as if someone died. "What's with you two? You look like someone stabbed your favorite pet."

William looks at Tia for a moment and she can't stop looking at the deck plates. Looking back to Crystal. "It's about that spell you used."

Tia interrupts, bringing all attention to her. "That was necromancy, wasn't it?"

Crystal stands there as if nothing she did was a problem. "Yeah, so?"

"And you don't think that using it is wrong?"

"We've been over this. There is no law out here."

"That's not the point Crystal." William steps forward. "It's inherently evil and completely immoral to use."

She softens in her stance. "If I hadn't used it, we would be facing a surprise attack tonight. At least we can minimize the loss of life." She turns and picks the tome up off her desk, feeling the power within it begging to be used. She holds it in front of her. "The power in this book can turn away any army used against us." She steps forward, getting Tia to step back. "I've learned many of the secrets it holds. With it, I can destroy the Black Rose and preserve the Empire, live forever, and even raise armies." Tia can feel the evil exuding from the book and recoils away from it.

Tia speaks up in fear. "At what cost Crystal?" This catches Crystal off guard because Tia has never called her by her first name before. "The book is evil. I can feel its evil. It's corrupting you."

"This book saved Williams' life. This book just helped prevent an immense amount of death. This is how I'm going to crush the Black

Rose and make sure anyone who even thinks about going against the empire is too afraid to."

William pleads with her. "I, we, know what they did to you and how they hurt you. I want nothing more than to destroy the Black Rose for what they did to you." He steps forward and kneels before her, taking her right hand. "But this, this isn't you. This isn't the woman I fell in love with." He puts his head down on top of her hand. "Abandon this evil, please."

"Please, Ms. Hellstromm. You're taking a path that is wrong. We are loyal to you, but you're being corrupted."

Crystal withdraws her hand and steps away from the kneeling knight. "Why can't you two see what I'm doing is for the good of us?" She continues to take steps back and grasps the book tighter with both hands in front of her. "With this, no one will ever harm any of us again." She looks at the book. "And if you can't see that, then I don't need you." She can feel the power in the book calling to her, to use it to destroy her enemies.

Tia, with tears forming in her eyes. "Listen to yourself. Are you willing to give up friendships, and the love of your life that you were willing to die for, over a book?" Tia places her hand on William's shoulder.

Crystal looks at the two and looks down at the book. She can feel its power calling to her, to use it to crush her enemies, to forge an empire of her own. It's her deepest desire and with it, she can realize them. *Immortality and an army no one can oppose. Dispose of the weak and take this power.*

She looks back at William still kneeling with his head bowed, unable to look at her and Tia crying. Crystal grits her teeth. "I can't believe I would keep counsel with people so weak." She holds her hand out, feeling the power surge in her. Then Olovira's words echo in her head. *Use them wisely as I did and heed their warnings.* She looks down at the book and realizes what Olovira meant. Olovira knew the power of the book and didn't use it unless she had to.

She feels it calling to her, pushing her. *Be dominant like Cline and live forever with the ultimate power over your clawed fingertips. Raise an army of the dead that can't be stopped and destroy the Black Rose and all other enemies.*

I've never thought of them as weak before. Her dark thoughts break. *William is the strongest person I ever met and I love him to death. Now I'm ready to dismiss his love for this? Tia's right, it's trying to take over my soul!* Crystal tosses the book across the room and collapses. Tia does not understand what's happening but knows it's the only chance she has. Praying to Daniel, her hands glow red and a lance of holy fire strikes the book, destroying it and its contents. She whimpers "I'm sorry." William slides up to her, embracing her again.

"That's the woman I fell in love with. She's back from the darkness."

Tia stares at the burning evil book of necromancy. *Good riddance.*

Crystal just repeats, "I'm sorry," over repeatedly. "I didn't mean what I said." She can feel the grip the book had over her disappear as it burns. She cries and apologizes. "I was the weak one, not you two. I wanted to give up and then I compounded my problem by giving into the power of the book. I was contemplating committing the most heinous of acts." William helps her back to her feet. "I was going to raise their own dead to fight against them."

Tia is in shock. "Their dead?"

Crystal sobs more, as it all is still fresh in her mind. "And in my head, I had it justified. I almost did it." She sits on her bed and buries her face in her hands. "I, I almost ended up cursed like Cline."

William looks at Tia, not understanding. "What do you mean, honey?"

"In that book was the ritual for becoming a Lich. To trap a soul and keep it from departing so the body could live forever. I was studying it, knowing full well what it would do."

"I made a promise to stay by your side, and if that means rescuing you from the depths of the void, the middle of the desert, or even from yourself, I'll be there." He sits down next to her, wrapping his arm around her.

Tia sits opposite William. "Ms. Hellstromm, we love you and will always look out for you."

Crystal speaks up but still rests her head on William's chest. "I love you guys too." She looks at Tia. "And put that chain-mail on."

They land outside of Portstown and disembark. They head back to the embassy to get troops geared up and ready. Crystal and Tia head to the Baron to warn him. They cross into the courtyard and Captain Motsana intercepts them. "What's going on, ladies? The festival doesn't start till midnight. You're a bit early."

"Captain, there isn't going to be a festival tonight if I don't get to see Baron Tenishar. There is going to be an attack tonight by the Black Rose."

"You have proof of this?"

Crystal presents him the plans and map she found from the chest in her torture chamber. He looks it over and nods.

Tia pleads with him. "It's very important that we save as many lives as we can. Please, Captain."

He waves them on. "Let's go then."

They head up to Baron Tenishar's office and enter. He stands up, grinning. "What do I owe the honor of you arriving early?"

All three bow their heads. "Baron Tenishar, the Countess bears a warning for you."

Crystal looks up. "We went back to the battle site and where I was held captive and did some investigating and found that the Black Rose was going to attack at the next festival disguised as New Haven troops."

Baron Tenishar looks at her, dumbfounded. "We did our own investigation and found no evidence of this. How do you know?"

Crystal looks to Tia and back at the Baron. "We got the information from a member of the Black Rose who was there and had decent inside knowledge of what was happening." She hands him the map and letters. "We found these in a secret chest in the torture room I was in."

"How reliable is this source?"

"I would bet my life on it."

Baron Tenishar looks at her. This isn't a small thing she says since a Black Rose member almost tortured her to death and it took a month to recover. "But why disguised as New Haven troops and not Rose Harbor?"

"To push you into a war with New Haven before we could finish our negotiations, and possibly get me and my retinue killed in the battle. This would make Rose Harbor also hostile to you if a representing member of the First House was killed under your care."

"That would make sense. It's very sinister." He waves a hand dismissively. "But they won't get past the gates."

"I believe they are already inside your gates. Tyra caught the scent of their members already here. In Black Rock, they were inside the walls there, too. It's the same tactic."

"You know what to expect?"

"They killed all the standing guards first in the town, then assaulted the barracks. It was fast and brutal. Completely caught us by surprise." She bows her head again. "We lost a lot of good people in that battle."

"Well then, we must prepare. You're welcome to join me and my staff in the bunker while the troops handle everything."

"Thank you, Baron. We appreciate the offer, but I must be there for my own troops. Captain Blakely is going to be contacting Captain Motsana to coordinate efforts and set an ambush for when they strike, I'm sure." She continues confidently. "And we need to make it look like the festival is still going or they will know there is something up. So, if I'm missing, they will stay hidden. I'm the obvious target."

"You're going to the festival knowing they are targeting you?" The Baron's whiskers twitch. "That's mighty brave of you, considering what you've been through."

"I'll be fine. Captain Blakely will be there to protect me, and I will have his back, too."

"But you could die out there. You should be in here with us."

"If I die, I die at his side. I accept that and wouldn't want to go any other way."

Tia just turns her head to look at her, then back to the Baron. "And I'll be there too. We started this together. We will end it together if we have to."

"Captain Motsana, escort the ladies back and prepare. We are going to feast and we will all fight tonight. If this little girl is going to fight, then I can't see why I shouldn't."

"But sir, you can't."

"Are you presuming to tell me what to do, Captain?" The Baron glowers at the smaller Catfolk. He looks back to Crystal. "It's been a long time since my claws have gotten some blood on them. Let it be the blood of our joint enemies Countess."

William and the others walk into the embassy. "Tyra, Tom, round up the staff and other non-combatants and get them into shelters. We don't have long to react." The two monks take off, not questioning orders. "Penelope, I need you as a scout and to identify important targets. If we can pick off their leadership or how they are communicating, we should be able to turn the tide of battle much easier. Also, alert the guards in the streets and tell them what's happening. We need to minimize losses here." She nods and takes to the streets.

He goes to the barracks and alerts everyone. "We need everyone ready to go. Gather around and I'm going to explain what's happening." Troops form up and William lays everything out.

CHAPTER 37
(Battle of Portstown)

Night falls and the moon rises. Crystal and her staff are at the Baron's table set up in the courtyard. William wears a cape over his armor to disguise him wearing it. Captain Motsana is doing something similar with an oversized festival robe. The Bastion is off the ground and behind the castle, where it can't be spotted. William surmised the tactic. "It wouldn't be good if they captured it and turned it against the town." The Priestess of Tatiana starts her prayer as the moon starts its approach to its zenith. As she gets to the end, the noise of the clashing of blades, gunfire, and the toppling of street carts can be heard. As predicted, Black Rose troops wearing New Haven colors on their armor storm the embassy and enter the courtyard of the fortress.

They all jump to their feet. William and Captain Motsana pull their swords, Portstown guard draw their Talwar's and put on their Patas from under their festival robes. Tyra and Tom toss off their robes and take their stances, and Tia steels herself for the upcoming battle. Rose Harbor troops stationed along the walls take aim, ready to fire. There is no retreat today.

"CHARGE!" William and Motsana shout with Catfolk troops, hidden about the area, and spring forth from their hiding places. William dons his helmet and they charge at the surprised Black Rose, who stop and back up, only to find the gates to the fortress have shut behind them, closed by the powered suits that came to life disguised as statues.

Crystal stands on the table and starts an incantation, feeling the power in her blood as it builds. She holds out both red glowing hands in front of her and a large ball of ice forms in front of her. Finishing her incantation, the foot and a half wide ball of freezing energy flies out like a ballista and hits the front rank of Black Rock troops, and explodes. High-velocity shards of ice and the force of the blast knock down those closest to the point of impact. Lances of ice lacerate and smash the forward line. Those at the point of impact are killed instantly. Crystal gets lightheaded and falls over, but Tia catches her.

"Are you alright, Countess?"

"Yeah, that took a lot out of me, but I'm still good. Just need to catch my breath."

"I've never seen you use that spell before. What was that?"

"You know what a fireball is?"

"Yeah, of course."

"That's what happens when you channel ice instead of fire into it." She laughs, getting back to her feet.

William saw the ball of frozen death fly just over his head and collide with the enemy. The ones closest to the blast froze instantly and shattered into thousands of shards and knocked over many. The next line drops as fire from the troops from hidden locations in the fortress open. William takes advantage as he rushes into the fray, stabbing into the stunned enemy. Flashes of blades and shields collide and the ringing of metal on metal as the battle turns into a complete melee.

William holds up his shield, catching a blade meant for his head, and Motsana slashes across with his huge Moplah, almost cleaving the man in half. William nods in appreciation and lashes out at another enemy, but he intercepts his blade with his own shield. The trooper takes his own swing and, with William's shield out of position, contacts his armor, but a familiar blue sheen absorbs the blow. *Thank you, honey, for watching my ass.*

Tyra and Tom fight back-to-back. A long sword swings at Tyra and she intercepts it with her lajatang she had Tom bring back with him from his visit with Master Monzulo. She counters with the one side of the Crescent moon blade with such force that not only did it nearly cut him in half but sent his body flying several feet away. She brings it back over her head and stabs it downward in a fluid motion, cleaving another man's leg clean off.

Tom lashes out with his sai, catching swords and disarming his opponent, but not before he takes a strike to his left shoulder. He stabs the man in the gut with a sharp point, and it sticks out to the other side. He pushes the dead man away when a spear comes to his left, but sticks into Tyra's flank. Tom grabs it and kicks the assailant, doubling him over, then brings his elbow down, bringing the man to the ground. Tyra whips her lajatang around and decapitates the man on the ground.

Tia notices Tyra is bleeding, looks at Crystal and she nods her approval. "Help her, I'll be fine. If anything, I'll stab someone with a wishbone."

Tia runs to Tyra, and Tom covers her, and she prays, healing Tyra's wound. Her hands glow blue and the blood stops and the wound closes in front of her. Tom intercepts a sword strike that almost hits her in the face with his sai and stabs him with the other, but not fatally. "Looks like you're stuck here." Tom grins, intercepting another blow. "Know any good fighting songs, Tia?" She shakes her head and Tyra's lajatang intercepts another blow meant for her.

With a flick of the Minotaur's wrist, the arm holding that sword comes off. "Hey, pick that spear up and poke things with it while you're here."

Penelope surveys the battle, and she notices there are a few Black Rose troops better than the others. One is a well-armed and armored man, but she can't tell what he is. *That must be their commander, but there are a lot of sharp, pointy things between me and him.* She pulls her revolver and takes aim. Firing a few shots, she watches in dismay as the armor turns the shots away, causing no damage. "Well, that option is out." A few Black Rose soldiers are escaping the battle and she runs along the battlement behind them, and pulls her daggers from their hidden locations. She leaps, blades flashing in the full moonlight, and plunges them deep in the rear man's back, riding him to the ground and rolling. They stop and turn and look at her and advance.

Crystal surveys the battle and Baron Tenishar stands close to her, taking down anyone who approaches too close. His claws, razor-sharp, cleave through the leather armor of a Black Rose soldier who advanced on them. She watches Penelope dive off the battlement onto some Black Rose near to her and see's she's bitten off more than she can chew. Crystal takes off running towards her. The Baron shouts a warning not to leave, but she ignores him. She starts a new incantation and the power in her blood responds as she points at those attacking Penelope. A ray of solid ice fires off one after another in quick succession, striking one of them, pinning them to the mason wall, dead on impact. Penelope doesn't look up, knowing exactly where that came from and tries to stop a blow from the remaining man, but the blade nicks her right arm, cutting through her black leather.

William hears the Baron shout at Crystal and turn his attention to her. He sees she's away from the table and that several Black Rose troopers have broken off to kill her. He gives chase, taking a strike across the back, finding a small spot in the armor by the pauldron. He turns to face the attacker, but Captain Motsana has already moved to protect him. "Go help the Countess, I've got it from here." He takes another blade on his Moplah and returns the strike. William nods in appreciation and rushes at the men stabbing one through the back but not stopping, running straight into a second, knocking him down.

Blades are coming in fast at the big Minotaur. Cut and stab wounds are building up faster than Tia can keep up with. With every swing, Tyra sends men flying, but it's not enough. A crossbow bolt lands, hitting her in the right thigh. Tom isn't much better, but he's hanging on. He's shattered several blades with his sai, but even broken blades can still cut. Tia is trying her best with the spear but she's not trained to fight, so she just takes pokes at anyone who gets too close. A crossbow bolt comes out of the darkness and Tom reaches for it, but it slips through his fingers, hitting Tia in the chest. More gunfire erupts from the battlements and more of the Black Rose troops fall outside the gate.

She looks down, and the bolt bounces off and falls to the ground. She grabs her chest and feels the chain-mail under her robe. *Thank you, Crystal, for making me wear this thing.*

Tom quips. "No fair, you have armor on." Tyra takes another shot to the body, pissing her off, and she reaches out with her hand and grabs a Black Rose trooper and uses him as a shield to intercept more incoming fire.

Baron Tenishar gets to Crystal at the same time William does, clawing another man's face off. A personal guard takes a bolt to the back, taking it for the Baron instead. "Sir, we are exposed here. We need to withdraw."

Baron Tenishar looks at him and then back at Crystal. "Let's go Countess." She ignores him, running up to William and kissing his helm.

"Let's do this together."

William readies his shield and sword and intercepts a blow meant for Crystal. She turns her bracelets off, and her claws come out and she lashes out, stabbing the man and rips his chest open. Blood splatters over her face and dress and onto Williams's armor. "You sure you need me?"

"Every day for the rest of my life." He covers her with his shield, taking a crossbow bolt to the shoulder. It doesn't go deep with the armor, stopping it mostly. William takes another blow, but he answers in kind, stabbing the man clear through the chest with his star metal sword, then kicking the body away. "Why are they using such old weapons? Don't they have access to guns, too?"

"I don't know. Makes little sense unless these are magically enhanced. Can't enchant bullets."

"That would explain how they are finding a way past my armor. Just be careful."

Penelope sees the big man cleaving his way through the Catfolk guard, giving Black Rose an advantage. She takes a sword on one of her daggers and tumbles into the man, slashing inside his legs causing him to fall. Then she stabs him in the back of the neck, her blade passing through the other side. He gurgles and blood pours from his mouth as he falls to the ground. *I must warn William about the enemy commander.*

The Black Rose commander swings his long-sword cleaving through a Catfolk guard, armor and all, with little resistance, and blood sprays into the night air. Captain Motsana moves to intercept the guy, bent on ending his bloodbath. The Captain swings his Moplah and the other man catches it with his shield, then his blade flashes, passing through the captain's sword, splitting it in half. Motsana looks in shock as the large man rears back with his shield and sends the poor captain flying onto his back. He brings his sword to bear on Captain Motsana, but Penelope slams into his leg with her daggers, knocking him off balance.

Captain Motsana stands brushing off. "Thanks." The enemy commander grunts and reaches down, plucking the Halfling off him and flinging her through the air. She comes crashing into the ground and feels a snap. Pain radiates from her right shoulder, and she drops the dagger she was holding in that hand. She rolls as another enemy soldier's sword stabs the ground where her chest used to be. She realizes her right shoulder is dislocated or broken, and she can fight no longer. She flees into the mass of fighting diving between combatants.

Tyra and Tom fight with Tia between them, but she's quickly becoming exhausted. Tyra pulls another crossbow bolt from her arm, throwing it to the ground. She swings her lajatang, arcing to the side, catching three opponents at once, sending them to their backs. Flipping the long weapon around, she stabs down with it, cleaving the arm off, holding the sword. Tom sweeps his leg, bringing another man down, but before he can finish him, he catches a sword with his sai, preventing them from stabbing Tia. She prays to Daniel to burn her enemies and holy fire lances out, burning two other men and setting them on fire. *Looks like I'm getting stronger too after healing Ms. Hellstromm so much.*

William stands with Crystal behind him. She starts an incantation, and he lifts his shield, giving her a way to see her target. A ball of ice forms at her red glowing fingertips and launches itself, hitting a man in the face and exploding into shards. As he reels back, William lunges forward, stabbing him through the chest, finishing what she started. A crossbow bolt comes screaming through the night and ricochets off his armor, but it hits her. She cries out and grabs her arm where the bolt has passed through. William turns to check on her. "Pay attention to them. I'll live. I've had worse." Portstown, Rose Empire, and Black Rose bodies litter the area and William spots the enemy commander, cleaving his way through their troops. He looks in their direction and marches towards them. His shield bashes a Catfolk guard smashing his face and comes in swinging at Will.
William holds his shield up and takes the hit, but the force behind it causes his arm to hurt. The shield splinters under the force of the man's blow. William brings his own sword around and the Commander catches it with his own shield, forcing it out of the way. William knows he can't back up because he's protecting Crystal. He shoves the Commander back, who takes another swing, hitting William's shield again. More wood splinters away and William swears the guy will break his arm like this. "Crystal, RUN!" William yells

intercepting another blow with his own sword, causing them to lock their blades.

A deep, gruff voice comes from the other man's helm. "I'm going to kill you, then I'm killing the woman." He pushes William back. Crystal gets some distance but doesn't go far. William swings, sliding along the man's blade, and lands a blow to the man's lower right abdomen. He grabs Williams's sword hand and head butts him helmet to helmet, knocking William backward and forcing him to drop his sword.

Tyra and Tom advance with the Rose Harbor and Portstown guards. The tide of battle is sinking in with the Black Rose, but they still fight on, even though they know it will lead to their deaths. More crossbow fire comes in and Tom plucks them from the air, but Tyra isn't so lucky, taking a few more hits and unable to dodge them. She falls to a knee with bolts sticking from her chest. She looks up at Tom and her eyes roll back into her head and she collapses. Tia prays to Daniel and her hands glow yellow, pulling the most powerful of healing she can, enveloping Tyra's body. She concentrates on repairing the damage. "Pull the bolts out!"

Tim does as he's told. "Stay with us Tyra."

The enemy commander raises his weapon and a black bolt of lightning strikes his chest, causing him to stagger back. He looks down and his sword trembles in his hands. "That's right, I can fight too." William takes the opening and gets up, slamming into him and bringing him to the ground. The commander's sword clatters away as the two wrestle on the ground. Crystal knows she can't fire into the fighting as she could hit William by accident. She looks down at her hands and knows a spell she can use, but it's from the book of necromancy.

The commander rolls on top of William and punches him. *Even with some of his strength sapped, he's able to do this damage?* William reaches out, trying to push the man off him but can't. William tilts his head to look at Crystal and she speaks an incantation, and vanishes from his sight. *Good girl, hide and run. Survive for me.* The distraction is all the enemy commander needed and rips Williams's helm off, causing it to clatter across the ground. He reaches back and strikes him again, but William can get his arm in the way, intercepting the strike.

William can't keep this up against this brute. They continue their struggle, and the commander beats William down, slamming his fists into the young knight's face. He reaches back to finish the job when a claw, wreathed in a black glow, melts through the man's chest, armor and all. Crystal's voice comes from behind him, dripping with a deep-seated hatred. "Get your hands off my man." Her claw closes and pulls back passes out of his body, leaving no wound and the Commander's body falls limp. William looks and Crystal is standing with a shadowy-looking figure that looks like an ogre. She waves her blackened claw, and it dissipates like smoke, having only lasted a moment, and she kneels, wrapping her arms around him.

William looks up at her. "What was that?"

"Don't ask questions you really don't want to know the answers to." She pulls him to his feet, and he grabs his helm. William looks down and pulls the guy's helmet off, revealing him to be an Ogre. "That explains why he was hitting so hard." The approaching dawn replaces the night as the fight winds down.

The Black Rose is surrendering, seeing the body of their commander on the ground. Sounds of fighting in the streets continue, but they surrender in time, unable to counter the might of the power suits. Crystal and William climb atop the battlements and look over, surveying the destruction. The Bastion is still in the air, having never fired a shot, knowing it would cause more damage than help.

The surrendered forces of the Black Rose are rounded up and locked away, led by Captain Motsana. Interrogations of their leaders will be done over the next several weeks. Crystal pulls the crossbow bolt from her arm and William has holes all over his armor. They make their way to Tia, Tom, and Tyra, who is recovering and eating some of the food from the festival table. "You two look like hell."

"Us?" She rolls her eyes.

William chuckles. "You and Tyra look like porcupines with all those bolts sticking out of you."

Tyra glances at them but continues to eat. Tia's robe has tears in it. Bloodstains are all over it as she comes over to treat Crystal's wound on her arm.

"You ok?"

"Yes, why Countess?"

"You have a lot of blood on you, like you were swimming in it. Are you hurt?"

Tia reaches up and taps her robes and the ring of the chain-mail can be heard. "I put it on like you told me and it saved my life a few times."

"See, I know best, don't I?" She pulls a bolt from William's armor and Tia heals him. She speaks an incantation and her eyes glow purple. "They are magically enchanted. Whoever is funding this knows our armor is bulletproof, but magical bolts bypass the non-magical armor." She drops it to the ground.

"That must have cost a lot of money." William winces as Tia yanks another one out.

Baron Tenishar walks over with the few remaining bodyguards. "Well fought. Had you not warned us, this could have gone differently."

"I see these as my people too, in a way. I've spent a long time here now and look forward to continuing learning about this place."

"If I know you, you're going to want to retire to your room soon. It's going to get hot out here." The Baron waves his arm around the area. "I wouldn't want to see you get hurt after surviving all this. Let us talk again tomorrow."

"Tia, you have things handled here?"

"Yeah, but where's Ms. Penelope?"

This causes them all to look around. Penelope is missing. Tyra stands up. "I'll find her dead or alive." They go searching through the area calling out to her and Tyra finds her laying on the ground with blood around her with other bodies from both sides.

Crystal is stunned. "Shadow, no." She kneels and grabs her friend, lifting her up. She wakes and screams in pain, causing Crystal to drop her and scramble backward.

She falls back to the ground. "That hurt!".

Crystal fires back. "I thought you died!"

"I did too. I was trying to run, and bodies started landing on me." She lets out a wince, trying to move. "My right shoulder is busted, AGAIN!"

Tia kneels next to Crystal and feels the surrounding area. "It's dislocated."

"Fix it with your healing magic, then."

Tia nods and holds Penelope up. She places her hands on either side of her shoulder and prays, then presses hard, snapping it back in, causing her to scream in agony. "I didn't know healing magic hurt so much."

"It doesn't. I didn't use magic, I just popped back into place. You should feel fine in a little while."

Penelope stands up. "Yeah right, like hell."

"I, for one, am going to take the Baron's advice and retire to my room." She takes William's hand. "Come along, Will. They can handle things from here."

William takes his place at her side as she hooks her arm in his. "I'm going to need a bath to get all this blood off."

William and Crystal get to her room, and she takes the blood-soaked dress off and tosses it aside like an old rag. He starts to unbuckle his armor, and she saunters over. "I don't have time to wait for all that." Wrapping her arms around his neck and uttering the incantation that he's very familiar with, he doesn't resist as the armor clatters to the ground. Both are still dirty, but they kiss passionately. After a few moments, she pulls back. "Let's continue this downstairs in the pool, and the first person to walk through those doors dies." William still can't tell if she's serious or not, but doesn't challenge her on it.

Tyra and Tom go back to their rooms and Penelope heads to the kitchen with Tia in tow. They grab a snack and talk about the battle and everything that's happened lately. Tia keeps the incident about the book to herself, thinking it would be best if Penelope didn't know. "So now what?"

"Back to negotiations, I guess. It's not over till they sign the paperwork, but this little joint venture will push us closer to an agreement and should knock some time off." Tia takes a drink of water.

Penelope glimpses William and Crystal walking in bathrobes, heading down to the bathing pool. "If you want to prevent some more injuries, I suggest posting a sign the pool is closed until further notice."

Tia leans on the counter. "Those two have been through a lot together."

Penelope drinks some coffee. "Do you think he will ask her, or will he stay quiet with his honor, holding him back for being from a lower house?"

Tia shakes her head. "I can't see the future, but you can tell those two will kill and die to stay together."

CHAPTER 38
(Epilogue)

Months pass as the negotiations go on. Tom and Tyra pass the time teaching some of their martial arts to the local military and citizens who are interested. Tom gives some serious thought to opening his Dojo permanently here, having rented some space. Tyra reminds him they still haven't stopped the Black Rose. "Maybe after this is all over, we can open one together. We can call it the Bull in the China shop!" Tom laughs till Tyra slugs him.

Penelope trades recipes and spends time with different food vendors learning new dishes to take back to Rose Harbor. Exotic foods make good money in places like Rose Harbor and she's sure Jack will invest in her restaurant. Crystal lets her know she will force her father to if she must.

Clerics from Rose Harbor arrive as part of an exchange program with Portstown. Tia came up with it, helping strengthen the bond between the towns. "The moon and the sun are in balance with each other, so why not the towns?" So, she and the priestesses of Tatiana teach each other about their gods.

Late fall rolls around, and with harvest season well on its way, the negotiations and the treaty are finally officiated. At a public meeting with the townsfolk of Portstown and officials from Rose Harbor. Baron Tenishar and Countess Crystal sit at the table in front of hundreds, if not thousands, of people. The Rose Empire and Portstown standards sit behind them respectfully. She's nervous as the first time she has ever done something like this. Baron Tenishar stands up and addresses the crowd as they quiet down. "Citizens of Portstown." His voice echoes, helped by magical enhancements. "Ever since Rose Harbor first graced our presence many decades ago, we've been peaceful with them, but separate as a people, a culture, and as governments." He gestures with his hands holding one behind Crystal's head and looks at her, then back at the people.

"Rose Harbor grew as it accepted others and has advanced in the ways of magic and science as we stagnated. As you are all aware, many months ago, during the spring planting season." He gestures skywards, looking up, reenacting the moment. "A great ship of iron flew over our heads, to the amazement of all of us." He pauses, looking down at the people once again. "And it flew the colors of Rose Harbor." There are murmurs from the crowd, and some also look up as he did in remembrance.

He then gestures back to Crystal and William. "It carried our honored guests here today who have learned of us. Learned of our ways and shared their own with us." He looks back at the people. "Many of you have seen them in the streets acting like one of us. They feasted and celebrated with us, and taught us their ways." He continues to be dramatic. "At first, I will admit, I was leery of their intent, but as we talked and enjoyed each other's company, I became convinced of their intentions." He turns and looks back at Crystal. "I, Baron Marou Tenishar, will sign the agreement, bringing us all under one standard." He turns back to the people. "We will keep our autonomy, but being under one banner, they will heed our call if we need them, and we will heed theirs. Today, we become a member of the Rose Empire and will prosper from their knowledge as they prosper from ours."

He pauses as the crowd cheers. Taking his cue, he reaches down for signs and officially puts his seal on the documents for the joining. He then smiles, bearing his fangs at Crystal, and motions to her, indicating it's her turn to speak. She glances at her friend in short order, seeing them all joyful on this occasion. Crystal is so nervous that her stomach churns. *But this is what I wanted this since I was a little girl.*

She stands and the crowd claps and cheers, then quiet down as she speaks. "Citizens of Portstown." Her voice is also carried by magical enhancement for all to hear. "When I was given this opportunity to come here, I knew in my heart that fate was calling. When we flew over your city and its pristine white buildings, it was a beacon of purity. I was curious about your ways, of the people who called Portstown home."

She takes in the crowd and swallows, as they are looking at her to speak to them. "Since the day we landed, you've treated me and my people with warmth and hospitality. Taught us your ways, your beliefs, and just how wonderful your food is." She smiles, getting a few laughs from the crowd.

That could have gone better. "For many months, we've shared each other's stories and tragedies, shared our joys and sorrows together. Learned and grew together. I know that the Rose Empire will grow with you, supporting each other as a family." She opens her arms spread wide. "My companions and I feel welcome here, as if part of my family is here in Portstown. I would like to share something that I've learned from spending so much time with you all." She closes her eyes a moment and takes a deep breath. She speaks in felinese. "I am grateful for spending so much time among your wonderful people and I feel that you have welcomed us as part of your family here. I sign today welcoming you all to our family so we will grow together as one people." She bends down, signs the documents and officially seals them. The crowd cheers and the Baron stands again, shaking Crystal's hand leading to a big Catfolk hug.

The Baron turns the citizens. "Let's celebrate today, and tomorrow a new dawn shines on us all."

They sit and Crystal talks with the Baron more. "Now that we're done here, I must deal with the matter of New Haven. The Black Rose must be stopped, or everything we worked so hard to build here could be in jeopardy."

"Yes, The Black Rose cult showed what they were capable of. I'm glad we didn't side with them." He can see her eyes go distant. "Are you going to be ok, Countess?"

She nods solemnly. "I will be eternally grateful to you and your shamans for repairing my body and keeping me alive and pain-free while I recovered, but now we must put these guys down for good." She takes his furry paw. "Don't forget to select a representative and staff to go back on the Bastion. The signing of the paperwork is only the beginning. Now you get a say in the empire's inner workings, so you have much to learn."

The Baron grins with his fangs showing. "I will, and as a sign of our new friendship, I will add to your complement of guards to New Haven, two squads of our troops led by Captain Motsana. He has agreed to take orders from you and knows he and his troops represent us. So, he will defend you as best they can."

She looks over the town with the Baron. "I'm not leaving just yet. Once the paperwork is delivered, along with your representative to Rose Harbor, maybe I'll think about moving on." She turns back to him. "But I appreciate the offer and welcome them to be with us. You've done much for me and Rose Harbor."

William stands up, and she takes his hand. "We are off to enjoy some of your fine food. Would you and your wife like to join us, Baron Tenishar?"

The Baron knows she is being polite and puts a hand. "No, thank you. You two go and enjoy yourselves. I'm sure you have much to talk about in your future."

(TO BE CONTINUED...)

The world doesn't end here. Check out more of Delveon with Legacy's, Chronicles, and Tales coming soon. Books 2 and 3 will be out soon, and the others will follow shortly after.

Timeline of Delveon

- 1850 Expanded Chronicle: I am Shadow (Coming soon)
- 1865 Hellstromm Legacy, Book 1: The Knight and the Half Dragon (Available now)
- 1866 Hellstromm Legacy, Book 2: Love, War, and Divinity (Coming soon)
- 1868 Hellstromm Legacy, Book 3: Fate of an Empire (Coming soon)
- 1886 Hellstromm Legacy, Book 4: Secrets of Titania (Coming soon)
- 1887 Hellstromm Legacy, Book 5: Wayward Journey (Coming soon)
- 1887 Hellstromm Legacy, Book 6: (To be determined)
- 1888 Dominex Tale (18+): Devil's Bounty (Coming soon)

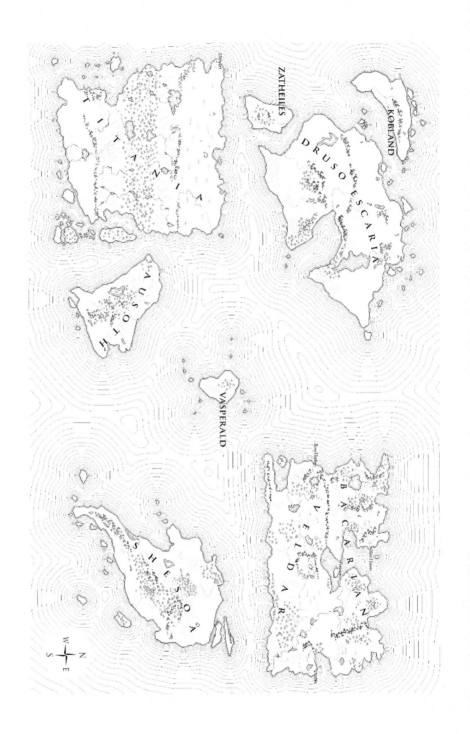

Made in the USA
Monee, IL
10 February 2023

27452439R10187